KNIGHT REDEEMED

THE SHACKLED VERITIES

BOOK TWO

TAMMY SALYER

KNIGHT REDEEMED

Knight Redeemed
The Shackled Verities (Book Two)

ALSO BY TAMMY SALYER

SPECTRAS ARISE SERIES

When all other options run out, never let go of your gun.

In a few hundred years, the Algol system becomes humanity's new home. The question is: Is it a better one?

THE SHACKLED VERITIES SERIES

In a Cosmos-wide war between celestials, humans are as expendable as pawns. Until Ulfric Aldinhuus, leader of the Knights Corporealis, uses the celestials' weapons to fight back.

OTHERWORLD OUTLAWS SERIES

A sawbones fae with a supernatural-sized grudge, a necromancer gnome obsessed with pixie dust, and a hoodoo cowgirl with a Sharps buffalo rifle and damn good aim—the Tuatha Dé Danann will never know what hit 'em.

COLLECTIONS

A Scorpion's Heart: Four Twisted Tales of Love and Lust

SHORT STORIES

Artificial Fate * Creepers * No Suede Soles in Hell

Visit my website to see if anything new has been released since this publication.

www.tammysalyer.com

INTRODUCTION

Hello and thank you for being here! Should you enjoy the words on these pages (and I hope you do!), I encourage you to join my Book Club and visit me at:

www.tammysalyer.com

I occasionally send newsletters to my Book Club with new releases, special offers, and other bits of news. As a special thanks to new members, please enjoy a handful of novellas and short stories from my many and sundry universes FOR FREE.

CHAPTER ONE

Knight Corporealis Eisa Nazaria, known in the Empire of Dyrrakium as the Nazarian Most High, stepped out of her dragørfly ship docked next to the black waters of Himmingaze's Never Sea onto the barren rocky shore of Isle Stonering. The glittering sheath of lights and glowing particles of dust and rock swirling endlessly overhead, from the sea to the chaotic sky beyond, caught her attention immediately.

"Well, Griggory," she said aloud, speaking into the cold emptiness of the dying world, "if you've found a way to reverse this doom, it seems you haven't done so. But I still have faith in you." To herself she added, *I have to, for Vinnr's sake.*

Abandoning the familiarity of her ship, she paced along the island toward the bereft temple in its center, surprised to find the structure still standing. The one-time shrine of Lífs had already been abandoned when last she'd set foot in this world seven hundred and fifteen turns ago. Before her arrival, the Himmingazian Mystae, servants of their Verity similar to the Knights, had blasphemed against their maker and forbidden any commoners of the realm from coming there anymore. The contemptible Mystae had made that choice—a poor one it turned out—just as she had made the choice to send Knight Evernal here through the starpath two days ago.

As Eisa looked around her, seeing how close to utter loss Himmingaze was, she wondered: Had her choice been as poor? Had she doomed Mylla as Himmingaze was doomed?

Her first task now was to learn if her fellow Knight, despite Mylla's failings and faults, was still here.

She reasoned that if she hadn't sent the novice, the fool would have gotten herself killed. Eisa had done what she did only to save her from herself. The rest of the Knights had been captured, and there was nothing noble about following them into the usurper's warship, where all of them were certain to be killed—if not something worse. But Evernal was too dumb and too young to figure that out on her own. She'd fired an emberflare cannon at Eisa in the skies over Magdaster, probably thinking Eisa a traitor. True, perhaps Eisa had reacted a bit more...*strongly* than she'd needed to, resulting in Evernal's exile to Himmingaze. But at least she had saved the novice's life.

Or had she?

Before the temple's entrance lay a mass of carcasses of what appeared to be giant sea worms. They littered the decrepit structure's steps and the ground outside. Obviously a fight had occurred, recently by the looks of the still-seeping carnage, and it looked like the worms had taken the brunt of it. Yet the sight of them put her on edge. Whoever had done this may still be present. Probably Evernal, but if it wasn't, who else might it have been?

One of the black worms wriggled, its great, alien head aiming toward her as if it smelled her. She reached for her curved Dyrrakium dagger and casually flung it, impaling the head. The worm fell with a heavy thump, and the creature lay still.

She retrieved the knife and with a twist of her wrist and a silent command, slipped her klinkí stones from her vambrace to create a shield of light around her. It might attract attention, but it would not be easily penetrated by any commoner weapon, and she knew no Mystae of Lífs existed in this world. She knew this because seven hundred and fifteen turns ago, she had killed the last one.

So where was Mylla now? As she paced along the outside walls of the crumbling shrine, Eisa called to her through her Mentalios lens but got no reply. Sending her klinkí stones darting out in intervals to light up what lay at the edges of her vision, she searched the island for signs of the novice or anyone else. When she'd nearly reached the rear of the structure, a reflection of the stones' lights drew her focus sharply. Where the slick, craggy rocks met the unrelenting waves, something glinted. Upon reaching it, she needed barely a moment's inspection to realize what it was: the ship Evernal had flown, now destroyed.

Hurrying to the wreckage, she found it empty. If the novice had escaped, she'd sought shelter from the unceasing rain that now drenched Eisa too in the temple. The cold feeling in her guts, though, told her she'd find it as empty as the wrecked scout.

Eisa made for the temple doors, and as she pushed them open, another crack of purple-green lightning barraged the shore, strobing the shrine's interior in ominous hues. She sent a salvo of wystic stones throughout the spacious chamber to confirm what she already sensed —the interior contained nothing moving, and nothing living. Evernal was not here.

And if the novice's fate had been forever death in pieces inside the gullets of those giant sea worms, Eisa acknowledged, the fault lay in part with her.

How many lives would her rashness cost? Would saving Vinnr atone for them? The answers could only be had if she wasted no more time contemplating them.

She withdrew her Mentalios lens from inside her breastplate. It was time to call Griggory Dondrin, old Knight and old friend. Together they would save Vinnr. And if the Verities would smile on them just once, maybe the time had come to restore Himmingaze as well.

...SSSSSSAAAAA...

...ssssssssssaaaaAAAAA...

The sound Eisa was hearing, buzzing sibilants and drones, had been filling her Mentalios link for some time before she finally recognized it as a voice. Griggory's voice.

She stood inside the dim abandoned temple summoning the long-lost Knight through her wystic lens, amplifying her call through Vaka Aster's Fenestros, and had been for long enough for the strange sky outside to dim, grow lighter, and dim again. Without a guide through this foreign world, it wasn't as if she could go and look for him, and it didn't seem as if there were many places left to look. This realm had become nothing but stormy skies and endless water, and it wasn't hard to conceive that this single lone island might be the last remaining. All she could do was use the Fenestros to create a beacon of sorts and hope he found her. Fortunately, the Fenestros made a powerful beacon. She couldn't be certain Griggory even still dwelled in Himmingaze, but something told her he did.

...eiiiiiissssAAAAAA...

And this, finally, was him. His voice grew louder as he approached, nearly yelling her name now. He was close. Casting her klinkí stone shield around her, she left the shelter of the shrine to wait for him beneath the magnificent Glister Cloud. *It's a fitting name,* she thought.

EeeeeeiiiiiiiissssSSSSAAAAAA!

The sky had again brightened a tiny bit, allowing her to see farther. Beyond the rocky shoreline at about the distance she could run in five breaths, the water seemed to be swelling. It looked as if a bubble at least as big as her dragørfly scout was rising from beneath, forcing seawater before it in a perfect sphere.

And it was coming fast.

Griggory? she tried. *Is that you?*

He responded at once. *Sour child, bitter girl! It is you. It is Eeeeiii-issSSAAAA!*

She chuckled without glee. After all this time, he still thought of her as cold and bitter. And he still called her "girl."

Briefly, she wondered if coming had been a mistake. Griggory was a force, and as unpredictable as he was uncontainable. In her years of training before he'd left Vinnr, no one had come as close to leveling her as her ancient tutor, mentor, and superior, Knight Griggory

Dondrin. He was the eldest living Knight, already old when she'd taken her oath, even when Ulfric had taken his.

The hardships she'd endured as a fledgling, then a warrior, then a priest in Dyrrakium, which was still Lœdyrrak then, had prepared her for anything the Resplendolent Conservatum could subject her to, or even the Knights Corporealis—but Griggory Dondrin had always made her feel as if she barely grasped the enormity of the responsibilities and obligations she bore. Of all the Knights she'd known, most who'd come and gone, he was the only who had ever awed her. Not because of his strength, though he'd been dauntless as a Knight, and not because of his faith or his wisdom, both as unimpeachable as any Dyrrak's. It was because of his compassion—for her, the cold, distant Knight who loved no one. Eisa had been taught since childhood she could only love one thing: her duty. Griggory had taught her that loving and being loved were more important than duty.

He had become more than just her teacher when she'd left her home and joined the Conservatum in Ivoryss. He'd been like a father, someone who often encouraged her, even after a failure, and believed in her inner strength, even when she felt weak. Not like her real father, a Dyrrakium descendant of the Sixth Line whom she'd long since forgotten. Like all Dyrrak fathers, hers had used Eisa's weaknesses as lessons to make her stronger, make her faith deeper. But Griggory had never cared about her faith or her role as a Knight. He had simply cared for her.

As she watched from the foot of the shrine's steps, the bubble suddenly breached the waves and rose from the water. For a moment, she caught sight of a man's silhouette inside a clear globe astride what seemed to be an animal or water steed of some sort. The creature leaped onto the shore, something from depths unimagined. Then the globe was gone, and only Griggory and the creature he rode remained.

Twice the girth but easily ten times the length of a horse, the creature's body resembled an eel, although one large enough to swallow a person in one gulp with room in its belly for seconds. Pure-black scales covered it, and at least a dozen gossamer beryl-colored fins of varying lengths and shapes trailed along its hide. Eisa struggled to take in its strangeness, but she had no trouble with its features. The beast's leap from the water had put it directly in front of her, and its head now hovered just an arm's-length before her own. Its skull seemed equal parts canine and salmon, with nose slits and a lower jaw that protruded beyond the upper. Many teeth, as silver as her armor and spiked like a game trap, protruded from the hooked lower jaw. Ridged horns that resembled ears swept back from the sides of the long skull far enough that Griggory could grasp them from where he sat on its back.

Its gray diaphanous eyes stared down on her with a predator's gaze, then it took a step forward and lowered its head closer. A feeling so unfamiliar she almost didn't recognize it twisted in her—cold fear— and she suddenly doubted the strength of her own klinkí stone shield to hold the thing at bay.

"Come, Hither, don't crowd the star-walker. She's come so far, so far. She's traveled too far to know what to make of a sight as pretty as you."

Griggory slid from the creature's back and closed the distance to Eisa in two long strides. She didn't dare spare him a glance. The creature's eyes hadn't wavered from hers. From experience, she knew better than to blink first. Even if Griggory somehow controlled it, as it appeared he did, once a killer's instincts were triggered, nothing could stop its natural inclinations. All one had to do was ask this world's dead Mystae to know this was a fact.

Her ancient mentor stopped beside the beast's head and reached up to scratch beneath its substantial lower jaw, which caused it to blink two sets of eyelids as if pleased with the affection. As he scratched, Griggory eyed her.

"Yes, it is Eisa, the girl turned doom-bringer. She brings the dark with the night, the blood with the knife, the death with the life. This is our girl, Hither. I knew she would come back, I knew she would. But now I must ask her why. Excuse me."

As he approached her wystic shield, she took in the sight of him. He was completely dry. The glowing bubble he'd been ensconced in must have been some wystic barrier to hold the water out. But the clothing he wore was unlike anything she'd seen. Ragged and threadbare, to be sure, but made from a strange, form-hugging material that she could only compare to a glove that had been cut to fit him as close as skin. This showed how gaunt he'd become, almost nothing but bones. The suit's collar rose to cover most of his chin, but she could still see how hollow his cheeks were, how his eyes seemed lost in their sockets, and his short, bulbous nose now looked like a mushroom cap sprouting from his skull.

"Griggory…" she began, then stopped, surprising herself at how meek her voice sounded.

He seemed not to notice. "Eisa Nazaria," he said, "why have you come back to Himmingaze so long after sealing its fate and leaving redemption to time? Is now that time?" He placed one of his palms against that light of her shield and pushed his face as close to hers as he could. "Because, I warn you, time itself is about to end."

He sounded as if he were…mad. It was impossible, she knew. A Knight Corporealis could not lose their wits. The Verity spark within them kept their minds as stalwart and constant as the eternity they inhabited. Yet, spark or not, he appeared to be, for lack of a better word, demented.

"What do you mean, time is about to end?" she asked, searching for the right footing to take with her long-exiled former teacher.

"Dark Eisa, daughter of Lœdyrrak," he said, not breaking eye contact for a moment, "you must be hungry."

She noted that the faded blue of his irises was still as clear and direct as the first day they'd met, some fifteen hundred turns ago. "No, I'm not hungry. Griggory—"

But he'd already turned and scooted up close to the sea monster, and he now appeared to be whispering to it. A moment later, the great beast slipped back into the sea without seeming to displace or disturb a single drop of water. It was disconcerting to watch something so large move with such agility.

But with it gone, she was a bit more at ease. Beckoning with her fingertips, she pulled her klinkí stones back to her palm and released the light shield. The damp immediately pressed in again. Griggory turned back to her and grinned with his skull face in a way that made her wonder if she'd been too hasty with removing the shield.

Before she could speak again, he rattled, "Hither will be back soon. She prefers the chewy fleech for herself, naturally, being a slangarook —they all love fleeches, you know—but she's the best at hunting down my favorite Never Sea delight. I'm sure you'll love it too. Not as good as the syke drink of the Lœdyrraks, of course, but then, what is?"

She couldn't be sure what all the words he said were, some being spoken in the Himmingaze tongue, but she caught the gist. "As I said, I'm not hungry. Griggory, I know it's been a very long time since we last saw each other, but focus, please. I'm here on extremely urgent business. I'm sure you know why I've come." Then, after taking another look at him, she had to ask, "How long has it been since *you* have eaten?"

The corners of his mouth turned downward. "What is the use, what? Eating now, so close to the end, is meaningless. There isn't the time. Not for Himmingaze."

The heavy mist looming over the ocean was thickening into a salvo to what felt to be a long-lasting rainstorm. "Come inside the shrine with me," she said. "We need to talk. And you're right about that, there isn't much time." *For both this world and our own, it seems,* she thought.

Whatever wystic contrivance he'd used to keep himself dry beneath the waves on the back of his beast must have worn off, because his silvery-blond mane had begun to droop and grow wet in the drizzle. But he did not move to join her. At a loss, she stepped to him and put a hand on his shoulder, meaning to pull him inside if she had to.

Shark-fast, he gripped her hand and yanked her forward until their noses nearly touched. "How many turns, Eisa? How many have passed? Do you realize what you did, what you caused and cannot undo?"

Twisting her arm free, she fought the impulse to strike him. But it immediately gave way to pity. And shame. How could he ask her if she knew what she'd done? She'd lived with that mistake for as long as he had—but she hadn't gone mad. Why had he? Was it simply because he was from the Yorish bloodline, never as strong as she, a Dyrrak, to begin with? If she let it, her pity would unravel. If she let it, she would despise him for reminding her of her shame.

Instead of giving in to anger, she grasped him this time by both shoulders, feeling the ridges of his bones beneath his strange costume, and spoke calmly, enunciating precisely. "Griggory, if Himmingaze is doomed, then it was because of the innate weaknesses of its maker's creations. Lífs was banished by her own creatures. Their own unworthiness and faithlessness condemned them, and I only did what was right in trying to avenge their Verity. You know why, too. Because we are not weak like they were. You are a creature of Vaka Aster, a Knight Corporealis, and I have never seen the taint of faithlessness in you. If this realm's time is over, then it is their fault, not ours. Do you understand me?"

She released him and swung her glaive over her shoulder, holding it out parallel to Isle Stonering's rocky earth. "Now, on my hallowed weapon, renew the faith in our fight and give me the answers I seek. Did you find it? Did you find Lífs's Scrylle?"

His eyes took in the glaive, then he glanced back over his shoulder to the sea. A multibranched fork of lightning that seemed to fill the horizon flashed, illuminating him from behind for a moment as if he were a Verity himself. He finally said, "Yes...yes. The Scrylle, all the celestial stones, except the one you keep. I had them all, and I could have brought Himmingaze back from the eternal ocean."

"You could have? Do you mean...do you know the way to reverse the banishment? And more importantly, do you know how to cast it?"

"Oh yes, I know that I knew, but I don't know now because I no longer have the Scrylle."

The rain became sheets, flowing from the sky as if the air itself had turned to water. Eisa hardly noticed. "What do you mean? Where is it?" The fool, his lunacy had totally undermined the mighty Knight he'd once been. She wanted to rage at him, but it would do no good. Griggory was beyond being intimidated; he had to be waited out. "Tell me what's become of the Scrylle."

"Inside." He pointed toward the shrine's door. "You'll catch your death." Then he snorted, amused. "Catch your death—Eisa the dark daughter of Lœdyrrak. Catch your death, ha! Unless it catches you first!"

He brushed past her and went inside, still chuckling, the sound of the quiet but sinister feeble-minded. She remained in the rain for another moment, gripping the glaive hard enough to press the delicate designs of its metal shaft into her palms, then followed.

From a seat in the center of the chamber, directly atop the stonework marking Lífs's symbol, he gripped his long hair and wrapped it around his free hand, wringing water from it. An illumination charm whispered into his Mentalios, still around his neck after so many turns, cast his face in a soft light that smoothed its grooves and hollows enough to remind her of the hale and hearty man he'd once been. When he spoke next, his voice seemed softened too, the edge of madness no longer punctuating his tone. "There were creatures, servants of another Verity, here. Nearly two thirty-nights ago. In Himmingaze, that is a quarter of an anni-cycle. Everything has changed here, Eisa. Even the way they count time. And—"

She cut in. "I don't need an education on Himmingaze. About the Scrylle, and these servants of another Verity?"

"One," he went on. "Then two. So pale, so tall. Almost like the Yorish, but they were not from Vinnr. They called themselves Flesh Casters, but it was my doings that took their flesh."

Balavad's minions! She started to interrupt again, but stopped herself. He was talking at last. She had to let him, even if it was barely discernible from gibberish.

"I finally found the artifacts, Eisa, but then these men, if men they were, found me. They told me they were sent by the Verity of Battgjald as emissaries to Himmingaze. *Emissaries*, they said. Lies, of course. I could read it in their thoughts—Lífs's Scrylle taught me many secrets— like poison leaking from their wounded minds.

"I learned Balavad's plans. The Battgjald Verity will come and make this world his own, make Lífs bend to his will before the five once again became the one—you know it? The Syzyckí Elementum? He doesn't want to reunite with his fragmented quins, for all the Verities were originally one Verity, and the Syzyckí Elementum is their reunification. I fear that time is coming, too, whether Balavad wishes it or not." He held up an empty hand that seemed to be grasping something that wasn't there and looked thoughtfully at its absence. "There were many secrets in Lífs's Scrylle. Many." His hand fell back into his lap.

What he was saying rang true to her mind, or at least familiar. This is what Balavad had told Ulfric, in a way. So the usurping Verity's plans went beyond Vinnr. All the more reason to stop him there. If only she could force Griggory to stop speaking in riddles and tell her where the artifacts she needed were.

But he went on and she waited, biting her tongue, clenching her fists. "I tried to use these poor servants of Balavad, tried to make them help me restore Lífs to Himmingaze, but they were too frail and too unwilling. They fought the Fenestrii and burned like candles, their skin crackling from their bones like leaves from trees. Their screams were…like nothing I've ever heard. I lost heart, Eisa. Lost it for a time."

She had no idea what he meant, but she knew his nature had never been cruel. Nor had his actions ever been needless. She trusted that if these Flesh Casters of Balavad had died by his hand, they had deserved it. The important thing was: "So you know how to restore Himmingaze and undo the banishment." She knelt down and looked him full in the face. "Tell me how. And then"—in a flash of insight, she promised—"then we'll stop this. Together, we can restore Himmingaze. But first, we must return to Vinnr to defend it from Balavad. The usurper wishes to do the same to our realm as he would have done here. But you know how to stop him, Griggory, if you'll just— wake up."

She gave him a tiny shake. She knew the strength the Knight had once had, though, and had no desire to arouse his anger. And, of course, this was Griggory. She couldn't hurt the first person in all the worlds who'd ever shown her true kindness, the love of true family. Selflessly, he had given Himmingaze hundreds of turns of his life, trying to restore the grave wrong done to it, just as he had selflessly taken her under his wing when she was still so young and needed someone to show her what it was like to be cared for.

For a moment, his eyes focused on hers, the ancient clarity and wisdom he'd once had perfectly brilliant in them again. "You have the Verity of Battgjald's vessel?"

She released him, a feeling like acrid smoke replacing her insides, hollowing her. "Why?" she asked flatly.

"That's what it is, Lœdyrrak. The Glister Cloud..." He paused and reached into a bag he wore around his neck, withdrawing his own klinkí stones. With a childlike smile, he tossed them over his head and sent them spinning and twirling in a spiral, much like the balls of light that comprised the Himmingaze sky. "The Glister Cloud *is* Lífs's vessel, or it was. Her Knights used her own spark gifted to them to shatter her vessel, creating this Cloud from her pieces to shield them from her celestial self. When they broke the final Fenestros, the one you keep, it broke the vessel and sent it aloft. As time passes, the vessel is disintegrating. As it does, Himmingaze is destroyed with it."

As he was speaking, he'd pulled his wystic stones into a tight ball hovering before them, then allowed them to explode and rise high up to the chamber's ceiling. On completing his description, he guided the stones in a slow descent until the lay scattered along the shrine's floor and began to dim until they were colorless crystals once more. A display to match his description of the Glister Cloud's origination and eventual elimination.

"Soon, very very soon," he went on, "it will all be gone. Himmingaze is only being held together by what remains of Lífs's spark, but it's running out, dissipating as much as belief in their maker is dissipating among the Himmingazians. And without Lífs's Scrylle and all her Fenestrii to undo the banishment, and a Himmingazian Mystae with a strong spark to perform the steps necessary, the vessel cannot be restored."

These fragments of knowledge about how the banishment worked fascinated her. She hadn't learned any of this before the last Mystae had hidden the Scrylle and then died—or rather been killed. "And where are the artifacts?"

He waved his hand vaguely toward the open door. "Gone. Stolen from me."

"You're telling me that the only way we can replicate this banishment to force Balavad out of Vinnr is to shatter his vessel and turn it into some kind of...of barrier that shields our realm from his sight. But we need his vessel and Fenestrii and Lífs's Scrylle to do it." She turned and paced a few steps away, then came back. "Do you know who stole them? Can we get them back?"

"The grandling of a dear friend. A precocious busybody with an imagination fit to beat the best storytellers in Vinnr. Vreyja once told me about a time when he was still a child and he'd tried to invent—"

She cut him off. "Who is he, Griggory? How do we find him?"

Griggory stood and began pacing a pattern among his fallen wystic stones as he told her a curious story. Sometime in the recent past—Eisa guessed just a day or two ago based on his description—he'd heard a voice in his Mentalios. The voice had been calling out from Isle Stonering, seeking Ulfric, and unfamiliar as it was, he'd known it must have belonged to a Knight he'd never met. He'd come to the island as quickly as he could, riding on Hither beneath the surface of the sea.

Evernal, Eisa thought.

As he got close, from under the waves he'd witnessed a monstrous flying ship, blacker than the blackest ocean's deepest depth, and knew from the flying Ravener fighters accompanying it, like the ones he'd witnessed when the Flesh Casters had come, that it belonged to the Battgjaldic Verity. As he and Hither watched, the black behemoth consumed two Himmingazian ships. They belonged to the Glisternauts, which he explained were Himmingazian explorers. One ship belonged to the Glisternaut he knew well, the one who'd stolen two of Lífs's artifacts from him. Some short time after the ships were swallowed, a starpath had appeared, spearing right through the heart of the black starship. Then there had been an explosion, and the starship and everything it contained had been obliterated and scattered throughout the Never Sea.

Eisa listened closely to the story. "So you think this Himmingazian who stole the artifacts from you was taken by Balavad, and now everything is lost or destroyed," she confirmed. "Were all the artifacts stolen?"

"Lífs's Scrylle, of course, and a Fenestros. I gave them to Vreyja for safekeeping. I've known the lovely woman for many cycles. She and others like her are doing their best to keep Lífs's lore alive, but secretly, and I help them remember what's almost been forgotten. They know Himmingaze can only be saved one way, through renewed belief and trust in the Creatress. And re-forming her vessel, of course. But I learned a new bunch of Balavad's Flesh Casters were hunting me and the artifacts—it's why I stay below the waters with Hither, you see. I couldn't think what else to do with the Scrylle. Vreyja's grandling, clever boy, so clever, took them. I should have known he would guess their power and wouldn't be able to resist such splendid things. And now they are lost to the sea. Without the Scrylle map, I'd have to live another hundred lifetimes to find them again. As you can see yourself, Himmingaze will be forever gone before that happens."

Eisa stepped away from the old Knight, staring into the shadows of the shrine without seeing. Balavad's warship had been here, and, she had to assume, the Knights she'd witnessed taken captive in Vinnr were still his prisoners. The voice calling for Ulfric, that had to have been Mylla. But why would she think their Stallari was here? Her mind would have been muddled by her unexpected journey through the starpath, and she most likely wouldn't have known what realm she was in unless she recognized Lífs's symbol in the shrine.

She turned to Griggory. "Do you know where Ulfric is?"

"My old friend." He smiled wistfully. "He was the much better choice for Stallari. His resolve, even after he met Acolyte Lutair—oh, you could see how in love they were..."

He began rambling and Eisa ignored him. If Ulfric were in Himmingaze, surely Griggory would have sought him out. And if he'd been aboard Balavad's ship—but his ship was destroyed. So what of the Knights? *Are they all dead?* she wondered as a cold feeling that had nothing to do with Himmingaze's rain drenched her. *Verity's tears, not Roi...*

Too many questions, and no way to answer them. She paced back to Griggory and gripped his shoulder to force his attention to her. "Where is Balavad now? If he came here, does that mean he succeeded in Vinnr? Could he have instead failed?"

Griggory said nothing, eyeing her in that old way he had when he wanted her to think things through and come up with answers to her questions on her own.

Eisa grasped the hilt of her dagger and seated it more firmly in its sheathe. She had been here long enough. Himmingaze was beyond saving, but Vinnr might not be. There were too many unanswered questions for her to linger here.

"Griggory, come back with me to Vinnr. There's nothing left for you in this place. If my fears are correct, only Dyrrakium stands between the salvation of our world and the end of it. You and I must return and stand with them."

She reached into the bag she carried that contained Vaka Aster's Scrylle and Fenestros, preparing to open the starpath. Griggory paced toward the structure's entrance as if he hadn't heard her.

"Griggory?" she called. "Your world needs you. Your Verity needs you. Your faith—"

He turned back and looked at her, the same kind eyes twinkling in the light of his Mentalios that she'd first seen when joining the Conservatum in Asteryss at the young age of twelve. Eyes containing wisdom far beyond any Dyrrakium priest's. Eyes that knew compassion as well as power that went beyond human limits. Eyes that had seen things inside the Howling Weald no other person of Vinnr had. Griggory had fed the hunger she'd had as a young Conservatum acolyte for greater things than her heritage and traditions and had made her come to realize that service to her Verity was far nobler and more honorable than the fate of being a Dyrrakium leader, a destiny she would otherwise have chosen. But that had been eons ago, it seemed. Forever.

"Eisa, daughter of Vinnr, my faith is not in your fight, but in my own."

As he said that, the monstrous head of his slangarook pushed through the doorway behind him, its eyes coming to rest menacingly on hers. A limp grayish sea creature fell from its jaws and landed at Griggory's feet. The old Knight retrieved the animal and bit into it without hesitation. Eisa's stomach flip-flopped.

Looking over his shoulder at her and still chewing, Griggory went on. "I will not abandon Himmingaze until its last drop of water has fallen from its shrinking sky, and I with it. You do what you have to do, what you've always done. Just remember to do it with the honor and faith I taught you. I have known more living than you can imagine, and love, and loyalty. I know that you have all of those within you still, even if you have forgotten them. If you succeed in Vinnr, remember me here. Remember what happened and spend the rest of your life, however long it may be, seeking redemption within yourself. Then perhaps you can begin restoring your own faith."

He stepped into the storm, the slangarook backing out with him, and disappeared.

CHAPTER TWO

U lfric's eyes opened.

The light shining into them was almost too bright to take, washing straight down on him through a broken ceiling.

Dear Verities, no! I'm not back in Himmingaze, am I?

The shrine of Lífs had been the last ceiling he'd looked on…but no. This was bright daylight, Halla bright, in fact.

Vinnr. Vaka Aster told me we are in Vinnr. And the Knights are here.

Following this was a thought that brought both indescribable relief and a sense of heavy weight. *I am me, once again,* he thought. And he felt it, from his thoughts to the warmth of his toes in his own worn leather boots. Ulfric looked across the chamber and experienced a momentary sense of disequilibrium. He recognized the room, the sanctuary at the peak of Mount Omina, but had never seen it from this vantage before. He'd been in the dark of his mind for…how long? Days, turns?

How did I get here? What has happened?

It all came flooding back in that moment. All of it. The duration of his journey through Himmingaze, the engineer Bardgrim, the warship capturing them, his wrathful tirade at Balavad, speaking through the memory keeper to Crumb, then demanding Mylla give him Balavad's

Fenestros so that he could look into the Scrylle and find the way to unmake the cage.

Mylla…

She had struck him—he would never forget that. He'd gone into the black. Then…?

He groaned and pulled himself up into a seated position. Of course the vantage was unusual. He'd never occupied this position. None but Vaka Aster, or the vessel the Vinnric Verity inhabited, had.

The chamber wavered, and he saw the shapes of people around him, his weirded vision distorting and fracturing their forms as if he were looking through a prism. At some point, he'd been given a robe of heavy, pristine wool, the kind that had customarily been draped on Vaka Aster's vessel. He rubbed his hand against the fiber, carded to a softness that would put a baby to sleep, then pulled the robe open. One of his own drab brown tunics covered his torso. The ceremonial tunic of dark blue and his armor that he'd been wearing when he'd been transported to Himmingaze were missing. This information concerned him. How long had he been here? How long since Symvalline and Isemay had been sent to Arc Rheunos?

"Ulfric? By the fickle furies of fate, is that you?"

It was Stave's voice, and a moment later, his wide form was visible approaching from farther back in the chamber.

"It is," he said aloud, then quietly to himself, "and it isn't."

Stave had him by the shoulders, his whiskery face a hand's-width distant. "Verity's light, your eyes! Look like bruhawks' eyes, they do! All swirly and wystic."

Ulfric reached up and patted one of Stave's shoulders. "I know. Believe me." More figures approached, and he saw Mallich and Safran clearly a moment later.

"Stallari," Mallich said and tipped his head while touching his fingertips to the center of the nine-pointed star on his chin.

Ulfric returned the salute. "Mallich, Safran, you're well? I've missed some things, I know. But you're all well?"

We are, Ulfric. And you? Safran sent by Mentalios, projecting for each of them to hear.

"I'm…" He almost confirmed that all was right with him too but stopped himself. That description didn't fit, so he finished with: "Back."

Mallich asked, "And Vaka Aster?" The man's topaz eyes didn't waver, piercing even the fractured chromatism through which Ulfric saw everything.

He sat silently for a moment, pondering how to answer that. After so many long turns a Knight, and most of those as Stallari, he had developed a default condition that had never yet failed to serve him, though he couldn't always say it served him well. Blunt pragmatism.

"Vaka Aster is still shackled, and until that is resolved, nothing else can be. Do we still have Balavad's Scrylle?"

Safran sent: *We don't know where Balavad is now, but we were fortunate that the Himmingazian Bardgrim retained his artifacts. We have them with us.*

"That engineer was full of surprises. I'll . . . miss him," Ulfric said, realizing he'd grown fond of the precocious stranger.

"You don't have to miss him, you don't," Stave said. "He's turning out to be quite the fit among us, even as green as he is. Along with about thirty others like him."

"I don't understand."

"Stallari." The urgency in Mallich's tone grabbed his attention. "The *Vigilance* has been destroyed. And our numbers are down to five. We must think critically about where we'll be safest. We must plan."

A great deal of news was coming at him, and he was struggling to fit all the pieces together. But Mallich was wrong about something.

"Seven, Mallich. We are still seven Knights. Symvalline is not lost to us. She is in Arc Rheunos with my daughter. Vaka Aster showed me. And Eisa is still—"

Stave cut in, his voice a burning ember. "One other thing we can be sure of, none of this would be happening if Eisa hadn't betrayed the Order. There is a reckoning coming, there is, if she ever dares show her face again."

"No, Stave," Ulfric said and shook his head. "We don't know Eisa's purpose. We can't until she is found. In Himmingaze, Mylla told me what happened aboard the *Vigilance*, that she took Vaka Aster's Scrylle.

It was reckless, but I've known Eisa longer than any of you. She never acts without purpose." *But is that true?* he thought, remembering all he'd read in Lífs's Scrylle. *The doom of Himmingaze, how much was she responsible?*

Safran wrapped a hand around one of Stave's, halting further arguments from him as a fourth figure approached and squeezed himself between the Knights.

With another shake of his head, this time to clear it, Ulfric at last asked, "Bardgrim?"

The engineer—as unbelievable as it was that it was him—grinned amiably. "Glad you're back, Aldinhuus. Er, Stallari rather, is it?"

Ulfric's usual composure failed him. At first, all he could think to say was: "Just Ulfric."

His Himmingazian companion gave him a quick nod and continued. "I'm sure you've all got a lot of catching up to do and you're looking forward to some home-cooked meals and whatnot. But I need a quick hand with something. Shouldn't take a moment, given your particular proclivities."

Ulfric's eyes widened as a vague, shadowy memory passed through his mind. Bardgrim aboard the warship, fighting all around, Bardgrim leaping...

"I know what you've done," he said.

The way that statement hung in the still air pulled the engineer up short. "...And?"

"Tell me why."

Uncertainly, Bardgrim looked to the others for a clue.

"You saved me. Saved *Vinnr*," Ulfric stated.

A blush of modesty Ulfric wouldn't have guessed Bardgrim capable of spread over his face, and he stammered, "If you want to put it that way...you see, well, there was a Ravener—really, it was this Balavad sprite fellow, and he'd somehow gotten control of the Ravener—made the poor sod one of these vessel things, I guess? And he had Knight Evernal's sword and was about to, you know, *kill* you. So I..." He shrugged and cleared his throat. "I stopped him with the first thing I had on hand."

Ulfric broke into a grin, wide and authentic, and stepped off the platform and over to Bardgrim. He put a hand that felt as hot as if it had recently come from a forge on the man's shoulder and gave him a squeeze that was hard enough to make Bardgrim wince. "You mean you took the blow that was meant for me. You're one of the most extraordinary—"

He cut himself off, his eyes fixed on the man's face. His chin, the Himmingazian's chin—it bore the star of Vaka Aster, the star that proclaimed that he was a Knight Corporealis of Vinnr.

"Extraordinary," Ulfric repeated quietly, then finished his statement. "One of the most extraordinary *Knights* I've witnessed in my long turns. Truly."

Bardgrim continued to look flustered. "Not exactly a Knight, really. See, I haven't taken a vow of chastity or perpetual irritation, or whatever it is you do."

"It's an oath, Himmingazian, a promise to uphold our duty to protect the vessel from all enemies. And you have been ordained as a Knight Corporealis by Vaka Aster, one of the Five Verities, creators of all things," Mallich cut in evenly.

Stave added with a twist of his usual gruffness. "It's the greatest honor there is in any realm."

Bardgrim's eyes widened a moment as Ulfric observed him digesting this. The Himmingazian was more than changed. Ulfric sensed he was *greater* in some way, stronger, resilient. A Knight, in other words. And what's more, he no longer harbored the same fear or timidity, even toward Ulfric, who'd treated him roughly indeed. For that, Ulfric found himself surprisingly grateful.

"Perpetual irritation, like I said," Bardgrim confirmed. "Not an *oath* I'm likely to make. Or is it take?"

"It's not something to quip about," Ulfric started, then put a halt to his shoddy righteousness. Who was he to speak to this man about honor? Bardgrim may have caused him more than a few headaches in the past days, but in the end, he'd been the bravest of them. He'd had no idea what he was involved in, no training or even a basic familiarity with the archaneology of Verities, just a list of forbidden rumors and whispered half-truths to bring him from disbelief to acceptance of the threats they endured, all in a matter of only a few hours. And he'd stood up to everything they'd faced, coming through it not only with his life but also having been ordained, *chosen*, by Vaka Aster. What other endorsement could be that resounding? Ulfric would never again have cause to find fault with the Himmingazian.

"I'm sorry, Bardgrim. I'm not myself and it's been a difficult few days." He swept his hand out to encompass the Knights. "There is no word in our realm or any other to express the depth of the Knights Corporealis' gratitude. Nor of my own."

With a short forced laugh, the engineer said, "It was nothing, just a tickle and a strange trip through a dimension of space or stars or something I couldn't describe if I tried, and, you know, here we are. I don't even have a scar, though it would have been a great story to tell. I'm sure no one back home will believe me now, with—well, anyway, let me get to the point."

"Anytime," Stave grumbled.

"Send us 'Gazians back home and we'll call it even. What do you say, Master Knight who became a sprite? Deal?"

Ulfric glanced at his three companions before answering. "We could use you here, Bardgrim. We are not yet entirely free of this threat." As he said this, he could read in Bardgrim's eyes that he'd known what Ulfric's response would be.

"Ah, yes, well," the man jabbered. "Don't mistake me, I am ridiculously grateful that you and your brighter self brought us—and by 'us' I mean me and the crew of the *Bounding Skate*, do you remember them? —here, obviously, and rescued us from the warship, but all us Himmingazians, we'd really prefer to go home now."

"Speaking of going home," Stave cut in, "Ulfric, we need to discuss getting back to Vigil Tower."

One thing at a time, Ulfric thought. *I'm not actually the damned Verity, I can't manage everyone's fates!*

But he said, "Stop, wait. I need some gaps filled in first. Things that happened on the warship, and what's happened since. Start from the moment Mylla brained me." He glanced around, still fighting with his

Verity-enhanced eyes. A sudden thought struck him like a blow, making him blink. "Mallich, you said we were still five Knights strong, excepting Eisa and Symvalline. Was that including Bardgrim?"

Mallich nodded slowly.

"Then…where is Mylla?"

The wounded look in Safran's dark eyes answered him. She sent: *She didn't return with us. Mylla, our sister, was lost in Himmingaze.*

CHAPTER THREE

Mallich tasked Jaemus with standing at the damaged front entrance to the mountaintop enclave the starpath had brought them to and keeping an eye on the rest of the refugees from Balavad's ship. Vaka Aster had rescued a few hundred captives and brought them back to Vinnr when she'd defeated Balavad, though only a few were still there now.

Wasn't that a fine thing, Jaemus thought, going from being one of the most decorated engineers in Himmingaze to a—what was he exactly? A lookout? What specifically was he looking out for?

Whatever it might be, the simple fact was that after living his life among nothing but rain and a glittering horizon that was sure to kill him, and everyone else, someday, he couldn't keep his eyes off the vista that spread before him. He'd never seen so much land. Rocks, dirt, things called trees, they were all nothing but myth in Himmingaze.

Footsteps sounded behind him and he glanced back. Knight Glór was approaching, and she smiled when he noticed her. She was hard not to look at and not just because she was Vinnric. Her hair was as black as Knight Evernal's had been, but glossy and straight, and her big eyes, so dark they were nearly black as well, shined playfully. He guessed from the fine lines that swept back beside her eyes and mouth she was older than him by a few anni-cycles, or turns, as they called a long passage of time here in Vinnr. But there was also such wisdom in those lines and the steadiness of her gaze that he instinctively thought of her as ageless.

She carried a Fenestros and used it to speak to him, her voice like crystal through the stone. "Is all well, Knight Bardgrim? Can I bring you anything?"

Oh, that's right, he wasn't a mere lookout, he was a *Knight* now. Was that better than being a Glisternaut?

"I'm fine, I think," he responded, marveling at just how fine he felt indeed. He wasn't tired or hungry, and most of all, he was not in any pain after having a sword plunged through him. There were definitely perks to this Knight thing. After all, a Glisternaut couldn't survive something so, well, hideous. "There's only one group of Vinnrics left, and I think they'll be headed down the mountain soon," he finished, inwardly repeating what he'd just said. *Headed down the mountain.*

No Himmingazian in his lifetime, or several lifetimes before his, had ever seen a mountain, much less *walked* on one. All his home's mountains stood deep beneath the turbulent waters of the Never Sea now, where no one who didn't want to become a feast for fleeches dared go.

Safran glanced over the encampment the Vinnrics had made for themselves. Only a few fire circles remained, all carefully covered with snow to put them out, gathered from the intermittent snowbanks that remained from winter. "Ulfric and Stave are working to repair the interrealm well. We may be back indoors by dinnertime, and then you and your friends will see what the cities of Vinnr are like."

"I'm assuming they'll be on land?"

She grinned. "On land, yes. And they don't—how did you describe the Himmingaze cities?—hover."

He smiled back. She was, by far, the most amiable of his new companions. Warm, quick to smile. She reminded him of his gram-sirene, though she looked far younger. He was having a hard time understanding the match between her and the far coarser Stave. "Tell me what this interrealm well is," he said. "Is it like the starpath? Much as I want to get home, thinking of being discorporated and blasted through space and time on a beam of starlight again has . . . less appeal than one might think."

"Not to worry, Jaemus. They're like doorways. You simply step through and you're in the next room. But the room can be a dozen or a hundred leagues distant. Ulfric and Knight Dondrin built them long ago to help the Knights protect the Fenestrii and come to each other's aid quickly if needed." She stopped at his look of, what he imagined was, over-rapt fascination. These kinds of wonderous things were the sweetness in his chuffee.

"A portal, then?" he asked.

She nodded. "Exactly. A portal only a Knight can open."

"And how does it work for those who aren't?"

"We'll take your people through in smaller groups with us. It's quite simple. They will take one of our hands, then each other's. Anything touching the Knight who opens the well will be pulled through with them."

"That's a relief," he commented, not sure if he meant it. There was so much he didn't understand about this world, its physical properties not the least of them. It would take lifetimes to learn it, if he wanted to. Which they were telling him he now had...

He heard a familiar buzz in the sky outside and looked out. One of the Vinnric flying crafts, what they called dragørfly scouts, flew over-head, heading down the face of the mountain. Scouts from their capital city Asteryss had found the refugees shortly after their return. Knight Roibeard had spoken with the first scout pilot who landed and learned that they'd been watching the starpath continuously since their city had fallen. Expecting either Vaka Aster—or their final doom.

The Ivoryssians had steadily been evacuated in small numbers by these crafts and others brought from the city. Jaemus's mind itched to get a closer look at the scouts, pull them apart and see how they worked. Those among the refugees from Balavad's ship who'd felt up to the task and didn't want to wait for a ship that could carry them had started walking back toward their homes and cities, leaving only a handful still at Mount Omina.

He noted Safran watching the scout closely. When it was out of sight, she sighed. "The Ivoryssians will be happy to return to their homes. And those who survived the Ravener attack on Asteryss will be happy they are back. Despite the many sacrifices and lives lost throughout the realm, Vinnr is fortunate."

He glanced at her, wondering if she was attempting to be funny, but saw the seriousness in her firmly set features. Jaemus had heard that the city most of the refugees had come from had been defeated decisively and many taken captive. Before that, another kingdom called Yor, east and north of here, had fallen to Balavad too. If Safran thought that was lucky, he couldn't imagine how much worse she thought things could have been.

But that wasn't true, was it? He'd seen with his own eyes the way Balavad changed and distorted people, turning them into the mindless and marauding Raveners, gangly and hideous. He thought of his friends inside the mountain, Cote and the rest of the Glisternauts, and imagined what they'd be like if that had happened to them. It sent a shudder through him. Safran put a warm hand on his elbow.

"Don't worry, Jaemus, I think the worst is behind us. And once we're back at Vigil Tower and we have a chance to consider all options, I'm sure we'll get your people back home without further delay. You too. That is"—she caught his eyes with hers—"if you still want to leave."

His mouth opened to say the obvious, *Of course I do*, but something in her gaze stopped him. *Don't I?* he thought and closed his mouth again.

"I have something for you," she said and reached into a pouch she wore at her waist. She drew out a pendant with a circle of crystal in the center. He recognized what it was instantly. A Mentalios lens, like all the Vinnric Knights wore.

"We have a few extras of these in case one of us loses ours. This is the last we had here in Mount Omina. The lenses are useful beyond imagining. Well, perhaps you can imagine it. I've already seen the nimbleness of your mind." She handed it to him and gestured for him to put it around his neck. "Let me show you how it works."

He took it without question and easily memorized the Elder Veros phrase she taught him that would allow him to focus his mind. *Cæcra ad resrs, boromcad bea dord. Kucik kea kesrs, emsu kæ lœkra. Cycle of light, balanced by dark, focus my sight, into my heart.*

He repeated it after hearing it once, and she gave him a knowing grin. "Nimble, as I said. It isn't the words so much as their resonance that clears your mind and allows you to hone your focus," she said.

Then something extraordinary happened. Spoken words, in Safran's voice, ran through his head, as if he'd thought them himself. *Do you hear me?*

His shoulders jerked just a hair. "That's just...water and lightning! That's incredible!" he said aloud.

She held up a hand. *Use the lens. Send your voice, your thoughts, into it.*

He cleared his throat, realized how silly that was, and a moment later thought: *Having someone else inside my head is a lot like having someone else in my underthings drawer. I don't really care what you see, but I'm pretty sure you're not going to like it.*

With a snort, she sent: *I can only see into your mind if you leave it unguarded. Learning this will come with practice, like anything. You will get better at it the more you do it. Eventually, you won't even think about it anymore, it will become natural. Now, I'm going to let the others know you wear a Mentalios as well.*

"Wait. I don't really think that's—"

But Safran was already channeling: *Knights, I've given Jaemus a Mentalios. From now on, if you send to all of us, think to include him as well. And he's a very good pupil. He's already learned the basics.* She pointed at him, inviting him to try it out.

Um, hello? This is Jaemus. He warmed to the experience quickly. *Borrowing the words of a famous Himmingazian, let me say, "Even the farthest of friends who knows your mind is closer." I paraphrased a bit, of course, but the sentiment seems to apply.*

Jaemus Glunt! Stave sent, his rough voice striking inside Jaemus's skull like a blunt instrument. *Time's right that you'd step up to the Order. I knew you'd become one of us eventually, I did.*

And Roibeard: *Welcome, novice.*

Then Ulfric: *Take it slow. It can be overwhelming at first.*

He clutched his head in both hands and pressed his eyes closed to block them out. When the Knights stopped speaking, he reached beside him to put a hand against the wall and steady himself. "That was like having a school of fish fighting in my head. How in Himmingaze am I supposed to get used to that?"

"It gets easier, as I said," Safran said aloud, putting a reassuring hand on his shoulder. "Normally, you wouldn't receive one until you'd been ordained by the maker herself. But circumstances being what they are… Keep it close. It may seem frivolous or cumbersome to you now, but you never know when you'll need to warn others of danger. Or be warned."

Jaemus forced a smile to his lips that felt as fresh as ten-cycle-old smookshark and grappled with the urge to remove the lens and give it back. His mind was an…*active* place, and he wasn't entirely comfortable with the idea that someone else might be able to explore it without his control. But then, how wonderful was it to be able to speak without being heard by those you didn't want listening?

Perks to being a Knight, indeed, he thought and realized Safran had heard it by the way she smiled broadly at him. *Oh, this is going to take some getting used to.*

Don't worry, she sent. *It will take some time to learn to manage your thoughts, but I'll show you how to do it. The interrealm well won't be done until evening. That gives us a few hours to practice before we travel back to Vigil Tower. First lesson, think of your mind as a kórb fruit where others only see the outer layer.*

"Yes, right. Now, what's a kórb fruit?"

CHAPTER FOUR

The words Eisa wanted to scream—*You're a traitor to your Verity!*—died on her lips. Griggory was gone. Nothing she said or did would change that. What he'd said, that she needed to restore her own faith, had shaken her, and now the knot in her guts clenched and burned. She knew what he meant: how her rage against the blasphemous Mystae had doomed Himmingaze and its Verity, what she'd done to Lillias…

But the burning inside would abate, as it always did eventually. She would not fail her own Verity or her people.

Casting her klinkí stone shield, she strode back to her dragørfly ship, already holding the Scrylle and Fenestros scepter and murmuring the incantation that would bring her back to Vinnr through the starpath well.

The experience of slipping through stars and realities was bracing, energizing, and she arrived near the top of Mount Omina in what felt simultaneously like a moment and an eternity. The dragørfly ship hit the ground hard, its engine failing, as she'd feared it would. Despite being Knight-made and reinforced with techniques only Knights knew, no nonliving object could travel the starpaths for long before they became crippled and ruined. It had probably been the reason

Mylla's own scout had crashed, stranding her to be done in by those disgusting sea worms.

Eisa abandoned the ruined ship and surveyed the mountainside—what she could of it, anyway. Complete darkness enclosed her, the hour close to Hallumbrum as she surmised from the stars. With one hand, she launched her klinkí stone shield, and in the other, she held up the Fenestros. With a few whispered words, the celestial stone was illuminated and cast a globe of light around her nearly as bright as day.

Shadows bounced and skittered from the light, almost as if alive and craven, hiding from her. The effect was far eerier than any Glister Cloud–ridden sky in Himmingaze could be. The place looked blasted and ruined for as far as she could see. The avalanche of a few days ago had ripped away whole trees and sent countless tons of rock skidding down the mountain's face. Snowbanks looked melted and dirtied, probably from the Raveners' ships. Down the mountain's slope lay the avalanche's path, leading to more darkness where, she knew, it had killed Symvalline and Isemay, Ulfric's daughter.

The shadowy slope of devastation held her gaze for a time. As she thought of her fellow Knight buried under hundreds of feet of snow and broken trees and rubble, she suddenly grew woozy, as if all the blood in her body was sinking to her feet. Her vision narrowed, her stomach heaved.

Almost as if it were happening to someone else, Eisa felt herself fall to a knee, heard a wail escape her lips. The loss of her friends, the loss of Griggory, the loss of another entire world—nothing in all her hundreds of turns had prepared her for this much loss.

She stayed there for she didn't know how long, her chin sunken to her chest, eyes closed, the Fenestros and klinkí stones doused as her limp arms hung at her sides, shaking.

She heard Griggory's voice in her mind. *Faith in the fight, Eisa.*

Yes, there was always a fight. Of that, she would never lose faith.

With an angry swipe of her wrist across her mouth, she rose. No more weakness. She was a Knight Corporealis, the strongest of the Verity's creations. She was a Dyrrak, the most faithful of all the people of Vinnr. And she was a Nazarian, the worthiest of the six founding lines of the people of Lœdyrrak.

The walk to the Knights' sanctuary would be rough, their paths obliterated by recent events. She started there anyway, at least to be under a roof as the night passed. The skies were clear, with no enemy in sight, and she arrived at the hollowed mountaintop sanctuary not long later.

The Fenestros cast light around the main chamber. People had been here since she and the other Knights had taken the vessel aboard the *Vigilance*. Fallen stone and debris had been cleared, signs of a recent fire still lay in the modest hearth. With a sudden suspicion, she hurried to the rear of the main chamber and saw…

Yes, the interrealm well had been restored. Not just people of Vinnr, but the Knights specifically had been here.

A sudden burst of excitement filled her chest. This was a clue, possibly a confirmation that they must have survived the usurper! Griggory had seen a starpath open from the usurper's warship, destroying it in the process. Did that mean all aboard the ship had been destroyed, or had some escaped? If some had, the starpath well might have brought them home. If they interrealm well was fixed, now they were likely back in Vigil Tower.

And who had opened the starpath? Only two things were possible: either someone on the warship had a Verity's Scrylle and Fenestros, or a Verity itself had done so. The fact that Vinnr had not been destroyed told her Vaka Aster's vessel, wherever it was, was still sound and that the fight against Balavad may have gone in the Knights', and Vinnr's, favor. *With no help from me,* she noted, and that knot in her stomach wrenched tight again.

But how did she know this for certain? How could she? Wasn't it also possible that Balavad had more than one warship, that his forces even now were rampaging through Asteryss and Magdaster and beyond, taking Ivoryss one city at a time as she suspected they'd done in Yor? Mylla had described the creatures Balavad's minions were transformed into. When last she'd seen the rest of her Order, they'd been taken captive by the usurper. What was to say they hadn't become slaves themselves and had simply rebuilt the interrealm well at Balavad's bidding?

If she went directly back to Vigil Tower, she could be stepping into a trap. As far as she was aware, she and Ulfric were the only remaining free Knights, and she didn't even know what had become of him. He'd simply disappeared. Where was he? *What* was he?

She pulled her Dyrrak dagger clear of its sheath and flipped it back and forth over her knuckles and around her palm like an allurer lulling her observers, thinking. Nighttime on the mountaintop was a cold, silent affair. Even the wind seemed unwilling to witness the desolation. Her mind was not at ease, and the preternatural quiet wasn't helping. She would wait until tomorrow morning when Halla lit and warmed the darkness to decide on a reasonable course of action. Until then she would consider: Whom could she trust?

The answer was simple. The same people she'd always been able to trust. Her own people, the Dyrraks.

The rest of Vinnr judged them as traitors, but the commoners of the lesser kingdoms were wrong. None were more worthy of Vaka Aster's favor or more willing to do what was necessary to prove it. The Dyrraks were pure in their devotion, as faithful to the Verity as Eisa was herself. Only once had Eisa's faith ever been tested, only once had it ever wavered, when her lover Lillias had betrayed her. She'd nearly failed that test, but in the end, it was Lillias and her plot that had failed.

It was funny in a way that all that had befallen Yor and Dyrrakium all those turns ago, and the doomed realm of Himmingaze, all the suffering of their peoples, could be blamed on her, the beautiful Acolyte Lillias of Yor.

Lillias...

Eisa spun her knife faster as she thought of the Yorwoman. If Lillias had never betrayed her, Eisa would never have pushed Dyrrakium to forsake its alliance with Yor and Ivoryss, and she would never have been in Himmingaze, filled with rage and despondency, ready to strike out against anyone who crossed her. And oh how the blasphemous Mystae had crossed her, and how they had paid—not only for their mistakes, but for Lillias's. Eisa had learned her lesson: commoners were weak, commoners were faithless, and never again would she trust anyone but the Knights and her own people.

Decided, Eisa abruptly sheathed her dagger, dispelling thoughts of Lillias to the pit of rage deep in her mind, and heart, she always did. When morning came, she would take the well to Dyrrakium and bring an army back to Ivoryss. If the usurper's forces ruled the city, they wouldn't for long. The Dyrraks were undefeatable.

She leaned up against the wall next to the interrealm well. Removing her Mentalios lens from around her neck, she carefully placed it inside the brass ring that made up the well's center. With it hanging there, no one else could come or go. She let her back slide down the wall and stared into the darkness, her mind as restless as her conscience.

CHAPTER FIVE

Oh, Mylla, Ulfric thought. *Why you?*

For that matter, why did they have to lose anyone to something as unthinkable as a war between Verities? Much less someone who had such promise, such vitality? She, above all the hundreds of Knights he had known in his long service to Vaka Aster, had been special. A star that shone brighter than many others in ways that defied both her youth and her start of life as a Dyrrak exile and orphan. She'd shown an aptitude for the rigors of the Order that surpassed most of her peers, and, above all, an innocence that had endeared her to him as if she were his own daughter.

Now, gone. Most likely dead.

In the short time he'd been back in Vinnr, the Knights had filled in the final pieces of what had occurred since he'd caged Vaka Aster. Not only was Mylla gone, Eisa had not returned from whatever inexplicable and unexplained pursuit she'd set herself on either. Yet he didn't, *wouldn't,* believe she'd betrayed them. Her devotion to Vaka Aster came not only from her oath as a Knight but from her heritage as a Dyrrak. Dedicated, devoted, and devout, almost to a fault. There must be more to her actions than they yet knew.

But he'd learned, hadn't he, that she had secrets. Such as the chaos she'd caused in Himmingaze.

Griggory had recorded it all in Lífs's Scrylle, what Eisa had done to their Order of Mystae, and Ulfric had stumbled across it trying to find the starpath to get back to Vinnr before he and Jaemus had been apprehended by the Glisternauts. Hundreds of turns ago, the Himmingazian Mystae had performed a wicked act of sacrilege to banish their Verity from Himmingaze and take power for themselves. Eisa, because she was Eisa and could not stand for such apostasy, had slain them to the last man. And because of her thoughtless frenzy of punishment, their Scrylle, and thus the way to save Himmingaze, had been lost. Griggory had been there since then, seeking the Scrylle. And Eisa had never spoken of any of it.

Yet still, for the life of him, Ulfric could not figure out why she had sent Mylla there. He sensed the mystery of Himmingaze's decline went much deeper than he yet knew, but concerning himself or the Order with it now was an impossibility. Balavad could be back, and Vaka Aster was still caged—as was he.

These thoughts weighed on him as he and Stave finished carving the final sigil into the wall of Mount Omina's sanctuary. He'd smashed this wystic doorway to the interrealm well on his way through last time in order to keep Balavad from following him to Vaka Aster's vessel. Now, he reflected darkly, by some twisted irony he was that vessel.

"Bogtrottin' slag!" Stave cried beside him and dropped his chisel. He stuck a dirty thumb in his mouth, speaking around it. "You finish that last bit, Ulfric. First thing I'm doing when we get back to my forge is drop this blunt bastirt into it."

Tapping gently with his own tools, Ulfric listened to Stave whisper curses at the hapless chisel and reflected, *I never knew how much I would miss them, the Knights, until now. But oh Verities, that's nothing compared to how I already miss Sym, Crumb.*

Thinking of them, where they were, what dangers they may be facing, doused any momentary amusement he felt at Stave's creative language. He was as trapped like a fox surrounded by hounds with his unsought Verity inhabitant. Freeing himself and Vaka Aster of this predicament as quickly as possible came before all other considerations. He didn't want to be responsible for a world. He simply wanted his family home again, safe and healthy.

Getting to Vigil Tower was the first step. The ancient fortress's stout walls and chambers stocked with weapons and wystic defenses to keep him and the Himmingazians safe were vital. The Vinnric commoners, history had taught, could be unpredictable in times of unrest. Since they'd arrived at Mount Omina, Ivoryssian scouts had been coming and going constantly, and the mountain sanctuary would no longer suffice as a stronghold.

The final piece of stone crumbled from the wall, leaving behind an ancient Verity rune few but a Knight could read. Ulfric backed up a pace. "Done," he said.

Stave looked it over, then gave the wall a smack with the flat of his hand. "That's that, then. Should get us home, it should. So who goes first?"

Ulfric looked around at the bedraggled and mystified Himmingazians resting in the chamber. Though two days had passed, none had yet come fully to grips with the reality of their situation, and he couldn't blame them. Four spins around Halla ago, the idea that celestial beings were responsible for the creation of all was not only foreign to them but forbidden. And now they lived and died by the whims of two of these Verities that weren't even their own. He would send them back to Himmingaze if they chose to go once he had the chance to examine Balavad's Scrylle. It was the only Scrylle now available to them and would be the key to opening a starpath well back to Himmingaze.

"We can't send the foreigners until we know it's safe," he told Stave, gesturing with his chin at a group. "We need a scout to go ahead and ensure the tower is not compromised."

"I'll do it," said Mallich, approaching from the chamber's anteroom.

Ulfric nodded. "When can you be ready?"

"The last of the Ivoryssians are walking toward the glades farther down the mountain to meet their retrieval ships. We're alone here now, so now I'll go."

Stave turned and rummaged amid a pile of weapons and tools that had amassed around him like dunes. He gripped two axes and a rock hammer and said, "I'll come with you, I will. Safety in numbers."

Mallich shook his head. "I'd like to have you, but the numbers need to stay with Ulfric. He's our duty now."

Stave's heavy eyebrows cocked in annoyance, but he nodded. "Aye."

"If I'm not back before High Halls, something's gone awry. Which means you'll need to find a way off Mount Omina and go somewhere safer," Mallich said.

He paused, knowing, as they all did, that nowhere within a hundred leagues would be safe if the right, or wrong, enemy came looking for Ulfric. Stave handed Mallich one of the axes, and Mallich seated his own heavy greatsword, Ruin Hammer, firmly in its scabbard. Without a second glance, he held his Mentalios lens up to the brass ring inset in the wall and spoke the words on the ruins carved around it. The stone face of the wall began to shimmer like Halla light on water, and a moment later, he stepped into the shimmer and disappeared.

Ulfric exchanged a glance with Stave, who gave a short nod. The waiting would always be the hardest part of any mission like this, but there was nothing else to do now but wait.

Ulfric considered what came next. It all hinged on him searching Balavad's Scrylle. He knew it would be dangerous. The last time he'd done it, Balavad had nearly taken control of his mind. But it was the only way he knew to end this catastrophe.

Fortunately, Mallich was back sooner than either expected. Not an hour had passed.

He stepped through the portal, his usually sanguine expression tense. "The gates on the outer wall have been demolished. I didn't visit every tower, but Vigil Tower itself has been ransacked," he said simply before Ulfric even had to ask.

"Ivoryssians?" he asked.

"No, I think it was Raveners. I can't see the people of Ivoryss causing such destruction to a part of their own city."

"That means the tower isn't nearly as secure as we would want it, eh?" asked Stave.

Mallich shook his head. "We can still bar the doors, which I did before leaving, but there are plenty of weapons that can get through them if the wielders are determined enough. We'll need to prioritize shoring up our defenses. And if another flying force arrives…"

Ulfric scratched his chin in thought. "The interrealm well and the catacombs are still accessible to escape if needed."

"They are," Mallich confirmed.

"But we don't know how many other wells remain unbroken or undiscovered."

"We don't."

Safran, listening through the Mentalios, spoke. *Should we even risk it?*

"We may be safer among the Ivoryssians than out here on our own," Mallich said. He looked at Ulfric. "But the city of Asteryss…it's been badly damaged. They will be busy enough restoring it without concerning themselves overmuch with our affairs, or Vaka Aster's."

The people of Ivoryss had gone over three hundred turns, many generations, without seeing the living vessel. For many, belief in their maker had gone from strict to tenuous, to, in many cases, outright disbelief. Ulfric thought back to the day this all began and the skepticism he'd seen in the leader of the Dragør Marines, Commander Brun. How far had it spread? Were things different now after what Balavad had wreaked?

Since returning two nights ago, Ulfric had remained secluded inside Mount Omina, unwilling to risk the reactions of the Vinnrics at seeing him in the flesh, no longer the Stallari of the Knights Corporealis, but now the living vessel itself. The Knights, too, had kept their distance, telling the commoners only that the vessel was safe and they needed to return to their homes. Their recent traumas—the transformation into Balavad's Raveners, the battle for first their city, then their lives aboard his warship—had rendered them pliant, in too much shock to argue with the Knights. But how long would that last?

His companions were waiting for whatever Ulfric advised. Resolute, he gave a curt nod. "We go back to Vigil Tower. At least there we can protect the Himmingazians and provide them with more suitable shelter until we send them home. Have Jaemus prepare them. We'll go as soon as they're ready."

CHAPTER SIX

Pebbles grated beneath boot heels, shattering the silence as loudly as an emberflare petard. From where she sat with her back to the wall, Eisa remained motionless, not even breathing. Someone had entered the chamber. The question was, did they know she was there?

The steps moved quietly, cautiously, toward her. Was it another Knight? No, a Knight wouldn't skulk in the dark like a rodent.

She said nothing. Perhaps it was an animal. The bears on Mount Omina were five times larger than a person, and this late in the spring, they would be hungry.

She gripped her nine klinkí stones in her left hand, but with her Mentalios engaged by the interrealm well, she couldn't use them. They were nothing but thumbnail-size rocks now.

Another step, just as cautious, getting closer. Whoever it was hadn't bothered with a light. Did they think she couldn't hear them? The careful steps told her that whoever it was, they were as blind as she.

Slag it. She was already bored with this game.

With a lunge, she flung herself forward off the ground, dropping her klinkí stones and yanking free her dagger. Whoever was there threw themselves sideways, but not before her legs and theirs tangled. She went down on her stomach and instantly wrenched her leg free to roll to one side. She heard her enemy do the same, and then it was silent in the chamber again.

A scrape of stone, a swish of cloth—the enemy was moving, circling. She danced with them. A moment later, she knew their back was to the wall she'd been leaning on. Wraith-silent, she lunged again, planning to pin the assailant against the wall with her own body and stab the life from them. They, too, could have a knife, but she could recover from a few wounds, if the enemy was lucky enough to land them.

But they were quick, much quicker than she'd expected. Her dagger arm was parried aside with enough force to slam her wrist into the wall. The dagger's hilt, adorned by the broken piece of Fenestros, struck the wall too—and a light flashed throughout the chamber, bright enough that it felt like spears thrown into her eyeballs. She disengaged from the attacker, her arm involuntarily flung over her eyes, hearing him cry out too.

Scooting away as quickly as she could, she swiped madly at her eyes, trying to regain her sight before he did. Cracking her eyelids a fraction, she saw nothing but great red and black spots dancing before her. One of the black spots might have been the shadow of a man on the other side of the chamber.

"Whoever you are, I'll build a cage for your head from your bones and keep it as a trophy," she warned. "Lay down your arms and drop to your stomach if you wish to avoid such a fate."

She heard the man's breath hitch as if surprised. Then a voice that was vaguely familiar called, "Knight Nazaria?"

After blinking hard a few times, she forced her eyes to stay open despite a lingering glare in the room. What was still illuminated? She blinked again and swiveled her gaze around the chamber. There, the center of the brass ring of the interrealm well was emitting a slowly fading glow. It was coming from her Mentalios.

Of course, the fractured Fenestros in her dagger's hilt must have struck it, the combined energy from it and the wystic interrealm well had been channeled through the lens, creating a spark as powerful as a dozen torches.

Her sight was coming back, and she could clearly make out the figure about twenty paces across from her. Definitely a man, though he was still shrouded in shadow.

"On your stomach!" she demanded.

It was her turn to be surprised. Slowly and without question, he did as told, splaying his arms by his sides, hands empty, but keeping his head up enough to watch her. Without taking her eyes from him, she sidestepped to the Mentalios. When she reached it, the glow had dimmed enough to leave the rest of the chamber in the dark. Only the circle that had been the lens itself still held any light, but she could see the crack that now split the lens in two from top to bottom.

"Oh, you are going to pay for this," she promised the familiar stranger.

"Knight Nazaria, I didn't know it was you. It was so dark, I thought all the Knights had left. I would never have fought if I'd realized who you were."

That voice, now she had it. "Wing Rekkr?"

Relief turned his voice husky. "Yes, it's me. May I stand up?"

"I don't think so, commoner." The light was gone again, the room swathed in blackness that was only broken by the glint of stars through the rent in the chamber's ceiling. Eisa reached into her bandolier and withdrew Vaka Aster's Fenestros, enticing it to wash the chamber in a much more tolerable low light. She saw his face clearly now. The Wing Marine who'd helped Mylla recover the final Fenestros after Asteryss had fallen, and her paramour. If Eisa had thought of him at all, she would have assumed he was dead like she'd heard so many others were. "What in the name of Vaka Aster are you doing here?"

"Scouting," he answered. "Watching the starpath to see who—and what—might come through. We're rotating from Asteryss with what's left of the Dragør Wing Fleet. The other Knights were still here when the Wing I was to relieve left earlier this evening."

She snorted. "Scouting won't do much good if you have gaps in your rotation."

Despite her refusal to permit it, he seemed to be willing to risk his life to stand and rose to his feet slowly. She ignored his indiscretion.

There was news to be had—he'd said the other Knights were here. She wanted the full story. If he needed to stand to tell it, she'd let him.

"Tell me, Wing, from the beginning. What's happened in Vinnr since Mylla left you in Asteryss—or, remind me, was it you who left her?"

CHAPTER SEVEN

Within a handful of hours, the Knights and Himmingazians arrived at Vigil Tower.

It was a bittersweet moment for Ulfric. He was, for whatever it was worth, home once more. But what he felt acutely, like an ache in his heart that could not be cured, was that the true meaning of home was out of his grasp as long as his family was not present.

Though the Himmingazians had regarded the journey through the interrealm well back to Vigil Tower with more than a hint of anxiety, Jaemus rallied them quite well, assuring them they would be safe and warm if they trusted the Knights. Now, being once again indoors seemed to relax them more than being at Mount Omina. The Knights found them rooms in the northeast tower that had only suffered minor disorder, and Ulfric wondered how much of their returning calm was based on their particular tower overlooking the Verring Sea. They were a people who lived on water, and he guessed being close to something familiar helped set their minds better at ease. Overall, he was impressed with how readily they seemed to adapt.

After a thorough check to ensure the main tower was free of imposters and the gates and wards of the fortress were as secure as they could be, the Knights and Ulfric now gathered inside Vaka Aster's erstwhile throne room at Vigil Tower's peak.

Ulfric reached for the pouch with Balavad's Scrylle and Fenestros and pulled them out. The touch of them was no different than Vaka Aster's or Lífs's. Still, his flesh crept with loathing. So much suffering and harm had befallen this world, and who knew how many others, because of this Verity, this calamity of a celestial, to whom these artifacts belonged. He briefly wondered what would have happened if he'd never looked into Balavad's Scrylle in the first place, then pushed the thought away. What did it matter? There was no wisdom in looking backward, only lessons. And what he did next would prove whether he'd ever applied wisdom to these events or was simply cursed with foolishness he mistook for wisdom.

"Is this wise, Stallari?"

Ulfric looked up. Mallich stood beside him, and like always, his words were uncannily close to Ulfric's own thoughts.

"We know what happened when Mylla tried to see into the wicked one's Scrylle," Mallich continued. "She was young, her resolve and fortitude still waxing. Do you know what Balavad is capable of if your mind is opened to this?"

He did know, all too well. Inside Vaka Aster's sanctuary on Mount Omina, when he'd performed the spell to cage her, he'd lost Balavad's Scrylle in the furor her return from the Cosmos had caused. But then, compelled by Balavad, he'd reopened both it and his mind to the usurping Verity. He could still feel Balavad's alien voice creeping through his thoughts.

But in the end, he had overcome Balavad's influence and thrown himself into the cage he'd erected with the Fenestrii. As a result, he'd made himself the thing he'd been trying to unmake. Yes, he knew the dangers of this Scrylle all too well.

Looking from the artifacts in his hands to Mallich, then to his other two companions, he said, "What else can I do? There is only one way to right all these wrongs, and it lies within this Scrylle."

There was no argument to be made.

The silence in Ulfric's mind was unnerving after feeling Vaka

Aster's presence whispering at its edges, and sometimes booming through it, prior to their deal to leave him to resolve this problem on his own. The absence of his maker's intrusion should have been welcome, but in some ways, it wasn't. Instead, his mind felt hollowed out and drained, like one's stomach after rejecting something bad. His thoughts, as sharp as always, still carried a burden of knowing too much, of having seen and heard too much for his simple human shell.

He considered calling to her, but decided against it. She could hear his thoughts, he was sure, and knew the danger he now faced. In truth, with her inhabiting his being in this way, did he really have anything to fear?

He looked at his Knights again as if searching their faces for solutions, but their expressions mirrored his own uncertainty. Pacing to the opened window, he took a moment to breathe deeply of the fresh air, feel Halla's rays on his face again. His heartmatch and daughter awaited him, his freedom awaited him. Hope, perhaps, awaited him.

With Balavad's Scrylle and one of the pitch-black Fenestrii in his hands, he said, "I don't know what might happen. Be prepared for anything. Anything at all. If you have to restrain me, do it."

His fellow Knights glanced at each other uncertainly, and he almost smirked. Within him, after all, was a celestial being. It would take more than a few Knights with ropes to restrain him if Vaka Aster didn't want him to be.

Affixing the Fenestros to the setting within the Scrylle cylinder, he breathed deep once more and let his eyes fall to the now glowing stone.

Allowing one's mind to penetrate the lore of a Scrylle wasn't terribly complicated. He could have done it in his sleep. But as soon as the world within began to spread before his mental sight, claws began shredding his brain, bringing tears to his eyes. His fingertips and the skin of his face tingled, first lightly, then fervidly, as if each tiny fiber of flesh was vibrating faster and faster. Then, unlike any other time he'd peered into a celestial cylinder—save once—a sudden blinding illumination burst inside it, around it, all throughout his mind. He jerked, though he didn't know if it was his body or just his mind, and realized he couldn't escape it, he was trapped inside the light

Then, just as suddenly, it shrank into a concentrated beam. With an arrow's speed, it shot directly to the core of his mind, knocking him backward. His jaw clenched so tightly he felt a tooth crack.

Still gazing into the Fenestros, he concentrated. As if he stared into an optiscope that could view things hundreds of miles distant, his mind's eye peered through the singular beam to its terminus.

Where he saw absolutely nothing.

The Scrylle was empty, as if it had been reamed out until hollow. Only one thing could cause that. The realm it had belonged to, and everything it had once been a record of, had ceased to exist. The realm of Battgjald was no more.

Which meant—

And here you are, Stallari Aldinhuus, creation of my quin, Balavad said in his thoughts. *I wondered if you'd managed to retain my artifacts. You must hope you will be able to use them to unmake the cage you wrought and restore yourself to nothing but a man once more. A frail, weak, trivial creation. You had hope, didn't you? Hope. One of the many strange things my quins gave their creations. A simple but useless thing.*

Overwrought with the realization that an entire realm and all who'd inhabited it had ceased to exist, Ulfric couldn't speak.

Are you surprised to hear me again? It's no matter. Your last chance came and went, Aldinhuus. And your actions will not go unpunished, Balavad promised. *There will be a reckoning for this breach. Vaka Aster cannot destroy my realm without expecting the same be done to her own.*

Ulfric felt something shaking and realized it was him. His body lay writhing and shuddering on the floor in a fit he had no control over. He heard shouting—so far away and all around him. Then the light beam shattered, fragments of it exploding and becoming embedded in the meat of his brain. Vaka Aster's voice whispered, *You cannot take this one, quin.*

A rushing, pulling sensation erupted behind his eyes, as if his mind were being sucked into a tunnel, then it went black.

"Breathe, Ulfric!" Stave growled. "Just open your eyes and breathe.

He can't get in there, in your head. Not if you don't let him, he can't. Open your eyes."

Stave's voice came from right by his head. He tried blinking and barely managed it. His body quaked again, but less violently as the shaking gradually subsided.

Mallich crouched beside him. "Stallari?" And through the Mentalios, *Is it still you, Ulfric?*

His brain was too raw and he jerked, flinging a hand at Mallich to stop him from using the lens to speak again. He couldn't take another voice in his mind right now.

He tried to speak, but at first his voice would only catch in his throat, like a stuck bone. Mallich pushed him up into a sitting position and thumped his back, as if he were choking on mis-swallowed water. Across the chamber, Safran had spun her klinkí stones into a brilliant blue net that held Balavad's Fenestros inside, separated from the room and everyone in it. The Fenestros had gone black again, dormant. The Scrylle cylinder itself lay on the dais next to him. A harmless, hollow device now.

With another attempt, he finally gruffed, "Battgjald is gone, completely gone. Destroyed as if it never was. And the Scrylle is empty."

The others stared at him wordlessly.

"I can't..." he murmured. "I can't reach Symvalline and Crumb now."

WHILE ULFRIC CAUGHT HIS BREATH, Mallich went to the scullery to find something to refresh them. All he knew was that Crumb and his heart-match were in Arc Rheunos and that Symvalline had "been taken." What that meant, how dire their situation was, were utterly unknown. And until he was free of Vaka Aster, he could neither learn more about nor intervene in their fates.

By the time Mallich returned, Ulfric's mind was made up.

"So, you saw him again, you did, did you?" Stave asked, shaken but hiding it behind a brow that was creased so deeply in a frown his forehead seemed to have caved in.

Sitting at the base of Vaka Aster's throne, Ulfric tipped a mug of lind wine over his tongue, feeling its delicious flavor, both hot and cold at the same time and heavily fermented, slide into his stomach. It was a relief to know he could still experience such a pleasant sensation, but he barely tasted the nectar.

He'd clamped down on the despair rushing through him and turned his mind to seeking a new answer. Balavad might say hope was useless, but he knew it wasn't. Hope was all he had left.

Now wholly focused on how he would get back Symvalline and Isemay, he promised himself he would do whatever he had to. He may not soon be free of this cage he'd created of himself, but they weren't beyond reach yet. There had to be a way. After all, he was not the only Knight Corporealis in Vinnr who could travel by starpath.

"Yes, Balavad was there," he said, his throat constricted as he recovered from the ordeal. "Brutal and cold and vicious, like always. He'd have had me if Vaka Aster had not intervened."

Safran had tucked Balavad's Fenestrii and Scrylle safely inside their carrying pouch and stood across the chamber near a window. Mallich and Stave sat beside Ulfric in seats they'd pulled up to contemplate their next steps.

You're sure, Ulfric? Sure Battgjald is no more? Safran sent.

"I couldn't be more sure if I'd been there myself when it ceased to be." The closest he'd ever come to such complete negation of a reality was reading Jaemus's Scrylle map and seeing the missing Fenestros of Himmingaze. It was an odd sensation, like a puzzle piece that lacked a puzzle. Where his mind knew something had to be, there was nothing. And the more he thought about it, the odder, more disconcerting it became. It was beyond what a human mind could truly grasp, even one as stalwart as a Knight's.

Safran, looking troubled, pressed: *But didn't Vaka Aster tell you the key to undoing this cage was in Balavad's Scrylle? Can that mean she doesn't know she destroyed his realm, along with his vessel?*

Ulfric wiped his brow with the back of his hand, feeling clamminess. "She must not have before, but she does now." He didn't want to entertain the thought, not even for a moment, that she might have let him discover this calamity for himself just to see how he'd react. She might have been removed from their human plights, but she wasn't malicious. Not in the way Balavad was.

"That puts us in a troubling position," Mallich stated. "You are vulnerable, and while you are vulnerable, Vinnr is as well."

"I'm aware," he replied.

Safran began to pace before the window. *I think we now understand better what happened on the warship. While your mind was dark, Ulfric, Vaka Aster chose to destroy Balavad's vessel in order to stop his assault and the fighting that would surely have resulted in the deaths of every Vinnric and Himmingazian aboard. In doing this, in destroying the vessel, she ended his world with it. It was a matter of him destroying you, or Vaka Aster destroying him.* She stopped pacing and looked at them. *So does that mean Balavad still has his mind on us, and on Vaka Aster? If he can't conquer Vaka Aster, will he seek revenge instead?*

"It'll take him time to rebuild his world, more time than any of us will be alive, we can be sure of that," Stave offered, then looked quickly at Ulfric. "*Most* of us, anyway."

Rubbing the nine-pointed star on his chin, Ulfric pondered what it all meant. "He may still have forces or spies in other realms. Those who weren't there will not have ceased to be when Battgjald was lost. We must be prepared and remain vigilant, but I don't think we should be as concerned about him as we were."

That leaves getting you back to yourself, finding a new vessel for Vaka Aster, and bringing back Symvalline and Isemay, Safran sent, already working through the problem. *The answer is to find the other Verities' Scrylles. Ulfric, you said Symvalline and Isemay are in Arc Rheunos. There's a strong chance they would have attracted the attention of Mithli's servants when they were delivered by the starpath and may still be with them even now. If one of us were to go to Arc Rheunos, perhaps we could find them, both Symvalline and the Arc Rheunos Knights. If we can explain our needs to them, and if we are persuasive, they may allow us access to Mithli's Scrylle. And since you cannot leave Vinnr, we will bring both what we glean from their Scrylle lore and our sister and your daughter back with us, if they remain there still.*

This is exactly what Ulfric had been thinking. He said, his voice stronger now, "Vaka Aster has assured me they are there. When we were on Balavad's warship, I...spoke to Isemay for a moment."

Mallich eyed him, waiting for what Ulfric wouldn't say. Ulfric hadn't spoken to Symvalline, only to Isemay, because she and Isemay weren't together, because she may have been in danger. Ulfric didn't need to say it. The perceptive Knights could read enough from his silence. Knowing what little he did of Symvalline and Isemay's situation, Ulfric had to admit how tenuous Safran's idea was. But tenuous was better than nothing.

After a moment, Stave said, "But leaving your side puts you at risk, it does, and our oaths to Vaka Aster are unbreakable..." He trailed off uncharacteristically.

"You won't be breaking your oaths," Ulfric said. "Finding a way to release Vaka Aster from this trap I've made of myself *is* fulfilling our oaths. Taking no action is failing them." He spoke bluntly, but this was no time for nuance. "Yet," he hesitated, hating to say it, "with only Balavad's Scrylle, it may not be possible to open a starpath. It's too dangerous to use."

"I'll try it, I will. Let that worm-slurping celestial try to face me," Stave said.

"No. If I can barely keep my wits while sharing my mind with our maker, not to belittle your sturdiness, Stave, but Balavad might damage your head beyond your spark's ability to heal."

Stave sneered. "Blargin' Eisa, that traitor. If she'd not take Vaka Aster's Scrylle, we'd have you turned back into your old self by now, we would. When I see her again, I'll—"

Much as we are all concerned what Eisa's intentions were, and may yet be, she's not here now, Safran cut in. *And we can only speculate why she did what she did, which gets us nothing at the moment. We must focus.*

As it always did, her calmly delivered advice cooled Stave's less harmonious temperament. He quieted and scratched at his voluminous mutton chops.

Mallich said, "What about Himmingaze's Scrylle? Could the new novice know something?"

Ulfric nodded. "Actually, I had their Scrylle in my hands shortly after I was sent there, but—wait, the one called Captain Illago. Stave," he said, excitedly, "can you go and fetch him? The taller one, looks a bit like…just ask Jaemus which he is. He may be able to tell us where their artifacts are."

"Got it," Stave said and made off.

While waiting, Ulfric considered Griggory's account of Himmingaze from the Scrylle. Should he tell the others what knew? He discounted the idea. Safran may be willing to give Eisa the benefit of the doubt, and Mallich would always trust his long-time companion, but Stave was an if. And under the circumstances, further exposure to actions of hers that, by some interpretations, could be considered questionable would not improve things should Eisa reappear.

Besides, many other things required his focus now. Playing mitigator to the Knights' ire toward their fellow Knight didn't need to be one of them.

Captain Illago, Jaemus by his side, stepped into the chamber. His gate was slow, as if the stairs to the tower top had tired him. Jaemus, however, was as spry as could be. Ulfric hadn't known him long enough to judge whether that was just his usual way or if his new ordination was the reason for his gusto.

"Aldinhuus," the Glisternaut captain said amiably enough. If nothing else, he seemed willing to forgive Ulfric's threats from their short encounters on Isle Stonering and his ship, *The Bounding Skate*.

"Captain, thank you for coming. Please, Jaemus, can you translate?"

"Pleasure," the engineer replied.

In a few brief words, Ulfric came to learn that after he and Jaemus had made their escape from *The Skate*, Illago had taken the remaining celestial artifacts, one of Lífs's Fenestrii and the Scrylle, and locked them inside a secure box aboard the ship. From there, Ulfric gleaned, the craft had likely been destroyed along with the Knights' own, the *Vigilance*, when Balavad's warship exploded. *They are lost now, scattered throughout the Himmingazian ocean no doubt.*

He thanked the captain for his information. Illago nodded, and Ulfric could tell from his expression he could see the news hadn't been what they'd been hoping for. Jaemus was about to leave with him when Stave put a hand on his shoulder.

"One moment, novice. Would you be able to spare me a few minutes after we're done here?"

"…Sure," the engineer said. "What about?"

"Just want to get you a bit more acquainted with the Knights, I do."

Looking dubious, Jaemus rubbed his new chin adornment, then nodded and the two Himmingazians stepped out.

Ulfric looked to the others. Their next step was obvious.

"We must find Eisa," Mallich said. "And once we do, someone must go to Arc Rheunos."

CHAPTER EIGHT

Being thought of as important had always mattered to Jaemus, but that was when it came to such things as how to keep cities afloat above the thrashing waves of the Never Sea's endless storms or devising new schemes to penetrate the Glister Cloud surrounding Himmingaze and find the 'Gazian people a new home. The Glisternaut fleet was his second home, and he'd believed he'd never leave it or betray it. To travel the stars and seek a new destiny, these had been his goals, his personal path to prominence.

But he'd always just assumed he would do these things *in* Himmingaze and his achievements would be for the sake of his *own* people.

Not here, in this hot, bright, stony world filled with towers and streets and daylight and earth and mountains—all things he'd heard of, read about, but never actually *seen* on his water-soaked world. *Not* as a Knight Corporealis. And *not* for a celestial being whom he'd never even heard of just a few days prior.

Yet, as anxiety-producing as these thoughts were, they were dwarfed by what was coming at him at that moment.

A swinging wooden practice ax being wielded by a Knight who

seemed to be more motion than man forced Jaemus to duck, his breath abandoning him like a traitorous scoundrel.

"No! Not that way," Knight Thorvíl warned, scooting bent-kneed backward and out of range of Jaemus's wild, unskilled defensive swing with his own practice weapon. "You're not trying to fell a tree, Bardgrim. I can move; a tree can't. And I'm fast—see."

Swooping in, Stave swatted him with the flat of his ax blade across the stomach, then spun away to his unarmed side. Jaemus "oofed" and doubled over, wondering what exactly the properties of a tree were.

"And I'm nimble," Stave gruffed.

Jumping forward again, the Knight planted his free hand against Jaemus's shoulder, his right leg behind his, and shoved. Jaemus went down on his back like a bucket of dropped stones.

"But like a tree, I, your enemy, am also incapable of mercy."

With that, the ax in his right hand plummeted toward Jaemus's head, then slammed into the sawdust beside it with an ominous thunk.

Standing over him, Stave looked into his horrified face and chuckled. Jaemus turned his head aside and spit blood from his bitten tongue into the dirt.

"Did I hurt you, novice?"

Swiping his mouth with the back of his hand, he said, "My tongue may be bloodied, but my pride is most definitely broken."

"C'mon, up you come." Stave bent forward and grabbed his hand, hauling him to his feet. "You must remember to think fast and anticipate your foes. Don't ever be lulled by their words when it's their weapons you should be watching, it is."

"Right, right, I'm fine. Just a bit flustered. You know"—he dusted off his legs—"I'm not a man for stabbing and smashing things. I keep telling you that."

Nothing about Jaemus was warrior-built, not physically, not instinctively. Training him in the ways of the Knights Corporealis had become an obsession for Stave and Safran it seemed since they'd arrived in Vinnr two days ago. First Safran with the Mentalios lens, and now Stave with his blunt instruments. They'd barely let him rest.

To his surprise, though, he'd found he didn't seem to feel much need to rest, and he'd noticed they rarely seemed to either. An effect, the pale one named Mallich Roibeard had told him, of his Verity-given spark. And though protecting Verities' vessels was the job of the Knights, Jaemus had not yet decided if this role was one he intended to adopt, short- or long-term. He was still Himmingazian. He still had his own home to one day save.

And it all came down to Verities, it seemed. Which meant, like it or not, for now, he was where he had to be, even if it meant tolerating the bruises and bumps of this crazed ax-wielding Knight while they tried to figure out what had become of this rogue Knight they called Eisa Nazaria.

Jaemus heaved a breath and lowered his arms, practice weapon and all, then leaned up against a stout metal pillar in the midst of the training yard. "I think I'll take a break now, my dear, sweet, tender tutor. That or simply die."

Stave quirked a wooly eyebrow. "That's a curious thing to say, that is. You're a Knight now, novice. You can't die from a little scratch or two. Will it help if I promise not to hurt you too much?"

"It was a figure of speech," he said. "What I mean is that training with you is making me feel like death is preferable. Have you ever heard of the theory of ramping up difficulty levels in accordance with a pupil's development?"

He delivered the words lightly, hoping Stave would take the hint without Jaemus running the risk of irritating him. It was hard enough dealing with the swarthy Knight when Stave was cheery. He didn't think he would survive him being irritable.

To his relief, it seemed to work. Stave gave a little shake of his head and began walking toward the exit to the arena. Just as he reached the doorway, he turned back. "As a matter of fact," he growled, "you under-estimate just how much pain and suffering you can endure, you do. But we'll fix that." He reached toward a two-bladed battle-ax leaning on another pillar—most definitely *not* a training weapon—and turned, arcing his weapon in a ruthless throw toward Jaemus that was intended to cleave.

And then Jaemus did something that, despite a total lack of intention, remedied his wounded pride. With fleech-fast reflexes he didn't realize he had, he ducked under the ax as it flew overhead, then, still in a crouch, sprinted toward his attacker, smashing full-bodied into him like a battering ram.

There, he stopped cold. Stave's physique rivaled an anvil's and was just as immovable to the comparatively wispy Jaemus. He couldn't have weighed more than one of Stave's beam-like legs.

"Get off me, ya mad man!" the Knight said, shoving him in the chest, but his tone was good-natured, even pleased. "See there? You did that right, you did. Thinking on your feet, reacting from your gut. Well done, novice Knight. Well done. Now, when is it that you'll be taking your oath so you can be a proper Knight Corporealis like the rest of us?" He regarded Bardgrim with mild scrutiny, then added, "As like the rest of us as possible, I mean, being that you're green like a kórb fruit, you are."

The training yard's stout doors opened and Ulfric stepped in. Jaemus could see the lines of care carved on his face. One notable feature was missing. The hollows beneath his eyes that one would expect to see. At some point, Ulfric had replaced the goggles Jaemus had given him (or rather, the ones he'd *taken* from Jaemus) with something that was his own design. The lenses were thick, dark, and huge, covering from just below his cheekbones to halfway up his forehead. His appearance was nearly comical, but the apparatus did conceal Ulfric's exceptionally strange Verity-enhanced eyes, which Jaemus supposed was the point.

"Ulfric," Stave greeted. "Come to show the novice a few of the old fighting techniques, did you?"

His voice was slow and heavy when he spoke. "Not at the moment. If you don't mind, Stave, I'd like the yard to myself for a bit. I need some time to think."

Jaemus heard what had happened when the Stallari looked into Balavad's Scrylle. At some point, an entire world had somehow ceased to exist, and now Ulfric's fusion with their celestial sprite was irreversible. And, worse, it appeared the man's family was still missing and the means to find them lost. It was no wonder the fellow looked so morose.

And, of course, Jaemus had also learned that he and the 'Gazians were stuck here for the while due to the Battgjald Scrylle's shocking blankness. Yet, if Aldinhuus did harbor a Verity within, perhaps there were other ways to get back home…

"C'mon, Glunt," Stave said, slapping him on the back. "Let's give the Stallari the yard."

"It's engineer, and my name is…oh, why don't you just call me Jae?"

The two brushed by Ulfric, who seemed lost in his own world. When Stave peeled away with a comment about wanting to beat on some metal, which Jaemus took to mean…well, he wasn't quite sure, he headed up the main tower's stairs, overwhelmingly happy to have escaped the Knight's torture, er, *training*.

Halfway up, though, he paused. Ulfric had largely been absent for the last two days, and Jaemus had decided it was better to let him alone to grieve his family's loss. But now the man was out and about. It was time to have the chat he'd been putting off. He just hoped what he was planning to ask didn't wind up leaving him in worse shape than his training time with Stave.

CHAPTER NINE

Halla rose over the chamber atop Mount Omina as Havelock Rekkr finished describing the events that Eisa was sure would come to be known in heroic terms as something like The Great Salvation of Vinnr or The Days of Vaka Aster's Blessing. Commoners enjoyed their overblown descriptions of events, even those bordering on the mundane. But the truth, as Eisa could discern it from what she'd seen and what the Wing had explained, was simple: Vaka Aster had found a new vessel. Those who'd been taken captive aboard Balavad's great warship had seen her appear and defeat the usurper, thus ending his designs of ruling Vinnr for himself. Then they'd all been delivered to Mount Omina through the wystic starpath, something none of them fully understood. As far as the Ivoryssians and Yorish were concerned, they were saved by their maker and all would be well again.

Upon questioning him, Eisa also learned that the Knights had been seen amid the fight on the warship and had also been returned to Mount Omina. All of the commoners had disembarked for home before them. Had anyone seen the new vessel? The Wing thought not. It was assumed the Knights protected whoever it was inside the mountain sanctuary.

It was all so convenient, Eisa thought, but she could find no reason to believe his story was untrue, even if it wasn't the full story. The commoners lives, and the fact that Vaka Aster had saved them, Eisa guessed, were simply a byproduct of the whole affair. Commoners did like to think they were special somehow, but once one lived as long as Eisa had, one came to realize that few things were special—or even mattered at all. Time passed, Verities created and destroyed, and all the little, pointless lives that flowed in between these two intractable pillars were happenstance at best.

But she didn't say any of this to Havelock, though it wasn't hard to imagine how he might respond. How could a Dyrrak, someone who claimed to be among the worthiest and most faithful of Vaka Aster's people, have such a bleak perspective about their maker? The answer was simple. A Verity was the greatest of all things. What choice did one have in the face of such greatness but to submit to it and be honest about one's own worth? Imagining Vaka Aster, or any of the Verities, as compassionate beings who cared for their creations was as foolish as it was absurd. If you didn't understand that and lived your life expecting something from Vaka Aster—compassion, mercy, anything —just because her celestial kind brought you into existence, you were destined for nothing but misery. One's role as a selfless servant to the Verities was the only honest role one could play in these worlds.

Eisa had taken a seat on the dais to listen to Havelock's tale. She now stood, wiped a bit of dirt from the blade of her glaive, and stepped to the storage chest where the Knights kept a few wystic implements. She needed to replace her Mentalios with a spare and get back to Vigil Tower now that she knew it was safe.

Aside from some books and a few mechanical and crystal odds and ends Ulfric frequently tinkered with, the chest was empty. *Fickle fate,* Eisa thought, realizing she would have to pursue other options for returning to Asteryss. She turned to the commoner. "Where is your Wing scout, pilot?"

Havelock, blood dried on his face from a cut to his cheek and beginning to show wear after his long night under scrutiny, asked coolly, "Why?"

She glanced at him, surprised at the challenge in his tone. "Why?

Can't you see? You've broken my Mentalios lens and left me without the ability to open the interrealm well. It's time I return to Vigil Tower with haste. So I'll be taking your craft." At his scowl, she couldn't help but taunt him further. "But don't worry. You won't be derelict of your duty. You'll still be here, *guarding* the starpath." She wanted to laugh at the self-deceit of the Ivoryssians to think they could mount any kind of resistance if another foreign force came through the well. Hadn't they learned anything the first time?

"I'm not guarding it. I'm *watching* it. And I need my scout to report back to Asteryss if anything comes through again."

She grew serious. "Take me to the scout, right now, or I'll find it myself and you'll be reporting the loss of your eyes next time you *see* Asteryss."

Jaw tight with resignation, he rose from where he'd been sitting against the wall. He grumbled something that, though she couldn't make out the words, definitely did not sound like, "It would be my pleasure to assist you, Knight Nazaria."

Before she could question him, he said, "Follow me," and paced toward the outer chamber and exit of the mountain sanctuary.

In Halla's full light, the mountain's face looked far less forbidding. Though the avalanche's path was still clear, many of the high peak's larger rock promontories hadn't been disturbed, and snow still lay in blankets around the dome. Enough of it remained that she could trace Havelock's footsteps from the night before, which appeared to come from the same direction as her own.

They moved downhill, passing the hillock her ship had come to rest behind. "Landed" would be too polite a term for it. One of its wings had come loose and now lay beside it in the dirt, and the landing gear looked warped and unreliable. Havelock glanced at it but didn't ask questions.

When they found his scout a little farther down the mountain, Eisa could see its condition was almost as rough as her own scout's. The metal fuselage bore scrapes and gouges, some blackened as if hit with something burning, and there were visible nicks on all four of the wings, along with cracks in the cockpit windscreen.

When he stopped walking and turned to her, she asked, "You flew that here? Did you expect to arrive in one piece?"

"All the fleet has damage. We barely have two dozen scouts that are still flightworthy," he said simply. Then added, "You're welcome to walk if it suits you better."

"Don't push me, commoner," she warned.

"Right, or you'll have my eyes."

She approached the damaged ship. She knew how to fly it, of course, as the dragørfly scouts belonging to the Dragør Wing Marines of Ivoryss were modeled after the Knights' own design. But when she got the windscreen pushed open, she found herself glancing back to the commoner. "When does your relief arrive?"

"Two days."

"And you're provisioned accordingly?" She caught the slight widening of his eyes at her apparent concern as he nodded. "Then fare you well," she finished and climbed inside.

Charging the engine by a hand crank would take a few moments, but she could tell in just a few turns that something was wrong. The gears clanked and thudded against each other in a haphazard way, and she detected no hum as the energy center accumulated power. "Slagging bastirt," she murmured after giving it far more time than was needed to know the ship was going nowhere. She slammed the windscreen open again and jumped out.

"Lying to me was a monumentally stupid thing to do, commoner. And now it looks like I'll have no further use for you." Her hand went to her dagger hilt as she approached him, ready to ensure he never tried a silly ruse to waste her or any other Knight's time again.

He backed up a step and held out one hand. "Wait! I told you it was damaged. I figured it would give in sooner or later. It's not my fault it was sooner. Obviously I didn't know it was grounded permanently."

She eyed him, not sure herself whether she'd really meant to harm him or just scare him. "Obviously," she said flatly. "But you have ensured your relief won't find me in such a reasonable mood."

Bringing his hand to scratch the scruff on his chin, he thought a moment. "Perhaps we can fix it." She followed his eyes as they tracked back toward her own dragørfly scout. "Between yours and mine, we may have all the parts we need."

"How long?" she asked.

"How long…?"

"How long will it take you to fix it?"

He gazed toward Halla and then around the mountain. "With *your* help, we could be flightworthy by late tonight, I'd guess. Tomorrow at the latest."

Eisa considered. It was get this craft back in the air or wait for two days before another Ivorýssian arrived. If everything in the commoner's story was true, and she had no reason to believe he'd lied, the Knights were safe. The Stallari, by some unimaginable twist of fickle fate, had been found, and it seemed the world was clear of Balavad and his Raveners. She had no reason to go to Dyrrakium now, other than perhaps to inform the Domine Ecclesium that the threat had ended. Therefore, the only imperative she had was to reunite with her Order and resume her duties as protector of the celestial vessel. Explaining herself to her companions wouldn't be easy, but what did she care what they thought of her actions? She'd done what she thought was necessary, as was the Knights' duty.

She looked back at Havelock. "All right then. Tomorrow at the latest, or—"

"Yes, I know." He sighed.

CHAPTER TEN

A day and night had passed as the Knights discussed plans and options for seeking out Eisa and Vaka Aster's Scrylle. The discussion had come to two options. One, wait at Vigil Tower and hope she came to them. Or two, start their search in her ancestral home, the one other place in Vinnr she had threads of allegiance. Dyrrakium.

Ulfric had finally sent his companions away for a while. The discussion had strained all of them, both from not knowing where to start and from not knowing Eisa's intentions. He was starting to lose his grip on his agitation and needed time to think before he began raving with anger, grief, and fear.

The training yard where he'd spent untold hours had always been as much a place to perfect his fighting skills as it was a place to get his mind clear. As Jaemus and Stave left, he took a breath and approached the yard's first pillar.

Forgoing armor, shield, and helmet, he pulled free his klinkí stones, preferring the lightness and lack of being inhibited by the defensive uniform. Simple objects composed of celestial elements, just as the Scrylle and Fenestrii were, the klinkí stones were no bigger than a thumb knuckle. In the light captured from Halla and reflected down to the courtyard between the lofty walls of the Vigil Tower fortress, they looked like radiant ingots of lead in his palm with Elder Veros runes etched along their sides. Yet once he whispered the words of power through his Mentalios, their hearts flared with a cerulean glow, and they became not stones but weapons—or armor or a shield or any number of other uses the Knights could make of them. The true gift of the klinkí stones was more than their form, it was the wystic core of power that came from the Knights themselves, extensions of the celestial spark gifted to them by Vaka Aster.

Gifted, Ulfric thought, bending his knees into a fighting stance and sending the stones floating lazily toward the first pillar, erected in the courtyard for this purpose. The drumming the stones made against the hollow metal tube sent a resonate *doon...doon...doon* echoing across the yard. *What kind of gift makes the receiver wish they'd never laid eyes on the giver? Our duty is to Vaka Aster, but the ends are not to "save" a celestial being. Their nature is eternal; it's ridiculous to think we affect that. The ends are to ensure continuity of the world and all the people in it. We Knights protect not our maker. Rather, we protect this world.*

And these celestial "gifts" have become too much of a burden of late.

He flicked the recovered stones harder and faster this time, first into the original pillar, then into a wider one farther away, creating a louder *doon-doon-doon...dun-dun-dun* echo, then summoned them back to his palm.

The spark within me is Vaka Aster's gift to me, and it isn't in my nature as only a tiny part of the greater Syzycki Elementum to understand the full meaning of it. But a gift received becomes a gift that can again be given, and I can still position myself to aid Symvalline and Isemay. If I cannot serve both my Verity and my family, my family is who I choose.

But if I cannot serve both Vinnr and my family, am I ready to sacrifice an entire world? Vaka Aster was. Why shouldn't I?

Recovering the stones, he grew still, staring off into the distance, but unseeing. He wasn't ready to know the answer to that. He knew Symvalline would tell him not to be a fool, that her life wasn't worth the whole of Vinnr. But he suspected she'd stumble over making the same claim of Isemay's life. Was there no correct course of action to take?

From the south side of the courtyard, seventy paces distant, he heard the rhythmic sound of a hammer on metal. Stave in the smithy, beating out what was undoubtedly a new weapon, just another to add to the hundreds already stockpiled within these walls. The Knights could arm every man and woman in Asteryss with the volume of weaponry they'd amassed over hundreds and hundreds of turns. Stave, a blacksmith by trade before Knighthood, found contentment and escape in his old profession as much as Ulfric did when creating music through martial dances with klinkí stones.

He resumed. Until his family was safe, he would not find a lasting peace, so he would create a momentary one through this comforting exercise.

Eyeing the nine variably sized pillars interspersed throughout the training yard—though he didn't need to; by now, Ulfric could toss a stone from anywhere in the yard in his sleep and hit every pillar—he committed to the old movements.

To anyone but a Knight, the discipline of the Singing Pillars might have seemed an elaborate dance of enviable grace and flickering lights. But all the Knights knew the steps as well as Ulfric did. The ancient training sequence was meant to be practiced and practiced and practiced again until even a Knight's fleshless bones could perform it if they had to.

Mastering the steps required more turns than most commoners lived, but the result was part of what made the Knights so indomitable. Just one of their Order could fend off dozens of foes with nothing but a handful of wystic klinkí stones. The melodic pillars served as targets, and if the practitioner's steps were timed and followed perfectly, the sounds they made created a vibrating hum that seeped into the fortress's walls, as well as into the flesh and mind of the Knight, imbuing him or her with a sense of harmony, of calm. Two things Ulfric needed desperately.

As he practiced, Ulfric's worries gave way to deeper senses, ones that perceived things from a distance and granted his thoughts a wider, greater clarity.

Symvalline is among the most capable of the Knights I've ever known, a fighter, but even more, a tactician. Whatever's become of her in Arc Rheunos, she's strong enough to handle it. And Crumb said she's being aided by someone there. She is safe...

Regardless, two people, two foreigners in a foreign realm that's already been corrupted by Balavad won't be able to stand against threats alone. Not for long. I will send Safran and Stave. Together, they have more wits and strength than a hundred people.

He listened to the drumming of the pillars, punctuated regularly by Stave's hammer, and spun his body, moved his feet, flung his stones. His breathing barely sped up, and his heart beat strongly and evenly. *The nature of a Knight,* he mused, *is not all that different from the nature of a Verity. We are a duality. As Verities are divided by attachments to their corporal and incorporeal selves, we are divided by allegiances to both our maker and our world. And to those we love.*

Safran, Stave, Mallich—they love Symvalline too, as a friend, and as a sister in the Order, as their own family. As did Mylla. They must leave for Arc Rheunos soon, but how can the starpath be opened?

But that answer was easy. Vaka Aster. Ulfric had no choice but to try to recall her, to beg for her aid. Not even his pride, not even his unwillingness to be used as her puppet would dissuade him now.

"Thoa's aufaorrfaro."

Jaemus's voice cut through his meditation. Coming to a halt, he gathered his stones to hover over his open palm and turned to face the entry arch where Jaemus stood. Though, he admitted, the interruption was welcome. It was time to take his mind off his lost loves. He knew what he had to do.

The Himmingazian had spoken in his own language. Though Vaka Aster had given Ulfric the ability to understand Himm, he hadn't used it in days and wasn't immediately sure what Jaemus had said. The naked wonder in the engineer's expression was enough to give him a hint, however.

"What was that?" Ulfric asked.

"Oh, sorry. Slipped into Himm. Not surprising, given that I am, in fact, from Himmingaze. Which is the reason I'm here, conveniently enough. But also let me just repeat: what you were doing just now was amazing. Simply *amazing*. Do you have any idea how quickly you were moving? It was almost like watching a water spout spinning. And the sounds—glorious! They could probably hear it halfway up the towers."

Jaemus had a tendency to prattle, not a habit shared by any of the Knights, who most often channeled their thoughts directly and succinctly through their Mentalioses. It was even unlike the acolytes of the Conservatum, who were trained to revere the Knights as teachers whose time was valuable and not to be squandered with idle or superfluous talk. Ulfric hadn't spent more than a few moments among anyone besides the Knights and acolytes in many turns. Thus Jaemus's long-windedness tended to alternately fill him with an expectation that some news of great importance would soon be imparted or, when none was, confuse him as he parsed through meaningless chaff to get to the man's verbal wheat.

"You want to discuss Himmingaze?" Ulfric posed.

"Indeed. Well, more or less. You see, my crew and I are feeling a bit, how do I put it, confined, I suppose, and would like to know when we can go home. Himmingaze, home."

"Why? It remains unsafe there," Ulfric replied. "The Glister Cloud has left your world close to its end." Did he need to state the obvious? The 'Gazian was much smarter than that.

Jaemus rubbed his chin thoughtfully, his fingers tracing the raised edges of a nine-pointed star there as if he were discovering a new and surprising feature. "Neither, according to all of you, is it entirely safe here. Which leaves the Himmingazians where, exactly?"

Ah, now he understood, and when put that way, it seemed obvious enough. "You wish to speak to Vaka Aster and ask to be sent back to your realm. Perhaps even request she intercede on Himmingaze's behalf?" Maybe he was putting thoughts into Jaemus's mind now, but it seemed quicker than waiting until he presented them himself.

Jaemus clapped his hands together and shook them as if waving in victory. "Yes! We'd like to go home. And well, yes? Do you think your

Vaka Aster the Magnanimous might be persuaded to, oh I don't know, put in a good word for us with the Creatress? Or Lífs, if I should use the formal name. It seems that as a peer, Vaka Aster may have a bit of sway among the star-walking elite. And since you share your, erm, brain with her…"

The vibrations of the melodious pillars had faded to a low hum Ulfric felt along the fine hairs of his arms and neck, as well as deep in his bones, but were no longer audible to the ear. He relished the serenity this brought him, a feeling he'd often wished he could bottle and take with him everywhere he went. Jaemus's words bordered on irreverent, though his tone was all seriousness—at least as serious as he ever really sounded—but Ulfric took it with more *magnanimity*, to use the 'Gazian's word, than he might ordinarily have.

But how to explain to him that a Verity was not a being given to granting wishes? Vaka Aster had brought them here instead of leaving them behind, after all. She must have had some reason for that choice, whether they knew what it was or not.

He tried the indirect route and had to hope his tone was convincing. "You must learn to trust things you do not yet fully understand, Jaemus. We call this 'keeping the faith in the fight.'" Even as the words dissipated in the air, he realized he sounded as disingenuous to his own ears as Jaemus's face showed they did to him.

"Is that right…What exactly does 'fight' refer to? From what I've learned, your Order's primary role is to *stay out of* fights—though you don't seem to be good at it. It appears you lean more toward solitary confinement and"—he looked toward the opening to Stave's smithy—"creating an excessive volume of sharp objects."

"No, you're taking it too literally. What it means…" He paused to think it over, realizing he'd never had to define the aphorism aloud. "To the Knights, the fight we all face is the temptation to give up. We fight to stay true to our convictions, and our duty, despite all the battles time brings us. It's choosing to remain strong in our certainty that whatever happens is surmountable, and that together as Knights, and even alone, we will never be beaten as long as we remain faithful to this certainty." *That certainty used to be Vaka Aster's fidelity to us and to Vinnr. But is it really? Has it ever, really, been so?*

Jaemus's face grew thoughtful for a moment. "So you mean it's just a saying that reminds you to keep up hope despite whatever odds you face."

He'd never thought of it that way, but it fit. "Exactly." Jaemus's astuteness once more caught Ulfric off guard, and he decided the man deserved a straight answer. After all, he liked the 'Gazian. Dropping his klinkí stones into a pocket and straightening his tunic, he said evenly, "Regarding Himmingaze—the Verities aren't given to involving themselves with commoners' affairs."

"According to what you've told me, the Glister Cloud is hardly a 'commoner' affair," he countered.

And Ulfric had no argument for that. His own dilemma was nearly identical to Jaemus's: he needed Vaka Aster to send Safran and Stave after Symvalline and Isemay, and Jaemus needed her to send him and his people home. Maybe the maker would help if Ulfric asked, yet the 'Gazians wish for Vaka Aster to try influencing Lífs's realm…well, that was surely unprecedented and presumptuousness. Worse, wasn't it similar to Balavad's own actions, if not his ends?

What did he have to lose by asking, though? He already intended to reverse his agreement with Vaka Aster, ask her to interfere when he'd explicitly forbidden her to—as much as any man can forbid any celestial being anything. He would help Jaemus, too, if he could.

Before he could give the 'Gazian a response, the largest of the pillars rang with a drawn-out base note that rose up the walls of the inner courtyard and could be heard throughout the fortress. A clapper inside linked to the main fortress doors, and the pillar's chime indicated a visitor.

He'd known the people of Asteryss would spot the smoke from their hearth fires and realize the Knights had returned, but they'd come knocking sooner than he'd expected. They *had* rung for entry rather than trying to break their way in, which was a good sign. How good remained to be seen.

Ulfric ran his thumb over his Mentalios and watched the 'Gazian attempt to think of another tactic to entice him to bring Vaka Aster into their affairs. *What should I say to him to keep him from setting his hopes too high?* he wondered. A moment later, Safran's voice came through the Mentalios.

We've had a messenger from Arch Keeper Beatte.

One moment, Ulfric said. He looked meaningfully at Bardgrim and tapped his Mentalios. "Focus on the mindlink, Jaemus. You're here and part of our affairs, for now at least. May as well get comfortable with it."

He scowled but reached for his own lens readily enough. "Speak, oh spritely Stallari."

Ulfric asked Safran to continue.

The Arch Keeper has requested an audience with Vaka Aster at Aster Keep.

Beatte wasted no time, Ulfric thought. She'd accused him of betraying Vinnr last time they'd met. Whether she'd been aboard Balavad's warship with all the other Vinnrics or not, she'd no doubt heard the tale of all that had happened there. The Knights and Ulfric had fought the usurper and his forces as hard as the other captives. It was enough, apparently, to sway Beatte toward a more favorable opinion of them. How long it might last was another matter.

He could imagine the many dozens of requests the kingdom's leader might choose to make of Vaka Aster, and none would be unreasonable. Except, again, Verities were not in the business of granting wishes, and the Knights were not in the business of serving as ambassadors between her and commoners. The Ivoryssian high seat was just a new tangle in a web already filled with them.

Everyone, he sent. *Join me in the meeting hall. We have much to discuss.*

CHAPTER ELEVEN

Jaemus followed Ulfric to the meeting chamber through the main hall. Though he'd been in it before (while exploring the fortress to find somewhere to hide from Stave) the size of it was enough to take his breath. Himmingaze's floating cities had large meeting spaces, but his definition of "large" was limited to space that held no more than a few dozen people. You could fit a few hundred in Vigil Tower's main hall, with room for a dance troupe and a feast as well.

This meeting chamber lay at the base of Vigil Tower. The soaring primary tower itself was topped by a domed oculus Jaemus had marveled at from the other towers. It was the largest of four that rose from equidistant points around a white-stone inner curtain wall, itself wide and long enough to contain a small village within it. A covered clay-shingled parapet ambled along the top of the wall. The three smaller steepled towers were tall enough to observe the entire city of Asteryss from. Jaemus knew this because he'd walked every nook and cranny he could since arriving, trying to find places Stave was sure to not be.

Safran and Stave beckoned to him and Ulfric to sit with them at an oblong table beneath a tapestry depicting a forest filled with animals. They were of all shapes and sizes, running through the trees and flying through the sky, a scene beyond Jaemus's wildest imaginings. Above the scene, the rays of Halla, the Vinnric shining daystar, beamed over all. Everything about the tapestry, from the fibers it was woven from to the flora and fauna it contained, awed him. Was this what Himmingaze had once looked like, before the Glister Cloud and its endless storms had nearly drowned the entire world?

"Just waiting on Roi to finish checking the catacomb wards," Stave said. "Kórb?" As Jaemus pulled out the seat next to him, Stave held out a bumpy-skinned green fruit the size of his fist. The twinkle in the Knight's eye was not lost on him.

He took it with a flat: "Don't mind if I do."

Safran gave Stave a stern sideways glance, then sent to Jaemus: *We harvest them from our own trees in the courtyard. Have you seen them? They are only as tall as a new sapling, something like our Stave*—she shot the short Knight another glance, this time while grinning—*but they grow fruit during every season. We never run out, but they're so delicious that we never grow tired of them either.*

"Do I just—"

No, through the Mentalios. You need to practice. Arching her thin eyebrow at him, Safran coached: *Remember, think of what you mean to say and let the words form. But know your own mind so that what you send is what you intend to send. If you want me to know about rain, don't let your thoughts dwell on how you feel about rain or something that's happened to you while it was raining, or you'll send that and I'll know more than you mean for me to.*

He'd had a similar lesson once or twice in the last few days and knew exactly what she meant. As she'd told him about the kórb fruit tree just now, he'd gotten a perfect image of it in his thoughts, even down to the color and shape of their leaves, the gnarly bark of their sturdy trunks, and the type of insects that made their homes in the tree's dense branches. More than just words were communicated in these marvelous mind lenses, but that was the danger. Controlling what you sent, and to whom, was where a level of mental discipline took over—and he'd yet to fully master that. Trying to communicate with the other Knights had been more than a little embarrassing as his thoughts at times were more naked than he'd intended. Still, he'd endure a thousand embarrassments for this amazing ability to speak with *his mind.*

Just bite into it, or does it need to be...? He paused, trying to think of the word he was looking for.

Peeled, came Mallich Roibeard's voice, and Jaemus turned to see the palest of the Knights enter through the hall's main door. He equaled Jaemus in height and walked with the calm assurance of a man who rarely found anything surprising. Jaemus found that when Roi's steady topaz eyes came to rest on his, they had a way of instantly putting him at ease.

Yet despite the Knight's composure, Jaemus saw the lines of tension in his face when Ulfric began addressing the group aloud.

"Acolyte Irrick of the Conservatum delivered a missive from the Arch Keeper today, as Safran has told you. Beatte requests, 'humbly' she puts it, to speak with Vaka Aster. The Ivoryssian court and Conservatum are planning a mourning ceremony for the city tomorrow and wish the creator to attend."

Are they aware that you are Vaka Aster's vessel now, Stallari? Safran sent. *The few I spoke with on Mount Omina seemed either too in shock or too confused by what occurred on the usurper's warship. I'm not convinced they completely comprehend what's happened to them, or to any of us.*

Ulfric said, "It's hard to say. I haven't wanted to mingle with the commoners to find out. Being the vessel is too...burdensome." The Stallari's face drew into a scowl, then smoothed as he went on. "The exact words in Beatte's message were, 'Vaka Aster and the creator's representatives.' Many people of Ivoryss were defiled by the usurper, consecrated like the Raveners from Battgjald, and conscripted into Balavad's army. That along with coming through a starpath would rattle even a Knights' wits."

"It makes sense, it does," Stave said. "Beatte and the rest of Ivoryss must be in a state trying to put things to rights. Asteryss was hit hard by that mongrel Verity. They'll be looking to their creator for guidance and, more than that, reassurance that they're safe from this happening to them again."

Ulfric nodded. "The invitation sounds genuine, but we can't give ourselves to confidence in the commoners or the Arch Keeper in times like these, nor can we meet Beatte's subterfuge with openness, lest we give ourselves into a trap."

Safran's features were dour. *Aye,* she sent. *That and Beatte will want to know she still rules. With Vaka Aster's return, her leadership will be dependent upon knowing she is favored—and the rest of the realm knowing it too.*

"She seeks Vaka Aster's endorsement," Roi stated matter-of-factly.

Yes, I believe that is her intention. Choosing her words with intention, Safran went on: *The people of Ivoryss have suffered. As short-lifed commoners, their loss sits with them differently than our own, and we should honor that. From the towers, we've all seen the damage to Asteryss and how diligently they're working to reorder and rebuild this city, despite their recent losses. It is no wonder that they wish to grieve together and give this tragedy its due weight.*

Her gaze moved around the table to each of them. Jaemus felt an uncustomary need to keep silent, enamored by her calm authority and wisdom.

And perhaps, she continued, *we also should be honored to be invited to join. But the question is, after the events that transpired upon Balavad's incursion, and the Arch Keeper's quick condemnation of the Stallari, what do we truly owe her, or this kingdom?* After a moment to let that sink it, she finished. *We can't give her the audience she seeks. Their troubles are theirs to deal with. We can heal our own griefs privately.*

Jaemus wasn't sure if he was hearing it through the Mentalios or if he'd simply come to know the Knights well enough, but he seemed to discern the sorrowful whisper of *Mylla.*

Roi and Stave were nodding again in agreement, and Roi said, "And the risks right now to Ulfric are too severe. The people of Vinnr have faced fears they could never have been prepared for and now bear the stain of those fears. It isn't abnormal they would remain suspicious of all. The nature of Beatte and those Balavad imprisoned is now complicated and steeped in unknowns. We should remain sequestered until we better know their temperament and intentions."

Each Knight appeared to be in agreement without needing to say it.

Jaemus had quickly grown used to their subdued and controlled reactions and assumed the matter was settled. Therefore, he was surprised when Ulfric spoke up.

"Despite the commoners' grievances with us, real and imagined, we can't ignore this invitation." He glanced at Safran. She did not scowl, but the fine wrinkles around her eyes tightened. "As you say, we should be wary of the Arch Keeper's purpose. Balavad's spies were diligent before the invasion, and though Battgjald has fallen, the Scrylle tells us any Verity's living creations can endure if they aren't present when their realm is lost. Who's to say Balavad's spies are no longer among us —or part of her own court? We don't know the full extent or consequences of what's been wrought."

He tapped his knuckles on the table, and with a final hard rap, he said, "For this reason, we will accept the invitation to their grieving ceremony. Safran, I would like only you to accompany me."

"Ulfric, we won't be able to protect you—" Roi began.

"You won't need to. Between Safran and I, and the Fenestros we're taking with us, Beatte's court will have little power to keep us against our will. And I believe it's crucial that we see, that *I* see, what we're dealing with. I can't risk sending anyone to Arc Rheunos until we have reliable safety here."

The three Knights said nothing, though the air had grown thick with unease.

Ulfric continued, "You can use the Fenestros to speak for us, Safran, and channel all that happens back to Vigil Tower at the same time. I will attend as myself, at least long enough to see who they think I am, and imply Vaka Aster doesn't wish to meet. We need to know what the commoners know and do our best to discern their plans for the future, if possible even before they do. It's the only way we'll be able to keep control of the situation."

It has been hundreds of turns since I politicked, Safran mused. *And the commoners may find my voice, such as it is, unnerving.*

"Politics are politics," Stave said disdainfully, "and I don't suppose anyone could be tricky enough to learn to speak out of more than two sides of their mouth. Not even Beatte and her peons." He chuckled bitingly. "Well, that is unless they can also speak through a Fenestros, that is."

Safran chuckled soundlessly. *I see your tolerance for rulers and their courts has not lengthened commensurate with your life, love.*

"The exact opposite," he agreed.

She grew somber again, agreeing with Ulfric reluctantly. *I suppose it makes sense I speak for the Order. After all, I played these political games in the courts of Vinnr long before Beatte was a wisp of thought in Vaka Aster's designs. If anyone can get Beatte to reveal her aims, it will be me. But, Ulfric, why mask the fact that you're now the vessel?*

Ulfric took a bite of the kórb he'd peeled. "I'll avoid being known as the vessel for as long as I can. I need to be free to move, to breathe. Once the commoners believe me to be the living vessel, they will barrage me with requests for aid and audience—just like Beatte has. You will all be forced to fend them off perpetually, endangering and distracting us from what we need to be doing: finding Symvalline and Isemay, and finding a way to unmake this cage."

Everyone at the table nodded knowingly.

"If they don't perceive you as the maker, Ulfric, how will you escape if the politicking breaks?" Roi, ever the practical one it seemed, asked. "Vigil Tower's outer wall is already breached, and we don't have the time or means to restore it."

The sour expression on Ulfric's face showed his distaste for the whole affair. "They won't attack their own Verity." He scooted the goggles he wore up to his forehead, flashing his uncanny, swirling eyes for everyone to see. Jaemus had gotten used to the unusual sight in Himmingaze, but for the Knights, it was clearly something new.

Roi finally nodded in agreement. "You'll reveal your true nature if needed. I don't envy you. But we are vulnerable with the loss of the *Vigilance* and the means to travel by sky, though it seems as if their own sky fleet is now decimated. Our wards in the catacombs have never been breached. But they know about the interrealm wells now. They could have a force waiting for anyone who shows up at the Omina well. Never in a thousand turns have there been so few of us to protect the vessel."

"There are other wells throughout Vinnr, Mallich," Ulfric said. "But I truly believe we won't need to use them."

"And if Balavad returns? He may come to reclaim his artifacts." *Or seek revenge,* Roibeard sent through the Mentalios. The words were so loud and sharp that Jaemus nearly flinched. "And we also have the Himmingazians to think of. They are as much in danger as the vessel. Outside of these walls, they are foreigners. But keeping them here makes them prisoners," he finished.

Jaemus was quite clear about what Roibeard was getting at. After what had happened here when the last foreigners from another world arrived, the people of Vinnr would likely consider the Himmingazians a threat. And it wasn't as if they could blend in. The hue of their skin was impossible to miss among the Vinnrics. "It would probably be best to send us home, then, right?" he said.

Roi said, "If we could. But we don't have Vaka Aster's Scrylle. We can't open a starpath well without it."

Jaemus looked to Ulfric, who gave him a short nod that he didn't think any of the others caught. Did that mean he would ask Vaka Aster to send them home, or didn't it? Jaemus had as much trouble reading the Knight now as he had back in Himmingaze. But he did sense that the man wanted their recent conversation in the yard to remain between the two of them. Obliging, mostly out of curiosity, he averred, "You're saying we Himmingazians are stuck here, then?"

Stave clapped a hand that was like a shovel head on his shoulder. "Don't worry, novice. We'll keep you safe, we will. That is, until you can take care of yourself and your kin." Jaemus caught the look Roibeard threw Stave, and the nod Stave returned. Then he said, "Wait right here," rose, and left the meeting hall.

To no one in particular, Jaemus said, "I don't know what that was about, but I really, really hope I'm going to like it."

"You're one of us now, Himmingazian, whether you have yet accepted it or not." Roibeard's hand went to his long beard and pulled at it thoughtfully. "You're marked, chosen by Vaka Aster to be one of her protectors. It's an unusual manner of becoming ordained, maybe even unprecedented." He looked to Safran.

I've never read of it happening before, she sent. *All Knights since before the War of Rivening have risen through the Conservatum and chosen this path for themselves.*

Aren't I the fortunate one, Jaemus thought, keeping his misgivings to himself—he hoped. They clearly thought the "choice" thrust upon him honorable, but he sensed in them—perhaps through his own intuition, perhaps through the Mentalios lens link they now shared—an undercurrent of…something else. Doubt? Disbelief? Or were those just his own feelings? It was all a bit much.

Stave was already returning, pacing across the meeting hall carrying a sword like Mylla's in an ornate scabbard made of a gleaming metal that seemed to catch every light in the room and amplify it. He reached Jaemus and said, "Up with you. 'Gazian, are you ready to wield a real sword?"

"Come again?" Jaemus stuttered.

Stave wasn't about to win an award for patience. "A battle sword. Think you can fight with one yet, do you?"

"…Er, not so much. But I'm rather wicked with a torque wrench."

Because he'd said "torque wrench" in Himm, unable in his nervousness to think up a comparable word in Elder Veros, Stave appeared confused. "Is that a weapon?"

"If your enemy is a stubborn bolt, then definitely."

The Knight stared at him hard for a moment, then broke into a wide grin. Slamming his free hand on Jaemus's shoulder again, he said, "You're ready for this, you are, even if you don't think it."

Unable to think of a polite way to refuse, Jaemus stood, and Stave began affixing the scabbard around his waist. When he was done, he stood back and eyed Jaemus critically.

Safran sent: *Draw it, Jaemus. It's called Winter's Bite and was hallowed by Vaka Aster in the Dastrart Age. It is the weapon of a Knight Corporealis, and only we who have been gifted a Verity's spark may wield one. But caution, the power of your spark combined with its own is enough to destroy a vessel. Use it in service to our Verity. You are a protector now.*

Her coal-black eyes were hard as she held his, brooking no hesitation. He wanted nothing to do with the weapon and was about to say so when Stave reached into an inner pocket of his vest and pulled out a small object.

"And this, too," he said simply, and pushed the object into Jaemus's hand.

The geodesic chunk of crystal was the color of a leaden sea. "Is it...?" he breathed, then could say no more.

"Aye, you know what that is, you do," Stave said. "Your own klinkí stone. Your first. Once you master that, then you'll collect more. The better at wielding it you get and the stronger and more concentrated your own Verity spark grows, the more you can manage at once. After we're done here, I'll teach you how to attune it to your spark."

"Will this 'tuning' involve me getting bruised, bloodied, or broken?" he said.

"Only if you want it to. Itching for some more training in the yard, are you?"

"Not just yet," he mumbled. Despite himself, Jaemus felt himself beaming so wide the corners of his lips seemed to reach his ears. Unwilling to wait for Stave's directions, he focused his thoughts into the stone, willing it to rise from his palm. It came alight before his eyes, the crystal's heart pulsing a deeper blue. Tiny inscriptions, almost too small for the eye to read, flared on its surface. Elder Veros runes. The same that comprised the writings on the Scrylle maps he'd looked at.

"Born to this, you were, Jae. There's no doubt. Not a one," Stave crooned in his rough voice.

After another second, Jaemus swore he felt the stone almost move. Hypnotized by what he was doing, he suddenly grew self-conscious. What did the other Knights think of his childish wonder? He realized he didn't care. He had his own kinky stone!—though, he supposed, he should start calling it by its true nomenclature.

Now try Winter's Bite, Safran urged.

He closed his palm around the stone, feeling its heat reach all the way to his wrist. "Really, the sword is lovely, but I'm just not sure I'll ever be up for swinging one around and dicing people up into so much stew meat."

"You must—" Stave began.

Let him be, love, Safran cut in. *He will know when it is time. He must choose for himself what he wants.*

Grumbling, the stout Knight looked at Roibeard. "What have you got to say about it, Roi?"

Roibeard thought before he spoke, as he always did. Jaemus was still learning to keep his own mouth in check when talking with the quiet Knight, quashing his tendency to fill silences with sound, regardless of the need, or lack of need, for it.

"He came by this path differently from the rest of us. Safran is correct. We can't make this choice for you, Bardgrim. It's yours alone."

Jaemus sighed and began to unbuckle the scabbard.

"No," Roibeard said. "At least wear it for a bit, get used to its feel. We won't force anything on you, but meet us in the middle, if you would." Using the Mentalios, he said: *A time may come when we'll need you, when Vaka Aster will need you. Or when Ulfric will. But I promise, if that time comes, the choice will still be your own to make.*

But Jaemus knew better, and he knew Roibeard and the other Knights did too. He'd shown the kind of choice he would make the first time he'd jumped between Vaka Aster and her enemy. And would have died for it, if not for the Verity's intervention, or "ordination," as the Knights called it. It seemed his choices tended to lead to consequences that even death was too simple for. Not for the first time, he wondered what in the worlds he had gotten himself into.

Momentarily overwhelmed at these realizations, he suddenly wanted nothing more than to be in his room with Cote, curled up in his arms and trying to forget these last few days. Even having a klinkí stone of his own did little to reduce the weight he felt bearing down on him. *Just get through this meeting, Jae,* he told himself. *Then talk Ulfric into getting Vaka Aster to send us home. That has to be the best thing for everyone. It has to be.*

Roibeard's leonine eyes were lingering on Jaemus, making him feel as if his thoughts may not have been as private as he wanted.

Then Ulfric rose. "Tomorrow at High Halls, Safran and I attend Beatte's summons to Aster Keep." To Jaemus, he sent: *If I can impose on you one last time, Bardgrim, please stay until then. You may not wish to fight with a sword, but your intellect is a greater contribution. We—I—could use your insight afterward.*

Jaemus sighed. It wasn't fair for the man to appeal to Jaemus's ego—or, weakness, however one wanted to think of it—to get him to consent.

One thing about it though. It worked.

CHAPTER TWELVE

After the meeting with the Knights, Ulfric pushed Jaemus out the door in order to confer more closely with Safran about the coming meeting at Aster Keep. To occupy himself, Jaemus had wandered down an unexplored hallway that, by no coincidence, was as far from the training yard as he could get.

And he'd found something quite marvelous. The Stallari had been busy.

A door that had previously been locked now hung ajar. Sidestepping his better judgment, he went in and found a chamber stuffed with —simply everything his curious mind could wish for. Tools, machines, glassworks, devices, and sundry scaffolds and storage chests, all stacked, standing, hanging, and balanced from floor to ceiling. The sheer volume of objects was so massive that Jaemus could easily believe it had taken lifetimes to collect and create them. It was as if he'd entered his own glorious dreams and been handed access to treasures that surpassed them.

The "being handed access" part was, however, subjective. He had a sense that the Knights would probably disapprove of a stranger rifling through their belongings. Jaemus had little trouble disregarding this inconvenience, however, justifying the intrusion to himself with, *Ulfric owes me a set of goggles and the 'Gazians a couple of ships anyway. I'll just... poke about a little.*

Intellectual and inventive types are alike in many ways, no matter their walk of life, ilk, or age, and Jaemus didn't have to stretch his mind to guess this space belonged to Ulfric. The Knight had spoken some about his gadget-mindedness, and passing comments from the other Knights had given Jaemus a sense that Ulfric was, at heart, a tinkerer and experimenter—a bit like himself, actually.

As he thought over the current twist in circumstances, he browsed. But the items he discovered quickly overcame his attention, and soon he suspected he understood what a few of the incomplete projects were intended to be. One in particular caught his eye. A set of wings, sized in such a way he could see they were clearly intended to be worn by a person. And based on the rigging and devices attached to them, he was fairly certain they weren't meant to be simply decorative.

If I could figure this out, he thought, *I may not need permission to leave the tower. I can just jump out a window and take a look for—*

The door opened a crack. He flinched, knowing he was caught, and thought about making a run for it, but it was already too late.

To his relief, it was Cote who came in and closed the door quietly behind him after spotting Jaemus. "The training yard was empty, but the tall pale one said he saw you come this way."

Jaemus breathed a sigh of relief. "Just restless energy."

"As usual." Coming up beside him, Cote closed his arms affectionately around Jaemus's waist. "How did it go today?"

He turned and grasped Cote's cheeks between his palms, brushing each of his eyes with a light kiss, then returned his focus to the winged contraption. "I was attacked by a mad beast with an ax, then warned that this world might want to kill us, then given a new sword and a stone I could pierce metal with using only my mind. So, like most days, I would say."

He sighed, knowing Cote would never settle for his attempt at lightheartedness. His lifemate's interest was genuine, and not only because he worried about Jaemus but because of how Jaemus had become the de facto representative for them all.

He went on. "In all honesty, I'm not convinced they've chosen the right man for the, er, *honor* of becoming one of them."

Cote sat on a nearby crate and leaned back against a worktable, stretching his long legs out before him. He looked tired, which didn't surprise Jaemus. His tossing and turning the last two nights would have kept Jaemus awake if he hadn't been anyway. Oddly, he felt less urge to sleep than was normal, which contributed to his wandering about, a side effect of his newly acquired Verity spark. *I'm powered like an engine now*, he thought. *But what replenishes the engine when its energy is used up? Fascinating...*

Cote said, "As I understand it, it wasn't the Knights who 'chose' you, if you want to apply that word to the situation, but rather their...Verity did."

The way he almost swallowed the word before he could say it showed how little used to the situation Cote had grown. In Himmingaze, the old Verity worship and even speaking about the myth with anything but dismissal was outlawed as both foolish and a threat to their necessarily ordered and structured lives, lives dictated by rules of logic and the predictability of numbers and technology. Lives dedicated to survival and an escape from their doomed watery world.

As Jaemus considered Cote's statement, he lightly brushed the back of Cote's hand. The coldness of it surprised him, despite the warm breeze blowing in from the ocean outside. (And how marvelous was its aquamarine color! So deep and crystalline, nothing like the inky waters of the Never Sea. You could even see fish swimming in it! Fleeches would have no chance at a sneak attack in the Vinnrics' waters.)

"Chosen or forced into," he finally said. "It doesn't seem to matter when the chooser is some kind of mix of stars and unfathomables."

Cote smirked. "Unfathomables?"

"I'm an engineer, I make things, and that includes words. And it appears I'm not all that different than our host." He let go of Cote's hands and waved around the filled room, indicating its chaos of stacks and shelves.

"Vaka Aster?" Cote asked.

"No, I mean yes, that too, I suppose. Verities are the makers of everything, the Knights say. But I don't mean Starbright the Shiny. Rather Ulfric. I think these are his inventions."

Cote looked around, doing his best to appear to admire the morass of items as much as Jaemus did. "You told me they live dozens of lifetimes, right? I suppose that would give the brusque one time to make all these."

"Exactly what I was thinking."

Their conversation trailed off comfortably, Jaemus deep in his thoughts as he let his hands explore the set of wings. Flying with one's own wing set, now *that* was something else. The little tingle of excitement this thought gave him faded quickly as deeper, heavier thoughts took hold. *Is this it, Jae? Is this the way to save the Himmingazians? Instead of flying to the stars, we can fly through them, in a manner of speaking, to this new world? Instead of engineering and technology, should we Himmingazians rely on wysticism and celestial sprites to transport us to a world full of strangers with quirky habits and customs, where we might settle down and escape the Glister Cloud and the destruction it brings?*

After this afternoon's meeting with the Knights, it seemed the answer to this question was a profound no. The Knights had agreed there could be no trusting this kingdom's leader, Arch Keeper Beatte, leaving him to wonder at exactly what kind of person they were dealing with and why a world with such a big external problem, namely Balavad, would be so bent on creating unnecessary internal ones. It was nothing like Himmingaze, where every system, city, and group were collectively focused on one goal: to leave. Here, the world was their sanctuary, yet they seemed unable to appreciate it.

Lastly, the fact that the 'Gazians could not expect the Vinnrics to welcome them with open arms, even if the Knights would, troubled him more. And Jaemus did not want to be a prisoner here.

He turned away from the wings and sighed. "Cote, I've spoken to Ulfric, and when he's free today, he's going to ask their Vaka Aster to send us home. I should probably get the shiny one to remove this stardust endowment I've been given too."

"No," Cote said in a subdued version of his commander's tone, catching Jaemus by surprise. Cote's sea-green eyes—the most beautiful Jaemus had ever seen and half the reason he'd first pursued the Glisternaut—gleamed thoughtfully before he spoke again. "You may be the only one who can fix this, Jae, though I'm not completely certain what 'this' is. You're closer to these Knights, and to this Verity, than the rest of us."

Jaemus clasped his hands together tightly. "Fix it? See, that's the problem. I don't know *how* to fix it. Does that mean staying or leaving? Does that mean carving a neat little statue and asking the Creatress nicely to put Himmingaze to rights? Does it mean fighting battles with foreigners from other realms? I don't understand anything, Cote, and it's starting to make me...grumpy."

Cote spoke in his cryptic voice, the one that always made Jaemus want to pinch him. "Figuring it out isn't going to be easy, is it?"

After a pause, he heaved another sigh. "The Knights held a meeting this afternoon. They're concerned about how the people here will react to the Himmingazians. They were just at war with other-worlders, which makes them less trusting of new people like us, even though we're obviously not here to fight with them. And I for one don't want to stay here if it means one of the locals stabs me or any of the Glisternauts the first time they see us. So if the Knights can send us home, that seems the best less *uncomfortable* option."

"Going home isn't what we should be talking about," Cote said. "You know as well as I that staying or going isn't the heart of our problems. It's what's becoming of Himmingaze. And your 'stardust endowment' might be what's needed to intervene in some way. Perhaps you have the chance to reverse the Glister Cloud's encroachment through this...what is the word the Vinnrics use? 'Wysticism'? Anyway, this phenomenon of our old myths-turned-truths."

Jaemus frowned. "That's a bit heavy of a thing to put on me, Cote. I mean, yes, it's what I've been trying to do all along, but—"

"And now maybe you can. You survived being pierced by a weapon that they say has the ability to destroy one of these Verities. You're up to it."

Thoughtfully, Jaemus put his hand where the scar of Knight Evernal's sword should be. The truth was, he felt nothing, not even the tiniest of aches, as if it hadn't happened. But it had. He remembered it all too well, and the Knights often reminded him of it, congratulating him and thanking him for his courage in such a dire moment. The rest of the Glisternaut crew had their doubts about the story, but with so much to marvel at in this new world, they were willing to accept it, or at least not question it.

Still, the idea troubled him that perhaps he truly was, even though in his fantasies he'd always fancied himself to be, now the one who could save Himmingaze. The reality of it settled with all the weight of, well, *a world*, on his shoulders.

Cote coughed.

Jaemus patted him on the back until the fit ended. "That cold seems to be getting worse."

"It's lingering, true. Maybe a result of this new world—the exposure to things we've never been exposed to before. The food may not be agreeing with us."

"Us?"

"Some of the crew are feeling poorly, too. Nothing serious, and you seem as healthy as ever. I'm sure it will pass. I feel a bit better than yesterday. What were the Knights meeting about?"

Cote was too pallid, his rigid Glisternaut commander poise betraying a stoop in his shoulders, and Jaemus considered whether he should worry him further about the issue. He decided to go ahead and explain what he knew, which really wasn't much. Cote wouldn't let him sidestep it anyway.

"They've been asked by the local leader to grant her an audience with Vaka Aster. And they aren't inclined to trust the woman."

"Why?"

"Some kind of disagreement from before, or maybe worse than a disagreement, between them and the people of this, erm, legislative municipality." Himmingaze had no word for "kingdom," and Cote wouldn't know the Elder Veros term.

Cote looked troubled. "We're caught in the middle of something we have no means of getting out of. Meanwhile, Himmingaze grows wetter and colder by the day. Jae, do everything you can to learn what advantages you've been given, and quickly. You didn't ask for it, but not all luck is sought. And this *is* luck, but not luck alone." He grasped Jaemus's hand. "I'm sorry I doubted you when you told me the old beliefs were important. I didn't know better. You did. I won't doubt you again."

Even when I doubt myself? he wondered.

Considering his words before continuing, Cote went on. "We are grateful for this hospitality they've given us. But there comes a time when hospitality, especially the kind that confines you behind walls not of your choosing, becomes not generosity but prison."

His words echoed Jaemus's own earlier thoughts. Cote pulled his hand from Jaemus's and rubbed the back of his neck as if it pained him. "The rest of the 'Nauts will understand the dangers our differences could invite if we tried mixing with people from this world—especially after the people here have already been invaded by *another* group from elsewhere. But...we can't hide behind these walls forever. And Himmingaze doesn't have forever, either."

CHAPTER THIRTEEN

A warm breeze hinting at early summer carried through the tall oriels circling the throne room's walls rising gracefully into cross-vault arches. Ulfric sat at the base of the throne, lost in the stillness of his thoughts. He hadn't truly slept since awakening as the celestial vessel.

In the arches' apex, a crystal oculus that outdated Ulfric by eight hundred turns had been set. In those days before the War of Rivening, when Vaka Aster was still present in her corporeal vessel, the oculus illuminated the sky over Ivoryss like an earthbound sun whenever the Verity was in this chamber, inspiring awe in all commoners. Those days of long ago had been wonderous, indeed, prosperous for all of Vinnr, bringing a long peace that many had believed would be permanent. Since the Cataclysm and war with Dyrrakium, though, and the waning of and eventual abandonment by Vaka Aster beginning around the same time, wonder had been missing from Vinnr.

It was still early in the morning before the summit, and Ulfric was strangely ill at ease. The realization that in a way Vaka Aster's absence from her creations for so long had inevitably been what brought wonder back to Vinnr clouded his thoughts. Because it was a dark kind of wonder, arriving in the form of Balavad the usurper and desecrator of Vaka Aster's realm. Was there an inevitability to these events he just couldn't grasp, a balance in the Cosmos that was too great and terrible for even Knights as long-lived as he to fully understand? Did it matter?

Ulfric stepped to a window that looked out over the city and kingdom beyond. Peering below, he mourned the devastation. Buildings with collapsed roofs and broken doors, signs of fires and chaos everywhere. Balavad's doing, of course. How many had lost their lives? It was a reminder that today's summit with the Arch Keeper would be equally rough if her intentions were not genuine. And in his experience, they never were.

A knock at the door pulled him back to the present. "Come."

Stave entered with a customary sort of comment: "Try not to get hit in the head today, Ulfric. You know what happens when you do. Ready to go then? Safran is down at the main gate waiting for you."

"Let's get this over with—again," he said simply.

Ulfric retrieved his thick eye shields. He'd created them to use for working wystic metals in Stave's forge, the kind that could only be fully evaluated through specially designed lenses. Now they were repurposed to shield his eyes from onlookers and replace his chromatic Verity-enhanced sight with something more natural. He'd lost the ones he'd borrowed from Jaemus aboard Balavad's warship. The most interesting thing about them, though, was that although he'd specially designed these for wystic artifacts, and Jaemus had designed his for the practical purpose of seeing better in the dark, having no idea when he'd done so how to harness wystic arts to improve them, neither set was any better than the other. Jaemus's talents were impressive.

When they descended to the gate, both Mallich and Jaemus awaited them. Mallich wished him and Safran luck and held up one of the Fenestrii to indicate he would be waiting for word.

The engineer, looking almost self-conscious, gave Ulfric the Knight salute, then cleared his throat. "Ulfric," he said, "just a quick punctilio, if you don't mind. If things were to become...fraught at this meeting, would your Vaka Aster protect you?"

Would she? He had asked, no, *demanded*, that she leave him be to resolve these conflicts himself. How vulnerable was he now? How present was she?

Vaka Aster? he tested, but in his head, all was silent.

His discomfort grew, but he hid it and gripped the engineer's shoulder reassuringly. "Faith in the fight, Bardgrim."

Jaemus raised a dubious eyebrow but said nothing more.

"Luck, faith, and"—Stave rapped his knuckles on his own head—"keep your head down," he said as they pushed open the wicket door set inside the gate.

Ulfric gave him a good-natured clap on the back. "Keep your wits and your axes ready, old friend."

After Safran and Stave exchanged an embrace and Mallich tipped his chin in farewell, Ulfric and Safran stepped past Vigil Tower's broken outer gate into the streets of Asteryss and began a solemn march to Aster Keep. Unlike last time, no Halla-powered skimmer was available to take them, so they set out early, knowing most of the city was preparing for the ceremony. Safran called to Yggo and Urgo to keep watch over their heads and ensure their path was safe.

By the time they arrived at Aster Keep's steps that led to the rampart and the upper keep's inner courtyard, Ulfric had seen up close enough of the damage wrought by Balavad's forces to feel drastically less horrified at the thought that the usurper's entire realm had been obliterated. Asteryss would take many turns to recover, and the destruction by Balavad had been utterly unprovoked.

Two Dragør Marines met them at the base of the keep's steps. Exchanging a minimum of words, Ulfric and Safran followed them up.

Not yet midday, Ulfric sent to Safran, preferring to keep their communications not audible to the Marines, though there was no reason not to trust them, *and look how many people have already gathered.*

Around the city as far as Ulfric could see, newly sewn and embroidered blue-and-white banners depicting the kingdom's dragør emblem fluttered from towers and atop roofs that had either been restored or remained undamaged from the usurper's attack. Surrounding the keep's walls, small groups of people were already present, looking forward to the official ceremony led by the Arch Keeper that would allow them to publicly mourn and begin to heal.

Safran nodded. *It's a clear indication of how ready they are to put this behind them.*

Ulfric had to agree. As they reached the upper courtyard, the absence of the squadron of Dragør Wing fighters that had been there last time shook his nerves slightly. There were none because the entire fighter battalion had been destroyed. Not only Asteryss had been weakened, he was coming to realize, but the whole kingdom, and he wondered how close it had come to a fatal downfall.

No need to wonder, Ulfric, he told himself. *You know quite well how close they came. How close we all did.*

"You'll need to leave all of your weapons with us," the first armored Marine said, his voice not quite a command. "And the flying stones."

Ah, yes, their secret was out.

Leveling the dark lenses of his eye shields on the man, Ulfric said, "We will not comply, Marine. We are all allies here."

Their two escorts shared a glance, and Ulfric wasn't sure if their hesitancy was because they feared having to disarm the two Knights by force—and face a highly unequal fight—or because they were considering how true Ulfric's words were. *Allies.* It felt almost foreign on his tongue.

"Stallari Aldinhuus is correct," a voice said, and Ulfric looked aside to see Commander Brun, leader of the Ivoryssian Dragør Marines, approaching from the left. "If we cannot trust the Order of the Knights Corporealis that saved both Ivoryss and Yor from doom, we have no right to call ourselves a Verity-faithful kingdom."

She called me Stallari Aldinhuus, Ulfric sent. *Safran, it seems my role as the vessel is not known.*

She returned, *So it does. Still, we should remain cautious.*

He didn't disagree with that.

The stout Dragør Marine leader planted herself before the two lower-ranking soldiers, who both looked visibly relieved at having avoided a hard choice. She dismissed them with a wave. "I will accompany the Knights. Back to your posts."

Before they started their trek through the long courtyard, Brun appraised Ulfric and Safran a moment. Then she said, "You are welcome here, Knights, at least by me."

"Commander Brun, I'm very pleased to see you've come through this…war unscathed," Ulfric responded, unable to overcome his inborn stiffness with the commander. Their few interactions had been tense always, and unfriendly mostly.

Brun nodded shortly. "Though I didn't see for myself what you did, Stallari, my troops who were aboard the desecrator's ship have detailed everything that happened in full. I'm not going to claim I understand it —though I expect an explanation—but I can say without a breath of hesitation that I no longer doubt the existence of the Verities."

You'd be feebleminded not to, Ulfric thought but bit his tongue against saying it aloud. Instead, he gave a nod of his own. When Brun remained standing in place and said nothing more, Ulfric realized: "You mean you would like an explanation now?"

The commander's face tensed in a look that showed her patience was limited. "Let me be clear. *We,* as in the Knights and the Marines I command, *are* allies. Look at the troops along the walls up there"—she pointed to the crenellations above them—"and those here at the keep's steps. They are loyal to me. But neither of us knows what to expect when you meet with the Arch Keeper, and her new inner cadre of guards follow no commander but her."

Brun's eyes swept across the city, taking in the accumulating crowds whose voices were silent, unlike last time Ulfric had been to Aster Keep. "Things are different in Ivoryss, now," she went on. "I'm sure I don't need to tell you that. It helps us both to know all the plays, all the pieces, and all the facts of this game." The look on her face showed this was the furthest thing from a game that it could be to the leader of the Dragør Marines. "And the fact that only two of you came tells me you already agree with me, in theory if not in practice. Yet."

The tirade, sermon almost, caught Ulfric by surprise. He knew Brun was blunt, but her words and the implications of them bordered on tyranny against the Arch Keeper. Yet, though he *did* trust Brun's loyalty, to her troops anyway, he remained committed to keeping his secret for as long as he could.

As he started to tell Brun that no explanation would be coming, Safran sent: *Wait. Allow me to brush up on my old skills.* She withdrew Vaka Aster's Fenestros from the pocket in her cloak. "Commander Brun," she said through the stone.

To Ulfric, her voice was familiar—the same one he always heard when Safran channeled through the Mentalios link—if slightly distorted. But Brun's face showed frank surprise for a moment before she locked her features back into her usual scowl.

"We are friends," Safran continued. She held the Fenestros cupped in one hand before her and held out her other hand peacefully. "Our loyalty to our maker must still, as always, come first. In keeping with our oath to Vaka Aster and our duty to protect the vessel, the Knights are not at liberty to divulge some things." Her tone through the stone reverberated slightly when she stopped speaking, a hint of an echo trailing into the quiet spring air.

Recovered from her surprise, Brun said stonily, "Such as this."

Safran dipped her head in agreement. "Please, we are expected by the Arch Keeper. There are misunderstandings and conflicts to resolve, and alliances to be remade. Now is the time."

In an uncharacteristic show of reasonableness, Brun gave in. "Come," she said and started toward the main hall at a stiff pace.

CHAPTER FOURTEEN

Wing Rekkr's dragørfly scout had contained only the barest minimum of tools, making the process of scavenging Eisa's own scout for parts slower going than she'd anticipated or wanted. If threatening the commoner would have made the work go faster, she'd have done it. For that matter, if blinding him with her dagger would have been any use, she'd have done that too. She felt an unaccountable sense of urgency, an urgency that hadn't let up at all since Balavad's attack, despite the threat having seemingly dissipated. But the Wing was handy, and he worked diligently, so she kept her threats to a minimum. He may have spent a bit more time than was needed poring over her scout as he disassembled parts, and she suspected the Ivoryssians would soon be seeing their own upgraded scouts when he returned to his squadron. But she let him have this small prize.

Am I going easier on him because he was Evernal's paramour? she wondered, surprised at her own uncommon compassion for a commoner.

The whole time, she waited for the question she could see in his face he wanted to ask. But she said nothing. When he was ready to know, he would seek the answer.

Eisa stood in the shadow of a massive stone at the edge of the glade Rekkr's scout sat in and watched the sky. No hint of light on glass or a dragørfly scout wing had flashed, but the Wing's relief was due today. She wanted to be far enough gone before he or she arrived to avoid any altercation.

Just as she glanced back toward Rekkr, he was dropping the last tool back into its compartment aboard the scout.

He spotted her looking at him. "Ready to go?"

"You think it'll fly this time?" she asked as she approached to look the scout over.

"I do. And better than it did before, thanks to…" He let his voice trail off, and Eisa pretended not to know why. She'd have to remember to warn the rest of the Knights that any new Wing scouts should be considered with caution.

"Then, for what I hope is the last time, fare you well, Wing," she said and began to situate her glaive and the armor she'd removed inside the scout's small rear space.

The sound of his boots coming up behind her made her pause. When she turned, he was standing there, for the first time since their tussle inside the sanctuary not looking like he wanted to punch her in the throat. Here it was, then.

"Knight Nazaria, do you…do you know what happened to Mylla?"

Oh she knew, all right. And now, faced with the question, she realized she hadn't been sparing *him* by withholding the news of Mylla's fate. Rather, she'd been sparing herself.

Eisa didn't lie. Speaking untruths was a sign of feebleness, as well as failure of the Fourth Dyrrak Phase: overcoming weakness. But she'd had hundreds of turns to learn, and learn well, the subtler skill of avoiding admission of her…mistakes. And she used this skill again.

"Knight Evernal was lost in Himmingaze."

The commoner said nothing for a moment, but his face grew still as stone. He blinked and let his eyes drift away from hers. His pain was clear, but it was Eisa who felt as if she'd suddenly had a blunt instrument slammed into her gut.

The love in his face, and the loss, was so familiar, so wrenching that for a moment she didn't trust herself to speak again. She'd felt those things once, and she'd paid for it just like he was.

"She…" Eisa wasn't sure what she was going to say, but she tried again. "She was an honorable servant of Vaka Aster and a loyal Knight. Till her last breath."

Still looking away, he gave a brief tip of his chin. "I know."

There was nothing left for Eisa to say, and she'd already given her goodbye, such as it was. Turning to the scout, she climbed inside, closed the hatch, and began the task of getting power built up.

As she cranked the engine, she took a quick glance out through the window screen. The Wing was stepping back toward the shade-giving rock to escape any wash from the scout's oscillating wings. His shoulders sagged. *If you're wise, Wing, you'll remember this lesson,* she thought coldly.

In moments she knew the work he'd done had been effective. The gears cranked as fluidly as if made of water, and in no time she had the craft in the air.

When Omina had grown small behind her, and her dealings with Rekkr were over for good, her chest finally released the tightness that had overcome her while discussing Mylla's fate. The breath she drew wasn't so much relief as it was resignation. If anyone were to ever pass judgment on her for her actions, none would be harsher than her own.

The moment of ambivalence was short-lived, however. Within an hour, the scout's improved speed brought her within range of Asteryss City. Destruction spread out below her like a shattered clay goblet. She hadn't seen any town so riven in many hundreds of turns. Even Yor's own capital hadn't been hammered as hard as Asteryss after the coup her lover had started that led to the Cataclysm. Eisa had assumed Balavad would take over Ivoryss the same way he had Yor. Through subterfuge, manipulation, and deceit. This all-out assault showed he'd known he would find what he sought here and had no patience to acquire it through slower means.

But it was what she saw beyond Asteryss in the Verring Sea that captured her full attention.

The Dyrrakium fleet, hundreds of ships, was amassed off the coast south of the cliffs where Vigil Tower stood. And in the air, several hundred Dyrrakium attack crafts circled the city. It was a magnificent fleet, an indomitable one, and a fleet the Dyrraks had been building for hundreds of turns for one purpose: dominion.

CHAPTER FIFTEEN

Brun dispatched a messenger to the council chamber to announce the Knights when they arrived. Soon, the doors swung wide from inside to welcome them. Beatte herself, wearing a light shift of mail just visible at the collar beneath her fine robes, stood there to greet them. Her black hair, elaborately decorated with diamonds and ribbons woven into its complex style, was pulled back so tightly the skin over her sharp cheekbones and edges of her lips was stretched taut. She was much paler than the last time Ulfric had seen her, but makeup artfully enhanced the richness of her umber hue.

Immediately, she caught sight of Safran's two axes worn in her crossed baldrics and the hilt of Ulfric's sword. The ancient hallowed weapon was Star Spark, Mylla's sword and the sword that had helped them all discover Jaemus's new status as a fellow Knight. Ulfric had adopted it for now, as his own, Light Spell, seems to have gone missing. Upon asking Brun, he'd learned Acolyte Irrick had given Symvalline the sword the day that Balavad's Raveners has attacked Asteryss. Where the familiar weapon, one that had been by his side nearly as long as he'd been a Knight, was now, he couldn't guess. He prayed Symvalline had it with her in Arc Rheunos.

After taking in the armed Knights, Beatte's gaze fell on Brun, and none present could miss the censure in it. Her tone, however, was cordial. "I had hoped for the full complement of the Knights Corporealis, and our Verity Most High as well, to join this council, but I do not blame you for your caution. We must replant our gardens of peace one seed at a time. Welcome, Knight Glór and Stallari Aldinhuus, welcome. You do Ivoryss a great honor."

The Arch Keeper neither knelt nor cast her eyes down before any other person in Vinnr, but when she dipped her head in a show of courtesy to them, Ulfric was astonished. Was her action a habit of having been brought up in the Resplendolent Conservatum—all Arch Keepers were chosen from among the acolytes—or a genuine gesture toward reconciliation?

Or, Ulfric's cynical side offered, was she simply being cagey in order to lull them into easy manipulation?

Ulfric caught Safran's glance as she sent, *So, there's confirmation. Your true nature is still secret.* Nonetheless, neither could predict how this meeting would unfold.

The Arch Keeper had spoken in the Ivoryssian tongue, though it rang strangely to Ulfric's ear. The Knights had grown used to speaking in Elder Veros for Jaemus's sake.

Safran lifted her hand and held forward the Fenestros she'd brought, responding in Ivoryssian as well, "Greetings, Arch Keeper Beatte. I have not seen you since before you left the Conservatum. Almost thirteen turns ago, hasn't it been? I wish the circumstances were not so somber, and on behalf of the Order, Stallari Aldinhuus and I extend our sympathies for all who have suffered and fallen throughout Ivoryss."

The Arch Keeper's eyes flicked more than once to the Verity stone as Safran spoke. The effect of the Knight's voice echoing from within it would naturally take some getting used to, but Ulfric wasn't sure if that was the Arch Keeper's only cause for distraction.

Cagey, the word flashed through his mind again.

"Thank you, Knight Glór." She looked at Ulfric curiously. "Those are unusual eye shields, Stallari. I trust they serve some purpose?"

Ulfric nodded and said, "They do."

She waited a moment for more of an explanation but soon realized none was coming. "Very well. Please, come to the table. Refreshments have been prepared." She turned and led them to the grand oval council table. A dozen seats extended down each side, and once the Arch Keeper took the head, she motioned Safran and Ulfric to the two immediately to either side of her.

The chairs provided were well cushioned, plush by anyone's standards, and attendants moved smoothly from their posts along the walls of the room to assist them. A variety of court personalities, some graduates of the commoner branch of the Conservatum, whom Ulfric recognized but only knew by face not name, took the remaining seats. The far end of the table hosted someone unfamiliar, however. A Yorman, and clearly an important one.

Brun, not having received an invitation to sit, turned toward the west wall to take a position of waiting. The Arch Keeper stopped her.

"Commander, you are dismissed. See to it that we aren't disturbed," Beatte said crisply.

"Aye, Arch Keeper." Brun's reply was equally curt.

One less ally present. Ulfric cursed inwardly. This observation, as precise as it was, only brought greater anxiety. Silently, he thanked Brun for ensuring he and Safran had not been disarmed.

Once all were settled, the Arch Keeper spoke again. "I am sure most at the table here need no introduction." Her meaning was clearly: *I have no interest in introducing them.* "Except for our esteemed guest from Yor. Newly appointed Arch Keeper Fergus."

Both Safran and Ulfric rose from their seats and dipped their chins toward the round-nosed, ginger-bearded giant. "Arch Keeper," they said together.

As the Yorish went, the man appeared the epitome of their stock. Pale and built lithely but robustly, with flashing gold eyes that showed a ruthless wisdom. With the exception of the ruthlessness, Ulfric imagined he might be looking at some many-turns-removed descendent of Mallich, the resemblance was so keen.

The Yorman also rose. His uniform, though made of plush fabric by a commoner's standards, was purpose built. Woven in the deep greens and reds of his homeland, it was still equally suitable for fighting, working, or enjoying a dinner. Ulfric had a sense he'd like this man and his practical nature, though the Yorish had not been friendly with the Knights since the Cataclysm.

"Knights, I am most honored," Fergus said in Ivoryssian, tipping his chin in acknowledgment.

His husky voice carried weight that Ulfric felt sure could be leveraged to strike fear if he chose to. His presence and title confirmed that their previous Arch Keeper had not survived Balavad's sack of their kingdom. The Yor elected their leaders from among their own branch of the Conservatum, and only those who excelled in both leadership and scholarship were considered. Given Fergus's intimidating stature, Ulfric suspected his appointment had also been based on the kingdom's need for more than symbolic strength in the position, therefore they'd chosen the most formidable representative they could.

All this aside, the real question was, what would the Yorish Arch Keeper be doing at the Ivoryssian mourning ceremony?

Once Fergus sat back down, he and Safran did likewise.

What do you think this is really about, Safran? he sent.

We'll know in a moment, but based on the way Beatte eyed the Fenestros, I believe they are planning to invoke the old custom of the Armistice of the Stones.

The next moment, she was proved correct. "With deep sadness," Beatte opened, "I want to acknowledge how much we've all suffered— too much—both as the singular kingdom of Ivoryss, and as Vinnrics as a whole. I've requested Arch Keeper Fergus to join us because it is no longer a possibility to consider our kingdoms divided. The peril from beyond is much too dire, and we know too little about it. From what our Yorish friends tell me, the damage we Ivoryssians suffered was indeed grave, but Yor lost even their renowned former leader, Colnach, along with most of their own naval forces. Many of their people, like our own, were rounded up by Balavad the Desecrator.

"For this reason, Knights of Vaka Aster, we intend to once more, after so many turns, call a worldwide peace under the sanctity of the Armistice of the Stones." She looked to Safran, recognizing her position as speaker for the Knights with the ease of any skilled politician, and said, "Knight Glór, will you do us the courtesy of presenting the remaining celestial stones?"

She knows we haven't brought them, Safran sent.

We shall remain forthright, he responded. *Simply tell her the truth.*

"As you must know, the celestial Fenestrii were one of the usurping Verity's targets. The Knights have reclaimed them and will continue to guard and protect them against any such future threat. The one I am using today is the only stone among us." Safran completed her statement by lying the Fenestros atop the table, still tucked beneath her palm.

Beatte's lips pursed, pulling even more on the taut skin of her cheeks until no lines creased her face. She looked as though she wore a mask, a tool for concealment, though nothing about her simmering anger was hidden. She went on. "Our disappointment is heavy that the Knights did not have enough trust in us, in *me*, to fulfill my request to bring the Fenestrii to this meeting. No, don't say anything, for I understand."

She held up a hand to keep Safran from interjecting, though Safran had made no indication she was about to. The Knights would not bother giving platitudes or making excuses for the truth. The truth was, they *didn't* trust the Arch Keeper, and there was no reason to lie about it.

And the Fenestrii—Ulfric had vowed during the chaos of these past days that he'd never let the celestial artifacts into the hands of commoners again. There was simply too much at stake with the power they held.

"But again, as I said, I can understand your hesitations. I've heard," her tone dropped in sympathy, "that you also lost some of your own. Is it true?"

This gave Ulfric a start. Rumors had a way of growing like weeds, becoming more distorted as time passed, but he hadn't anticipated this. He would have preferred their reduced numbers and the vulnerabilities this created be not widely known. But worse, Beatte had hit a painful mark. He didn't need to be reminded of Symvalline or Mylla.

Beatte's words, again, were intentionally vague. Did she know who among them was absent, what their actual numbers now were? The thought gave him an uncustomary moment of paranoia. Did spies walk inside Vigil Tower even now?

Attempting to remain impassive, Ulfric held his tongue as Safran relayed what was occurring back to Mallich and Stave through the Mentalios-Fenestros link.

"Knights?" Beatte inquired politely.

Safran turned her dark eyes on the Arch Keeper. "Your information is understandably incomplete, Arch Keeper. Though both Knight Lutair and the Stallari's daughter are temporarily absent, the Order remains full strength, despite these recent events."

Many at the table shifted uncomfortably. A term like "temporarily absent" was widely understand in politics to simply be an attempt to hedge, and they certainly assumed Symvalline and Isemay were dead. Some cast expressions of sympathy toward Ulfric and Safran, others didn't bother to pretend. The Yorish leader Fergus remained quiet and still, but his eyes missed nothing.

Ulfric approved of Safran's tactic and sent: *We won't mention Eisa or Mylla, even if Beatte asks directly.* He doubted she would. Nothing in this court moved in a straight line.

"These recent events," a young court fixture repeated. Ulfric knew him as a child of privilege from Asteryss whose enrollment as an acolyte at the Conservatum most likely had been granted because of his family name instead of any of his personal qualities, which he'd heard were best characterized as limited. "We have chosen a name for these dark days. 'The Desecration of Vinnr' seems to fit the best."

Something told Ulfric the young man had been the one to suggest the name. Yet, despite the aristocrat's magniloquence, Ulfric thought it fit.

The Arch Keeper flashed the man a look of irritation, and he closed his mouth abruptly. Ulfric took this to mean that Beatte wanted no one else to speak, intending to control the conversation herself.

Growing suddenly weary, he recalled Stave's attitude regarding politicians and started second-guessing his decision to come. Speaking out of both sides of their mouths, feigning and implying, parrying and thrusting like combatants—this was politics, and it bored him. He'd been a lensmaker all those hundreds of turns before becoming a Knight, not a nobleman, and certainly not a politician. His attitude, much like Stave's, had always been that if the object was to defeat each other, it would be better to do it openly and honorably, in a fighting arena or through a straightforward competition. Lies, disingenuous flattery, and subterfuge were the trades of cowards.

He glanced over to see Safran smirking at him, and he realized she'd heard his thoughts. *Except you, of course, Safran,* he covered, having forgotten it was her trade once, long ago.

Don't worry, Ulfric. Why do you think I became a Knight? But that just means we have to be twice as careful. Even cowards, especially *cowards, are as dangerous as vipers.*

Sweeping away any last vestiges of pretend sympathy, the Arch Keeper finally came out with what she'd been waiting to say all along. "We can no longer afford to allow the Knights Corporealis to lock away the artifacts that we require to keep our world safe from another incursion. Arch Keeper Fergus and I request with *all* urgency that the Knights turn over the Fenestrii to us, where we can use and protect them, and allow us complete and unfettered audience with the Vigil Star as we please."

She placed both her palms firmly on the table and stared into Ulfric's eye shields. "You will open Vigil Hall to this court and to the Yor court immediately." With an actress's expertise, she softened her expression and tone just a fraction, ending with, "We request this in the Vigil Star's name and the names of the sovereign kingdoms of Vinnr. And if the Knights wish to maintain the goodwill of all, you'll cease further prevarication and submit immediately."

CHAPTER SIXTEEN

Jaemus had been pacing his and Cote's room since Ulfric and Safran left for the keep, watching over Cote sleeping fitfully on their bed. His lifemate's breath was more labored than it should be if he were merely suffering a touch of indigestion from too much Vinnric chelbiefin shark and lind mead (which Jaemus would have been happy to consume until his belly burst). Jaemus had nearly worked himself into his own fit of indigestion, worrying about what might occur over the next few hours. What if the Knights didn't return? Maybe he shouldn't have changed his mind and decided to stay.

He knew he wasn't the only one on edge. He'd only briefly crossed paths with any of the Knights during the previous evening. They'd been busy preparing their defenses, spending all their time checking gates and the wards, whatever those were. He'd stayed out of the way and avoided asking too many questions, as their agitation had seemed ripe enough to burst, and he didn't want to get any of *that* on him.

He needed no further evidence of how high tensions were running than Stave's reaction when he'd asked him what dangers they needed to be concerned about, and the Knight had replied, "The danger is a blargy power-hungry Arch Keeper whose guts I'll wring out like a moldy sponge if any harm comes to Safran, I will." Jaemus had seen in his eyes that he hadn't been speaking metaphorically.

Cote coughed in his sleep, a rattling sound that reminded Jaemus starkly of his mother's last few cycles in Himmingaze before she'd died. He stepped over to his beloved, brushed Cote's dark hair from his forehead, noting how much paler he'd become, and whispered, "I'll be back in a moment, my captain. Just need to see what's going on with Stave and Roi."

As he reached for the door latch, a quavering chirp resounded from the central courtyard. It was like the sound the Singing Pillars made in that it seemed to not just travel *up* the walls but *through* them. Yet there was a note of alarm to the ringing, not harmony. Cote startled awake.

"What is that?" he asked alertly, as ever. Cote's trait of instant readiness, no matter the situation, sent Jaemus into momentarily entertaining the thought that he would make a much better Knight Corporealis than Jaemus ever would. Then Cote coughed once more.

"You relax," Jaemus said. "Let me go see."

But Cote was already out of bed and pulling on his boots. Knowing there was no point in arguing, Jaemus waited. Together they made their way toward the landing at the end of their hallway, meeting a few of the other 'Nauts who'd opened their doors to find out what the sound was about.

Jaemus, his role as emissary between the 'Nauts and the Knights fully entrenched by now, assured them, "I'll chat with Knight Roibeard and be right back."

At the moment, Stave arrived at the top of the wide stairs to their floor.

"Oh good, Stave, can you—" Jaemus began.

But the Knight cut him off. "Novice, get your sword."

He could swear his heart had just turned into a block of ice, if ice could experience terror. "Come again?" he stuttered.

Stave wasn't about to win an award for patience. "Winter's Bite. Think you can fight with it yet, do you?"

"...Er—"

But Stave appeared to dismiss the whole line of conversation. He walked inside Jaemus and Cote's room and swept up the hallowed sword, which Jaemus had carefully and considerately placed as far in the room from anywhere he might sit, stand, or lie as possible.

As the Knight retrieved the weapon, he explained, "The wards are breached. Don't know by who or what, but whoever's here will be in our basement in a split. We'd best get your people—"

He stopped short when Mallich's voice rang through the Mentalios lenses, astonishing Jaemus to be hearing it too. *Stave, show the Himmingazians to one of the arms chambers and have them select weapons if they wish. Then bring Jaemus to the catacombs and meet me there. Quickly.*

The ice of Jaemus's heart was suddenly melting, turning him into a puddle of goo from the inside out. "I, uh, I think we should—"

Inexplicably, Stave slammed him on the shoulder with what he must have thought was a good-natured pat and smiled almost joyfully. "Don't you worry, novice. Swing this like I showed you and you'll be fine. You can't die, remember?"

"But what about—"

It was no use. Stave's frame, as impassable as any wall, was pushing him and Cote toward the other end of the hallway and the stairwell leading to one of the many storerooms of weapons as he hollered out to the other 'Nauts to join them.

WITH SCARCELY ANY memory of how he'd gotten there, Jaemus looked around the dim room many floors beneath Vigil Tower in which he, Roibeard, and Stave now stood. The floor was roughened stone, the ceiling the same, and the air was much damper than inside the great tower above. Clearly, this was the entry to some kind of tunnel or cave system. The heavy wood-and-iron door they'd entered through, cracked slightly open, stood at their backs, and the equally stout door before them apparently led to the things they called "wards." Or maybe the door was the ward, but Jaemus was too ruffled with fear to ask at the moment.

After bustling the Glisternaut crew and Cote into a chamber that had been filled to bursting with both sharp and blunt metal objects and many more of indeterminate danger, Stave had told Jaemus to warn them to stay put, then pulled him down the stairs after Roibeard before he could protest.

Now, Stave and Roibeard stood between him and the far exit of the small chamber, hardly big enough to add more than two or three additional people. They said nothing, both so quiet the sound of Jaemus's own breath nearly deafened him. He couldn't control his anticipation.

"Master Knights, if you would, please tell me again why I'm here." They'd laden him with an over-the-shoulder bandolier from which dangled a dozen round fist-sized objects, and he pulled one free from the loose binding knot to hold out as he spoke. "I'm a bit confused about the part I'm supposed to play with regard to these…er, balls."

Stave glanced over his shoulder, saw the object in Jae's hand, and contorted his half-brow in a look that was either subdued apprehension or frank irritation. "Careful with that now, Bardgrim. Treat it wrong, and ping-pang wiggle-waggle, it'll do to us what Halla'll do to a worm under glass. Crispy, if you take my meaning."

"Yes, yes. I'm hearing what you're saying, but I'm not understanding what you expect *me* to do with it. This whole idea of 'crisping' something is not settling well. If *you* take *my* meaning."

Abruptly, though calmly, Roibeard turned and took a step toward him. "Novice, your task is simple, but not enviable. If whoever arrives through that door puts Stave and I down and you can see we aren't going to get back up before they reach the door to the tower, you turn and you run. But first, you drop that bandolier, twist that emberflare petard in your hand till the top spins round, and throw it into the pile. You'll have the time it takes to draw maybe three sharp breaths to get back behind that door before it goes. And you *must* be on the other side of it. Understand?"

"And where exactly is it going?" he managed through numb lips. *Stop asking stupid questions, Jae, or he may spin* your *top around.*

"It's simple, it is. You know what a Vinnric looks like on the outside by now, do you?" Stave said, and Jae nodded, confused. "Well you throw one of those petards at them, and you'll know what they look like on the inside too."

Roibeard added, "No one—*no one*—gets through that door, Bard-grim. That's your job. You have to hold the fortress until Ulfric and Safran can get back. And you have to protect your own people. That bandolier will turn this room to rubble and buy you time." He put a reassuring hand on Jaemus's shoulder. "You can, and you must, do this."

"They're coming. I hear them now," Stave growled.

Roibeard turned back and took up a defensive position. Then they all heard it.

Rap-rapraprap. A pause, then: *Rap-raprap-rapraprap.*

Stave and Roibeard looked at each other.

"Eisa?" Stave said.

Roibeard closed his eyes as if concentrating, then said: "She would have disabled the wards, not tripped them. And she's not responding to me through the Mentalios."

The knocking was repeated. *Rap-rapraprap…rap-raprap-rapraprap.*

Stave shrugged. "Doesn't matter, it doesn't. She's traded the knock code to some enemy. And whatever they paid, they're about to get it back tenfold." He tossed a handful of his klinkí stones overhead, where they hovered and glowed like tiny blue moons. In his fright, Jaemus decided not to retrieve his own lonely stone. Who knew what havoc he might cause with one under these conditions. Their little alcove was too small to hope any stray flick would skirt his fellow Knights.

Fellow Knights, he marveled distractedly.

Roibeard looked at the door and called, "State your name and venture, stranger or strangers."

He'd spoken in Elder Veros, and a muffled, accented voice from the outside replied in the same. "The Dyrrak have arrived to serve our celestial maker Vaka Aster upon the direction of the Nazarian Most High. We bring our swords but have come in peace."

So what are the swords for? Jaemus questioned. *Trimming the hedge?*

The two Knights exchanged wondering stares.

"You've got to be riddlin' the feeble," Stave muttered. "Nazarian

Most High? Since when has Eisa been high anything, other than highly full of—"

"Now not," Roibeard cut in. "Eisa sent the Dyrraks."

"Yes, I hear that. Means we've got one more enemy horde to face, and the Dyrraks were always fight-crazy."

Jaemus almost asked what Stave considered a man who'd forged and assembled over a thousand battle axes to be but kept his mouth shut.

"The Dyrraks would not be here in small numbers. They'd know better. They'll have their army, probably. Their martial strength is—or was prior to the Cataclysm—primarily with ground troops." Roibeard spoke quietly, as if his mind were on other things.

"Doesn't matter if they're swimming, flying, or lurching—if they were sent by Eisa, they bring her deceiver intentions with them."

"It may be. It may be—but we don't know Eisa's will or what she was doing at Magdaster."

Stave nearly shouted, "She sent Mylla to Himmingaze—after firing on her scout!"

"Aye," Roibeard replied, still calm. "But she didn't kill her. She could have, she had two chances, but neither time did she. Maybe she was trying to protect her."

"Now *you're* riddlin' the feeble, Roi. Don't you go sticking your neck out for that blargin' traitor again, I tell you. Don't do it."

Though Roibeard's face was still perfectly composed, Jaemus saw one of his hands bunch into a fist. Caution being the bruiseless part of valor, Jaemus took a furtive step backward.

Roibeard's next words were as tense as his fist. "The one thing that has eternally been true of the Dyrraks is that they would die for Vaka Aster—"

"Bunch of barmy zealots, they are."

"Yes, but they are a kingdom that exists for the sake of their loyalty to our Verity. Who better to keep them—both Vaka Aster and Ulfric—safe from Beatte's machinations now? Eisa might have sent them here to protect the vessel."

"Or she sent them to kill *us* so *she* could take the vessel, just like her zealot kin probably want to do. Remember, she doesn't know what's happened, she doesn't know Vaka Aster is among us again."

The two fell silent, no sound in the chamber but their breathing. As little as Jaemus wanted to see the insides of a Vinnric, much less a Dyrrak, his mouth started speaking before his mind could tell it to shut up. "Just a quick point. Wouldn't someone who had the best of intentions simply have knocked at the front door?"

Both the Knights looked at him, then to each other.

Roibeard said, "If we can't find somewhere safe to take the vessel, then we are failing our first duty as Knights. We have to speak to them."

Stave squinted up at his still-hovering klinkí stones. "They could kill us first, they could. Or've been turned by Balavad."

"What other choice is there? They'll come through that door one way or another. After all, they were able to breach the wards."

"No doubt Eisa told them how."

"No doubt."

Finally, Stave swirled his empty hand, spinning the trove of stones around in the air, and nodded. "Always wondered if the rest of the Dyrraks are as ugly as the *Nazarian Most High*, I have." He spit on the floor. "Let's find out."

CHAPTER SEVENTEEN

Ulfric had to take a slow, considered breath to hold back his first response to the Arch Keeper's ill-considered demands, but his ability to draw from his Knightly discipline was diminishing quickly. Remaining still to allow Safran to work her charms was his last resort. They could never open the doors of Vigil Tower to commoners again. Or at least not until he had released Vaka Aster and the Verity was unhindered by human vulnerabilities once more.

Instead of Beatte, Safran looked pointedly toward the Arch Keeper of Yor. "The profundity of your kingdom's suffering and losses, Arch Keeper Fergus, shines like tears in your eyes." Her voice carried a resonate compassion through the Fenestros that soothed even Ulfric's agitation like a balm. "I can only guess at how vulnerable your people must now feel at having been so long under the usurper's occupation. The Knights heard rumors of the decimation of your militaries, and with the history of unrest between Yor and Dyrrakium, you must be desperate to rearm and rebuild before they learn of your weakness."

Ulfric turned, his curiosity to see Fergus's reaction equal to his curiosity about Safran's tactic. The flaring of the Yorman's cheeks reminded him of the low rumble one hears just before a volcano erupts, but his words were calculated and calm.

"You cut quickly to the heart of our troubles, Knight. And the answer is, we are."

Safran nodded and ran her fingers over the Fenestros, still lying on the table before her.

It was Beatte's turn for reddened cheeks. "Why do you hesitate, Knight Glór? Stallari Aldinhuus, what say you?"

Be ready, Safran, Ulfric sent, knowing he didn't need to. *I'll take it from here.*

He responded to both Arch Keepers at once. "What use do you believe the Fenestrii would be to you, Beatte, Fergus? They are not weapons. Never mind. Don't answer that, it isn't important. Experience, *recent* experience, has shown us that the kingdoms are not equipped to ensure the security of the stones, which are far more dangerous left among you than they will be with us—where they will stay. As for the Vigil Star, our creator is the only entity who may command us. And, Arch Keeper," he said directly to Beatte, "the Vigil Star cannot *be* commanded."

Ulfric rose and Safran followed as Beatte, Fergus, and the cadre of court attendees soaked in his refusal. Beside Ulfric, Beatte gripped the arms of her chair. He could nearly feel the heat of her rage.

He fixed the Ivoryssian leader with his eyes, though she couldn't see them, and finished. "The people of Ivoryss look to their leader to make the wisest and often hardest decisions to ensure their safety. They will need you today of all days to be both pillar and mortar for rebuilding their hopes and ushering in a safe and prosperous future.

"Have your mourning ceremony, Arch Keeper. The Knights will decline to attend for one reason: we do not serve Ivoryss. Our fealty is not given to you. Do not forget this. While you and your company from Yor negotiate peace between yourselves, the Knights Corporealis, as ever, keep you, all of you"—his gaze swept over the attendees—"safe from ultimate destruction."

He nodded to Safran, and the two stepped away from the table. "We'll take our leave now."

The Ivoryssian leader shot from her seat. "You will not!" With a quick jerk of her chin, she summoned the resident guards to readiness.

The moment he and Safran had entered the room, Ulfric had calculated the number of Marines present: twelve, an easy force to beat. However, the rear of the chamber contained a stairway, and at the top, a balcony fed by hallways leading elsewhere inside the keep. Any number of reinforcements could enter through there, though they'd be grouped tightly before they reached the lower floor.

Ulfric, show them your eyes, Safran sent. *Show them who they truly face.*

Not yet, he returned. And why not? The reason, he admitted, was simple. He was tired of Beatte believing she ruled over him and the Knights, and he wanted the satisfaction of making her finally accede to her own limits.

"Aldinhuus, you and the Knights Corporealis no longer get to decide our fates. Seize them," Beatte ordered the guards.

Ulfric had no desire to hurt anyone, either, at least none who didn't deserve it. Therefore, he cast his klinkí stones into a cerulean net of light, Safran doing the same. The entire group of attendees gasped, no doubt having heard, and some even having witnessed, the capabilities of the wystic stones.

"You mean to take us prisoner?" he asked, his tone one of mock interest. "You wish to go to war with our Order, the same people who saved you and Ivoryss, as well as Yor? What will the people you lead think of that?"

Fergus had not moved from his seat, and Ulfric noted that he watched the proceedings with a spectator's interest, not the interest of a commander being refused, and he had a sudden insight. The Yorish leader was not here specifically to ally with Beatte, but to ally with whoever offered the greatest benefit. *It's a wonder the kingdoms haven't clashed in all-out war again since the Cataclysm,* Ulfric thought distantly.

No time for pondering it now. The Marines had formed a circle around the table, their own weapons at the ready, and all but Beatte and Fergus had stepped outside their ring. None of the fighters were familiar to Ulfric, and none showed a hesitance to engage the Knights if necessary. *Foolish commoners.*

"The people of Ivoryss wish for nothing but peace," Beatte seethed, "and your Order seems to think you have a right to stand against ensuring we have it."

The delusions of youth and power, he thought. Had she always been so short-sighted and callow, willing to believe whatever convenienced her?

Safran met Ulfric's eyes. *Keep them distracted for a moment,* she sent.

To divert their attention—and maybe to speed things up a bit, as this summit was clearly over—Ulfric leaped onto the table with his shield net still active and drew Star Spark. Safran did a slow spin in place, as if she had suddenly decided to take in the room. But Ulfric saw the way the surface of her Mentalios had begun to swirl in a spectrum of iridescent colors. She was watching something outside from the bruhawks' eyes. Why was her attention drawn to the outside, when the real festivities were here?

The Knight stopped her slow spiral, and her Mentalios cleared as she looked first at Ulfric, then Fergus, then at Beatte.

"Perhaps you are right, Arch Keeper," she said. "It may indeed be best if the Knights Corporealis no longer remained an influence on Ivoryss. We will be taking our leave, I assure you. And it will be permanent."

Surprised, Ulfric sent, *What is this about, Safran?*

At that moment, the heavy chamber doors were pulled open so abruptly they crashed into the walls, causing everyone to jump and some to shout out in surprise. An out-of-breath Marine, one of those who'd met Ulfric and Safran at the base of the keep's rampart, plowed inside.

"Arch Keeper, the city is under attack! We must take up arms!"

"The Desecrator!" Beatte gasped, instant fear turning her voice shrill.

"No, not the Verity or Raveners," the guard cried. "It's the Dyrraks!"

CHAPTER EIGHTEEN

"If you so much as breathe loudly, I'll remove your lungs through the new smile I carve into your throat," Eisa said into the ear of a strange, remarkably green-in-color man who stood behind Stave and Roi, holding of all things an emberflare petard.

The man stiffened as her dagger pressed at his throat and her armor at his back. He let out a sound like a donkey choking, but quietly, and offered no resistance.

"Good," she said. And the moment had come for a reunion. "Roi, Stave, it's safe to open the door to the catacombs. I've spoken with the Dyrraks."

The Knights spun around so quickly they blurred before her eyes. Either they recognized her voice, or they knew it would be hazardous if they accidentally struck a man wearing a bandolier of petards with their klinkí stones, because they didn't attack. She wondered if they might, given the nature of her departure and what they knew or might suspect they knew of what had occurred between her and Mylla.

Slightly vindicated, she noted that by sheer surprise in their eyes that they hadn't known this pale green enemy spy was behind them. Her companions were slipping, which in turn surprised her.

"Don't worry, I've got this blaggard under control," she assured them.

"Let him go, Eisa," Roi said calmly.

"Not until he drops the—" Before she finished the sentence, there was a dull clunk from the man's petard hitting the floor stones.

"He's one of us," Roi continued and unexpectedly stepped up and pushed her blade hand aside.

She held it in place stiffly for a moment, then let him. The foreigner, obviously a Himmingazian, quickly scuttled away from her toward the far door.

"One of us?" She took a closer look and realized he was wearing Winter's Bite. But the weapon quickly lost her interest. The mark on the man's chin had stolen it. "Is that…is he a…"

"Yes, a Himmingazian. And a novice Knight Corporealis."

Roi had barely finished the sentence when Stave lunged at her with his ax raised. The chamber was far too confined for her to fight with her glaive, so she'd left that just outside the door after slipping down the stairway from inside the tower, but she still held her dagger. As Stave closed the gap and swung, she spun inside his reach and would have tickled his ribs with her knife, but Roi cried, his voice more powerful than the scream of a bruhawk lunging at its prey, "STOP!"

The sound of his raised voice was so rare that they both halted instantly. "You will not fight each other!" he commanded.

"Roi, damn you! She's a traitor," Stave said.

"No more than you ever were, you unworthy bastirt!" she hissed back.

Stave had recovered from his swing and taken a step to the side, his ax still raised.

"Lower it," Roi demanded. "Both of you."

Eisa's eyes hadn't left Stave, nor his her. They stared each other down, once again repeating a habit that had become so worn it had lost its power to truly threaten either of them. One of Stave's own ridiculous aphorisms came to mind: *You can't pull a man back from the lip of a cliff if he won't let go of his anvil.*

Dismissing him, she sheathed her dagger and turned to Roi, gesturing at the Himmingazian. "How did this happen?"

Roi glanced between her and Stave, waiting for the shorter Knight to follow her lead. Eisa didn't care if he did. She'd do what was necessary to restore the Order to only worthy companions if he forced her to, but out of respect for Roi's friendship with Stave, she'd hold back until that happened.

Stave repositioned his feet and straightened out of an attack stance, but his voice lost none of its threat. "Why've you led the enemy to our door?" he snapped.

"Enemy?" she scoffed. "The Dyrraks would have been the last people standing if Ivoryss had fallen. As it is, they remain loyal enough to Vaka Aster to have rallied their full might in her defense. They are here for Vaka Aster. Better to have them come through the catacombs than through the city where they'd have to slaughter anyone who got in their way. Or have you forgotten how the lesser kingdoms feel about them?"

Roi kept himself between the two of them, and his voice lowered to its usual register. "Eisa, you need to explain yourself. Ulfric and Safran are at Aster Keep meeting with the Arch Keeper at this moment. What are the Dyrraks' intentions?" In a tone that barely concealed an accusation—something she'd never thought she'd hear from her friend—he added, "And why did you take the Scrylle and leave us aboard the *Vigilance* to fight the usurper without you?"

Though Roi hadn't insinuated she was a traitor in definite terms, she knew the idea was there. They thought worse of her than she'd anticipated. *It isn't that surprising, though, is it?* she asked herself. But this wasn't the time to reflect on her mistakes. She had to explain the Dyrraks' presence quickly to avoid a route and to, perhaps, find common ground. *After all these turns, the Knights and Dyrraks will finally unite, as they should have from the beginning.*

Keeping her explanation brief, Eisa skipped discussing what had caused her to leave the *Vigilance*—there would be time for that later, when they were all convened—and recounted the moments since she'd returned to Vinnr. Using Wing Rekkr's ship, she'd arrived in Asteryss this morning and discovered the Dyrrak forces approaching Asteryss's largest harbor. She'd presumed they were preparing to storm the city, likely believing Balavad controlled it.

With the information Wing Rekkr had given her, she'd landed on the Domine Ecclesium's flagship to inform the Dyrraks of Ivoryss's turn of events. During their meeting, his own news had been revealing. As she'd suspected, they had come to Ivoryss with the intention of stopping Balavad's forces, and he'd seemed…disappointed when she'd told him the enemy had been defeated. She sympathized. Rallying an invasion force only to turn them back home without a single clash of blades was in itself a kind of defeat. The Dyrraks had been shunned by the rest of Vinnr for so long, she supposed they wished for a chance to once more be a force to reckon with in the realm.

Then the Ecclesium had shared more disturbing news. Their spies inside the Ivoryssian court had reported that Arch Keeper Beatte had called a summit with the Knights and Vaka Aster. But it was a trap. Beatte's intention was to seize the Order and charge them as traitors if they refused to comply with her demands or failed to produce Vaka Aster in her vessel form.

As Eisa had taken in this information, the commoners' thinking was all too clear to her. They hadn't seen the living vessel in hundreds of turns around Halla. If, even after the fight with Balavad, they were denied her presence any longer, it was easy to see how they would assume the Knights were somehow to blame for the maker's absence. In the simple minds of commoners, Verities could be that easily summoned and cajoled, or controlled. And, naturally, because commoners were powerless, a dangerous position for the weak, they needed a scapegoat, a villain they could blame all their troubles on and punish. If not a Verity—because how can you punish something as powerful as a celestial creator?—then the Knights Corporealis would do.

Foolish commoners, ever incapable of embracing wisdom, even if it were rammed down their throats.

Eisa had thought it over quickly and decided the Domine Ecclesium should continue the plans he'd laid—in part. She'd permitted him to march ground troops to Aster Keep and demand an audience with Beatte, but more importantly, provide the Knights backup if it came to that. Beatte had shown herself to be the Knights' enemy, and Eisa thought it justified that the leader of the Dyrraks should look upon she who had thus made herself the Dyrraks' enemy as well. If Ulfric had truly returned, Eisa was no longer Stallari Regent and didn't speak for the Knights, of course, and she couldn't force them to accept the Dyrraks' assistance. But she thought Beatte's reaction to the Domine Ecclesium's unexpected visit might be all that would be needed to show Ulfric who the Knights' true allies were. Because if Ivoryss was no longer safe for the Knights, it was no longer safe for the vessel. And because Yor had already fallen, that left one place, one empire, for the Knights to go. Eisa and the Knights Corporealis were leaving for Dyrrakium. She was going home.

Once the Ecclesium's troop had left for Aster Keep, Eisa had ordered a contingent to go through the catacombs to Vigil Tower while she came by scout.

Roi and Stave listened to her story unfold, Stave reluctantly, and she wrapped it up with: "Now we must warn Ulfric and Safran what Beatte has in store for them, if they haven't already seen it for themselves. The Domine Ecclesium leads enough warriors to put down any resistance, and they'll be there shortly. They will escort Ulfric and Safran back here, and we must make for Dyrrakium. Today."

Her companions took in the news. When she was finished, Roi asked, "Why come back to the tower through stealth, Eisa? Why not face us as our confederate?"

"My Mentalios was broken on Mount Omina, so I couldn't inform you of my approach. And," she added, for once aware of the coldness in her tone, "I had to see you first, see if you were still *you*. I watched the *Vigilance* get taken. How could I know you hadn't been turned into a slave like Balavad's others? We've been friends for many, many turns, Roi, but you know my first duty is, and will always be, to protect the vessel."

Roi nodded and stated as coldly, "There is more you must account for, Eisa." He raised the Fenestros he'd been using to link with Safran. "But for now, I'll warn Safran and Ulfric."

"Wait, you're just going to believe her?" Stave gruffed.

She sneered at him. "For what possible reason would I lie?"

Stave's lip curled like a mutt, but Roi, as always, stepped in. "I've known Eisa for three times the length of your life, Stave. She does not lie."

Stave and Roi locked eyes for a moment, and she got the sense they were speaking to each other through their wystic lenses. Damn that Wing for causing her to break her own. Losing the mindlink was like losing a sense.

After a moment, the two seemed to have concluded their conversation, and Stave turned his glare to her, burning through her like fire. But she was Eisa. She was ice, and fires lit by unworthies could do her no harm. She'd never wanted to admit Stave Thorvíl into the Order. He hadn't cared a whit about Vaka Aster before joining the Conservatum, and he'd only done that because he'd fallen in love with Safran, not because he'd found a higher calling, not because Vaka Aster had summoned him. He'd been a blaspheming, drunken blacksmith from the rustic alleys of Magdaster before, but Ulfric had refused to listen to Eisa's objections when he'd accepted him into the Knights. She'd insisted that an unbeliever could never truly have faith, whereas Ulfric had argued that those who found their faith late were the strongest with it. Overruled, her last assumption had been that Vaka Aster would deny him ordination, but about that, too, she'd been wrong. So now, though they may both be Knights, they would never be equal, and she would never treat him as such.

Her disdain didn't leave her expression as they glowered at each other. Finally, he growled and stepped aside.

She said to Roi, "I'll let in my kinspersons in now." Sparing a glance at the Himmingazian, who had said nothing during their exchange and stood with eyes as wide as the Verring Sea, she commented, "Keep that one out of the way or he might get hurt."

CHAPTER NINETEEN

I n the moment it took those present to comprehend the arrival of the Dyrrak force, Ulfric jumped off the table to join Safran and now stood back to back with her.

Care to fill me in? he sent through their Mentalios link.

Eisa has returned. She is with Roi and Stave within Vigil Tower. Apparently, she's negotiated with the Dyrrak people to take the vessel to Dyrrakium. Their full military force, some fifteen thousand ground fighters as well as water and airships have arrived by sea.

Ulfric was speechless, his mind teeming with hundreds of questions competing to be the first asked. More pressing, however, was the danger posed by the Dyrraks, who were trained from birth in the arts of combat. *Are the commoners in danger?*

Only if they take up arms. Roi tells me Eisa commanded the Dyrraks to spill no blood.

Ulfric had little confidence in the frightened people of Asteryss. *The Ivoryssian forces are already dangling by a thread. If they initiate a fight, they will be slaughtered.*

Yelling came from outside the meeting chamber, but it stopped short. The guards in the room scrambled to take up a defensive position to protect the Arch Keeper from both the Knights and whoever was coming.

Ulfric looked over his shoulder as a sepia-skinned man wearing a red irregularly-shaped gem the size of a child's fist around his neck entered the chamber. Dozens of armed Dyrrakium warriors flanked him on each side, their numbers stretching outside the doors beyond the limits of Ulfric's sight. Then the sound of boots above him drew his attention to the balcony, teeming with more Dyrrak fighters.

"Which of you is the Arch Keeper of Ivoryss?" the Dyrrak leader said in Elder Veros.

Ulfric turned and stood beside Safran. They both waved their klinkí stones to hover around them, interlinking them to create a protective shield not even another Knight could penetrate.

Safran sent: *If a skirmish breaks out, let me stay ahead of you, Stallari. You should not engage if you can help it.*

The truth of this grated on Ulfric. He was a senior warrior and had been in more of these types of rumbles than he could remember, but his first duty was to Vaka Aster, which meant his body was not his, not really, to put in jeopardy. With clenched teeth, he held steady, waiting.

Fergus had risen and grabbed a set of eating knives, brandishing one in each hand. He stood at the ready, staring at the newcomers as if he meant to turn them into the main course. The rest of those assembled at the table had scattered, finding nowhere to go but to put their backs to the solid walls. The assembled Marines looked from Beatte to the Knights and then to the Dyrrak troops, at a complete loss about what to do. Without direction from Beatte, their own captain held up a hand and motioned for all to stay in place.

From where she still stood at the head of the table, Beatte demanded in Ivoryssian, "How dare you, Dyrrak. Your exiled and dishonored people have not been invited to Ivoryss. Leave immediately or—"

The Dyrrak leader cut her off. "Do not speak to me in that sullied language, unworthy. You demean yourself when you set aside the first gift of our maker for your lesser tongue. No Dyrrak will hear it."

This isn't going to go well, Ulfric began. *Safran, speak for the Knights.*

Ask the Dyrraks why they've come to Ivoryss. Perhaps their answer will help assuage the fears of the Ivoryssians.

Before Beatte could respond, Safran held out her Fenestros and stepped forward. "Esteemed Dyrrak, I am Knight Corporealis Safran Glór and this is Stallari Ulfric Aldinhuus. Please state your business in Ivoryss."

The Dyrrak leader looked to her. "Knights Corporealis of Vaka Aster the Creator, I am Starkas Nazaria, Heir Regent of the Sixth Line of Dyrrakium, Domine Ecclesium of the Dyrrak people. We have come to offer our protection to Vaka Aster in this time of strife and war with the usurper called Balavad. I request you take me to our creator."

Nazaria, sent Safran. *That is—*

Yes, Ulfric answered. *Eisa's Line.*

The clean-shaven, middle-aged man still had dried salt in his black hair and the creases of his unusual clothing, clearly having come straight from a long sea voyage. He and most of the others were built like Eisa, rangy and thickly muscled. The leader's tunic flared open at the chest, displaying raised and vicious-looking blackened scars representing runes and images that matched ones Eisa also bore. His head was shaved along the sides and his bared forearms resembled ropes made of beam-thick iron. A warrior priest, then.

He spoke again: "The Dyrrakium fleet awaits Vaka Aster's command and will rid the realm of any derelict and blasphemous army that attempts to thwart her will without hesitation if our maker so desires it."

The Dyrrak leader's statement could not have been further from what Ulfric had hoped he would say. The Ivoryssian soldiers in the room brandished their swords more threateningly, preparing to sacrifice themselves in futility if Beatte commanded it. They had no chance against an army the size of the Dyrraks'. Surely Beatte would know that.

A quick glance at the Arch Keeper caused Ulfric's stomach to roil in dread. She was looking to her guard captain, her face a rictus of rage. Would she truly give an order to attack this greater force? The Arch Keeper could not be that vindictive, that willing to die and take her kingdom with her, could she? All Ulfric could think of were the harried and frightened commoners throughout Asteryss, already beaten almost to death by a monstrous Verity, now about to be undermined by their own leader's foolishness.

He had to act. The Dyrraks had come prepared for battle, but he didn't wish to see any more Ivoryssians slain, not in Vaka Aster's name. Stepping clear of the klinkí stone shield, he spoke loudly, his baritone resonating throughout the hall, "Vaka Aster does not condone such actions."

The Domine Ecclesium's lips tightened. "And do you speak for the creator, Knight?"

"No," he responded. "I am the creator."

Dropping any further pretense, he pulled the eye shields from his head and let his eyes' wystic colors, the colors of the Cosmos, fall on those assembled. A moment later, the high ceiling of the chamber burst alight with a glow of thousands of dragørflies, the susurration of their wings a subdued cacophony that filled the room. Those who'd seen his eyes gasped, and the rest did when they dragørflies appeared, swooping and buzzing throughout the chamber.

The Domine Ecclesium along with the entire assembly of troops dropped to their knees in deference. "Vaka Aster, your Dyrrak servants submit themselves most humbly to you."

Ulfric was momentarily distracted by a strange tingling sensation that covered his skin from head to toe, as if he'd just traveled through a starpath.

Safran's voice came to him, slightly hesitant. *Ulfric, your skin...*

He glanced down at his outstretched hand that controlled his klinkí stones. The dark skin seemed to emit a bluish cast of pale light. *That's... something,* he thought.

We need to put a stop to this, now, Safran sent. *The Ivoryssians can't handle a new threat to their sovereignty.*

I agree. We're done here, for better or worse. The Dyrraks will come with us back to Vigil Tower.

"Arch Keeper," Ulfric said in Elder Veros, facing Beatte. Once he had her attention, he realized he had no idea what to say to her. Who was he? A Knight or a Verity? The absurdity, and enormity, of the role that had been forced on him chilled his guts. But he had to say something. "Your city has served Vaka—me well for these long turns. It would now be wise to see to your people. Rebuild, care for each other. Heal your wounds." He turned back to the door. "Domine Ecclesium, the Knights Roibeard, Thorvíl, and Nazaria await us at Vigil Tower. We welcome your escort."

"Stop," Beatte cried. "Vigil Star, the people of Dyrrakium are traitors, usurpers. You…cannot show them your favor."

The Domine Ecclesium stood and growled at Beatte almost predatorily. "Do you dare to speak to your creator that way?" He looked to Ulfric. "Vaka Aster, I will happily—"

Ulfric cut him off. "Lead the way, Ecclesium. There will be no bloodshed here today." He took Beatte in with a glance as well. "*None.*"

The Domine Ecclesium stepped beside the entrance and bowed his head. His assembly of troops stood and parted down the center, leaving a path for Ulfric and Safran. Safran looked at the Arch Keeper sadly, seemed about to say something, then began pacing toward the main doors.

Let's hope things did not go this poorly at the tower, she sent as she exchanged a glance with Ulfric, who followed.

Let's hope.

The Dyrrak fighters closed ranks behind the two Knights, keeping their weapons trained on those within the meeting chamber.

As they moved down the outer hall, Ulfric heard Beatte say, "Ivoryss will remember this, Dyrrak. This is not over."

And the Ecclesium's response: "We shall meet again, unworthy."

CHAPTER TWENTY

Safran conferred with Mallich as Ulfric and she made their way through the keep's main courtyard. Afterward, she quickly explained to him what Mallich had learned from Eisa on her return. While he listened intently, Ulfric's stomach soured from both what he heard and what he saw. In every direction, Dragør Marines stood guarded by more Dyrraks, their weapons at their feet. He saw no one injured, which slightly soothed his stomach, but only slightly. The Dyrrak forces had overcome the keep's defenses so swiftly and with such stealth it seemed none had even had time to put up any kind of fight. *What kind of force this large can do that?* he wondered. It was almost incomprehensible.

He and Safran were guided back through the city on the same streets they'd walked to Aster Keep. Everywhere Ulfric turned, he saw Dyrraks, hundreds of them, guarding every intersection and lining rooftops with weapons and crossbows in hand. Most disturbingly, overhead the sky teemed with Dyrrak attack craft. They ships were similar to the dragørfly scouts that had originally been Ulfric's design. But he'd come up with it only approximately fifty turns ago, and the Dyrraks had been exiled over seven hundred. Where had they acquired the designs?

But he knew, didn't he? *Eisa.* He was beginning to question his assumptions about her loyalty. Had she never given over her ties to Dyrrakium completely?

During his and Safran's brief audience with Beatte, most of the city's remaining residents had arrived at the keep and begun preparing for the mourning ceremony by setting up chairs or simply scouting somewhere to wait. Unlike during his last visit, no one had booths or stalls to sell drinks and food. The people of Asteryss had lost that sense of celebration. They simply stood in wait for the Arch Keeper to come before them and speak.

Now, these men and women watched both aghast and awed as the procession of their longtime assumed enemy the Dyrraks led a member of the Knights Corporealis and himself, a being who could no longer be referred to as simply a man, away from Aster Keep. He couldn't imagine what they were thinking.

And the way his skin now glowed along with his eyes—he knew this not as a mark of celestial divinity but as a symptom of becoming a vessel. In some turns—tens, hundreds? who could say?—he would cease to be a man at all and his spirit would dissipate little by little to rejoin the Great Cosmos, leaving his no-longer-a-man shell completely to their maker. To the world, he'd be a martyr of sorts. To his wife and daughter, he'd be as good as dead.

He still had time, though, and he shook this new fear off. Wishing he'd refused to visit Aster Keep altogether and remained anonymous, he watched the Ivoryssians as they marched through the city. One thing was clear. The people of Asteryss could not take another battle. Neither their hearts nor their minds were strong enough to endure more strife and destruction. Ulfric could see it written on their faces, their obvious fear—until they looked upon him. When that happened, he watched their shock turn to awe, then, to his dismay, even greater fear.

Maybe us leaving is what is best for the people of Ivoryss, and even of Yor, he considered. *To have Vaka Aster out of their lives for a time. Let them get on with things without a false hope that their maker will somehow come to their aid. Let them relearn reliance on themselves and each other, grow strong again on their own, so they will remember that they are.*

For a moment, he was buoyed by the idea of the people of Ivoryss, a kingdom he regarded as home, returning to its resilience and glory. Yet, his thoughts soon darkened. *Beatte, though—is she capable or too jaded? Too power greedy? Will she lead them astray?*

Don't think too much on it, he told himself. *There is nothing you can do for them now. Staying would only make them resentful. By leaving with the Dyrraks, and by showing it is my choice, or rather Vaka Aster's, perhaps they will come to accept that the Empire of Dyrrakium is not an enemy. It is a part of Vinnr, accepted and even included by the maker herself. This could be the first step to mending the divisions sown so long ago. Surely they will not continue their hostilities knowing the Vigil Star doesn't wish them to. I'll have to find some way to begin to mend this rift if I can—once we're away.*

The thought of this added burden made him wish he could put his mind in a cage like a bird and throw a sheet over it. *All I want is Symvalline and Crumb home safe. Why has this, all this, fallen to me to resolve?*

Shortly, Safran broke into his thoughts. *Ulfric, this isn't right. It looks as if the Dyrraks have completely taken over the city. This is an occupation force, not a simple rescue.*

He agreed. *We should have answers soon,* he sent. *Eisa has a great deal to explain.*

Safran said nothing more, and they continued their journey.

Soon they reached Vigil Tower, and Safran rang the cord to announce them through the pillars. Jaemus arrived at the tower's door to let them in. As they stepped into the main hall, only the Domine Ecclesium and two others followed. The rest of the Dyrraks remained outside, and Ulfric caught a glimpse of them setting up a guard as the doors closed.

"Welcome back, Safran, Ulfric...decorative newcomer and friends," Jaemus said, nodding to each, but keeping his eyes on the Ecclesium. "Glad to see you made it safely."

Opting for private communication, Safran sent, *Jae, where is Stave?*

Jaemus answered aloud. "The rest of the, erm, team, including the new one—Eisa, is it? real charmer she is—are waiting for everyone in one of the meeting chambers. They asked me to come for you."

But Ulfric knew better. Stave and Roi were likely ensconced on the balcony, crossbows in hand, waiting for any need to use them. Jae was likely the decoy, his unusual visage a ploy to throw the Dyrraks off in case their intentions were nefarious.

Jaemus began to turn away, but the Domine Ecclesium stopped him. "What is wrong with you?" he asked, or demanded.

"This again," Jaemus muttered, but Ulfric jumped in.

"He's a Himmingazian, from the realm of the Verity Lífs, and Knight Corporealis of Vinnr. My guest." Silently, he sent to Roi and Stave, *We are all well here, and I don't believe we have much to worry about. Join us.*

Safran, speaking through the Fenestros, said to the Ecclesium. "Perhaps we should all assemble before discussing any further matters. Domine Ecclesium, please follow me. We'll sit under the statue of Vaka Aster. Jaemus, please go and collect the others."

Seeming to understand their need for subterfuge, Jaemus made a show of dashing off.

From behind him, Ulfric heard: "Stallari, I'm glad to see you again."

Still bare of the eye shields, Ulfric turned to catch Eisa in his wystically enhanced gaze. She stood with her glaive in her hand beside the door, flanked on both sides by several more Dyrrak warriors, their backs to the wall. They were so quiet, Ulfric hadn't even known they were there.

When Eisa saw him, her face showed her surprise. *What...* she sent.

She wore a new Mentalios lens that had come from a variety he had stored among other tools specifically for the Knights' use. Somewhere during these last few days, she must have lost her old one. One of many stories she needed to tell. *I have the same question for you,* he sent, *and many, many more. But not now.*

In that moment, she'd taken in not only his strange eyes but the rest of him, too. The way his skin now shone like the wings of a dragørfly gave him away completely. In response, Eisa lost her composure for the first time Ulfric had ever witnessed. "You...you are..." she stammered.

The Dyrraks on either side of her suddenly seemed to realize who he was, and each of them dropped to a knee, their eyes downcast and heads bowed, the noise of their metal weapons on the stone loud enough to echo throughout the hall.

Yes, Eisa, I am the vessel. He could see her wrestling with this news, and after a moment, she followed the Dyrraks' in dipping her chin and dropping her eyes, though she didn't kneel. Ulfric suspected her response was less about reverence and more to do with her having to grapple with the realization that the man she'd recently accused of having lost his faith in their maker had, in a manner, *become* their maker. He turned away, letting her come to terms with it on her own. Internally, he was thinking, *It isn't what I expected—or wanted—either.*

In a matter of minutes, Roi and Stave had surreptitiously left their sentry posts and arrived to meet them beside Vaka Aster's statue on its dais. Ulfric's heart twinged thinking of the last time he'd stood before the simulacrum. When he'd given Crumb the memory keeper.

Though the Himmingazians had brought benches and chairs here, the light from nearby windows making the spot perfect for quiet respite, the only person who sat down was Jaemus. As soon as Ulfric stopped walking, the Dyrraks knelt with their heads bowed again. *Not going to get used to that,* he thought.

Jaemus's neck swiveled as he looked to the Knights, then to the Dyrraks. Apparently thinking he was breaking some kind of etiquette, he rose again and stepped backward toward the dais. As the only person moving, he drew everyone's attention. Even a couple of the overly reverent Dyrraks glanced up to see what he could be doing. After a second, he leaned against the dais awkwardly and pointedly looked away, as if his mind were on other things. *So out of his element,* Ulfric thought, sparing him a moment of compassion. He noticed that Eisa, too, stood away from the group.

Unused to, and definitely uncomfortable with, the deference given by the Dyrraks, Ulfric said, "Stand or sit as you prefer."

Once they'd all risen, he looked to Safran, and she quickly introduced the Knights to the Domine Ecclesium. Instead of introducing the Dyrraks in return, the Ecclesium waved to a more ceremonially clothed Dyrrak woman.

She stepped forward. "I am Seldeg Aoggvír, Heir of the Third Line, Chancellor of the Dyrrak Phalanx. We Dyrraks are at your service, ever faithfully, Creator." She then stepped back with the rest of the Dyrrak group, leaving the Domine Ecclesium to speak.

"The Dyrraks have kept our word to escort yourself and this Knight safely to your fortress," he said. "What now, Creator, can we do for you?"

Ulfric shared a glance with each of the Knights, and Roi gave him a tiny nod. With an internal shrug, Ulfric decided to keep things simple. "Passage to Dyrrakium, Domine Ecclesium, for both this vessel and my ordained Knights. We—I shall now honor the Dyrrakium Empire as my new residence."

The weight of the decision settled on his shoulders suddenly. "And one more thing," he added. "We have other-worlders, Himmingazians, among us. Will Dyrrakium welcome my favored guests as well?"

Though the Ecclesium's demeanor didn't change outwardly, Ulfric could almost feel the excitement that radiated from him. "It is done." He raised his head, though his eyes never rose higher than Ulfric's chin, and seemed to think about what to say. "Creator of All, the Dyrrakium people are prepared to walk your ordained path. We offer your vessel an eternity of sanctuary behind the impregnable walls of Dyrrakium. We shall unerringly follow your guidance and teachings and spread your dominion throughout Vinnr."

I don't like the sound of "spread your dominion," Mallich sent. *What does he mean?*

Stave barked, *Means they Dyrraks' fanatical zealotry hasn't abated a single bit since their exile, it does.*

"As your chosen ever-faithful," the Ecclesium went on, "we have amassed our fleet and await your command."

The skin on Ulfric's neck, cooled by the breeze outside, now tingled uncomfortably with pinpricks that started at the base of his skull and ran down his spine. "What command are you waiting for, Ecclesium?"

The Dyrrak leader's eyes flashed, the same silvery-gray as Eisa's, Ulfric noted. With his wide shoulders and broad back, his strength alone would make him a formidable foe, but the elation—or, as Stave said, fanaticism—galloping unchecked behind his mirror-like eyes could well make him dangerous.

The Ecclesium stared at Ulfric long enough that Ulfric wondered if he'd answer at all. Finally, he did.

"The maker's command to cleanse and purify the unfaithful from Vinnr. We shall bring the Dyrrak way of life to all the kingdoms, as we've been waiting to do for many hundreds of turns, and wage a war of dominion in Vaka Aster's name. No more shall the unworthy threaten our maker. We will make all the peoples of Vinnr as faithful and devoted as the people of Dyrrakium."

Ulfric was sorry he'd asked.

Ulfric, Mallich sent, *I know I don't need to say this, but we can't give these exiles leave to wage war on the commoners of Ivoryss. The people here are misled but not deserving of punishment. They have suffered enough.*

Stave put in, *They're about as trustworthy as my grandfather Serl, and he swung from the gaol of Magdaster for selling pig-iron swords to the Dragør forces.* As he spoke, his eyes never left Eisa. She stared back, unmoved.

Safran was silent, and Ulfric looked to her for her thoughts. She held his gaze steadily, deliberating but uncertain. *Whether we accept their offer of sanctuary or not, Ivoryss is still in danger,* she said. *The Dyrraks have been absent from Vinnr's wider affairs for so long, there is no telling what they'll do, who they've become. Could it be a trick? Are they under Balavad's influence?*

"My Maker," Eisa said aloud. "All will do as you command."

Ulfric's eyes darted to her, but she was silent through the Mentalios. What was she thinking? Whose side was she really on? It was no secret Eisa had never respected commoners, but Ulfric couldn't believe she'd want them brought to their knees.

"Shall I give my air fleet the order and put an end to the doubts of these faithless Ivoryssians, My Creator?" the Ecclesium asked.

"No," Ulfric commanded. "I will not see war among my peoples. We will return with you to Dyrrakium, and the Dyrrak people shall once again be my chosen, as the Nazarian leader was my vessel before."

Stallari? Safran sent. *Are you sure?*

Rook's balls, Ulfric! What—

But Ulfric cut Stave off. Too much and too many were at risk for Ulfric to choose any other path. *Mallich, Safran, take the celestial artifacts to Urgo and Yggo. Have them carry them and follow us on the journey. We must protect the artifacts first and retrieve them only when we are sure it's safe. Stave and Jaemus, gather the Himmingazians.*

Eisa, he turned to her, *you still have Vaka Aster's Scrylle and Fenestros?*

She looked back at him, her eyes filled with questions he didn't have to think too hard about to guess. Wouldn't he know where the artifacts were if he were the maker's vessel? She didn't know the limitations his action of shackling Vaka Aster had bestowed on them. But now wasn't the time to discuss that particular point. He didn't know if any time ever would be.

I have them, she answered simply.

Good. Give them to Safran. Aloud he said, "Ecclesium, leave your chancellor and twenty able bodies to assist my Knights in readying for the journey. You may go and prepare your fleet."

"It is done, My Creator." The Ecclesium turned and gave orders to his people, bowed, and left the hall through the front entrance.

He looked at Eisa. "Knight Nazaria, lead your kinspeople in packing the essentials the Knights will need to take to Dyrrakium. You know what they are."

...Ulfric? she sent. *You must explain what's going on. What...you've become.*

We will talk soon, he assured her. They had *much* to talk about.

Safran, Stave, Mallich, and Jaemus, each looking as troubled as he felt, set off. A moment later, Eisa gathered the Dyrrak contingent and followed.

Shortly, he was alone the in main hall. He tilted his eyes up to the simulacrum of the discarded vessel, the Dyrrak woman who'd been Eisa's and the Domine Ecclesium's ancestor. Looking into her face, a stranger's, he now realized she was closer to him than any other person who'd walked in Vinnr in two thousand turns. *Was it like this for you, Nazarian? Did you resent your station as much as I do?*

Ulfric thought of the thousands of objects within the fortress he and his Knights had collected and created, his chambers full of inventions and contrivances, the weapons Stave had painstakingly forged and crafted, the rooms upon rooms of books that held the history of Vinnr since the beginning.

They were abandoning Vigil Tower and all it contained, just as Vaka Aster had been made to abandon this relic of a vessel. He was deserting his home, not just the objects but also the memories, leaving it all to the commoners. Would the Ivoryssians respect the traditional sanctuary of Vaka Aster, or would they loot and destroy it? The next time he looked upon Vigil Tower, would it be as dilapidated and forgotten as the temple of Lífs in Himmingaze?

The Knights had, as Vaka Aster had, become so distant from the rest of the Vinnrics in the last many turns, he realized. He could no longer gauge the commoners' fidelity to their maker or her representatives. If they stayed, perhaps he could renew their faith, but not in the way the Dyrraks proposed. Yet now that he'd shown the Dyrraks favor in front of the Ivoryssians, how safe would any of them be? The blood between the kingdoms had soured too long ago to be easily remedied.

In a brutal wave, it hit him: in under a thirty-night, he'd lost his family, many of his friends and fellow Knights, his freedom, and now his home. Was anything worth such a price?

CHAPTER TWENTY-ONE

Fourth Phase Venerate Sveinkí Edizriis, son of the Fourth Line, pushed the pale foreigner he'd apprehended forward another step across the canal bridge toward the Citadel Suprima. The woman emitted a grunt but with a shrill hissing sound that made Sveinkí's teeth grind. This was the fifth Ravener of Battgjald the Dyrraks had found skulking through the city, and he knew how pleased the Domine Ecclesium would be at her capture. The last one hadn't lasted as long as they'd have liked under questioning, and this one gave them a chance to learn more about the foreign Verity. The previous spy's body had stunk like refuse when they'd immolated it after she died.

It had been foolish of this foreigner to try to hide within Elezaran, the Dyrrakium Empire's capital. Few knew the art of spycraft better than the Dyrraks, and they remained ever vigilant in flushing out those who'd come from the lesser kingdoms to spy on them. The Dyrraks' self-exile didn't mean they were foolish enough to believe those kingdoms would forget about them. This foreigner would have been rousted sooner if she'd not hidden in the gutters for so long, as if any information of use could be found there.

Unfortunately for Sveinkí, the Domine Ecclesium was with the fleet at the moment, once more spreading Dyrrakium's faith and devotion to the rest of Vinnr at long last. The Ecclesium had left the empire headed by his regent. The younger, albeit temporary, Nazarian had nothing to offer Sveinkí. She would only be in the seat of power for a thirty-night or so—the Dyrraks had placed many bets on how long it would take to subjugate the lesser kingdoms, but no one believed it would be more than a thirty-night—and was not endowed with the power to promote him, a promotion well earned by his unearthing of this Ravener. But he could wait until Ivoryss was tucked neatly into the folds of Dyrrakium's dominion, a fresh kingdom of people to make worthy of Vaka Aster's gifts. The Ivoryssians had fallen very far from their faith, according to Dyrrakium's spies, but that would change once they were embraced by Dyrrakium and taught true devotion.

The Ravener slowed again, and again, Sveinkí helped her along. If he had to guess, he'd say the woman was being stubborn, testing him. It was a little thing, a test like this. Sveinkí hadn't failed any of the Phases he'd tested in, he wouldn't fail a starveling prisoner's ill-advised trials. These foreigners, so strange, so pallid, so lanky—it was more than a little surprising to him that any Verity's creations could be so frail and so...*off*. But who was he to judge a Verity's creations?

"Push this body again, creation of Vaka Aster," the Ravener hissed at him, "and I will show you the true meaning of dominion."

It was the first time the Ravener had spoken, and it unnerved Sveinkí. Prisoners in Dyrrakium knew their place, and he'd never been spoken to before like this. But it wasn't the threat that sent a cold tingle washing over his skin, it was the way the prisoner seemed to have been listening to his thoughts. *Impossible,* he told himself. *She's clearly been in Dyrrakium for some time to know our ways this well.* It was unsettling that someone who stood out so much could have stayed hidden long enough to learn the Six Aspects of the Dyrrakium people. Sveinkí decided the first line of questions he'd ask would be how the Ravener had managed to do it.

But for now: "Silence yourself, unworthy," he warned, yanking the ropes tying the woman's wrists behind her back to pull her off-balance. "You do not speak unless required."

They reached the walls of the citadel, and he called to the wall guard. "Venerate, tell the Regent Ecclesium we have a new creation of Balavad in our midst. I'll take her directly to the vaults."

The young Third Phase venerate nodded at Sveinkí's command and yelled at the door guard to open it. Shortly, Sveinkí led the captive deep below the citadel's main floor into the dark, cold vaults where important prisoners were held.

"I'll be back to discuss your interests in Dyrrakium after I've taken a meal," he told the prisoner as he showed her into a cell. Unable to resist, he gave the woman a final shove. "You just relax for a bit, get cozy in your new home."

The prisoner stood staring at the back wall of the cell as Sveinkí locked it. She didn't move, simply remained upright and rigid, as if she'd become a standing corpse. She didn't turn around.

Sveinkí watched her for a moment, his nerve endings chilled once again. He was going to enjoy making this one talk, he decided. As he turned away, the prisoner spoke.

"Has the Domine Ecclesium returned yet?"

Sveinkí stopped and looked back at the prisoner, equally surprised she thought he would answer her as he was she knew the Ecclesium's status. "You can't be feeble enough to believe I'd tell you that."

"Then your purpose is served," came the Ravener's sinister hiss.

Infuriated, he stepped closer to the prisoner's cell, ready to teach the woman an early lesson about obedience and servility to a son of the Fourth Line. As he did, the woman turned toward him and somehow crossed her cell and reached the bars in an instant. Sveinkí had a moment to think the woman moved like a bat in the dark, lit only by torchlight, one moment on one side of you, the next it was caught in your hair, biting at your neck.

And of all frightening and dangerous things there were in the world, the only thing that made Sveinkí's skin crawl were bats.

He flinched away from the bars, but the woman's face was before him, looking down into his own. Her eyes had gone black, black as used-up embers, black as a starless night, and they transfixed him. Pale, almost transparent teeth, sharpened to points, flashed in a wicked grin. The woman's hand was suddenly around his throat, gripping vise-like, holding him in place. A black miasma began to fill the cell, seeping through the bars. It pushed itself like a worm into his nose, and it felt like acid. He opened his mouth to yell, and more vapor spilled down his throat.

He felt the hand release him, felt himself falling, and the last thing he heard was the creature's monstrous hiss...

CHAPTER TWENTY-TWO

Under Eisa's direction and with the Dyrraks' efficiency, they had the essentials from Vigil Tower packed and loaded aboard the Dyrrakium ships before Hallumbrum. Vinnr's cold moon, barely a sliver, and the few lights still remaining in Asteryss left the city feeling empty, almost haunted, as if Balavad had won.

Despite the city's foreboding pall, a sense of vindication pervaded Eisa's spirit. Everything she'd wished for was coming true. Vaka Aster had returned to Vinnr, the Knights Corporealis were relocating to Dyrrakium, where they should have been from the beginning, and she would once more be among her own people.

Everything she wanted—

So why did she feel as if more was wrong than right?

There was too much her companions weren't telling her. About Vaka Aster, about Ulfric. She knew it as surely as she'd known that day on the *Vigilance* that the vessel had been abandoned. The galling part was how long getting those answers had had to wait. The Dyrraks' timing may have saved the Knights from a nasty end, but it had left her further in the dark.

In the streets of Asteryss, most of the illuminate orbs had been broken, but a few remained to light the way to Asteryss's largest port, where the Dyrrakium ships awaited them. The commoners had gone home, seeking whatever broken and fearful sleep they might get. They knew they could not stand up to another hostile force, and their Arch Keeper had remained barred behind Aster Keep's gates. Like a coward. Who would lead these people once the Dyrraks had gone? She wondered. And why did she care?

At the main gate to the shipyards, they passed a squad of Dragør Marines. They were wisely not trying to stop the Dyrraks' procession, simply observing. She recognized Commander Brun, having crossed paths with the woman on occasion in the Conservatum. The commander looked as Eisa would have expected. Beaten, but not defeated. Unlike the Arch Keeper, Brun was one of few among the commoners Eisa had developed a grudging respect for. A woman with the unbendable spirit of a Dyrrak. It was a pity her faith was weak.

She peeled off from the line of Dyrraks and approached Brun.

"Commander," she said.

Brun scowled. "Knight Nazaria."

"I imagine you haven't sent any Wings in the air since the Dyrrak air fleet's arrival."

Apparently, Brun's sarcastic side was triggered by the impotency of her position. "And lose the last of our scouts when the Dyrraks decide to kill some innocent Ivoryssians? Whatever gave you that idea?"

Tempted to simply turn and leave, Eisa steadied herself. "You have a Wing Marine, Rekkr is his name, still at Mount Omina. I seized his scout to get here. When we've left the city, you'll want to send someone to retrieve him."

"You mean you left him alive? How civil of you, Knight."

Eisa looked over her shoulder as the last Dyrrak carrying the Knights' supplies passed by. Was it worth saying it? She decided it was.

"I know your people have suffered, Brun, and having your shores and city so easily overcome by people you think of as treasonous scoundrels must chafe you. But you're wrong about the Dyrraks. These are Vaka Aster's chosen, and our maker is simply returning to those who most deserve the honor. Perhaps, in the maker's absence, you Ivoryssians will finally learn what it means to be worthy." Brun's face began to pinch and wrinkle like a sour apple left to dry too long beneath Halla, and Eisa knew her famous fury would soon follow. Before that happened, she continued. "But remember, the Dyrraks could easily have decimated this broken city. Could have, but didn't. We, they, are not the people you think. The common history is wrong, and it always has been. The Dyrraks never tried to usurp the Yor throne, and they didn't cause the Cataclysm. They are not given to treachery the way the rest of the peoples of Vinnr are. It isn't their way."

"They certainly ran and hid like they did," the commander spat. Then she seemed to consider Eisa's statement. "Or so the history books tell us," she added, her tone flatter.

"Listen to me. I *am* history, not a book dictated and written by people who either don't know the full story or have reasons to change it. And I'm telling you, they were not guilty of what they were accused."

"Then why..." Brun stopped and seemed to reconsider her first question, then asked a different one. "Why are you telling me this, Knight?"

It was a fair question, but she chose not to examine the deepest of her reasons at the moment. "You're better than your leader, Commander. Watch her. Keep her in check as much as you can. Don't let her incite a war with Dyrrakium. Ivoryss, even Ivoryss allied with Yor, can't win. Rebuild and forget whatever insults you think Dyrrakium has given you. It's the only chance Ivoryss and Yor have."

"Is that a threat?"

"Don't act a fool. If Dyrrakium were going to take the lesser kingdoms' thrones, the dust would already be settling by now."

Brun held her eyes and after a moment gave her a curt nod. Eisa moved off without another word. Inwardly, she grunted at herself. Why had she told Brun so much about the Cataclysm? Maybe it was for the best. The world had changed. Ivoryss needed to be prepared for the new order of things, and perhaps that started with Vinnr's true history finally coming to light.

After the ships were loaded, Eisa returned to Vigil Tower alone to collect the Knights, as well as the unexpected group of thirty-three

Himmingazian commoners, and one Himmingazian...Knight? It was an astounding turn of events that Vaka Aster had ordained a man of another realm as servant to her, another of many such events she had yet to learn the full story of.

Yet, as she thought of the one called Bardgrim, something Griggory had said bubbled to the surface of her mind. *...without Lifs's Scrylle and all her artifacts to undo the banishment, and a Himmingazian Mystae with a strong spark to perform the steps necessary, the vessel cannot be restored.* This Bardgrim was now a bearer of a Verity's spark, a fully ordained Knight Corporealis. And what was a Mystae but simply another word for Knight?

Clearly this is the Bardgrim who stole the Scrylle from Griggory, she thought. *The pieces to restore Himmingaze seem to be coming into place. That is, if Bardgrim knows where the Scrylle is now.*

This new fact sent a slight tingle of anticipation through her. She'd given up hope of saving Himmingaze, but maybe she needn't have. Yet, as incredible as it was, Eisa put it aside for now. Vinnr and Vaka Aster came first. Once they were safe in Dyrrakium, she'd think more about it.

Stepping into Vigil Tower, possibly for the last time, she found the main hall occupied by the Himmingazians as if they'd been conjured by her thoughts.

Himmingazian *refugees.*

As the Cataclysm had scaled up after Yor's usurpation, Eisa had spent a short time in her homeland to prepare them for the skirmishes to come. While there, the Yorish and Ivoryssian traders and ambassadorial troupes had been rounded up and held in detention, either to be traded for Dyrrak hostages or sent back to their own homelands if the war they all feared was coming could be averted. The refugees had no doubt suffered. So many of the Dyrrakium people who'd been on the mainland in Yor and Ivoryss had been maliciously and unjustly attacked after the coup on Yor's throne that the Dyrraks had had little mercy left for the unworthy kingdoms' people in return.

These Himmingazians didn't look as bad as those captives had, but they didn't look good. Their green skin color made them look ill at the best of times, at least to her eyes. Yet a quick glance was enough to tell her they weren't at their best, despite having been treated well and given a safe place to await their return home.

"Knight Nazaria," Bardgrim called to her. He still wore the ancient blade called Winter's Bite, hallowed by Vaka Aster in the Dastrart Age, if she recalled correctly. Though, he wore it on his right hip, and she'd already noted he was right-handed. This man, whatever else he was, was no fighter. "Ulfric asked me to wait for you. Are the ships ready for everyone?"

She eyed him, fascinated despite herself. "You stole the Scrylle of Lífs from Griggory, correct?"

This caught him by surprise. "I, uh, well, I—you know, it was—"

She cut him off. "Where is it now?"

His brow creased and he sighed. "Gone, I suppose. When I saved Ulfric and the Ravener stabbed me, everything got a bit hazy, so I don't remember much. But they say Balavad's ship exploded, so I suppose the Scrylle did too."

Saved Ulfric? What would he need saving from? He's Vaka Aster. "Don't be daft. A Scrylle is as resilient to fire and force as a star. If it's not in Vinnr, it's at the bottom of your Never Sea. Pity."

His penetrating look told her he was having trouble believing it was truly pity in her tone, but she didn't care. He was just a Himmingazian, like all Himmingazians, and she'd already judged their worthiness.

At that moment, Stave's voice came from the far entrance. "I'm telling you, Ulfric, the interrealm well is the better route, it is. Stuck in the middle of the Verring Sea with a bunch of Fenestros-fondling Vaka Aster flatterers isn't a good place for—" He stopped abruptly when they saw Eisa.

Ulfric approached, his face grave. "Is the Dyrrak fleet ready to disembark?"

He'd put on a bulky set of eye shields, like the kind he wore when grinding lenses but made of a strange glass, flint glass perhaps? She could no longer see his eyes, and his skin had resumed its typical coloration, no longer glowing with a faint blue light. She could almost believe she was speaking to her old friend the Stallari again, if not for what she'd seen earlier that day.

"Vaka Aster," she replied, "the Dyrrak fleet awaits you."

One edge of his mouth turned down, the same way it always had when he was dissatisfied. "Just…it's still me, Eisa. I'm Ulfric, as ever."

"But—" She'd been about to say *You're not* but stopped. It was a relief to be able to think of him as the same person she'd known for fifteen hundred turns, after all. If he insisted on being informal, she couldn't refuse. "All right. Is everything ready here?"

Stave jumped in. "The well, Ulfric, like I said. The safer route."

"No, we're going to live among the Dyrraks. It's better that we begin now. And other than Eisa, none of us has gone through the inter-realm well to Dyrrakium in ages. Only she knows what awaits at the other end."

Though she couldn't see his eyes, she could feel their weight on her through his eye shields. "The well is unchanged," she answered. "The chamber in the Citadel Suprima hasn't been altered at all."

"See there," Stave said. "We could be in Dyrrakium before morning if we take the well, we could."

"Are you afraid of the sea?" Eisa mocked.

He scowled at her, seemed about to resist responding, then couldn't. "Let me put it to you this way. If those skin-maulers you call kinspeople so much as twitch the wrong way, me'n Ulfric and Safran and Roi are going to be sailing that ship on our own, and the sharks of the Verring Sea are going to feast like they never feasted before on an exotic Dyrrakium delicacy."

"What kind of delicacy?" Bardgrim cut in, uncannily naive for someone who'd been ordained by Vaka Aster.

Eisa's eyes shot to the Himmingazian, and Stave too shut his blustering mouth. Bardgrim merely stared at them as if to ask *What did I say?* She realized, to her surprise, he was feigning idiocy simply to distract them from another argument. *Perhaps not so stupid, then,* she mused.

"Stave, get Mallich and Safran. It's time to say goodbye." Ulfric put a hand on Eisa's shoulder, giving her the tiniest of nudges, then said to

Bardgrim, "The 'Gazians need to stay directly behind me. Follow close. We'll ensure their safety."

IN THE MIDDLE of the night, the walk to the docks was uneventful. The Dyrrak soldiers still stood as sentries along the streets, keeping those curious enough to brave a look tucked away in their homes and the Knights' procession unhindered. The whole of Aster Keep's upper courtyard overlooking the city was ablaze with light. They were watching, of course, witnessing the humbling of their once great city. Eisa could feel Beatte's hostility like a toxic fume all the way to the sea.

The Dyrrakium flagship, the *Gildr*, was far too big to bring into the narrow harbor that served as Asteryss City's main port. The main deck itself was at least as broad and long as Vigil Tower's main hall. The Knights, Ulfric, and the Himmingazians were taken to it onboard smaller ten-person crafts, one Knight staying with the separated groups of Himmingazians for their protection. Eisa noted, however, that the Dyrraks paid very little attention to the foreigners, good or bad.

Once all were aboard the *Gildr*, it promptly drew anchor and set off under the light of the stars. The darkness of the Verring Sea's horizon swallowed them almost immediately, leaving the backlit silhouettes of the smaller Dyrrakium ships against the remaining lights of Asteryss to slip behind them.

Until the night was shattered by the brilliance of an explosion.

Eisa and the Knights rushed to the deck rails and peered toward the bedlam. Several more explosions followed, and off the stern of the *Gildr,* they saw the docks of Asteryss's ports aflame with huge fires that burned as tall as houses. Along the coastline, to the north and south, more explosions followed.

"Verities fury..." Roi whispered. "They're destroying Asteryss's ports, their ships... Ivoryss will be completely defenseless, cut off."

Eisa looked at Ulfric, whose hands were clenched around the railing so tightly his knuckle bones looked ready to burst through his skin. "I told the Ecclesium this wasn't to be. I've got to stop this." He was about to stride off when Roi grabbed him by the arm.

"No, Ulfric. You can't confront him." Ulfric turned back sharply as if to berate Roi, but the Yorish Knight continued. "Think about it. Why would Vaka Aster ask the Dyrraks to do anything, when Vaka Aster could simply make her, *your*, will so? Ulfric, what do you think will happen when they realize what you've done?"

And here it was, the secret she knew they were keeping from her. She took a step in front of Ulfric, blocking him, and planted her feet.

"And what exactly have you done, Stallari?"

CHAPTER TWENTY-THREE

Ulfric faced Eisa. The fires behind them, reflected in her silvery eyes and illuminating the hard lines of her face and black hair that seemed to blend into the night surrounding her, reddened her sepia skin further. The effect made her appear uncannily dragørlike. For a moment, Ulfric had the impression he was facing a creature from the Howling Weald rather than his old friend and compatriot.

The two stared at each other a moment, eyes locked. He now read Eisa in new ways, saw her actions of the past through a new light. After what he'd read in Lífs's Scrylle—Himmingaze's fate that Griggory had recorded, fate sealed by Eisa herself—he no longer felt he understood his old friend the way he once had.

The other three Knights stood next to him, facing Eisa. After a moment, Safran sent through the Mentalios link, trying to placate Eisa's clear edginess, *Eisa, just take a moment. Listen to—*

"I'm done waiting, Stallari," Eisa cut in. "You need to explain what's happening now, explain what…you've done."

"Am I interrupting?" The Domine Ecclesium materialized from the foredeck as if he'd been blown in like smoke. None had heard him come.

Ulfric glanced at the man. How much had he heard?

Shooting Eisa a final *This will wait* glance, he stepped in front of the Dyrrak leader. "Ecclesium, explain your actions here. Why have you ordered this attack?"

The moment Ulfric looked at him, the Ecclesium had dipped his head and dropped his eyes. At Ulfric's confrontation, his eyes rose, slowly, almost questioningly. "Creator, what better way to ensure Dyrrakium's haven remains safe from intruders than to hobble them?" His eyes wandered to the fiery horizon, then back to Ulfric's chin. "I assumed you knew our plans, Maker, as you know all that we do and intend. I could only think you'd have told me if you'd not wanted me to give the order."

Oh, the man was shrewd, very shrewd. Ulfric was perilously close to giving himself away. How much would the Ecclesium understand? Could he even conceive of a Verity being, as he'd put it, "hobbled" the way Ulfric's actions had hobbled Vaka Aster?

Mallich's warning was correct. In the eyes of the Dyrraks, what Ulfric had done, even if unintentionally, would be seen as the worst apostasy. Shackling one's own Verity, one's celestial maker—they would see it as depraved. Ulfric was certain he could best any Dyrrak who tried to retaliate against him for what he'd done. Yet...he'd been removed from their kingdom for so long. How could he know what they were capable of? Without Vaka Aster's intervention, he was still only a man, and any man could be brought low with enough force. And if Vaka Aster felt a threat and stepped to the fore again to protect him, protect Vinnr—

No, he didn't want that, not yet. He was unwilling to risk not being his own master if she chose not to retreat once more. Ah, but he was not his own master, was he? Not while his fate was in the hands of the Domine Ecclesium.

Ulfric looked away from the Dyrrak leader and pointed a finger to Eisa. "Knight Nazaria, from this moment forward, you will be my representative among the Dyrrak people. Domine Ecclesium, if you wish to see me, speak to me, or relay information to me, Knight Nazaria will act as your voice."

"My Maker, if I have offended you—"

Farther along the deck, the Himmingazian group milled among the few possessions they'd brought from Vigil Tower, mostly food and clothing. Jaemus was with them, his limitless energy now being put to the task of making them as comfortable as he could. Ulfric went on before the Ecclesium could finish. "Now, see to the Himmingazians. Ensure their quarters are as comfortable as can be."

His tone was dismissive, and the Dyrrak leader understood. Ulfric caught the scowl that washed over his face as Ulfric turned away. He was a man of power who'd reigned unchallenged in his own empire for many turns. A man now usurped by his own faith. A man who represented a new danger, if Ulfric's guess was right.

To his back, the Ecclesium said, "It is done, Creator."

He heard nothing as the Dyrrak left. He only knew he was gone when Safran visibly relaxed beside him.

Jaemus, Ulfric sent, *the Dyrrak leader will be sending someone to help the Himmingazians get settled. Would you join the rest of us here?*

Mind if I just—

They'll be safe, I promise. They must be tired. Let them rest.

It must have taken effort to channel the sound of a disgruntled sigh through the Mentalios, but Jaemus managed to do it. A natural to the Order, indeed.

Eisa, quiet during the Ecclesium's visit, didn't hold back any longer. "Ulfric—"

He held up a hand. "It's time you know the full story."

"It's time she finishes explaining why she betrayed her own oath," Stave interjected.

"We'll get to that," Ulfric said.

Jaemus arrived, rather hurriedly, and cut in as if no one else had been speaking. "Look, sorry to break up this lovely deck party, but we need to chat, Ulfric. Cote, and the rest of the 'Nauts are getting sicker. We need to get them back to Himmingaze, even if I'm going to stay."

Surprising Ulfric, it was Eisa who spoke. "There's no Himmingaze to go back to." Jaemus looked at her incredulously, and she went on. "Or there won't be for much longer."

"Speak plainly, Eisa," Mallich said, not unkindly.

Her gaze moved over those gathered, seeming to assess who was a foe and who was still a friend, then said, "A few days ago, after we collected Vaka Aster's previous vessel and brought it aboard the *Vigilance*, I discovered Vaka Aster had abandoned it—and us as well, it seemed at the time. We didn't yet know what had become of you, Ulfric. So I went to Himmingaze to speak to…" She hesitated, uncharacteristically. "Griggory."

Griggory Dondrin? Safran sent, though the question was in each of their eyes. *The one they used to call the Dragør Tamer? But he disappeared a long time ago.*

"Aye," Eisa said. "Ulfric and Roi knew him. He's been in Lífs's realm since the Cataclysm. It was Griggory and I who discovered the cause of Himmingaze's ruin, this Glister Cloud. When the Yor rebels attempted their coup—"

"Yor rebels?" Stave interrupted. "It was the Dyrraks who tried to overtake Yor and started the coup, it was."

Eisa shifted position, widening her feet a fraction as if preparing for a fight. "That's the common history, Stave. And since neither you nor Safran was even born yet, you know little of the true history of Vinnr."

Before Stave could respond, Mallich pressed, "Go on, Eisa."

A beat passed, then she did. "After Lillias Grannd of Yor betrayed her kingdom, Griggory and I traveled to Himmingaze together. The turbulence of the coup, the fights it caused throughout the realm, the exile of Dyrrakium—I was a novice enough Knight then that my faith…wavered. Griggory, though, is and has always been peerless, and he took it upon himself to help me forge a stronger faith by proposing we widen our knowledge of the Cosmos together. To better serve Vaka Aster, he promised. He said Himmingaze was a quiet realm, one of peace and unique people. He'd been there before, you see. You remember his wandering ways, don't you, Roi?"

Mallich nodded, and she continued. "I agreed to go with him. It seemed…a good way to put the three kingdoms' troubles behind."

She went silent a moment, her eyes far away with memories of a long-ago time. Ulfric knew the pain she hid and suspected Mallich did as well. They'd known Eisa's love for Lillias, the noblewoman from the Conservatum who would have been the next Arch Keeper of Yor—if she hadn't succumbed to her own greed and desire for power. Eisa's wrath at learning of Lillias's plot had made her wild, for a time, unpredictable. Griggory, the only Knight whose authority Eisa had never questioned, must have taken her to Himmingaze for her own good, maybe even for Vinnr's good. But his plans had gone awry. Ulfric had read in Lífs's Scrylle what she'd done there, how her rage had been inconsolable. How she'd killed their Mystae upon learning of the sacrilege they'd committed. He wondered if she'd confess to that now.

"There, we met Lífs's Mystae and discovered what they'd done—their execration of their Verity," she went on. "They had discovered some kind of banishment curse. I don't know how. It allowed them to fracture Lífs's vessel, and upon this sundering, the vessel became the Cloud that now surrounds the world. It acts as some kind of veil, hiding the world from Lífs's celestial sight, exiling her from her own realm. Through some wystic power we don't know, Himmingaze itself remained intact." She looked to Bardgrim, whose own face was slack with disbelief. "But not for much longer."

The Knights took this story in. It might have seemed unimaginable, but, then, so had caging a Verity only days ago.

Safran asked, *But why would Lífs's Mystae do this?*

"Simple. The same urge that drives unworthies like Lillias drove those blackguardly Mystae. They wanted to rule, uninterrupted, with allegiance to nothing." Her voice creaked like breaking ice. "They desecrated everything sacred and dishonored themselves and their oaths. Griggory has remained there ever since, seeking to undo their sacrilege. And because of this, after Ulfric disappeared, I went to find out if Griggory had learned the secret of their banishment curse. I reasoned that if we had it, we could use it against Balavad."

"And did he?" asked Stave.

She shook her head. "No, the secret is lost, along with their Scrylle. And with each moment that passes, the Glister Cloud, Lífs vessel, disintegrates more. As it fails, so does Himmingaze. It will be undone within a thirty-night, maybe mere days."

Jaemus had been growing paler and paler as Eisa spoke. At her last statement, he made a choking noise. They glanced at him.

"Bit queasy," he muttered, then asked, "And the Scrylle, does it show how to fix things, glue the vessel back together, as it were? Can Himmingaze be saved?"

"Griggory tried. He searched for all these turns for the celestial arti-facts. When at last he did find them, the Scrylle was stolen." Ulfric almost pitied Jaemus for the way her gaze cut right into him. "As you know, Bardgrim."

"And they were lost when Balavad's warship was destroyed," Ulfric stated, knowing they'd been aboard the *Bounding Skate*, which was now destroyed as well. "Eisa, is Griggory still there now?"

She nodded. "Griggory has…chosen to remain in Himmingaze."

"Why? Why didn't he return with you?"

"You'd have to ask him." A troubled look passed over her face before she went on. "So you see, my actions were, as always, in service to Vaka Aster. I knew we as Knights could not defeat Balavad, not with Vaka Aster still absent, but I also knew the Himmingazians had found a way to at least *misdirect* a Verity. I just didn't know how, but I was sure Griggory did. There was neither time nor need to explain myself. I had to act for the vessel's sake. And Vinnr's."

And what about Mylla? Safran said.

"I sent her to Himmingaze because I was trying to save her. The novice was going to attack Balavad's ship after you all were taken. She'd have died if she did, so I stopped her to save her from her own foolhardiness."

"And now she's dead, anyway, she is," Stave growled.

"That isn't my fault. She hadn't the strength to win her final battle."

Ulfric grimaced. "She had more strength than you know, Eisa. She fought Balavad single-handedly, to her last breath."

"Then she did her duty."

"You wretched—" Fists clenched, Stave started toward Eisa, who squared her shoulders to face him. Safran grasped his arm.

No, she sent. *This isn't our way. Knights, we are in this together. Our fate and our faith depend as much on our loyalty to each other as to Vaka Aster.*

Eisa's actions, though rash, were no less necessary than ours. She's right. Vaka Aster and the vessel are what we swore our lives to protect. You two must put aside this endless, pointless squabble and remember the oaths you've taken to Vaka Aster—and your loyalty to each other as Knights, for Verities' sakes.

Both Stave and Eisa backed off, their loathing for each other at least temporarily corked.

Ulfric approached Jaemus, his lined face set in an expression of deep sympathy. He touched his chin with one hand, then held it palm forward in a gesture Jaemus was now familiar with. "Bardgrim, I promise, we will find a way to help your people. I don't yet know how, but we have Vaka Aster's Scrylle once more. I will scour it for the answers to preserving your realm. If there's a way, we'll find it."

Jaemus, silent for once, could only nod his thanks.

"But first," Ulfric continued, dropping his hand and looking at Eisa. "You and I need to speak alone."

CHAPTER TWENTY-FOUR

With a measure of reluctance, the four Knights went in search of Chancellor Aoggvír, who'd been tasked with seeing to them and the Himmingazians. Safran had to give Jaemus a tug on the wrist to get him moving. He seemed frozen to the spot at the news of his realm's imminent demise. Eisa had little trouble imagining how he felt. Vinnr had so recently been facing the same sort of threat.

But no longer. And despite the fact that she'd chosen to pursue a different avenue for attempting to constrain the tyranny of Balavad—and had, in the end, been ineffective—Eisa would not stand to be accused, if that was what Ulfric had in mind.

Thus, she attacked him first.

Facing him rigidly, she demanded, "What heretical thing have you done, Ulfric? Have you spit on everything you swore to defend?"

Her tone was blazing; he met it not with his own fury but with a reserved coolness Eisa wasn't prepared for. Slowly, he spun away from her and walked to the railing, gripping it roughly as if to keep himself from jumping over the side. When he turned again to face her, he spoke in a voice gritty with regret.

"I never in a million turns, a million lifetimes, would have chosen this, Eisa. What did I ever do to turn your opinion of me so bleak?"

He wasn't accusing her of anything, yet she couldn't have been caught more off guard. His blatant sorrow—about *her* deeds? about his *own?*—had an edge to it that cut deep. And there was more, a depth of compassion that reminded her of the Stallari in his prime just after he'd met Symvalline. He'd become a changed man then, a man of level-headed, reserved judgment, giving all commoners and even the occasional wayward Knight the benefit of a doubt before accusing them of misdeeds. Eisa would have, and had, followed that man to the ends of Vinnr. Until Lillias had ripped the last shred of any compassion, any love, she'd had straight not from her chest but from her very spirit.

As Ulfric waited for her to respond, a crack of lightning flashed across the sky and rain began to fall. For some reason, Eisa's thoughts remained on the Yorwoman, and the searing crack of lightning mimicked the pain that seared her own spirit still.

"Eisa?"

She pushed the thoughts away with an effort and brought that old bitterness to bear on something present—the Stallari. "You lost your faith, Ulfric, you and Symvalline both, and intended to forsake your oaths, leave your companions, and quit the Knights." She eyed him, taking in the shields he now wore over his eyes, the way he faced her but hid at the same time. "Instead, you—"

"You don't know what I did."

The level statement stopped her. Here she stood, accusing him, yet she hadn't been there. *She* was the one who left her companions. He said he hadn't chosen this. Should she believe him? Shouldn't she, at least, hear his full story and how Vaka Aster came to choose him to be the vessel?

He'd have done so for her, and right now, he was the only Knight who still had faith in her. "Tell me what happened," she said at last. "I… I must know."

Removing the eye shields to gaze at her with his celestially enhanced eyes, he said with a weary sigh, "It was a terrible, unintended mistake."

As the *Gildr* sailed south into the night's unknowns, he explained the plan he'd devised upon meeting Balavad in Aster Keep. With grave assurance, he explained that his only intention had been to summon Vaka Aster using the cage, as he'd told her and Roi that day on Mount Omina. Their celestial creator had to be shown Balavad's destruction, then, Ulfric had been sure, she would face Balavad and protect Vinnr from ruin.

But Ulfric hadn't realized that shackling her in Balavad's cage was only one part of things. Once she'd been summoned, he hadn't known how to unmake the cage to free her to act against their enemy. And when he'd looked inside Balavad's Scrylle a second time in search of answers, Balavad had been there, toying with his mind. Unwilling to let himself be used as a pawn, Ulfric had thought he could sacrifice himself for the good of everyone by throwing himself into the ring of Fenestrii that acted as Vaka Aster's prison, hoping it would release her. Instead, his actions led to this—to him becoming Vaka Aster's vessel, and her becoming caged. The only way for Vaka Aster to free herself was to destroy Ulfric, which would destroy Vinnr. Until this curse was broken, her power was limited, and he still didn't know how the cage could be undone.

"The consequences of this catastrophe are worse than if I'd done nothing. Vaka Aster can't aid us unless I give my will over to her. Even then, she can't leave my being, and I am more vulnerable than any vessel in history." He sighed. "I never asked our creator to become part of me, I promise you that. I was only doing what I thought was right."

As Eisa listened, his glowing eyes held her still. And though ages had passed since she'd seen a human with so much celestial power within them, she could still read the regret, the worry in his familiar face. And the burden of leadership he'd been carrying like an anvil on his shoulders since his and Symvalline's daughter had been born? That was still there, too.

"So you see," he finished, "all I want now is to put this event behind us, free Vaka Aster and myself, and find my family."

Like a splash of cold water, Eisa suddenly understood that she and Ulfric were very much alike. He was fallible. And so was she.

The difference—he freely admitted it.

As if her voice had a will of its own, she heard herself say, "I know what it's like to curse yourself by trying to right wrongs, Ulfric."

He looked at her levelly, but she read no question in his face. As if he knew what she'd done. "Would you like to tell me what you mean?" he said.

And for the first time, Eisa confessed what she'd done, how the discovery of Himmingaze's Mystaes' desecration of Lífs's vessel and their creation of the Glister Cloud had made her lose her reason. How she'd slaughtered them to the last person as punishment for their crimes, and how in doing so she'd doomed Himmingaze. And because they'd lost or hidden Lífs's Scrylle, Himmingaze remained doomed.

When the last word left her mouth, Eisa felt as if she were suddenly waking from a dream. Tense, she waited for Ulfric's admonishment, one that she deserved.

He approached, his celestial eyes holding hers. Stopping just before her, he raised both arms, his intentions unknown. She hesitated, unable to throw a blow at him, not at her leader. But she didn't have to.

He laid his hands on her shoulders, their searing heat seeping through her armor, and said, "I failed you more than I ever knew, Eisa. I was supposed to teach you wisdom and temperance to balance the great warrior in you, and I didn't fully succeed. Your spirit is indomitable, and you will be a greater Knight than I am someday. There is still time." She heard through the Mentalios link what he failed to block, *Endless time.*

Unsure what he was getting at, she questioned, "What do you mean?"

"All curses—like all cages—can be broken. Remember that."

Her heart's fast beat began to abate. He had accepted her faults without judgment, without anger. He even took some of the burden of blame, unnecessarily, on himself. Eisa had always told herself that her deeds were not her fault, but rather the fault of Himmingaze's faithless Mystae who had forced her hand. She had judged them and found them condemnable. She'd even relished being the one to condemn them. And since then, she'd condemned everyone who had dared take a misstep. Commoners; Mylla, the child of cast-out Dyrraks; weak and unworthy acolytes of the Conservatum; even Stave Thorvíl, her own Knight companion. Even Lillias.

But in her heart, which now beat at a slow, steady pace, she knew the judgment she placed on others was misdirected. She was the one to blame for Himmingaze.

And Ulfric, her Stallari, forgave her. Trusted her still and showed her a way to get free of her cursed judgment. She hadn't realized it would matter this much. Seven hundred turns of wrath—at herself—could finally recede.

He released her shoulders and began to pace in a tight circle, rubbing his thumb around his Mentalios lens. "We have two tasks now before us. First is to find a way to unmake this cage and get Symvalline and my daughter back home safe."

Drawn back to the present, she said, "Is there a way?"

"There must be, but it won't be easy," he said. "Balavad's Scrylle is useless. Vaka Aster destroyed his vessel and thus Battgjald when she fought him in Himmingaze, and his Scrylle is blank as a new slate. Nothing remains, including the rite to unmake the cage. Now that Lífs's Scrylle and whatever lore it contained is likewise gone, that leaves us with Vaka Aster's, and"—he drew a deep breath—"that of the Verity of Arc Rheunos, Mithlí, whom I have seen is likewise shackled."

She drew a sharp breath. "Balavad has been there too?"

"Yes, his plans to prevent the Syzyckí Elementum are more advanced than we could have guessed. And that's where Symvalline and Crumb are now. Whoever caged Mithlí must know a way to reverse it, or if not, their Scrylle may contain what we need." He stopped pacing and looked at her. "I intend to send Safran and Stave there to find the artifacts and the cage-makers, and Symvalline and Isemay, and bring them all back to me. Unless—" He eyed her closely. "Do you think this task should fall to you and Roi?"

So, he still trusted her. Relieved, she thought it over. Choosing her words with care, she said, "No, Ulfric. I can't do that. I serve Vaka Aster, and I'm a Dyrrak. Besides yourself, I am the most capable person in Vinnr to keep the vessel safe. I can't leave Vaka Aster's side again. It was a mistake to do it once."

He nodded. "Safran and Stave then."

"Are you certain of Balavad's Scrylle?" she asked. "It could be that your current state inhibits you from seeing into it clearly. We know the Verities can't see each other. Perhaps that is true of their Scrylle lore as well."

He shook his head forcibly. "It's blank, I'm certain. And no, I'm not inhibited. After I arrived in Himmingaze, I looked briefly into Lífs's Scrylle and saw all that was recorded there, even what Griggory has added. If Balavad's own Scrylle contained anything, I would have seen it as well."

So Griggory had recorded her deeds. That must be why Ulfric had seemed so unsurprised by her confession. He already knew. And now he seemed certain Balavad's Scrylle was a dead end, but they needed to explore all options before giving this task up. She pressed, "What if all of us Knights looked together, at once? With our combined—"

"No," he cut in sharply. "You must swear never to look inside Balavad's Scrylle, Eisa. He can see your mind through it, and he'll take control. I've attempted to peer into it twice and barely managed to escape as myself both times. If not for Vaka Aster, I wouldn't have last time. His vessel and realm may be gone, but Balavad is still a Verity. He is still out there in his celestial form, and he is still malevolent. None shall ever look into his Scrylle again while I live. Swear to me now that you won't be that foolish."

The anger in his tone was that of the Stallari with whom she'd faced wars and skirmishes between the fiefdoms of each kingdom. Commoners too petty and dumb to know better than to fight each other for the Verity's artifacts, the Fenestrii, the vessel, the Scrylle. They all wanted to control the celestial gifts, as if that would give them power, and the Knights had been forced over and over again in olden days to fight them back. Ulfric had been indomitable then, a warrior of no compromises. But then the Cataclysm happened, and most of the Fenestrii were taken back to Vigil Tower, and the Knights had closed themselves away for the most part. Vaka Aster had slowly faded from them, attending to Vinnr less and less, her vessel becoming an inert statue. And as she had, the Conservatum drew fewer and fewer acolytes, fewer and fewer devout, and eventually, the Knights' ranks had dwindled to just seven. Seven to fight the world, should the world bring the fight to them, and protect Vaka Aster's vessel from the ignorant and faithless.

She still admired that Stallari, and she promised herself she would never again doubt him. "I swear it."

He peered at her, then nodded.

"And what's the other thing we must do?" she asked.

"Find a way to give the Himmingazians their home back and bring Griggory back to his own."

These words hit her in the guts, and she almost reeled. Was he mocking her, or worse, planning to punish her after all for what she'd done?

"I told you, it's finished, Stallari. There's almost nothing left to salvage."

His lips curled into a spare smile. "Have you forgotten? I am a Verity, or close to it. I won't, can't, leave Dyrrakium while I'm...like this. But between us Knights here, we have thousands of turns of experience, knowledge, and wisdom. And we have Vaka Aster's Scrylle once more. If it's not possible to save their world, then we'll find a way to bring them to ours."

"But you heard Bardgrim. Those who are already here are ill."

"And the spark we all carry can extend life."

She nearly laughed. "You're joking, Ulfric. You want to ordain them all as Knights, bring them into the Order?"

He did not laugh. "Wouldn't you say we owe them something for what's become of Himmingaze?"

She stared at him closely but could still see no judgment or mockery in the set of his jaw, the lines around his eyes. His sincerity was genuine and unselfish. Helping the Himmingazians was the right thing to do, and it didn't matter that she was the reason for their world's slow decay.

Still, she choked back the arguments against such absurdity. Their own Mystae had committed the ultimate sacrilege. The Himmingazians could never belong in Vinnr. They weren't acolytes of the Conservatum, much less capable warriors. They weren't even Vaka Aster's creations. Perhaps being Vaka Aster's vessel was having unforeseen effects on Ulfric's thinking. For now, she would leave it. The Himmingazians were a faithless race that hardly warranted more than this moment of her thoughts, and she'd give them no more.

But what was it Bardgrim had said? Something about saving Ulfric? Could that be why he'd been ordained a Knight? There was still a mystery with regard to that particular Himmingazian, and she was more than a bit curious to solve it.

Ulfric looked past the horizon. "It's almost morning," he noted. Weariness of the mind or heart coated his tone. "Eisa, you have to swear something to me."

She nodded when he glanced back to her.

"The Dyrrak people can't know the whole truth about the vessel, about the cage. If they perceive this vulnerability..." He let the statement hang.

"Are you accusing the Dyrraks of treachery?"

"I'm accusing humans of being human. You and I know there is a vein of weakness in every rock. Until all is righted, there's no reason to go hammering at that vein. Swear it, Eisa."

After a moment, she nodded once more. "Faith in the fight, Ulfric. Faith eternal."

CHAPTER TWENTY-FIVE

From a hatchway aboard the *Gildr*, Jaemus let his gaze sweep over the well-lit though uncannily quiet troop hold. For the past two days, he'd barely left this berth, spending all his time tending to the Himmingazians.

They were sick. He couldn't deny it. The cough Cote had shrugged off three days ago not only hadn't healed, it had spread to them all. A dry, deep-in-the-chest rattle that sounded like the air they breathed was filtered through gravel.

More than helpless, Jaemus was scared. What ailed them was subtle and could potentially have been simple seasickness, but Jaemus knew it wasn't. It was as someone, he couldn't remember who, had said—this wasn't their world, and despite the many similarities between the constitution of the Vinnrics and the 'Gazians, their bodies were not thriving here.

Conditions were crowded in the sleeping dorm, as the Dyrraks had had to make room for the extra passengers along with their own complement of two hundred or so warriors. Those not on duty or training on other decks, which left only a small group of fifty or so, maintained a sedate, disciplined composure that Jaemus wasn't used to.

The Himmingazian people tended to be more jovial, and far less... *formidable*.

His attempts over the last Halla cycles (he suspected he'd always think of periods of light followed by dark repeated as "cycles") to speak to any of the crew always resulted in a similar outcome: reverence for his rank as Knight manifested by an unwillingness to meet his eye, followed by quick withdrawal.

They did seem curious about the other Himmingazians, though the language barrier and the other-worlders' obvious illness made any sort of cross-realm sociability impossible. Jaemus had tried being friendly, even solicitous, but the only thing the Dyrraks seemed to respond to were requests for something to comfort the 'Gazians, food and what have you, which they snapped to fulfill as if he were an officer giving them an order. It was frustrating to be treated as some kind of superior rather than as what Jaemus was accustomed to, a peer willing to collaborate equally on assuring a necessary outcome. A Himmingazian, in other words. Such distance between him and these people didn't bode well for making a smooth adjustment to the Dyrrak way of life.

And that's what they faced now, wasn't it? A life in Vinnr. The story Eisa had told of Himmingaze—only a few more Glister Cycles until the end...

He couldn't imagine it. He just couldn't see it. His life, his history, his world wiped out of existence. His family, Jovus his dad, Vreyja his gramsirene, gone. He simply couldn't accept it.

And forget telling the 'Nauts this unbelievable news. They had enough troubles right now. Once they got through this sea voyage, maybe they'd feel better. Then, perhaps, he could explain this...this *inconceivability*.

He would try again to push Ulfric into doing something, *anything* he could to help the 'Gazians as soon as they made land and Ulfric took back all the celestial artifacts from the bruhawks. The ferocious-looking birds, big as a person with wings that spread three times as wide, rarely came aboard the ship and never together. They'd carried the satchel containing the Verity artifacts for the last three days, passing it off between them and never bringing it near a Dyrrak ship.

For someone who'd put his life in the Dyrraks' hands, Ulfric seemed awfully untrusting of the southern peoples.

The reason Jaemus saw so little of Ulfric was Ulfric's seclusion from the Dyrrak crew. He and the Knights shared a large cabin in the warship's sterncastle next to the Domine Ecclesium's. He didn't leave that space and was flanked at all times by the other Knights. In one of the few meals Jaemus had taken with them, they had decided that until Ulfric was able to release Vaka Aster, the less exposure any of the Dyrraks had to him, the better. The Knights couldn't risk Ulfric's so-called heretical truth being uncovered, or even suspected. The Domine Ecclesium appeared to be in his middle years, *fit-looking* middle years, but had a cunning wisdom in his eyes that seemed much older. Jaemus didn't mind admitting the man unnerved him. He, above all, needed to be kept away from Ulfric.

Cote rolled over on his bunk and gave a small groan. Jaemus would have known it was his lifemate even if he'd had rocks in his ears. Stepping away from the hatch, he pulled a stool to Cote's side.

"Good day to you," he said in mock formality. "I'm guessing that noise is your way of protesting not being the captain in charge of the ship you're traveling on, eh?"

Despite his illness, Cote's facility with Elder Veros was improving rapidly, and he insisted, stubbornly, on using it when they spoke. It came so naturally to him, in fact, that Jaemus wondered if Vaka Aster had intervened with him slightly as she had with Jaemus.

"Jae," he said through his increasingly dry, pale lips. "Just one more cycle, no...*day* from land now, that is right?"

"That's what I've been told. Eager to get off ship already?"

"It agrees not so much," he managed.

Attempting lightness, Jaemus offered, "I, for one, have never been so glad to lack the nag of hunger, which is apparently a side effect of being sprite-sparked. Have you tried some of that brittle, powdery brick they call 'food'? It's like trying to eat a desiccated carcass that's been molded into a *veeshock*."

Cote's grimace said he quite agreed. The warship's rations left more than a little to be desired, and it gave Jaemus added insight into the coldness, bordering on surliness, of most aboard.

"But you must eat what you can," he went on seriously. "It may taste like fleech castings, but it's important to keep your strength."

Cote sat up, struggling a bit as Jaemus watched, feeling helpless. His features, strong and set, showed the fire in him, the spirit and drive that made him a natural leader among their people. Jaemus would happily have given every drop of whatever celestial energy he'd been endowed with to end the struggle against this wasting of stamina and strength that was afflicting all the 'Gazians.

"I'd rather eat the fleech castings," Cote said, and Jaemus could have kissed him for showing the spark of humor.

"One more day," he said again. "Whole meals and a new ho—" he cut himself off. The 'Gazians weren't seeking a new home; no more than he had been.

"Jae, you've been hovering over me like my mother used to. Go outside, enjoy the…the Halla, is it? I'll be fine. We all will."

"I think I'll—"

"That's an order, Glint." His tone was strict, but the corner of his mouth turned up.

"As you please, Captain." He sighed. With a kiss to Cote's forehead, he stood and left the berth.

The hot sun, the dry air, the cool breeze—he stepped into the cornucopia of everything that was opposite of Himmingaze and couldn't help but smile. For just one moment he let his mind taste the word: *Home.* It wasn't so bad here, was it?

He wandered across the main deck, taking in the sights. The *Gildr* stood four decks high, bristling with weapons along each deck and off the sides. The things had barrels that reminded him of shelksies in a way, just hugely oversized. And he doubted that whatever they fired would simply stun whoever they hit. The weapons, along with the uppermost deck being packed with their small flying crafts, reminded him uncomfortably of the brief glimpse he'd gotten of Balavad's warship in the sky of Himmingaze.

The Vinnrics had a word the 'Gazians didn't: war. The concept was easy enough to imagine, though the idea any peoples would wage one was beyond him. Yet the dozens and dozens of similar ships in the Dyrrak fleet that he had seen from the topdeck told him the people of Vinnr did not share his trouble with the idea of blasting each other to bits.

A ring of rope had been erected in the deck's center, encircling a section of boards covered in sand, and sometimes blood. Jaemus had passed it once and learned the Dyrraks held fights, both hand-to-hand and with weapons, within the ring. It seemed to be a training ground much like the one Stave had used to try to teach Jaemus fighting techniques. With nothing else to occupy him, he grabbed a skin of water and paced to the ring to watch. *Wouldn't my mentor be so proud?* he thought without real humor.

Four combatants faced off within. Two were clearly masters—one, he realized was their military leader, Chancellor Seldeg Aoggvír. Each of the Dyrraks' skin was covered with the deeply inked markings that he was coming to realize denoted either a level of skill or a rank of some sort, and each master had paired with someone lower in position and skill, judging by their less-adorned skin.

"They are testing on their Fourth Phase today. Alfríl is a son of the Third Line. His family's honor will be continued through him."

Jaemus looked to his right, surprised to find the Domine Ecclesium beside him. The man moved with remarkable stealth, even when there was no need. It brought to mind one of Stave's many sayings: "Silent spiders enjoy quieter meals."

"Phases?" he asked with cautious curiosity.

The Dyrrak's mouth turned down at the corners, disapproving of Jaemus's ignorance, but his face smoothed again quickly. "It's easy to forget how alien you are to our people and our customs, Knight Bardgrim. It is to be expected, but your being here now I consider to be the deepest honor. And it's my duty to teach you the Dyrrak ways myself."

Jaemus twitched a bit in surprise. "Teach me...sorry?"

"Yes. You and your people, people of a foreign realm with no connection to ours, were chosen by Vaka Aster, brought to Vinnr, and you in particular granted such a generous gift. To be so foreign yet so favored, I could almost say you are even *more* worthy than the Knights of Vinnr. We Dyrraks are privileged to get to share our ways and our empire with you." He looked toward the ring of fighters, and added, "Certainly you will honor us in return, by honoring our own customs."

As he spoke, the fighting in the ring escalated. So much so that Jaemus soon realized he'd only been watching a warmup before. The two novices, though they hardly looked new to the arts of fighting, were taking beatings that would have left even Jaemus's spark-infused hide bruised and battered. But they continued without complaint and with barely a sound of pain or grunt of rage. Blood dripped and flew.

Watching their fight, Jaemus's head reeled. This was a Dyrrak custom? And *he* was expected to learn it? He swallowed and tried to keep his tone conversational instead of verging on horrified as he said, "You know, the Knights have mentioned that the Himmingazians might not be welcome in Vinnr, given our foreign nature, after what Balavad's, erm, people did to Ivoryss and Yor. And we don't exactly, you know, blend in."

The Ecclesium's lips pressed together, and he rolled his head across his shoulders as if to loosen up for a fight of his own. "The lesser kingdoms are given to prejudices. And why shouldn't they be, as low as their own failings have brought them? But we do not judge the Yorish or Ivoryssians. They are simply peoples whose fires of faith have been nearly quenched. Dyrrakium is a devoted empire, and we have waited patiently for the days that are now ahead of us. The faith of the peoples of Ivoryss and Yor will soon be reforged once Vaka Aster commands it. And you and your Himmingazian brethren will be here to aid our charge."

Jaemus gave the tiniest of nods to acknowledge the Ecclesium's statement, then stood as rigid as a pillar, keeping his eyes trained on the fight. Distantly, he hoped he looked attentive, as if he were simply pondering the words that to the Ecclesium must have seemed totally reasonable. Inwardly, he was quaking. Stave had used the word "zealot" more than once to describe the Dyrraks, and Jaemus no longer had to guess why. Was it some kind of Cosmic joke that he'd left Himmingaze's utter renouncement of anything to do with Verities only to fall in with a culture that treated forcibly shoving anything Verity-related down others' throats as a kind of sacred duty?

The Ecclesium seemed to take his silence for interest and continued explaining what they were witnessing. "Each Dyrrak begins learning the Five Phases from the day they take their first steps. It starts with purifying the body; second, the mind; third is to learn to release all attachments; fourth to overcome all weakness; and finally, each Dyrrak surrenders themselves to complete devotion, faith, and loyalty to Vaka Aster. Today, our Phase fighters Alfríl and Osnald will suffer. They may even die of their wounds. But if they survive, their final physical weaknesses will have been bested. Pain is weakness, you see. And their teachers have the utmost talent in doling it out."

Jaemus squeaked out, "You mean this is a fight to the death? What good would that do anyone?"

"Not necessarily to the death, but it may be." Jaemus felt the Ecclesium's keen stare on his face but didn't look at him. "Knight Nazaria has told me of the events in Himmingaze aboard the foreign Verity Balavad's warship. How you freely offered your own life for our maker. Did you not?"

"Well...yes?" he said, not sure he'd characterize his actions quite that way.

"Then why shouldn't we Dyrraks? How can one's faith be trusted if one's faith hasn't tested? The Knights Corporealis must prove themselves in the eyes of our maker to be chosen to serve. It's the same with our people."

Jaemus had no response to that. The reasoning was sound, he supposed, even if the methods by which the Dyrrak measured their worthiness were cripplingly harsh, literally.

The Ecclesium continued, "When you pass the Phases, Knight Bardgrim, you will join the ranks of those worthy of the greatest honor possible among our people."

Now he did face the Ecclesium, and his mouth forged ahead of his reason as it so often did. "When I—? My generous if muddle-minded friend, even if you were Vaka Aster her-him-*itself*, I'd sooner get swallowed by a fleech than do *that*."

As he flung his hand out to point to the fighters, the distinctive snap of a bone, and a large one, tore Jaemus's attention from the Ecclesium. His eyes shot to the ring, and the man who would have been honoring his family writhed on the deck, gripping his right thigh, his face a rictus of agony.

"Perhaps Alfríl will not pass the Fourth Phase this year, if ever," the Ecclesium said flatly.

Surprised at his emotionless tone, Jaemus looked at him. A set of twin grooves running beside the Ecclesium's mouth deepened until he was nearly grimacing.

"Excuse me, Knight Bardgrim."

As he swept off, Jaemus turned back to the ring. Several Dyrraks knelt around the fallen man, tending to his injury. One of the healers shifted enough for Jaemus to see the man. His thigh bone jutted through the skin, its end an uneven, shattered yellow and white spear.

With all the grace of a gutted fish, Jaemus bent over and deposited his last rations on the deck beside the ring. *Might as well have been veeshock for all the digesting of it I managed.*

CHAPTER TWENTY-SIX

J aemus the Himmingazian showed extraordinary courage. I was injured when Balavad took us captive and brought us aboard his warship. Even so, when Mylla, Ulfric, and Jaemus were captured as well, he appeared meek, and I saw nothing in him that suggested what he was capable of. But there was nothing meek in the way he stepped between Ulfric and Balavad's vessel before the usurper could strike Ulfric down.

Safran had said this to Eisa yesterday as they'd stood watch outside Ulfric's cabin together. It was an incredible story, the way this Himmingazian had sacrificed himself, apparently not even knowing he was ordained. Safran had said she didn't think he'd done it out of any great affection for Ulfric. It had simply been an instinct to protect those he cared about, the Himmingazians aboard that ship, which perhaps came from an innate understanding of the stakes everyone faced if Vaka Aster's vessel had been destroyed.

But now, looking at the Himmingazian doubled up and hurling his guts out on the *Gildr*'s deck, she had trouble really believing the story, though she'd conveyed it to the Domine Ecclesium when he'd questioned her about Vaka Aster's expectations for the treatment of the foreigners. It had seemed a relevant point to bring up. Despite her misgivings about the foreigners, if Vaka Aster had chosen Bardgrim, the Dyrraks needed to show him the respect due all the Knights.

After speaking with Ulfric the first night at sea, Eisa felt…lighter. She hadn't been this unburdened in centuries. For the first time in more turns than she could count, she caught herself looking forward to the future rather than simply being resigned to play her role in it. Ulfric's acceptance of the things she'd done, without for a moment making her feel as if she'd dishonored her oath or the Knights Corporealis, made her realize how deeply she'd buried her fear—fear of being unworthy.

Nevertheless, after these two days at sea, she was itching for a fight, something to relieve the dullness of sea travel. Maybe they should have listened to Stave's point about traveling through the interrealm well. In any case, she'd been heading toward the Phase ring to seek out someone to join her for a practice contest when Bardgrim had stepped out of the hold his fellow other-worlders were berthed in. She'd followed him out of curiosity. Under ordinary circumstances, she'd have known any new Knight of the Order long before they were ordained, and would have helped to train them in the Conservatum and cast one of the deciding votes as to whether they deserved to seek Vaka Aster's acceptance. His situation was unique, unprecedented as far as she knew.

His uncontrolled purging did not allay her misgivings about him. When he looked finished, she stepped up to him while he surreptitiously kicked some sand from the Phase ring over the mess he'd made.

"Water and lightning!" he yelped as he straightened and found her standing nearly eye to eye with him.

"Knight Bardgrim," she said flatly in greeting. Her eyes flicked to the ring as the wounded man from Phase contest was being carried away. She'd traveled home to Dyrrakium and passed her own Fourth Phase when she'd been twenty, and still bore scars from it.

He took a step backward until he was pressed against the ring's rope, startled. "Knight Nazaria? I'm sorry, I didn't recognize you for a moment without your…rage."

She eyed him, then jerked her chin toward the ring. "Care to spar?"

"I'd like to spar right now about as much as that poor fellow who just had his leg broken," he said, wiping his mouth.

"A Knight doesn't shun a fight. A Knight takes every chance they have to improve their skills, sharpen their mind as much as their weapons, in eternal service to the Verities."

"And serving our Verities is my top priority, believe me. So long as I get to keep everything inside and outside my skin in its proper place and configuration."

She scowled. Was he a coward, then? It didn't seem to fit the story Safran had told. As she scanned the nearby Dyrrak crew for someone else to challenge in the ring, she said offhandedly, "If you truly have serving a Verity in mind, you should return to Himmingaze and undo the calamity your forebears wreaked."

"About that, actually, and the story you told us the other night. You see, Ulfric's been a bit…distracted, and now that it's clear Himmingaze is in direr trouble than we thought, what do you think I should do with this?"

She let her attention shift back. "With what?"

From inside his vest he withdrew a folded parchment.

But it wasn't merely a parchment. "Where did you get that?" she asked.

With a quick, guilty glance around him, Bardgrim said, "Ulfric left it sitting on the table inside my Glisternaut ship just before he was, er, temporarily mistaken for a criminal, I suppose you could say. I didn't want it to get lost, so I kept it with me."

"You have Lifs's Scrylle map. Bardgrim, you hold in your hands the one way to find all the Fenestrii of Himmingaze." She gripped his wrist tightly, pulling him close enough to stare directly into his eyes. "Do you realize what you could do?"

He tried to step away from her but her grip held him in place. Instead, he leaned back. "…Find the Fenestrii?" he suggested.

"Put that away and come with me," she finished, releasing his wrist. "Now."

"About the map," he said and cleared his throat, "Ulfric has a bit on his mind and…well, could we maybe just not tell him about it for now?"

Ignoring him, she whirled and paced toward the hold where the Himmingazians rested. He followed a few steps behind. The Scrylle map would be illegible to any Dyrrak, being written in starcrafted runes that only a Knight could read. But that didn't mean such important artifacts should be toted around among the nonordained like an everyday book.

Once inside the hold, she led him to a steerage-level storeroom, well below the waterline where nothing they said would be heard. The Himmingazian's extraordinary possession could change everything for his realm. And—it could put her one step closer to getting redemption for what she'd done.

She slowed for a moment. *Redemption? Is that what I think I need?*

The last words Griggory had said to her in Himmingaze blazed in her mind. *"If you succeed in Vinnr, remember me here. Remember what happened and spend the rest of your life, however long it may be, seeking redemption within yourself. Then perhaps you can begin restoring your own faith."*

She snorted to herself. Perhaps, once again, the old Knight had been right.

Inside the dark, damp storage room, she turned back to Bardgrim. "To save Himmingaze from its doom, five Fenestrii and the Scrylle are needed, along with a Knight with enough faith and strength to see it done. It's not simple chance that you were ordained, Bardgrim, or that you somehow stole that map while Ulfric wasn't looking."

He started to protest, but she went on. "When we get to Dyrrakium and Ulfric gathers Vaka Aster's artifacts, I just need to collect one thing, then you're going back there, you're going to find Griggory, and you're going to right the wrongs of your Mystae."

"…Right wrongs? Right, well, see Ulfric said that one of the five Fenestrii is missing. It's not even in the realm. And I thought the map only showed where the stones are. There's still the Scrylle to find, if it's even still in one piece."

"I've told you, the Scrylles are unbreakable."

"Okay, sure. But are they also unloseable? Because…"

"With all five Fenestrii and the map, the location of the Scrylle will be revealed."

"You're…you're telling me the map also shows where to find the Scrylle?"

"All five and the map will help you find the Scrylle," she repeated as if he were feeble.

"But Ulfric never said—"

"Why would he? Last time he saw the map, he had the Scrylle, yes?"

Jaemus's brows rose as if to say *Good point.* Then he said again, as if he were an annoying mimic bird, "*Five.* Ulfric said the map only showed four."

"You can leave retrieving the fifth Fenestros to me."

CHAPTER TWENTY-SEVEN

From his confinement within the Knights' suite of cabins on the *Gildr*, Ulfric wondered if—and dreaded if so—the Domine Ecclesium had some grand ceremony in mind once they reached Dyrrakium. Verities knew he didn't want that. Or *any* of this, for that matter.

Four days had passed, and they'd sped to Dyrrakium in under half the time Ulfric had assumed it would take. The Dyrraks' advances in mechanics and industry that had given their ships so much speed confirmed his suspicions: Eisa had been sharing the Knights' inventions with the exiled empire.

When he'd asked her about it, her response had been characteristically blunt. "I always knew the day would come when we couldn't trust the commoners of the lesser kingdoms. I made contingencies, and it was good that I did, as you can see."

He'd let the conversation flag then. What good was pursuing it when she was so demonstrably right? Yet it was becoming clearer that someday Eisa's freewheeling decision-making could become a problem. At the moment, however, too many other problems vied for his attention. He pushed this one away.

Halla crested the eastern horizon as the *Gildr* sailed into a vast bay off the coast of Dyrrakium and docked. Upon hearing the shouts of the crew, Ulfric and the Knights left their cabins for the top deck and caught their first sight of the great shunned empire.

His eyes couldn't widen enough to take it all in. The shores of the bay contained enough docks for a hundred ships, with piers built on stone pillars reaching to the ocean floor and stretching out into the calm waters for hundreds of paces. Trade and storage warehouses extended a short distance back from the piers until butting up against a tall stout red-stone wall that looked sturdy enough to outlive the world, a fortified bastion along the bay's entire shoreline. An unbroken string of heavy armaments decked the wall, appearing capable of holding off a full-scale invasion.

The wall's three enormous drawn porticos gave him a glimpse into the city beyond that stretched so far past the limits of his vision that it appeared to have no end. Six immense statues rose above the city like watchtowers and towered ten times higher than the sea wall. Massive and imposing, each was the shape of a regal-looking man or woman, armed with Dyrrak weapons, their dress carved in the simple yet refined elegance of the Dyrrak people he'd met. He quickly took in that the statues were built in a V-shape stairstep pattern leading to a distant tower that seemed to glow with a reddish haze in the overhead sun. Even from this distance, the structure loomed large, and Ulfric guessed the tower's purpose. Something that formidable had to have been built for a ruler—or a Verity.

Thousands of people thronged the port as the Dyrraks tied off the fleet. The Knights and Ulfric returned to his cabin.

Safran said, *This city is huge. I've never seen anything like it. There are at least as many people outside to meet the ship as there are in Asteryss. If they're not as devoted to Vaka Aster as they say, we're in real trouble.*

Their faces all reflected the same mixture of readiness and caution, and no one, Ulfric noted, looked to Eisa for her reaction at Safran's implied doubt in the Dyrraks.

After a moment, she continued: *Shall we then? I will take the lead.*

"No." Ulfric stepped toward the exit, doffing his eye shields and handing them to Mallich to carry. He needed to be recognized in the role he was playing. It would be...safer. "I will. It's me, or who they think I am, that draws them."

Just as he finished, the shadow of the Domine Ecclesium appeared in the hatch. He didn't take a knee this time, merely bowed his head and did not meet Ulfric's eyes. Foregoing the direction that he speak through Eisa, he said, "Vaka Aster, your people await you."

Ulfric gave a brief nod, and the Ecclesium went on, speaking to the assembled Knights. "The ever-faithful Dyrraks have waited so very long for the opportunity to be witness to you, Great Creator. Their excitement, I assure you, will remain respectful. You and the Knights Corporealis shall be escorted through Elezaran, our capital, to the Citadel Suprima. I hope that our program suits you."

He remained with his head tilted down, awaiting Ulfric's response. So Ulfric had guessed right. Some kind of unlooked-for ceremony would herald this new chapter in his long life. He couldn't let this continue for too long or he truly would go—how was it Jaemus put it? —muddle-minded. A pause drew out, then he answered, "It is good, Domine Ecclesium," and said nothing more.

The Ecclesium seemed to expect more, however, and waited another few heartbeats before dipping his head in acknowledgment. Then, addressing the Knights, he said, "Follow me."

"Have a care for the Himmingazians, too," Stave gruffed.

In the short time they'd been in the cabin, the ship had come to full rest and was anchored to the dock so securely that the gentle waves breaking against it didn't rock it in the least. As Ulfric and the Knights proceeded toward the lowered gangplank, he breathed deeply, noting the coolness of the sea breeze that mixed headily with the otherwise warm air. Halla beamed brilliantly, almost scathingly, from above, lighting everything with stark rays. The beauty of the architecture and the obvious skill and devotion to the craft of construction its makers had shown while creating this city affected Ulfric. Dyrrakium's imposing aestheticism hadn't waned in the least during their exile, and the people filling the port appeared dignified to the last person. They carried themselves upright, tall, their postures without a hint of docility or servility. "Proud" didn't come close to describing them, and "noble" only touched on their features and carriage. He could see that their immense statues were in no way an exaggeration of their nature.

Not a whisper or cough came from the crowded port or walls, as if the empire were inhabited by mutes. The Knights waited on the deck as Dyrraks aligned themselves in ranks three deep from the base of the gangplank to the nearest portico through the city wall, creating an enclosed gauntlet of sorts for them to pass through.

Hearing footfalls ascending from belowdecks, Ulfric looked over his shoulder. Aoggvír, or more precisely, in the habit of the Dyrraks, Seldeg Aoggvír, Heir of the Third Line, Chancellor of the Dyrrak Phalanx, passed by. The sight of the woman trailing her made Ulfric reach for his sword—which, in order to uphold the charade of being Vaka Aster, he was not wearing. For a heartbeat, he thought he was staring at a Ravener.

Then he realized that, although the trailing woman's skin was as gray and lifeless-looking as the Raveners' had been, she was different. For one thing, she wasn't as gangly as the Battgjaldic soldiers, and for another, she was even less animated than they had been. Her steps were halting slides, as if walking did not come naturally to her, and her body moved stiffly and unnaturally, with neither her arms swinging nor her knees appearing to bend. She was dressed from head to toe in a hooded crimson robe, a few shades darker than her hair, that hid all but her face and hands—completely unlike the short breeches and abbreviated tunics of the Dyrrak people—and her unblinking eyes were a filmy blue. Her face…something about it was familiar.

"By my faith…" he heard Mallich whisper. "Eisa, what did you do?"

As Ulfric tried to place the strange woman's familiar features, the Ecclesium said a few final words of preparation to the Dyrrak crew aboard the ship, asked the Knights to wait a few moments while he addressed the crowd, then stepped to the top of the gangplank, positioning the woman beside him.

Putting a hand on her shoulder, he began to speak. "My devoted Dyrraks, today the faith and loyalty with which we have lived for thousands of turns has reached its pinnacle, for we, the worthiest creations of our divine Vaka Aster, have become unified at long last with our maker. Vaka Aster had chosen us!"

The words blew by Ulfric nearly unheard, for it was not the words but how they were spoken that shocked him. Though he could hear the Dyrrak leader's voice, the speech was repeated by the woman before him. Not only repeated, but projected louder than any human could speak. Her voice rang from her mouth like a tolling bell, washing over the crowd and echoing from the city wall. It was uncanny, a wystic affect. But how? The Ecclesium was no Knight, nor was the strange woman.

The Dyrrak ruler concluded his speech. "No longer do we declare the Six Aspects of our devotion to the void, but now we may do so directly to the Creator himself." He stepped to the side, lowered his head, and swept a hand toward Ulfric.

"Declare it to our maker, people of Dyrrakium!" the Ecclesium commanded.

As one, every Dyrrak yelled back, "Faith! Strength! Wisdom! Duty! Loyalty! Dominion!" The port went immediately silent once more as the last syllable died on the calm breeze.

That word again—dominion, Ulfric thought. He stepped forward reluctantly and looked at the crowd. Again, nearly in unison, every person knelt before him.

Verity's tears, Ulfric thought. *This was never what I wanted.*

The Ecclesium stood and with his eyes still lowered said, "Great Creator, we've prepared a palanquin to bear you toward the citadel. It lies just inside the city gate. Please, follow me."

He turned and began pacing down the gangplank, but Mallich stopped him with a hand on his shoulder. "Is there no quieter and less attended route, Ecclesium? Vaka Aster prefers solitude."

The Dyrrak leader turned back slowly. "But Knight Roibeard, don't look so worried. You are among devoted servants. There is no danger to our maker anywhere within the borders of this empire. Your role as the vessel's protector, such as it is, is all but obsolete in Dyrrakium." He looked at Mallich's hand still gripping him, then pulled his arm away.

"Besides, our maker is more than capable of meeting any challenge offered without assistance from you."

Did Ulfric hear an insult in those words?

Mallich looked at him, and Ulfric gave a brief nod. *For now, we should follow the Ecclesium's lead to the citadel,* he sent.

I'm beginning to think we might have been better off in Asteryss, I am, Stave said.

It is their way, Safran supplied, *and unfamiliar to us. They have been exiled for too long, cut off from Vinnr and the cultures and histories of the other kingdoms, and have lost their reverence for the Knights Corporealis. Even Vaka Aster is little more than an idea to them now. We have to be leery, but they've shown us no reason to suspect them of malicious intentions.* She paused. *Yet.*

Ulfric looked to Eisa, expecting a sneer or cold scowl from her for the suspicion the Knights held for her people, but what he saw surprised him. Her face had gone pale beneath the bronze burnish, and her unbroken stare rested on the pale woman who'd delivered the speech.

Eisa? he sent. *We will follow your lead.*

With an expectant look, the Ecclesium turned to face them.

The warm sun began to grow too hot, uncomfortable. They needed to get moving before whatever engineered calm they were experiencing fractured. He said aloud to the Ecclesium, "The Himmingazians shall accompany us. After you, Ecclesium."

The Domine Ecclesium nodded, then said, "Speaker, return to Chancellor Aoggvír."

The gray-skinned woman turned around in stilted jerks that caused her robe to part, giving Ulfric a view of her torso. A pearly crystal about the size of a large walnut was embedded in a metal setting in the woman's chest, just where her heart would have been. The crimson tunic the woman wore beneath the cloak was sewn into the edge of the setting, as if neither the stone nor the clothing was ever removed, giving the impression the woman was an elaborate doll with a strange jewel-like organ.

Fate's fury, sent Stave, *is that what I think it is?*

It was. A Fenestros, or part of one. Exactly like the one he'd used to look into Lífs's Scrylle back in Himmingaze just days ago. This was a piece of the realm's missing Fenestros. Griggory had not recorded *that* in the Scrylle, at least not that he'd read. And there was only one way it could have come to be here.

He looked at Eisa. Her face, wooden with tension, revealed nothing of what she was thinking. She stared at the back of the retreating Ecclesium as he walked down the gangplank. Without even glancing at Ulfric, she sent: *Are you coming?* and stepped after the Dyrrak leader.

PALATIAL YET AUSTERE, the Citadel Suprima's foreign architecture and unusual stonework defied Ulfric to guess its age. Pyramidal in shape, it rose to half the height of Vigil Tower, giving the impression it was more solid and ancient than the earth beneath them. As the procession had drawn close, he'd noted patterns in the structure's red blocks created by a rust-colored yet gleaming type of stone. It could have been mistaken for a metal, but it was much too rough for that to be the case and clearly unworked by hammer or anvil. The way it caught the sun and refracted its light gave the citadel its reddish haze from a distance. The effect was almost ethereal, as if Halla at sundown illuminated the citadel from within.

The trip to reach the citadel took much longer than Ulfric wanted. The beasts transporting his palanquin and the Himmingazians' carts were stout, lumbering, lizard-like quadrupeds just a bit smaller than an average-size horse, but far slower. All along the route, the Dyrrak people had lined the streets and bowed their heads in respect. Safran had guessed their reverence for the Order and their maker had diminished during their long exile, but they seemed to have reclaimed it for the time being.

Even before the Knights had been given a tour of the full citadel, Ulfric required they be shown their quarters and left alone. The Ecclesium tasked Chancellor Aoggvír with providing for them and took his leave almost immediately. She showed them to a massive hexagonal chamber at the pyramid's peak with a dais near the back that rose five heads over the tallest Dyrrak, upon which was anchored an ornate carved-stone throne. Six fountains encircled the chamber's periphery, and the sound of flowing water, colored a dull red from the ever-present red-stone dust that lightly coated the entire city, created a harmonious susurration throughout. This was to be Vaka Aster's chamber.

Or prison, thought Ulfric.

Before the chancellor exited through the chamber's heavy iron doors, Ulfric asked, "Where are the Himmingazians now?"

The Ecclesium had shown the foreigners little more than indifference, but *respectful* indifference, if such a thing existed. Jaemus watched the woman with anxious eyes. He'd wanted to go with the Himmingazians, but Ulfric had requested he at least see where the rest of the Knights would be first.

"They've all been shown to a suite on the lower floor of the citadel to settle in and try to recover from the voyage," the woman responded, head bowed. "We will provide for them as our own, Great Creator."

Jaemus, unable to hold himself back, pressed, "Take me to them." He shot a glance to Ulfric, and he gave him a slight nod. He couldn't very well expect the Himmingazian to be kept from his own people. He had never asked for this duty either, after all. Ulfric was uniquely sympathetic.

"This way," said the chancellor.

Jaemus followed on the woman's heels, and just as the doors swung shut, Eisa said, "I'll go and ensure the chamber and the citadel are secure," and followed them.

Mallich looked to Ulfric. "Would it best for me to go with her?"

Ulfric shook his head. "No. She'll keep us apprised through our lenses."

Mallich was silent, and Safran and Stave followed his lead, each adjusting to their new confines in their own ways. He didn't know who besides Roi might have guessed who the revenant creature on the docks was: Lillias Grannd, Eisa's former Yorish lover. What had Eisa done to her? And in the name of the Verities, why?

In a moment, Safran sent: *I am worried for them, the Himmingazians. They are doing poorly and have grown worse on the journey here.*

Ulfric eyed her. "What do you mean? Their world is entirely water. It seems unlikely they would get seasick."

They are having trouble adjusting to Vinnr. They seem to be suffering from a wasting condition. Like a disease, but I believe there is no cure except to be returned to their own realm. She looked past the doors where Jaemus had gone: *Jaemus seems well enough. The spark he carries protects him as it would us. An immunity of sorts.*

Ulfric felt cold, and he turned away from the others. *Isemay.*

It was easy enough for the others to follow his thoughts, and Stave said, "Sym will know what to do, Ulfric, she will. And that girl of yours is as tough as her parents anyway. We'll find them, and they'll be as fit and fine as a bruhawk with a gullet full of hare. You can be sure of it."

Ulfric looked at Stave and tipped his chin briefly, acknowledging his words if not Ulfric's confidence in them.

Ignoring Stave's last statement, Mallich said, "What do you think, Ulfric? Is it time to send someone to find them?"

Ulfric nodded decisively and turned to Safran. "Now that we've reached safety, will you see to Yggo and Urgo and have them come?"

Nodding, she paced to one of the chamber's tall windows and raised her Mentalios to link to the bruhawks. The creatures had stayed within range of the ships throughout the entire journey, carrying the satchel containing the celestial artifacts of both Vaka Aster and Balavad within their claws, only leaving them briefly with the Knights on their private deck when they needed to hunt. When Safran called, they swooped in the chamber and alighted on the tall dais within moments, leaving the satchel at its base.

Safran released the sightlink and gently scratched beneath their neck feathers as she praised them quietly. They bent their heads, crooning low at the welcome attention. *They'll want to be fed soon, or they'll hunt on their own,* she sent. *And the Dyrraks must be informed that they are allies so no one attempts to catch or kill them when they're away from the citadel. Yggo and Urgo won't be as tolerant of misplaced aggression as we might be.*

"I'll spread the word." Stave had already started toward the chamber door and spoke briefly with a guard posted outside. He came back in a moment. "Won't be long, it won't. I asked for some grub for us as well. We'll get that burly chancellor to formally brief the Dyrraks once we're done here. She looks like someone nobody in their right mind would dare defy, she does, " he finished and eyed Ulfric expectantly.

"Ulfric," he went on. "Who was that gray lady and why was a Fenestros punched into her like a dart?"

It was Mallich who answered. "Her name is Lillias Grannd, and she is the reason for what Dyrrakium has become. The Fenestros, though, I don't know where that came from." He turned to Ulfric with an eyebrow raised questioningly.

He shared his theory with the rest. "I believe it may be part of the missing Fenestros of Himmingaze. When I was able to read their Scrylle map, I could only find four. How and why this one is here is a mystery."

A mystery Eisa could answer, Safran said, her assumption right on point as it usually was.

Ulfric nodded. "Perhaps, but that is a matter we can wait to discuss, preferably with Jaemus present. It's his world's artifact, and he should be consulted. One thing we'll all agree on is that it will need to be... retrieved." *One more problem for us to resolve,* he noted with an internal sigh.

The Knights agreed without saying a word. Stepping to one of the windows, Ulfric gazed over the city. His eyes stopped on a swath of empty land a short distance to the north before the plains rose to the mountains. No, not empty. The field, small from here but he knew it was the size of the city of Asteryss at least, was filled with the returned force of Dyrrakium airs ships. Their numbers were staggering. Not a defensive force—an invasion force.

In his head, he heard the citizens of Dyrrakium chanting at the city's wall: *Faith... Strength...Wisdom...Duty...Loyalty...Dominion.*

Dominion. Through war, if necessary. How long would the Ecclesium wait for Vaka Aster's blessing to fulfill the Dyrrak's desire for dominion? He had to get himself and Vaka Aster free of these shackles before that happened.

He spun around. "Between Urgo, Yggo, Mallich, and Eisa, I'll be as protected as I can be. Safran, Stave, will you go to Arc Rheunos?"

The heartmatched couple exchanged a brief glance and Safran sent, *Of course. We'll find them if they're there.*

"Good. And thank you. Tonight, we all prepare. Gather what supplies you think you'll need for at least a half-thirty-night, and tomorrow morning you'll go." *Before it's too late,* he thought, stifling an urge to curse.

CHAPTER TWENTY-EIGHT

"Chancellor Aoggvír, wait a moment," Eisa called to the retreating daughter of the Third Line.

She turned. "Yes, Nazarian Most High."

"Take me to the Ecclesium, if you would."

She had some things to discuss with the Dyrrakium leader, particularly what the empire's plans were should Ivoryss retaliate for the hobbling of their shipyards. It would take them dozens of turns to prepare for such a thing, of course, but the Dyrraks need not wait to prepare their own defenses.

It was curious that the Ecclesium had ordered the shipyards to be destroyed. There were only two reasons to wound an unsuspecting adversary: either you feared they'd attack you, or you intended to attack them. Upon leaving Vinnr to seek Griggory in Himmingaze, she'd told the Ecclesium to take Dyrrakium's forces, fully battle prepped, to Ivoryss to meet Balavad's invasion. She had *not* suggested the Dyrraks use that opportunity to invade the lesser kingdom themselves. So what had his intentions been? Now that they were far enough away from Ivoryss to ensure it was out of reach, she intended to find out.

Aoggvír led her to the Ecclesium's chamber of rule at the citadel's base. As they entered the long, soaring hall, he was speaking with a Fifth Phase venerate. He looked up and caught her eye as she approached, and she heard him tell the warrior, "Tell the vault guards I'll be down to meet the new prisoner as soon as I'm finished here."

The venerate gave a bow and retreated.

"Starkas," Eisa said as she came to a stop before the council hall's oblong meeting table. Seven seats surrounded it, one for each senior of the six noble Lines, including the Nazarian heir, and one for the Domine Ecclesium. It occurred to her that she, being the true senior Nazarian, had no seat.

"Nazarian," he said. "I'm pleased you're here. I've been hoping to meet with you privately." He waved a hand and the remaining Dyrraks in the hall retreated to leave them alone.

"It seems beneath you to have an audience with criminals. This prisoner in the vaults must be significant," she commented.

His face remained neutral. Carefully neutral? "Just a spy from a lesser kingdom found recently in Elezaran. They will never learn. But they have useful information often enough that I like to question them personally."

She nodded, not really interested in the day-to-day workings of rulership.

The Domine Ecclesium was her descendent, some sixty generations removed, though their family resemblance was unmistakable in their deep-set eyes, wide jawline, and looming, stocky build. The Nazarians had ruled Dyrrakium in an unbroken line of succession since Vaka Aster had chosen a Nazarian ancestor to serve as her corporeal vessel. The continued allegiance of the people of Dyrrakium to the Nazarians, Eisa had to admit, was impressive. *What place could I take among the Dyrraks now that I'm once more in my homeland?* she wondered. *I could rule quite easily if I chose to.*

But the thought was idle. Since becoming a Knight, she'd never desired the role of Domine Ecclesium, her only ambition to continue in her unfettered faith and devotion to their maker. She didn't need to take her place in the line of succession to achieve that.

Starkas Nazaria had managed rule deftly, though he'd begun to fade toward late middle age. His days as Dyrrakium's ruler were waning. Soon challengers for leadership by younger Nazarians would come, as would, she realized, Fifth Phase masters of the other five original Lines. Now that Vaka Aster's vessel was no longer a Nazarian, they had a right to challenge. And one day, Starkas would lose. No doubt, the Ecclesium would not be one to give up leadership easily. Many other Dyrraks would die or be permanently disabled by his hand in the challenge of the Conquestum Ecclesium before he did.

She decided to get the simple things out of the way first. "It's time to relinquish the Fenestros shard I gave you."

His silvery eyes glittered. "You wish to…retire the Speaker?"

Always thinking several steps beyond what was on the table was one of his many astute qualities. For a moment, Eisa entertained a doubt. Would Ulfric would be able to keep the secret about what he'd done with Vaka Aster long from this man? If it were known, the Dyrraks would see it as an unforgivable transgression. But what could they possibly do about it?

"The Speaker has served her purpose. Dyrrakium has achieved indomitability in Vinnr, and there is no force that can oppose it. The Speaker and her Yorish lessers are bygones of an age that has faded to irrelevancy. I prefer the future to the past, which means burying it."

"As you say, Nazarian." He reached up and lifted off the heavy chain and pendant he wore around his neck. From the weight of her own dagger, Eisa knew the pendant was lighter than it looked. The Fenestrii, despite how solid they felt to the touch, seemed more feather than stone.

As he handed it over, this particular chunk of Fenestros remained deep red in color, an enchantment to hide its true nature that she'd given it when she'd provided it to him. Only a trained eye would know it for what it was. But when he spoke the incantation she'd taught him that would allow him to use the Speaker as his voice, it took on a pearly glow from some wystic inner light. Ulfric and the Knights had seen how it lit up inside Lillias's chest as they'd disembarked from the *Gildr*. Through her Mentalios, she'd heard and felt their horror at seeing a Fenestros used in such a way. Later, perhaps, she'd give them a single moment to express their approbation, but no more. She knew what she'd done, the abomination it was. And now, she was going to rectify it, their judgment be damned.

She collected the shard of Verity stone and put it inside her bandolier. "After I've released the Speaker, I'll want her buried in the Nazarian Line tombs."

The statement caught him off guard. "But, Nazarian, she's a traitor to her own kind, a heretic, and Yorish. It is against our laws and a corruption to—"

"We can put her at the other end from where your own dais will be when you die, Starkas, so you are not tainted by her corrupt corpse. As the Nazarian Most High, my command will be followed. Yes?" The steel in her voice carried a promise of swift punishment if he questioned her again.

Though his expression gave no doubt about his feelings on the matter, he simply nodded.

"It is good," she said.

Before she broached the next subject, he said, "There are concerns among the empire that may be dire enough to warrant your immediate attention, Nazarian. We should speak about them."

"What concerns?"

Now that the Ecclesium had her attention, he took a few paces toward the back of the chamber, hooking his thumbs into the belt of green metal links he wore, an adornment of immense value in Dyrrakium. In a measured, leisurely tone, as if his concerns weren't so important at all, he said, "The fact that Vaka Aster has taken a new vessel who is not a member of the Nazarian Line is first among them. What insight could you lend the people of Dyrrakium to help explain why not only our Line but the Dyrrak people as a whole have lost this unique favor?"

The Ecclesium, warrior that he was, knew how to slip a knife right into the guts, even the verbal kind. Vaka Aster had had little to do with her new choice of vessels, but Eisa wouldn't tell the Ecclesium this. Additionally, she didn't like the challenge she heard in his tone. "Is it the fact that our maker has taken the form of another that bothers you?

Or is it that the Nazarian Line can no longer claim the honor for ourselves?"

"You think my interests in the matter are personal," he said, turning back to her. "Perhaps I am concerned the Nazarian Line's rule will be challenged." He made the statement matter-of-factly, recognizing that his tone would dictate Eisa's responses. She had no patience for insinuations, and he knew it.

Surprised at how close to her earlier thoughts about Dyrrakium's future ruler the conversation had come, she said, "Your days as Ecclesium are numbered, Starkas, but Dyrrakium will exist forever. You can put your worries to rest. Vaka Aster has chosen us, the entirety of Dyrrakium, to protect her now. It's less important what vessel she inhabits."

He gave her a short nod as if accepting her response, then continued. "This is true. But we have a greater burden than ever—along with the greatest honor, of course. What better way to protect the vessel of our maker than to spread true faith once more throughout Vinnr? By tolerating the kind of uprisings and impiety that we saw in Asteryss, we indulge the other kingdoms in their dangerous ideas. Only the Dyrraks are faithful, are *worthy*, enough to protect the vessel, but we are also strong enough as an empire to compel all of Vinnr to come back to the maker's graces, to force worthiness on the other kingdoms, if necessary." His fist rose and clenched tightly as he said "force."

This was it, then. The Ecclesium—all of Dyrrakium, perhaps?— wanted, as she'd suspected, to conquer the lesser kingdoms. They'd had centuries to prepare for a war. It shouldn't surprise her that they were more than ready to fight one.

"Ecclesium, when I persuaded your forbearer some seven hundred turns ago to exile Lœdyrrak from the lesser kingdoms and accept blame for the coup started by Lillias and her greedy rats, I did it to *avoid* a full-scale war with the lesser kingdoms. But more, to remove Dyrrakium from the unworthies' endless squabbles and weaknesses. Their broken devotion to Vaka Aster is their concern, their *lack*, not ours."

"Could it be you've forgotten, Nazarian? Dominion, it is our Sixth

Aspect, our fate, which Vaka Aster has supported since she created the Dyrrak people from the dust of the Cosmos."

"Dominion is what *you* want," she said. "But you know almost nothing of what Vaka Aster wants, Ecclesium. You are no Knight Corporealis."

He paused, his face a well-controlled rictus. "And perhaps you are no longer a Dyrrak."

With the grace of a dancer, she shifted her stance, no longer discoursing but readying for a fight. "I wouldn't have believed you had it in you, Starkas, to challenge not only my authority but also my heritage. Is there anything more you wish to say?"

Their eyes remained locked, mirrors of each other. He said nothing.

Without looking away, Eisa yelled, "Chancellor Aoggvír, attend us!"

A moment later, the hall's doors opened and the chancellor stepped inside. "Yes, Nazarian Most High."

"You are witness." She almost smirked at the way the corner of the Ecclesium's mouth twitched. He knew what she was about to do. "Spread word among the Dyrrak people that tomorrow the Nazarian Most High will meet the Domine Ecclesium in the Citadel Suprima to challenge each other in the Conquestum Ecclesium." She looked to the chancellor, whose own eyes were wide. "Tomorrow, at High Halls, Dyrrakium will see its true, most faithful Nazarian take the throne as Dyrrakium's new Domine Ecclesium."

CHAPTER TWENTY-NINE

In the gaol vaults of Citadel Suprima, deep underground where no light of Halla had ever shone, the rooms were barred, cold, and lined with stone. They held unworthies who had been judged and sentenced. Dyrraks rarely strayed from their faith or devotion, and few had ever been left to be forgotten in these cells. But their most recent prisoner, a spy, was no Dyrrak.

As Eisa challenged the Ecclesium above, the woman's eyes shot open. They were a murky, featureless gray, as colorless as her skin, and her robes, now tattered, had once been an opulent velvety black. The robes worn by Balavad's most revered servants, the Flesh Casters.

You have served me well, priest, came the voice of her master, both from inside her mind and seemingly suffusing the air itself. *Now it's time again that I take your form for myself. This time for good. And you will fulfill a Flesh Caster's highest honor—you shall become my new flesh.*

*Willingly and with all my—*the Flesh Caster began, but her response was cut short by a lightning bolt of pain...then nothing. Darkness pooled in her open eyes.

The door at the chamber's far end opened, and a voice yelled, "Rations! Stand at the backs of your cells until it's served, or starve."

Shuffling noises and grunts came from the few cells containing other prisoners, followed by footsteps and the sound of food trays being slid under the bars.

A venerate guard reached the Flesh Caster's cell. "I said get back or starve, vermin."

The prisoner remained standing where she was, unmoving. The guard had a moment to be surprised at this. The Battgjaldic had been in a near comatose state for the last several days. It was widely believed she'd killed Fourth Phase Venerate Edizriis, but no one knew how—and since then, none had chosen to question her. The guards had placed bets on how long she would last without food before she expired, but she was from another realm, so no one quite knew for sure.

Fits of the faithless, the venerate thought. *I thought she'd be dead by now. I never should have made that bet with Kòrmak. That's three barrels of syke nectar I'm going to owe—*

Before he finished that thought, the voice of the Domine Ecclesium echoed through the vaults. "Venerate, come here."

Taking the remaining rations with him, he hurried to the entrance. "Ecclesium, how may I serve?"

He dipped his eyes, but not before he'd seen the Ecclesium's face. The man was pale, as if something had unsettled him deeply. At first, it was difficult to place the look on his leader's face—it had never been there before.

"I'm told we host a new Ravener in the vaults."

"Yes, Ecclesium. In the farthest cell. She's been unconscious since she was gaoled but has just awoken."

"Show me to her."

"This way. Have you been briefed on the venerate she killed?" he asked as they began to pace to the foreigner's cell.

"I have. The method of murder is still unknown?"

"It is, Ecclesium. He was found collapsed. But there is no sign he was choked by hands nor rope. His body was free of any external wounds, except..."

"Yes?"

The venerate swallowed. "His hands, Ecclesium, they were...missing. And we haven't found them."

The Ecclesium stopped short of the last cell, and the venerate turned back to see why. His expression was a mix of intrigue and disbelief. "Missing?"

"Yes, Ecclesium, we've searched the entire vault. There's no way—"

"That will be all. You may leave."

"But—"

"Out, venerate, or I'll have you in the Birdcage for questioning me." The guard was halfway back to the entrance before the Ecclesium's last word had left his mouth. "And close the door. No one is to enter until I'm gone. Understand?"

"Yes, Ecclesium."

As the lock's tumblers rattled, the Ecclesium faced the prisoner and stared at her curiously. She stood in the same place she'd been, unmoving, staring back with unblinking ichor-black eyes.

Strange, thought the Ecclesium, *all the other Battgjald prisoners had gray eyes.*

It was the Ravener who spoke first. "Do you know who I am, Ecclesium?"

"You're a daughter of Battgjald, what they call a Flesh Caster. We've seen your kind before."

The Ravener gave a low hiss. Her next words carried the same sibilance the other Raveners' had, but it was underlaid with a heavy resonant quality that made the Ecclesium listen closely as if by command. "Come, you must be wiser than that. You know who I am. You may address me as Her Holiness."

It took much for a man as solid as a stone pillar both in body and in mind to succumb to shivers, and the Ecclesium was as solid as they came. Nevertheless, a closer look into the blackness of the woman's eyes, like a great void, and he felt his jaw quake when he tried to respond. He had to swallow first.

"Balavad…" he muttered.

"That's better. And do you know why I've come?"

The Ecclesium gathered himself with an effort. Perhaps this creature was simply a master trickster, a virus that clouded the mind and none in Vinnr had immunity to. He had to think of some test, some way to make this creature show proof of her claims. But deep in his mind, he wondered, *Am I fool to question a Verity? Will there be a price?*

His thoughts grew more disordered, and he said the first thing to come to mind. "If you are truly a Verity, why did you kill Venerate Edizriis, and what...what did you do with his hands?"

"This body requires little sustenance, but it does require some," the creature replied. "Now, Ecclesium, we have many things to discuss. It can be done by your leave or by mine. What shall it be?"

"What do you want?"

"Oh, I think you know that too. I want the same thing you want."

As she spoke, a thick miasma began to flow around her, appearing from nothing. The vapor moved like a snake into the cell's lock, and a moment later, it clicked open. The woman—Her Holiness—stepped before the Ecclesium, her body transforming into something taller, ganglier right before him. She bent her face down to stare into his, those inky orbs igniting with an inner fire. The Ecclesium was suddenly overcome with reverence. He was being addressed by a Verity, one of the Five, for the first time in his fifty-three turns. More than addressed, he was being drawn into her confidence, shown an understanding that Vaka Aster had withheld from him. From *him*! The most devoted of all her creations. He dropped to his knees and bowed his head.

Giving voice to his, to *their*, desires, he said, "To spread true faith among all of Vinnr. To bring the maker's dominion to every corner of the realm."

"Every corner of the Cosmos, Ecclesium. And now we shall decide *which* maker's."

CHAPTER THIRTY

Jaemus stood in front of an open window on the citadel's main story, far below Ulfric's coop, as he thought of it. The pleasantly warm breeze of Halla's early morning washed over him. Instead of staring out over the city of Elezaran, missing the glimpse of the sea he'd had in Vigil Tower, his focus and his thoughts were turned inward.

The chamber he stood in was large, interspersed in perfect geometric intervals by ornate columns, somewhat similar to the columns in Lífs's shrine, he realized. The floor was covered in vibrant woven rugs, and the ceiling arced high overhead. It was a luxurious chamber fit for a ruler, but he called it by what it really was. This was a sick ward for the ailing Himmingazians.

They were all assembled, most of them resting—or languishing—on austere but comfortable cushioned pallets. Each woman and man was quite clearly sick. Their pale green skin had taken on an ugly brown-yellow tinge, and their eyes were glazed and their manners listless, some drawing breaths that were too shallow. None bore sores or bruises, besides the hollows under their eyes. They just seemed to be… wasting.

Jaemus had stood vigil over them all night, unable to sleep while they suffered. He'd tried Eisa several times through his Mentalios, but she'd never responded. It was time, maybe past time, he leave and do what he could to restore Himmingaze. Vinnr, quite clearly, would never be their home.

By the time Halla's first rays filtered through the windows, he was determined: If today was going to be the day two of the Knights went to Arc Rheunos, he too would be leaving. He wondered whether Ulfric would try to pressure him to stay, in need of his Knightly endowment for protection with Safran and Stave off to another realm. He'd battle Ulfric for the right to go back to Himmingaze if he had to—though he didn't harbor a spot of hope that was a battle he could win. He didn't think it would come to that, though. Ulfric was, despite his grittiness upon their first meeting, a reasonable, sometimes even kind, man.

Jaemus's heart beat out of step for a moment as he wondered about Ulfric's family. Could the same sickness the Himmingazians suffered be happening to the Knight's own daughter? He could imagine the fear Ulfric must be enduring, though he'd said little about it.

He walked across the room to Cote, who seemed to be stirring. He hadn't yet told his lifemate what he'd learned from Eisa.

"Cote," he said, kneeling by his pallet. "How are you?" *What a point-less question,* he thought, but what else could he say?

"I'll say this," Cote whispered, no longer even attempting Elder Veros, "whatever it is we have makes the barracks bug feel like a tickle."

"If it's a tickle you want…" Jaemus playfully flicked his fingers along Cote's thigh above the knee, where he knew the Glisternaut was most sensitive.

Cote, as always, grabbed his wrists to stop him, but his grip was weak, his hands cold as ice. "Stop," he almost gasped. "…don't have the energy."

"Of course," Jaemus said. "I'm sorry."

Cote lay back and closed his yellowish eyelids. His breathing settled, but not without a quiet rasp coming from deep in his chest. Jaemus frowned and rested his hand on Cote as the man fell back into a restless sleep.

Enough. He rose, determined to find Eisa.

But didn't have to look far. The woman stood less than a foot behind him.

"Bardgrim," she said.

"Would you quit doing that?" he huffed.

"If you're going to be a Knight, you need to better train your senses."

"My senses got me this far in life as they are, and I'm only going to be a Knight for another couple of cycles, thank you. After the whole save-the-world experience, I'm thinking of retiring."

Eisa had stopped listening, he could see that. Her eyes had drifted to the pallets and the sick 'Gazians. Silence lingered for a moment before she looked back at him. "Are you done?"

"Apparently."

She reached into her bandolier and pulled out two pieces of stone, then held them out. He could see easily how their rough edges aligned in one spot. "Are they...?" he started.

"Yes, two of three pieces of the lost Lífs Fenestros. I'll have the third soon. You still have the map?"

He patted his vest.

"It is good." From another pocket on her bandolier—did she ever take the thing off?—she pulled out another piece of parchment. "The Citadel Suprima is ancient, filled with hallways and passages, rooms and chambers. You'll get lost if you don't know how to read a map." She paused. "You do know how to read a map, yes?"

He hesitated. "I'm very versed on the schematics of ship operations systems and, recently, the diagrams I found in—" He cut himself off just before admitting to all the snooping he'd done in Ulfric's craft rooms. "In, er, places I was most definitely allowed to be in."

She ignored his slip. "Take this, then. An hour before High Halls, go to the raised yard overlooking the arena outside the citadel, the one we crossed to the entrance hall. At the top of the citadel steps at the end of the arch-lined pavilion is a dais. Meet me there. The Dyrraks will be gathering for...an event. I'll give you the last piece of Lífs's Fenestros, and from there you can have Ulfric send you home."

"Why not you?"

"Other matters require me today. Do not worry, once you show the Stallari the Scrylle map and the Fenestros shards, he'll understand why you should, why you *must*, go."

He gave what he hoped looked like a sage nod, but inside he was hiding his confusion. Eisa seemed distracted, as if a simple matter of saving a world was a tiny concern. He decided prying would only result in getting his head chewed off and said, "I won't have any trouble finding the dais, obviously. So what's the map for?"

She ran her hand along the side of her head, where the hair was cut brutally short. The other side matched, though she had a thick untouched strip of hair in the middle that was plaited and fell midway down her back. Jaemus had seen the style on many Dyrraks while going through the city. Those who wore it all seemed older, with more than the average number of skin markings.

"If I'm not there to meet you, you'll have to retrieve the last piece of the Fenestros yourself."

It suddenly hit him what she was talking about. He'd seen the Knights' reaction to that unusual copper-headed woman on the *Gildr*, too. And he'd seen what she had stuck inside her chest. "You mean you want me to...to..." He couldn't even say it, much less do it.

"Yes, you'll have to retrieve the last piece, as I said. If you ever want to take your people home again." She looked around the ward meaningfully.

"But...why wouldn't you be there? I'm certainly going to make a point of it, aren't you?" *Because the last thing I think I'll ever be able to do is yank a stone out of a creepy living dead woman's chest.*

She shoved the map into his hand. "Look, the circumstances of my return to Dyrrakium have changed. The Domine Ecclesium and I are going to settle some things today that I know now I should have anticipated long ago. That is, unless he thinks to settle them by a knife in my back from the shadows first."

His brow wrinkled. "That doesn't sound like the kind of guardian for Vaka Aster's vessel that Ulfric and the others hoped for. I suppose that means we're not trusting the Ecclesium anymore?"

"No. It isn't. And we should not. That's why I'll be taking over. High Halls, the dais. Be there, Bardgrim."

"I will, but—"

She paced away without looking back and was gone before he could try to stop her.

He looked at the crumpled map in his hand. Between the violence and politics of this world—he could barely tell the difference between the two—he was far past realizing Vinnr was wholly unsuited for the ambitious but comparatively peaceful Himmingazians. Good thing he and the rest of them would be leaving soon. He just hoped he didn't have to perform some kind of unmentionable surgery on a revenant before they did. He hoped even more that this world and its deep-rooted issues wouldn't follow them back to Himmingaze.

CHAPTER THIRTY-ONE

Ulfric and all the Knights but Jaemus assembled at first light in the Verity's chamber overlooking Elezaran. One other was notably missing.

"Still no response, Ulfric, and no one's seen her all night," Mallich explained. "I'll go look for her."

"Slag it," Ulfric swore. "No, Mallich. Let's wait a bit. There must be a reason she's absenting herself now."

"I think I know where—" Mallich began.

But then Eisa's voice came to Ulfric through the Mentalios. *Ulfric.*

He raised a hand to quiet everyone. *Where are you, Eisa? You've been gone since yesterday.*

Listen, she sent. *I've been staking out the citadel all night, taking the pulse of things here and in Dyrrakium to ensure we are safe.*

He detected some hedging in her tone. *And are we?*

We will be more so soon. For now, you have to trust me. I will explain later. I have something to attend to today, but after High Halls, Dyrrakium will be the empire it was meant to be.

What are you doing, Eisa?

You'll understand more after High Halls. And one last thing. She sent her next thoughts to everyone. *Knights, watch the Ecclesium carefully—he has forgotten his place.*

Eisa, what are you talking about? Mallich asked. Several seconds went by without a response, and he tried again, but she was no longer answering their Mentalios link.

Ulfric and the Knights stood stiffly around the Verity's podium, not speaking. What was there to say? He looked at each of his companions, their numbers seeming to thin more and more by the day. Safran, calm but worried. Mallich, troubled. Stave…well, if nothing else, his disposition toward Eisa remained as surly as ever.

Jaemus, he called through the wystic lens. *Do you know anything about what Eisa is up to?*

…A bit?

What in the worlds would Jaemus know that Eisa wouldn't have told them? *Stay put, I'm coming to speak with you now.*

Turning to the others, he said, "Safran, remain with the artifacts and keep an eye on them. You two, see if you can't find Eisa. She's taking some matter into her own hands, I can feel it, and I want to put a stop to it before things get…"

"Slagged up the bahooky so far our tongues'll be tasting our last meal twice?" Stave offered.

They each looked at him with a level of horror usually reserved for the scene of a terrible accident.

He was unfazed. "Well, that's about the truth of things when it comes to Eisa, it is."

After a moment, Ulfric went on, "I'll be back soon. If no one finds her before High Halls, we'll all meet back here. And from there figure out what in Verities is going on and what next threat we have to face."

Before he could step away, Mallich stopped him with a hand to the arm. "Wait. Take Star Spark with you."

Ulfric shook his head. "No. The Dyrraks will wonder why a Verity would need to be armed. And it's a hallowed weapon. If it were used against me…" There was no need to finish that statement.

"Then I'll accompany you."

He was about to protest, when Stave said, "No saying no, Ulfric. You need at least one of us. I'll go look for that—for her."

They were right, but there was something he could make use of if needed. He stepped over to the dais and reached into the satchel containing the Verity artifacts, withdrawing one of Vaka Aster's Fenestrii and the Scrylle. Retrieving a hard leather map case from among the sundries the Knights had brought, he stowed them inside and hung the case from his belt. As he lashed the base of it around his thigh to hold it secure, he said, "These are staying with me. Just in case." In case what, he didn't bother articulating as he nodded to Safran and Stave. "See you back here by High Halls."

As they paced to the doorway, Mallich suggested to Stave, "If you see the chancellor, ask her where the one called the Speaker is. I sense Eisa will be with her."

"Right." Stave opened the door.

The Dyrrak guard posted outside immediately fell to a knee. "Great Creator."

Ulfric approached him and said, "Venerate, show us to the Himmingazians' quarters."

"This way, My Maker."

They arrived shortly and found Jaemus pacing back and forth in front of one of the large arched windows. When they stepped inside, Mallich posted himself at the doorway, closing it softly behind them to avoid disturbing those who rested.

"Good Bright, or 'morning,' as you say here," Jaemus said with very obvious fake cheer. "Do they have anything like chuffee in Dyrrakium, by chance?"

"Chuffee?" Ulfric asked.

"Never mind. Look, about Eisa..."

He trailed off, and Ulfric waited several moments for him to go on. When he didn't, Ulfric pressed. "Yes, about Eisa. What in Vaka Aster's eyes is she up to?"

"Well, see, I don't know *exactly*. She just said something about having a score to settle with the Ecclesium, apparently about something she should have seen coming a long time ago, and she'd have it all sorted by midday."

"She knew our plan was to send someone to Arc Rheunos today to seek a way to break—" He cut himself off. He shouldn't be speaking aloud about the entanglement with Vaka Aster. Not in this place where hidden listeners could lurk.

"Well, she didn't say *not* to go ahead with that." His eyebrows rose as if to say *It's fine, everything is fine, old friend. Why wouldn't it be?*

"Jaemus, do you know where she is now?"

With a half sigh and pursed lips, Jaemus reached into his vest and handed Ulfric a parchment. "She's given me a map to get to the chamber for that odd, er, *person* called the Speaker. She said to come find her there if she didn't meet me in the courtyard before midday."

Ulfric nodded and said over his shoulder, "You were right, Mallich." Then to Jaemus: "And why are you to meet her?" Jaemus got that look in his eye, a slight creasing at the edges that said he was about to use sixty words to say what only six were needed for. "Just answer me straight, and no waffling," Ulfric warned.

In what had to be record brevity—for the Himmingazian—Jaemus revealed a few other surprises: Eisa's intention to get the broken pieces of Lífs's missing Fenestros; her assurance that Ulfric would then send Jaemus back to Himmingaze to find Griggory and the Scrylle; and, after reaching inside the same pocket and retrieving another parchment, he revealed his final surprise.

"You had this the whole time?" Ulfric said wonderingly.

"Yes, since the *Octopod*, when you looked into the Creatress's Scrylle. I'm a firm believer in being prepared, even if you have to do so through craftiness."

Jaemus was working hard, and failing, to appear confident. But Ulfric had no desire to chide the novice Knight. He'd put him in an impossible position in Himmingaze.

Still, it rankled him. *In all my turns as Stallari, never have so many of my Knights been this able, or willing, to bluff and mislead me. Clearly, I've grown too old for this role.* He looked between Jaemus and the Scrylle map and said, "Crafty indeed. I won't bother asking why you never told me you had this." He rested a hand on Jaemus's shoulder. "Do you have any idea what this means?"

"Well, if I understood everything Eisa said, it means I just need to get back to Himmingaze and talk with Griggory—we go way back, you see. I hope he doesn't hold a grudge about me taking the Creatress artifacts in the first place. Then he and I collect the celestial stones and the Creatress's Scrylle again, and finally save the world. It's just another day in the Knights Corporealis, right? I mean, I could be back to bring the rest of the 'Nauts home before Cote even wakes up if things go well."

Ulfric snorted, mildly amused. "For a—what did you call yourself, a Glint Engineer?—for an engineer, you have a deceptively simple way of putting things."

"One of my many gifts."

"So Eisa's going to get you the final piece of the Fenestros, which is being used to keep the cursed Yorish acolyte alive. And you have the other pieces?"

Jaemus patted his tunic's deepest pocket. "Here. And once I get that last chunk, you'll send me back?"

Ulfric nodded. "You have my word." He eyed the engineer for a moment. "Though, I could send you back now if you wished it." Drawing back the edge of his robe, he showed Jaemus the map case.

The engineer, understanding what it contained, looked at it longingly, but only for a moment. With a shrug, he said, "It would hardly do me or any Himmingazian any good if I went without the fifth Fenestros, would it?"

"No, it wouldn't. This is incredible, Jaemus. There is hope for Himmingaze at last, thanks to you. Now back to Eisa—we still don't know what she's planning. Mallich," he called, "get Stave and take this map to find her. Bring her back to the Verity chamber immediately. If she won't come, do what you must. Something is happening at High Halls, something that may affect our safety in Dyrrakium. She knows what it is and must be made to tell us."

Mallich paced over to them. "Ulfric, I've known Eisa almost as long as you have. Whatever decisions she's made, problems she's caused, she's only done them for the right reasons. Everything, except for this…this revenant." He took a deep breath, then went on. "Let her have this last chance to right her most painful wrong. Let her take the Fenestros back and put Lillias to rest. After her long turns of service, her sacrifices, doesn't she deserve that?"

Ulfric couldn't help but catch how Jaemus stared wide-eyed at the Yorman.

"What is it?" Mallich asked.

"It's…well, it's just, I thought you had some kind of speech limiter or something that only allowed you to speak a handful of words at a time. You've just said more than I've heard you say in the whole time I've been here."

Mallich's lips hinted at a smile and he said, characteristically, nothing.

Ulfric thought Mallich's statement over. After he and Eisa had spoken the other night on the *Gildr*, and she'd had the chance to unburden herself of what had happened to the Mystae in Himmingaze, he'd seen an old fire in her eyes for the first time in hundreds of turns. It burned warmly, not coldly and almost cruelly like it had for so long. He realized then that he had overlooked the fight she'd been waging against her own inner dragørs for too long, too mired in his own burdens and battles—and, he admitted, in his own wishes to leave the Knights and be a simple family man.

We are not meant to live this long, he thought, not for the first time.

Was Mallich right? Was this something Eisa needed to do? He considered that light in her eyes more carefully. Unlike some of the Dyrraks he'd met in his long life, even long ago when they'd still been called Lœdyrraks, it wasn't blind zeal that drove Eisa but a depth of willingness and devotion to her oath and her Verity. It was why he trusted her so deeply, why he'd always believed he could rely on her when needed. So much so that he'd been ready to turn over the rank of Stallari to her when he and Vaka Aster eventually parted ways, believing Eisa would finally be ready to wear the mantle. Yet today, now that she was once again playing loose cannon, turning away from the Knights Order and toward her own agenda...he wondered, would she ever be ready? Would she ever be worthy?

"Ulfric?" Mallich urged.

He sighed. Perhaps, if she was finally redeemed from her long exile of the spirit through righting, as Mallich had said, this one last wrong, then she would finally be fit to lead the Knights. Vaka Aster knew he'd had enough of it.

"We'll give her an hour," he finally conceded. "One. After that, we'll need to go get her."

Mallich dipped his head.

"Let's get back to the Verity chamber. Jaemus, you hold on to the map. Come get us before you do anything else, should Eisa fail to meet you. Understood?"

"Of course. Just one last thing."

Ulfric nodded expectantly.

"You're going to send me back, right, once I have the Fenestros shards?"

"As I said."

"That's terrific. But I've been thinking. It's possible, though I hope remotely, that I could be there for a while. I don't know how long, and I don't know how much longer Cote and the 'Nauts can hang on." He swept his hand from one side of the chamber to the other. "But I can't take them with me while they're in this condition..."

"Jaemus," he said, "maybe there is something I can do. Will you allow me to try?"

"I'd let you dip me in smookshark blood and send me naked into a vat full of fleeches if you thought it would help."

Stepping around him, Ulfric dug inside the map case holding the artifacts and pulled out the Fenestros. Laying it on Cote's chest, he whispered the chant he'd used while kneeling over Mylla on the shrine's floor in Himmingaze. She'd been nearly dead from a battle with the flying sea worms of that realm, and he'd known Jaemus had assumed there was no hope for her. Yet she'd risen to fight on, none the worse for wear. Could it work on these Glisternauts?

Moments passed as the Fenestros came alive in his hands, a tiny sun of blue and green and yellow that swirled exactly as his eyes now did. He could feel the ambient energy of the room pouring into the stone, into his hands, into him, then back out through the stone into the sleeping Captain Illago's chest. He'd left his eye shields in the Verity chamber and watched in a kind of numb awe as brilliant light seemed to physically push through the sleeping man's chest, diffusing through his entire body once it seeped into him.

Though the Glisternaut captain didn't move, seemed unaware anything was happening, Ulfric stopped and withdrew the stone. The captain's breathing deepened into the breathing of someone who was soundly, and through welcome providence, peacefully asleep, no rattle or rasp remaining. Jaemus leaned toward him, about to speak, but Ulfric put a hand on his arm.

"Let him rest. He will feel restored—for a time. But I must warn you, it isn't permanent. The invocation I used works well on other Knights because the spark we hold can't be extinguished, only diminished or taken from us by our maker, unless we are outright hacked into pieces. Commoners, even Himmingazian commoners, don't have this. Their own lives, whatever spark sustains them, are finite and will eventually burn out. Do you see? I may have renewed his life temporarily, but it cannot last forever."

"If it buys some time, that's all we need." Jaemus looked back at his heartmatch and took his hand, adding, "What about the others? Can you do this for them too, or does it only work once?"

"I will do what I can."

Ulfric rose and began making his way to each Himmingazian. Within a short time, they all rested or sat at ease with the same peaceful disposition as Illago, better at least for now. Ulfric found himself feeling unaccountably renewed with each person he aided, as if part of the energy he absorbed stayed with him. Or perhaps he was just buoyed by a sense of renewed hope with each person he healed.

When he was finished, Jaemus paced beside him and extended the citadel map from Eisa. "Here, I memorized it while you were busy."

Ulfric glanced at him. "You memorized the entire citadel?"

"Don't act so surprised. I may not be adept at swinging a sword but that doesn't mean I can't swing some intellect. You don't become a Glint Engineer by being—" He cut himself off when he noticed Ulfric's impatient scowl. "Anyway, it's better that you keep it. It'll save some time if I don't have to bring it all the way up here. If, that is, Eisa isn't where she's supposed to be. Which she will be. She seems the reliable sort."

"Reliable," Ulfric said flatly.

"Erm, well, she seems like she'll be reliable for this *particular* thing."

Ulfric glanced to the window. "It'll be High Halls in a couple of hours. You should be getting to your meeting. If Eisa is there, let us know and Mallich and Stave will join you."

CHAPTER THIRTY-TWO

After leaving Jaemus, Eisa wound down a series of staircases, deeper and deeper toward the epicenter beneath the citadel, lower even than the vaults. Soon, the only light illuminating the stairway was from her own Mentalios. Like in Ivoryss, illuminate orbs that drew their light from Halla were spaced throughout the pyramid. But not in the depths. The Speaker had been exiled to a dark place, to fit her dark deeds.

Oil lamps were interspersed in alcoves on the way down, but Eisa didn't bother lighting them. The interior smelled smoky and carried a hint of dampness, despite the dryness of the countryside. She frowned at the confinement. She'd never grow used to the thickness of these walls, the way they closed everything off. She idly wondered if deep down she'd chosen to become an acolyte at the Conservatum in part to escape the citadel, with its many secrets and unspoken-of nooks, where she'd have lived out her life if she'd stayed.

Her steps were slow, as if her feet sensed her reluctance for the task she'd embarked on. Before seeing Lillias on the *Gildr*, she hadn't faced the Speaker in hundreds of turns. *Did Starkas intentionally reveal her without telling me? Was he trying to unbalance me?* It wasn't important. The Ecclesium's days of malice would soon, very soon, be behind him.

She'd made herself believe the woman who'd betrayed her, the woman she'd once loved, had ceased to exist, and the revenant Eisa had turned her into was nothing but a tool, as necessary in facilitating Eisa's distant role in ensuring the Dyrrakium Empire remained safe as ships were to traversing the ocean. Why waste moments considering a tool if the tool was doing its job without causing trouble?

Trouble. That was the word. Ulfric hadn't needed to look inside Eisa's mind through a Mentalios lens to see how troubled she was. How many of her fellow Knights had remarked—some to her face, most not daring—over the turns on how much she'd changed after the Cataclysm?

Eisa?

It was Roi through the Mentalios. She hesitated a moment before answering...but it was *Roi*. A friend and a warrior she'd always respected. As worthy as any Dyrrak to serve Vaka Aster. *I'm here,* she said simply, continuing her descent.

I want you to know, I understand why you did it. I've known you all these turns. We've stood side by side through so much. You're my kin, my sister. And when you've done what you need to do, we'll stand side by side again. As Knights. We will never forsake each other.

She paused on the steps, an uncomfortable tightness in her throat. She could think of nothing to say.

One last thing, sister. I hope you find that releasing one tortured spirit can release another.

Moving again, she said simply, gratefully, *Thank you, Roi. I'll see you after High Halls.*

For the next few steps, she thought it over. Roi was right. Dyrrakium had Vaka Aster now. What purpose could the Speaker serve any longer? Better to release her, for all and for good. *For my own good.*

Finally, the winding stairwell came to an antechamber with a single iron-reinforced door. Eisa studied it for a moment, one hand unconsciously clutching the hilt of her now incomplete dagger, the one she'd kept and had used to carve out Lillias's heart and replace it with stone. She opened the door and went inside the Speaker's chamber.

Unlike in the stairwell, the sconces around the walls of the pentagram-shaped chamber were lit, likely from when the Speaker had been returned here. A hefty, ornamental carved chair sat in the center on a stone platform. Small figurines and statues of various Vinnric animals dotted the platform, a menagerie of Vaka Aster's many creations.

A muted yellow glow illuminated the Speaker. Her tunic bunched around the pearly stone embedded in her chest, giving Eisa an unrestricted view of it. She stared at it, unwilling to lift her eyes to Lillias's face.

That night she'd learned of Lillias's betrayal came back to her. She'd returned to Yor after a short stay in Lœdyrrak. In those days, when the Knights' numbers were much greater, a few fulfilled roles as Keepers of the Fenestrii, which were still dispersed throughout the realm. As a Keeper then, her place was in her homeland, but she went to Yor whenever she could get away, seeking Lillias's arms. Her lover, her muse, her escape from the hardships of life. Lillias wanted nothing from her but affection in return, and Eisa had come to depend on the freedom, the frivolity, that came from such an undemanding love.

And she *had* loved Lillias. Until she'd learned the truth.

Through the interrealm well, she'd arrived in the Fenestros chamber in Umborough, Yor's capital city and home to its royal seat. The chamber itself lay at the heart of the Resplendolent Conservatum grounds in a building that could be barred and guarded effectively from all but the hardiest of outside sieges. In each kingdom, their respective Fenestros halls were the only places under the Knights Corporealis' strict control, a miniature kingdom within a kingdom. And, of course, only the Knights knew the secrets of the interrealm wells that connected to Mount Omina, allowing them to escape, unfollowed, with their protected Fenestrii should it become necessary.

Roibeard along with Allanach, another Yorish Knight who'd served the Order at that time, and Griggory, had the hall barred when she arrived, and the noise of upheaval and chaos seeped through the walls as if the entire population of the city was running rampant. Ambassador Sœrnec of Lœdyrrak and most of his entourage were with them. Wasting no words, Roibeard explained what she'd arrived to: the Arch

Keeper Connaugh had been slain. Word had spread that the murderers were Ambassador Sœrnec and the Lœdyrrak emissaries.

The news at first shocked her, but that had quickly turned to anger. "That's all lies," she had scoffed. "What point or purpose would there be in Sœrnec, or the Domine Ecclesium of Dyrrakium for that matter, having Yor's ruler assassinated? The Dyrrak want nothing from this kingdom, aside from trade and assurances of peaceful borders. Connaugh supported both those ends."

"There's more," Roi said and gestured to Sœrnec.

The ambassador, an elderly man whose black and red Phase brands had already faded to nearly the same color as his skin, approached her, holding out a sheaf of letters. Their wax seals were broken. "You need to read these, Knight Nazaria."

Coldness began to creep up from her stomach into her chest then. There was something else happening besides a ruler being killed, and she sensed danger, a cutthroat hiding in the dark. She pushed back at the feeling, and at her companions. "Later. I must see to Lillias and ensure she is safe."

"Eisa," Roi interrupted, taking the pages from Sœrnec and nearly shoving them into her hand. "You need to see these first. They contain information that will…will be difficult for you to hear."

She hadn't wanted to take the pages, but Roi was Roi. Always serious, grave even at times, and more grave at that moment than she'd ever seen him. If he thought she needed to be made aware of something in those letters, it wouldn't be wise to dismiss them.

And it was all there, half in Lillias's own well-known handwriting—how many letters of love and devotion has she received from the Yorwoman?—details of a plot by Lillias and her coconspirators to overthrow the Arch Keeper of Yor and an intent to blame the visiting Lœdyrrak ambassador as a traitorous spy who'd orchestrated it all.

They had gotten one thing right: Sœrnec was more than adept at spycraft. He'd uncovered the plot while attending events at the Conservatum the day prior. A hushed conversation between Acolyte Lillias Grannd, already expected to be the next Arch Keeper, and an unnamed other had set his well-honed perceptions, one could even say paranoia, alight. From a hidden alcove, he'd listened to them and seen letters exchange hands. A good ambassador knew the sounds of a conspiracy when he heard one, and a Lœdyrrak ambassador was trained in more than diplomacy. That night, Sœrnec paid a local asset to visit the residences of Lillias and the man he'd seen her speaking with and steal any correspondence the asset could find. Their contents had confirmed his suspicions, but it had been too late to matter. Connaugh was assassinated the following morning before he left his bedchamber. Perhaps the discovery of the missing letters had prompted the conspirators to action. Regardless, the Lœdyrraks were now on the run and the Arch Keeper was dead.

The letters contained enough hints and details of the coup and their reasons for Eisa to piece things together. With a new leader and a cabinet of advisors handpicked by the conspirators, and the Lœdyrrak exposed as traitorous and wicked enough to attack another country's leadership, the Yorish usurpers would then petition Ivoryss to relocate Vaka Aster's vessel in Yor where the maker's protection was most needed.

Of course, Eisa had thought when reading this. Lillias had suggested dozens of times that Yor should be the celestial vessel's residence, had implored her to ask Ulfric to see it done, but Eisa had never granted that wish.

Lillias and her coconspirators craved the power and prestige that Ivoryss now exerted through virtue of being the location of Vaka Aster's vessel. Any Knight would say that power and prestige were merely perceived, not tangible—Vaka Aster's will was not something any person or kingdom could prevail upon, no matter where the Verity was.

But commoners were too short-sighted and simple to know that. And with villainous Lœdyrrak closer to Ivoryss than it was to Yor, thus an immediate threat to both Ivoryss and Vaka Aster's security, it would only make sense to move the vessel farther from their reach. Even if the conspirators' lies touched off a war with Lœdyrrak, if Vaka Aster were in Yor, they assumed the advantage would go to them. Perhaps, the letters went on, even enough advantage to invade Lœdyrrak and take without compensation what they would lose in trade with the dishonored empire.

For what felt like an eternity, Eisa consumed the letters, over a dozen of them, each word stoking a wrath in her that steadily grew too hot to contain. The last outlined Lillias's own ambitions. As one of the highest-achieving and most respected acolytes of the Yor Conservatum—the very same qualities that had drawn Eisa to her—she intended to take the throne of the Arch Keeper herself. What role she had envisioned Eisa would serve in her schemes was equally clear. She'd use her as a pawn in the match against both the Knights and the Dyrraks, manipulating Eisa to persuade both to do Lillias's bidding.

She had assumed Eisa was totally devoted to her and would be easily led along her string of deception. No one in the history of Vinnr had ever so badly miscalculated Eisa's loyalties.

Eisa had laid the last letter on a table, using every ounce of her will to hold back the trembling she felt pulsing under her skin, to hold in the scream that threatened to choke her. She went silent as the three other Knights planned what to do. With the capital of Yor in full riot, which was likely to spread, and no legitimate Arch Keeper on the throne, the Knights quickly decided the Yor Fenestros should be moved to a safer place. Allanach had taken it through the interrealm well to Mount Omina and from there to Ivoryss to warn Ulfric and the rest of the Order of the Yorish treason.

"No one knows Sœrnec and the Lœdyrraks are with us," Roi had told her. "You must return to Elezaran and brief the empire. Take the letters. They can be used to prove it has had no hand in this deed. When the havoc dies down enough, Griggory and I will secure the Lœdyrrak entourage anonymous and safe transport back."

She considered his suggestion. Eisa had known pain in her life. No child of Lœdyrrak, and particularly not a child of the Sixth Line, grew up without experiencing the hardships and depravations of moving through the five Phases that made one worthy. But the pain she now suffered at Lillias's betrayal cut into her heart in ways nothing ever had. Not even close. She felt sick, poisoned from within, and recognized she had brought it on herself. She'd regressed on the Third Phase and grown attached to another person, a commoner no less, instead of her maker. It was a mistake she vowed to herself to rectify before Halla rose again.

"I will return after I see to her," she had rasped, and Roi and Griggory did not need to ask who.

They couldn't stop her. Perhaps they didn't try because they pitied her. As her fellow Knights, they went with her, leaving the Lœdyrraks safely hidden and barred in the Fenestros hall.

They'd found Lillias with a collection of the conspirators in a secret room of an inn built along the city wall, an establishment Eisa had frequented with the Yorish traitor. Eisa hadn't known about the room or the hidden passage that led to it, but she'd used her powers of persuasion, mainly the threat of shoving a burning candlestick into the innkeeper's eye, to wrench Lillias's location from him.

With the innkeeper bound and gagged to prevent him from warning the blaggards, she lit the passageway with her Mentalios, Roi and Griggory following soundlessly. On reaching a wooden door, she listened with held breath. Muffled voices, one of which she knew too well, came through it. Without consulting the other Knights, Eisa palmed her klinkí stones, kicked the door open, and rushed into the room. There wasn't time to blink before six men and two woman—Eisa recognized most as other acolytes—were dead. Only one remained alive. Lillias.

Wrapping the woman in a net of klinkí stones smeared with gore, Eisa croaked the only word that remained to her in her rage: "Betrayer."

Lillias blinked, then managed a sneer, the look of a woman who knew her fate was sealed and felt no shame in the reasons for it. "I am the betrayer? Hah. People of Lœdyrrak, your homeland, attacked my Arch Keeper, killed him. And you, obviously part of the scheme, killed acolytes of the Conservatum! Who is the betrayer here, Eisa?"

"Slag your lies, Lillias! I've read your letters. Every word you just said is false." She flashed back on the last dozen thirty-nights she'd spent with Lillias, all the gentle compliments she'd given Eisa, her sweet speeches and flattery. Had any of it been real? "Every word," she repeated.

"Are they? The evidence is everywhere. The Lœdyrrak ambassador's own knife is in Connaugh's belly, and witnesses heard the fight." She paused, staring at Eisa coldly, then seemed to realize she'd be unable to lie her way out of Eisa's fury. "You may have killed everyone here, Eisa, but did you think it was just us? We've been trying for so long to get you and your Order to make Yor the seat of Vaka Aster's reign. If you'd listened to us, to me, this could have been avoided. Yor doesn't bow to you, Eisa, your Order, or to any kingdom. Yor has stood aside too long while Ivoryss pretends it's Vaka Aster's chosen, holding the vessel hostage like some kind of prize. And you Lœdyrraks, ha! Pretending your devotion is pure. Zealots! If Vaka Aster favors the Lœdyrraks so much, why has she never stepped foot in your lands?"

Eisa had never felt such a lust for someone's blood. She had every reason she needed to kill the woman, the blasphemer who didn't even know that Vaka Aster's vessel was Eisa's own ancestor. She loosened the cage of klinkí stones enough for Lillias to pass through, inviting the woman to attack her. Wanting to make her suffer when she did.

Lillias stayed in place, and her expression softened. "Perhaps, it isn't too late, my love," she said, her voice no longer shrill but low and pleading. "Connaugh was a spineless, unambitious leader and unwilling to demand…"

Eisa wasn't listening to her, the pounding blood wrath in her ears drowning everything out. Then Roi spoke to her through the Mentalios, breaking through the beating pulse.

We need her alive, Eisa. The letters will prove Dyrrakium's innocence, and justice will be served, but keeping her alive will help ensure it. The Yorish court will need her to identify the other conspirators, as well.

Lillias was still speaking, the plea in her tone sounding nearly genuine. "And with Vaka Aster's sanctuary here, the Knights must relocate to Yor as well. Their longevity and strength can benefit Yor, too. If you persuade them to come, it will be enough to show where your fealty truly lies."

"Truly," Eisa said, "lies are all you're capable of, Lillias. The Knights' fealty is not a bargaining chip for fickle commoners to play with. Our duty is not to weak-minded chookters like you without loyalty or faith." She flicked her wrist and pulled back her stones, then said over her shoulder to Roibeard and Griggory, who stood in the doorway, "Wait outside."

"Eisa, what—" Griggory started.

"Wait outside," she said again, louder, her eyes holding Lillias's.

They went. When the door thunked shut against the jamb, Eisa pocketed her klinkí stones, all but one. She dropped her gaze to it and whispered an incantation. As she did, she felt the pull from within her, a wave of her celestial spark being sucked into the stone she held. It began to glow stronger, Halla bright, and Eisa's legs grew shaky.

Lillias backed away from her until her thighs smacked against the table in the center of the room. "What are you going to do to—"

Before the question ended, Eisa flung the stone, shooting-star fast, toward Lillias's chest, hitting her dead center in her heart. Lillias made a guttural noise and fell backward onto the tabletop, her hands coming up to grab her chest. Eisa stepped up to her, feeling nothing, her entire body a numb thing. The wound wasn't bleeding, and the stone remained luminous. It would hold that bit of spark, bit of Eisa, forever, or until Eisa drew it back. It wasn't until after the carnage she wrought in Himmingaze that she'd replaced the klinkí stone with the Fenestros shard and given the revenant she'd made of Lillias in service to Lœdyrrak.

"I know you wanted your name spoken in the halls of eternity as a ruler of Yor, commoner, but I'm going to give you something better. I'm going to make *you* eternal. You will not die while my stone remains in your breast, tethering your spirit to this unworthy body." Her mouth was drier than the deserts of Lœdyrrak as she looked down into her former lover's terrified, agonized face and watched her try to speak. She put her hand over Lillias's mouth. "No, you've said and done enough. From here forward, the only words you say will be mine. I'm going to teach you what even the Conservatum failed to. I'm going to teach you what it means to be worthy."

A sound came from outside, the rattle of metal and rustle of cloth. Roibeard and Griggory would come to check on her in moments. She didn't want them to see this. When Lillias choked and her eyes glazed over, Eisa stepped into the passageway, swinging the door shut behind her. She'd come back for Lillias's body later, alone.

"Eisa?" Roi said.

Repeating his words, Eisa assured them, "She's no more threat to us."

At that moment, she'd decided: Lœdyrrak was the only nation who truly put Vaka Aster before their own greed and selfish interests. She'd persuade them to cut themselves off permanently from these lesser kingdoms. And when she could, she'd take Lillias's undead body back there, enshrined in the dankness below the citadel forever to remind Eisa, and remind Lœdyrrak, what frailty they had escaped from. To remind them never to let themselves fall as low.

Blinking away the memory, Eisa finally looked into the shining eyes of the one she'd made the Speaker. There was no life behind them, but they gleamed as if there were. "You poor, common girl," Eisa said. "Your worst crime was to believe that true power came from rule instead of devotion and faith in our maker. But I see now it wasn't your fault. You didn't have a chance. Perhaps if you'd seen Vaka Aster in those days, in her radiance, you could have been saved."

She brushed the back of her hand against the Yorwoman's cheek, marveling as she used to at the way the rich red-brown of her darker skin contrasted with the pale Yorish coloring. She'd loved how Lillias's freckles matched her own hue, and how the white skin of Eisa's many battle scars was the same as Lillias's skin coloring, the way lind tree fruit was the same color as the petals of a dalla flower. She'd imagined they were two parts of one whole, a union like Halla and its moon, or a hero and her enemy.

But now, looking at Lillias, Eisa saw she was not her enemy and hadn't been in centuries. The broken woman was as empty and spent as Vaka Aster's abandoned vessel. Which meant Eisa was, as she'd always been, whole on her own, not contingent on being one part of a union. A Knight didn't have that luxury, and it was time to let that fantasy die with Lillias.

She backed a step away and raised a hand as if to pick a kórb from a branch. In a low voice, she called her klinkí stones from her bandolier and sent them forward. They attached to the Fenestros shard like magnets. With a gentle pull, she willed them back to her.

Lillias's body was jerked to its feet and staggered toward her, the stone so embedded it wouldn't break free. The revenant pitched into Eisa, who wrapped her free arm around Lillias's waist to hold her up. Her raised hand was pressed between them, directly over Lillias's missing heart. She could feel the heat of the Fenestros. Lillias's head fell into her shoulder, and Eisa's breath caught short at the scent of her hair. It was the same as it had been so long ago, a scent as fresh as Halla-warmed honey and cherries. A scent that was so lovely she'd dreamed of it ever since.

With eyes that burned with unshed tears, Eisa whispered into Lillias's curls, "I'm so sorry, my love. You can be free now. I'm so sorry."

Then, without warning, the Fenestros shard let go and fell into Eisa's grasp. Lillias's body collapsed against her, the residual life inside that had once animated her gone to forever death.

Eisa let her klinkí stones clatter to the ground but held the Fenestros shard. Gently, she draped Lillias over the chair, feeling suddenly brittle, as if the strike of a feather would shatter her.

Just a moment, she thought. *I'll just rest for a moment. My duty can wait for a singular suffering moment.*

She laid the shard in Lillias's palm and placed it upside down on her lap, then pressed her back up against the wall opposite the dead Speaker's chair and slid down until she was sitting on the floor. Her eyes closed, burning behind the lids with tears she would never be able to shed.

CHAPTER THIRTY-THREE

Ulfric took one last look at the Himmingazians resting peacefully before nodding to Mallich and leaving for his chamber once more. None stirred in discomfort or unrest. They were, at least for now, out of the woods.

And he was, at least for now, comforted. If through the wystic gifts of Knighthood he could share some of the spark in him to salve their illness, Symvalline could too. Crumb would be safe for a while. If, indeed, there was safety to be found in Arc Rheunos.

He glanced outside, noting Halla's slow climb to midday. Opening the starpath well would draw the attention of the Dyrrak people when Jaemus was ready to go, but the Knights would reassure them. They could inform the people of Dyrrakium before sending Jaemus home, which inadvertently showed him that there was some freedom in being thought of as a Verity. Everything he or the Knights did would be accepted without question or confrontation.

His frustration with Eisa notwithstanding, it wouldn't be long now before he sent Safran and Stave to Arc Rheunos. To do what he could not do. He had no doubts in his fellow Knights. Stave, for all his bluster, had an uncanny combat astuteness and indomitability that could defeat an army. And Safran, thorough, clearheaded, and precise, had been an unexpected boon to the Knights when she'd joined as well. And both had an unwavering devotion to duty. No two Knights were better suited to travel into an unknown realm together than Safran and Stave, and if there was any chance at all Symvalline and Isemay were still within hope of aid, they would see it done.

He and Mallich reached his chamber, where the lone guard remained at his post. Forgetting himself, Ulfric nodded to acknowledge the guard as he would have done any attendant. Then he realized the folly in that. Would a Verity show such familiarity, even a sense of companionship to one of its creations?

The guard blinked once, then knelt with his head bowed. "Great Creator."

"Venerate," he said, "have refreshments brought, whatever you think will please the Knights. And also a pitcher of that Dyrrakium liquor." Ulfric couldn't remember its name, but he couldn't very well admit this to the guard. Despite, or perhaps because of, how his current predicament enhanced his senses, he found the traditional Dyrrak beverage delicious.

"Syke liquor, Great Creator?"

"Yes."

"It is done, Great Creator."

The venerate remained kneeling until Ulfric began to pass into his chamber. He was not going to get used to that. He turned back, "And, Venerate, kneeling is unnecessary from here forward." He and Mallich passed through the doorway before the guard had a chance to respond.

Safran stood at the window, looking out over the city.

"Safran," Ulfric said, "has Stave said anything?"

She spun around, and her eyes were alight with many hues. *Not yet. But the bruhawks have shown me something curious.*

"What did they see?"

It seems the entire city is amassing at the citadel. There are thousands coming here for some reason.

Mallich ventured, "Do you think it's to see Vaka Aster?"

It could be. Perhaps the Ecclesium has planned another event. Has he said anything to you, Ulfric?

He shook his head, troubled. If worse came to worst, the interrealm well away from Dyrrakium was in the citadel—though he'd let slip his mind the need to locate it. They could escape back to Mount Omina if needed. Or use Vaka Aster's Scrylle to travel the starpaths. But he was so sick of running.

They were interrupted by the sound of a metal knocker on the wood of the chamber's door. "It's me," Stave yelled.

Mallich unbolted the door, and Stave hurried in, already speaking. "Believe you me, you may think you've heard everything our deranged Dyrrak companion is capable of, but I have something new for you that'll test even the hardiest imagination, it will."

"What is it, Stave?" Ulfric said, intrigued.

"She's challenged that Ecclesium fanatic to a takeover, a power play. Eisa plans to rule Dyrrakium."

No words existed in any tongue Ulfric had ever heard to express his shock. Finally, he found his voice. "Why in all the worlds...where did you hear this from?"

"Chancellor Aoggvír. She seems a mite distressed by the whole thing, but she's been running around since last night, apparently, getting arrangements made. They have a ceremonial fight—except I don't think it's a pretty tip-tap, pit-pat, on-your-way kind of fight. I think it's to the death. The Concubineum Ecclesium or some such."

Conquestum Ecclesium, Safran put in. *You never paid much attention to the studies of cultures at the Conservatum, love.* She looked to Ulfric, her eyes clearing to their natural dark as she dismissed the bruhawk link. *This is...unprecedented. But it could likewise be advantageous.*

"Not if she loses, it won't be," Stave mused.

"But that's impossible," Ulfric said. "The Ecclesium must know she is a hundred times stronger and more resilient than him. Her Verity spark will make her unstoppable. Why would he agree to this?"

"Way I heard it, there wasn't a choice. If the challenge is made, it has to be faced. Even if he simply stepped down and let her take the throne, he'd lose everything, become a servant to the Dyrraks instead of a member of the citizenry. It's about honor, or what the Dyrraks think honor is." Stave leaned toward Safran as he finished. "I paid attention the day they taught *that*. And that Ecclesium doesn't strike me as the type who'd shirk a fight, he doesn't," he finished, addressing them all.

Another knock sounded. "It's the venerate bringing drinks," Ulfric said.

Stave paced to the door and pulled aside the cover of a small peering portal. He turned back.

"The Ecclesium."

"Alone?" Ulfric asked.

Stave nodded and Ulfric took a moment to compose himself. "Knights, as much as I wish it were not so, we can't have anyone leaving for Arc Rheunos until this matter with Eisa is settled."

They nodded, but their faces showed they were as much troubled about the decision as him.

He looked toward the raised platform on which the Verity's throne sat but decided against taking it. He didn't want to look down on people he was speaking with. Playing this role had already grown tiresome. He put his back to the platform and gestured for Stave to open the door.

The tall head Dyrrak paced toward Ulfric, showing unceasing deference by keeping his head bowed, never making eye contact. The three Knights arrayed themselves around Ulfric in a protective circle, and the Ecclesium stopped a few paces short. He carried a tray of assorted fruits, a pitcher, and several ceramic mugs, which he laid on a nearby table.

Turning toward Ulfric, he said, "Great Creator, it is my hope you've found this humble hall satisfactory. I've come to inquire if there is anything else your servants can do to fulfill your expectations. I have many services and celebrations planned—"

"No," Ulfric cut in. "I have no wish for those." He cringed inwardly at the idea of being treated as anyone's spectacle of worship.

The Ecclesium remained awkwardly silent for a few moments, then said, "Surely the Vigil Star wishes to shine for his most faithful people."

"They have seen me, Ecclesium. They know I am here." He had to think about what to say. "The people of Dyrrakium will ever have my blessing for keeping their faith as strong as they have, even through an unjust exile that you did not seek." He plunged forward with the subject on all their minds. "But I've heard what's to come this afternoon at High Halls."

The Dyrrak nodded but said nothing.

Ulfric found his manner unreadable, inscrutable. What kind of game could the Dyrrak leader be playing? Was he so accepting of whatever fate was about to befall him because he believed it was Vaka Aster's will? Ulfric needed to understand what pushed the man, but Verities were not known to be so inquisitive of their creations.

He decided to try a sideways tact. "Have you any requests to make of me, Ecclesium?"

"What request could I make, Great Creator, when you have given us so much?" The Ecclesium's voice was as steady as a boulder as he continued. "The Empire of Dyrrakium is truly a flourishing land, as our antiquated name Lœdyrrak means. It has remained so since we cut ties to the other Vinnric kingdoms, as compelled by the Nazarian Most High. They diluted and tarnished our faith with petty allegiances to petty ideas. We are purer in our faith and devotion than ever, thanks to the wisdom of the heir of the Sixth Line. Should Vaka Aster will that she be the next ruler here in Dyrrakium, I would not think to question it."

Ulfric had used up the last of his patience for varnished diplomacy at Aster Keep and was about to revert to ill-advised bluntness. Safran, to his relief, took up the thread of conversation first. Holding one of Vaka Aster's Fenestrii in her hand, she channeled her voice through it. "It is a curious thing, is it not, that Knight Nazaria would push Dyrrakium away from the rest of Vinnr in a bid to retain the empire's purity—but advise the empire to accept blame for crimes against Yor that it didn't commit?"

The Dyrrak glanced to her, then his keen eyes did a sweep of the rest of the chamber, landing only briefly on the two bruhawks, who had alighted on either side of the throne at the top of the dais. His features quickly smoothed as he said, "The rest of Dyrrak cares nothing about the accusations of disloyalty and lack of honor made against us. Does a wolf care about the accusations of a mouse? Why would a great empire bother with the sentiments of lessers?"

"That why she challenged you for rule of Dyrrakium, is it? Didn't want to see it in the hands of a lesser anymore?" Stave growled, the Dyrrak's smug judgment of who was greater and who was lesser clearly getting under his skin.

Not rising to the bait, the Ecclesium said flatly, "You would have to take up the Nazarian's reasons with her."

"You can stake your prettied-up skin on it that I will."

"What Knight Thorvíl's concerns are, I believe," Safran cut in, "is that Knight Nazaria acted without conferring with the rest of us. Do—"

She caught herself, and sent through the Mentalios, *I'm sorry, Ulfric. I was about to ask him if he knew where Eisa was. He would wonder why I hadn't asked Vaka Aster.*

We've learned her whereabouts. I'll fill you in momentarily, he sent as he watched the Ecclesium's face closely, seeing no sign his suspicions had been aroused. They couldn't afford the Dyrraks to have even the slightest hint of Ulfric's actions toward Vaka Aster. The Domine Ecclesium struck him as a man who would not react to something he considered "lesser" than himself with mercy or understanding.

Safran picked up her thread. "Do you, a man of such deep devotion to our creator, agree with Eisa's decisions?"

Where are you going with this line of questioning, Safran? Ulfric sent.

We need to know who we can rely on, she returned. *Should Eisa fail to best him and the Ecclesium is elevated above her, a Knight, we need assurance that he and the Dyrraks who follow him will side with us.*

But there is simply no way she would lose.

Safran's stare remained leveled on the Ecclesium, but Ulfric could sense her doubt—he felt it too. The Ecclesium seemed too assured, too calm in the face of what could well be his looming death.

The Ecclesium stared back at Safran. In fact, he'd been appraising her with a hint of something beyond respectful attention since she began speaking, and Stave had clearly noticed.

"Your eyelids broken, Dyrrak?" he said. "If you need a good wallop to fix them, I can help you there, I can."

Bottle that, Ulfric ordered. *We cannot afford to start hostilities here.*

Stave's jaw shut with a click. The Ecclesium carefully contained a smirk, then bowed his head toward Ulfric again. "I will, of course, follow the commands of our maker to the end of all ends."

He'd sidestepped Safran's question, but she was not finished with the man. She paced closer to him, then circled him slowly. She was Ivoryssian but shorter than most. Her eyes fell level with the Dyrrak's chin, and she would have had to stretch to reach her arms around his barrel chest. Yet as a warrior her combat skills were formidable. Ulfric wondered if the Dyrrak would underestimate her.

"And what of that thing she created of that Yor woman, Ecclesium? Is a revenant not an affront, an abomination, to the life Vaka Aster has gifted the people of Vinnr?"

The Ecclesium waited for Safran to come around to his front before glaring at her in a manner that reminded Ulfric too much of Arch Keeper Beatte, the contempt rulers bestowed on those they deemed lower. "As her companions, I would have thought you'd know her mind and actions. What's curious to me is that she would not trust you with knowledge of the Speaker. The once-Yor woman has been a great gift to Dyrrakium and our safety."

Ulfric felt the tides of this line of questioning turning and didn't like their direction. *Safran, let's adjourn this here. He'll never answer you directly. It seems he's been a politician as long as you were.*

And like a politician, we cannot trust him, she responded.

Slag trusting him. I'm nearly ready to do to him what Eisa has in mind, I am, Stave said. *It could be that I like him even less than I ever liked her.*

You don't have to like him to maintain him as an ally, Mallich replied. *So think before speaking next time.*

It took much to rile Mallich. The strain of every moment since the events that had happened at Mount Omina was beginning to show, and something about the Ecclesium's behavior was increasing the strain, for them all. Would it be best to let Eisa challenge him? Or should they put a stop to it? Ulfric needed time to think. The rays of

Halla shining through the window reminded him he barely had any left. The Ecclesium needed to go. Now.

"Was there anything else, Domine Ecclesium?" he asked in the clipped phrasing he'd adapted as his Vaka Aster voice.

"You must know," the Dyrrak said, as if it were obvious. "My thoughts are open to you."

Ulfric put a bite behind his words. "Assert yourself, Ecclesium, like a faithful Dyrrak. And speak plainly."

"I am sorry if I have displeased you, My Creator." Moving unhurriedly toward the window, he said, "Perhaps a victory over your enemies will refresh your favor?" and swept his hand toward the fields to the south.

"Do you mean an invasion?" Ulfric asked, keeping his voice neutral. "I've already told you I do not wish for war among the Vinnrics."

"Keeping and spreading faith in the sanctity of the Verities will ever be our only purpose, Great Creator. That is what the Dyrrak people mean by dominion, and we will remain prepared to protect *our* dominion from those who threaten it, always." He tweaked the word "our" with such subtle emphasis that Ulfric wasn't sure he'd heard it. The Ecclesium's voice, smooth with pride and purpose, grew louder. "The force outside Citadel Suprima is the largest ever assembled in the history of Vinnr and at the ready of the right commander."

He turned to leave, his long strides covering the floor of the chamber quickly. From the doorway, he spun back and added, "And as we know, faith always spreads faster by force."

"And what of allegiance?" Ulfric said.

For the first time since the Dyrrak had arrived at Vigil Tower, he looked Ulfric in the eyes. "That too, Creator." With a final glance at the Knights, he said, "Enjoy your refreshments. And may Dyrrakium's worthiest enjoy a Verity's blessing at the Conquestum Ecclesium."

CHAPTER THIRTY-FOUR

Eisa knew she was dreaming by the way Halla's light gleamed over her full head of glossy black hair, even the sides, which she'd let grow out of the customary Dyrrak style after being in the Knights for some time.

She also knew she was dreaming because she was smiling. The innocent, happy grin of a woman experiencing life in the moment, without suffering, without regrets.

Eisa had not been that woman for seven hundred and fifteen turns.

Lillias, her own curls like an inferno trailing down her back, danced toward her barefooted on the shore of a secluded lake in the forest spanning from Yor to Ivoryss. The Great Lochanian Forest met the Howling Weald somewhere on the other side of the Morn Mountains, the two forests really just one. Eisa had felt that way too. Lillias and she, just one spirit shared between two bodies.

"Look at it, Eisa, it's beautiful!"

Lillias held up her hand. On it perched a dragørfly as big as her thumb, displaying the nine false warm-pink eyes, four right, five left, that adorned its wings. Glossy blue and yellow horns sprouted from its head and swept back along its thorax, and Eisa's semiconscious mind realized it resembled a much less threatening version of the Himmingazian slangarook Griggory had ridden.

"Gorgeous, darling, like you," she said. "Careful not to touch its wings. They are very fragile."

Lillias gave her a peck on the cheek and giggled quietly. "Softy," she said, then swirled in a circle and danced toward the waterline, sending the dragørfly aloft.

Eisa looked into the distance, something drawing her gaze there. Something…that felt wrong. "Come back, Lillias. Don't get too near it."

Her lover turned and gave her a queer look, smirking with lips she'd painted as pink as the dragørfly's wing spots, and Eisa momentarily wondered if it was a color Vaka Aster splashed all her most beautiful creatures with.

Lillias asked, "Near what? The water?"

She said something else, but Eisa wasn't paying attention. That feeling was growing, dread creeping through her and swelling like a bubble that would burst and flatten everything it spattered. Her eyes swallowed the horizon, but she could see nothing. Halla twinkling off distant leaves, a shimmer of rainbow where an afternoon rain shower fell. That was all. Where was this feeling coming from?

"Eisa?" Lillias said, facing her now. "What is it? What—" She stopped, and her head tilted backward. Her mouth opened wide as if to scream. Then, abruptly, she did, shrieking with a force that seemed as if it could split the heavens.

Eisa tried to run to her, but she was rooted, unable to make her feet move. The cry continued, getting louder, impossibly loud. So full of fear and hideous hate that Eisa trembled.

She jerked in her dream, waking herself up, and her eyes shot open.

Disoriented, at first she didn't know if she was still asleep. The room was darker now, some of the oil lamps having burned themselves nearly empty. Shuddering, she stayed put for a moment, trying to forget the dream and the ache it conjured. As well as the fear that seeped over her goosebumped flesh because of it.

Movement in the near corner drew her gaze. A man. The Ecclesium was here, too.

Eisa shot to her feet. "What are you doing here? It's not yet High Halls." She wasn't sure if this was true but decided she didn't care at the moment. She was not accustomed to being snuck up on, and her dream's dark tendrils were still writhing beneath her skin.

In the dim light, his eyes caught the lamps and glittered like roaches. He stepped toward Lillias, then faced Eisa fully. His bare arms, knotted with muscle, and the open chest of his tunic showed that none of his physical strength had diminished in his middle age. But Eisa felt no concern. She could best him—was looking forward to it—even if she had to do it weaponless and with the use of only one hand. One didn't live to her advanced age and not know every possible way a fight could go, every move an opponent might make.

Finally, he spoke. "I'm here to offer you this chance, one chance, Nazarian, to join me instead of fight me."

She snorted. "Never took you for a coward, Starkas."

In one of the few times she'd witnessed, his expression morphed from a flat, all-powerful, unquestionable gaze to a rictus of pure fury. No longer checking his substantial baritone, he raged, "You knew it, didn't you? Knew and did nothing. Vaka Aster first abandoned us, Eisa, then let herself be shackled by her own creation, her own servant! And you remained loyal? To both your desecrator of a Stallari and to the creator who mocks us with her frailty? Do not dare question *my* courage. I have just seen for myself that it's true. Ulfric Aldinhuus is a faithless, broken vessel and a liar."

So—somehow he knew. Eisa felt herself grow numb, her mind stepping away from her body to observe and control what came next. "What do you want, Starkas?"

Taking a moment to rein in his fervor, he reached a hand toward Lillias's body and ran his fingers along the hem of her robe. Eisa had to force herself not to rush to him and yank it away. "What I want is for the people of greatest allegiance and devotion to the Verity we've served without question or benefit to finally have what is owed us."

"Blasphemer," she spat. "Where is your faith? None of us is owed anything by our maker."

His voice lowered in mock placation. "My faith hasn't gone

anywhere. My faith is in the rule and order of the most powerful beings in all the Cosmos. The makers, those who both create *and* abide their own creations. Those who give us our will—and who share it."

"And who is it you think shares your will?" But she knew, didn't she? The way Starkas had avoided her question about the prisoner in the vaults when she'd met with him yesterday—was that prisoner a Ravener? And if a Ravener had escaped Battgjald before it ceased to be, he or she must still live. They could still serve as a corporeal vessel for Balavad to walk in. And Balavad knew what had happened to Vaka Aster and Ulfric, had probably filled Starkas's mind with the truth and hints of reward for helping Balavad fulfill his original purpose. Now, the usurper had control of the Domine Ecclesium—and Dyrrakium's army.

She let her tone simmer with the same fury as his. "You speak as if you've sold your faith like a lowly commoner. What did you get for it? A pat on the head? The promise of becoming a puppet ruler in *his* realm?" She lowered her own voice to mock him back. "Did Balavad not tell you? Battgjald is as much dust as memory. There is no Battgjald anymore. Vaka Aster destroyed it. As she will destroy you, if I leave anything for her to. What good is your faith now?"

Disquietingly, he didn't so much as blink at her taunting. "Why," he asked, "would I want a kingdom in Battgjald when I have two more besides Dyrrakium in Vinnr to command? Before the War of Rivening, Vinnr was unified. Why can't it be again?

"Now, Nazarian, because you are my kin and you are, or were, a loyal Dyrrak, you have a choice. Will you take your place with me in leading this world to the faith it has forsaken and give fealty to a Verity who won't *forsake us*, or will you be like Vaka Aster and turn your back on *your own people*?"

He was here somewhere, the usurper, in the citadel. She had to warn the others. Channeling with a fervency she hadn't felt since she'd been a novice, she tried to reach out to the Knights—but something was wrong. She glanced down. Her Mentalios was gone. For the first time, she felt the worm of fear wiggle at the base of her skull. Without her wystic lens, she could not summon her klinkí stones. How could the fallen Ecclesium have been that stealthy? No one had ever been able to take such advantage of her while she slept before.

That left only one option, then. The fastest way to get to others was often *through* whoever was trying to stop you. She reached for her dagger, but it too had been stripped from her. It didn't matter. She had all she needed with her fists and feet.

"I think, Ecclesium," she said, "your days of ruling have come to their end sooner than you expected," and charged him.

CHAPTER THIRTY-FIVE

"I'll see you soon, my love, I promise," Jaemus told Cote.

The Himmingazian captain was sitting up on his pallet, his complexion smoother and healthier than it had been at any point while in Vinnr. Around them, the other Glisternauts spoke and laughed with each other for the first time without inhibition or illness since reaching this realm. If any balm could soothe more than seeing your friends back in the pink of health after fearing for days you'd lose every one of them, Jaemus didn't care. This sight alone was enough. Except for this one last seemingly insurmountable obstacle he was about to face...

Cote took Jaemus's hands. "You look so worried, Jae. But you don't need to. We've gone over this already. If you're not back in three days, we'll simply have the leader of the Knights send us after you. This healing sorcery of his is, well, I've never felt better."

"Then come with me," Jae said. He was stalling, and he was scared. The only thing he wasn't sure of was whether he was more afraid of leaving his friends here in this radically unpredictable place or of taking them back to a home that was slowly disintegrating, and which he had no assurance he could fix.

"You don't need to be watching over thirty-odd Glisternauts while you're trying to fulfill your *destiny*." Cote smiled like a rake, and it plus the way he so clearly enjoyed taunting Jaemus reassured him that his lifemate was back to normal more than anything else could.

Cote had always found Jaemus's vain certainty that he would be the one to lift Himmingazian from its woes a bit too high-blown. And for the first time in Jaemus's life, he was equally lacking in confidence in himself. But Cote followed up his jaunty grin with a serious look. "You're the one who can do this, Jae. Only you. I believe in you."

Jaemus leaned in and hugged him with his whole body. They remained that way for several moments, then Cote gently extracted himself. "It's about time to find your new captain. Or Stallari is the term, I suppose. I'm sure I'll always be your only captain."

Jaemus stood. "You know that's a fact." Taking a deep breath, hoping to absorb whatever it was that gave the Dyrraks such boldness, he said, "Okay. Three days, then you have Ulfric work his starpath magic if I'm still not back. Oh, and did I forget to tell you? I love you, Captain Illago." With courage he definitely did not feel, he finished, "Time to slip into a world less comfortable."

The door to the Himmingazians' ward was the hardest he'd ever closed. But as he wound his way through the citadel toward the main hall's entrance, slowly he began to feel lighter, more assured. Perhaps it *would* be as simple as he'd made it sound to Ulfric. Nothing so far had given him any reason not to think so.

He walked a few hallways before he realized something was missing and took a step into the main hall before he knew what. The citadel was almost preternaturally quiet. He met no guards in the halls, heard no sounds of the city outside coming through the windows, and saw no Dyrraks.

When he passed through the entrance hall to outside, he saw why.

The arena before the citadel was shaped like an amphitheater, with seating that rose easily ten levels high directly in front of and to either side of the wide steps leading to the column-lined upper yard. Thousands had assembled and now sat and stood among the seats everywhere he turned.

He remembered the dais Eisa had mentioned from their arrival.

However, it took him less than a heartbeat to know he was not about to walk out to it before such a mass of people. The dais lay at the end of a long landing that resembled the prow of a ship, and everyone in Elezaran—indeed, the huge assembly appeared to *be* everyone in the empire—would have wondered what in the worlds he was doing loitering before them. Instead, he stayed in the shadows of the columns and moved a bit closer, then tucked himself behind one to keep an eye on the dais and wait for Eisa.

The unfamiliar smells of the city wafted to him as he waited. Unknown foods cooking, fires from forges and homes, but most unusual was the bitter dry dust that seemed to be everywhere. Himmingaze barely knew the meaning of dry, and it seemed Dyrrakium existed in perfect opposition to their home.

Jaemus grew more fidgety with each passing moment. Eisa had not shown up. Rising due south from the amphitheater's wall was a towering pole with a crescent lying on its side at its point. Halla would lie directly in the crescent's center at midday, and the sun was just beginning to touch the edge of it now.

He had to face it, she wasn't coming. And he needed to get that last Fenestros shard before whatever event she had planned kept her from ever getting it to him.

"Guess it's another trip into the earth," he mumbled to himself in exasperation. "Don't these Vinnrics know nothing but worms should live underground?"

The concept of "underground" was unique to Jaemus, in that the only underground Himmingaze's floating cities had was submersion in the Never Sea. Of all the marvels Vinnr held, the tendency to bore into and under the dark, close soil was one he didn't think he'd ever find he liked. Especially after he'd learned the Vinnrics also buried their dead in it.

After reentering the main hall, he wended his way from memory toward an inconspicuous doorway near the citadel's heart. It wasn't locked, and after a quick look to see if anyone was watching, he stepped in. Before him dove a narrow tunnel and staircase that seemed to drop endlessly down into the ground. No sound carried up from it, and the air felt damp. His skin suddenly tingled as if he'd been brushed by the cold, wet, rough skin of a fleech. He didn't want to go down there. But he had to.

Once he closed the door, the darkness swamped him immediately. Pulling his Mentalios over his head, he held it out and imagined it brightening as Safran had shown him, speaking the simple incantation that would illuminate it. It lit the stairs enough to see his way down, and he sighed in relief. Then he noticed the way the light glittered against red seams of a different type of rock to the main stones comprising the citadel. It looked uncannily like the walls were bleeding. His relief evaporated.

"Now, remember to count your steps and mark your turns," he told himself. "Stay in the main tunnel." He stopped talking to himself for a moment, wondering if he'd heard something. After listening for a few seconds, he couldn't detect much, perhaps a slight whispering sound. "A breeze?" he asked himself. "Maybe there's an exit down there."

Taking the first step, he counted, "One…"

Seven hundred steps and three turns into new tunnels later, Jaemus began to doubt himself. He'd passed a handful of passages, ones he had expected upon memorizing Eisa's map, but the consuming darkness unnerved him so much that he kept losing count and had to stop to think through each step of his journey again. Nothing else in the tunnel differentiated from what came before and what he could see ahead. Endless stone, darkness, and silence. Occasionally, maybe a slight whisper of air. After a while, a little voice in his head was warning him to turn back before he got too far to find his way.

"Nonsense," he told the voice. "I should be close now, and I have the Mentalios. If I get well and truly lost, I'll simply call Stave—no, Safran, and ask her to come find me. Ulfric has the map, after all. Oh, I forgot to tell them about Eisa—"

As if he'd cursed himself, Jaemus suddenly lost focus and stepped awkwardly, stumbling on an uneven divot in the floor. His Mentalios lens dropped from his hand and went dark. "Water and lightning," he spat. "Where did that—"

He heard footsteps. Most definitely footsteps. Every drop of water in his mouth evaporated. Even his eyes suddenly felt like hot, sandy balls rolling painfully inside the soft meat in his skull. He couldn't have said why the sound frightened him, but he could definitely say that it did.

He froze. The footsteps were getting louder, and he could hear more than one set. Two, maybe more. But how could he judge? The darkness was total, almost like a weight that shrouded him, and the tunnels were endless, causing echoes to echo each other. As he listened, the sound grew and grew. More than a dozen, definitely. A hundred? Two?

He was panicking, he knew. *Get a grip, Jae. It's just other Dyrraks. Maybe they're on stair-sweeping duty.*

The cold sensation crawling over his skin, however, didn't agree with that guess. He didn't know what to do. He had to call the Knights. Through the Mentalios. He was alone down here, but he wasn't alone in his mind. They'd hear him, send help.

Frantic, he dropped to his knees and began sweeping the stone floor with his hands, searching for his wystic ornament. Then, a muted light bloomed some distance down the stairs, bouncing up the red veins of rock to him, giving them a fluid, blood-like appearance once again. He heard a voice, a man's, but it was too distant to make out the words. In response came a sound that was low, sibilant, like a hiss. A sound he'd heard before, hadn't he? From the gangly minions on Balavad's ship. The sound of a Ravener.

Fleetingly, Jaemus wondered if the burst of sensation in his chest was his heart exploding in fear.

CHAPTER THIRTY-SIX

"That settles it," Stave stated when the Ecclesium had left. "I'll be the first to congratulate Eisa when she puts that cur down."

Ulfric ignored him, too troubled by the Ecclesium's veiled threats and vague statements to tell him to calm down. "Safran, what do you make if his comments?"

Her face remained impassive, and after a few moments she spoke. *Whatever specific intentions he has, I think Eisa would have warned us in plain terms if she suspected any kind of imminent threat.* Ulfric was about to expand on her statement, but she went on: *However, it would be a mistake for us to discount that fleet of ships we've all seen.* She waved her hand at the window and the field outside where hundreds of sky ships were amassed. Waiting to be put to use.

Ulfric retrieved the ewer of syke liquor delivered by the Ecclesium and poured himself a healthy gobletful. As he started to agree with her, she turned back to them.

But whatever the outcome of today's fight between Eisa and the Dyrrak leader—if we don't stop it—I think we have to be prepared to leave Dyrrak-ium. The Ecclesium wants a war, and though he is devout, he is also shrewd. The more cunning and dangerous a mind, the easier for it to persuade itself that what it wants is a right, perhaps a moral imperative. In the end, he may come to think his will is yours, Ulfric, whether you agree with him or not.

Running his thumb over the goblet's lip, Ulfric said, "Whether Eisa realizes the danger she helped put us all in or not, we'll let them fight. It's their custom and—" And what? Did he think it would be best, as Safran had said, to have Eisa rule Dyrrakium? Perhaps. Perhaps it would bring a stability the current Ecclesium seemed intent on undoing.

"Maybe you should use your sway as Vaka Aster to intervene," Stave suggested. "The warrior with the biggest ax has the fewest enemies, you know, and no one has a bigger ax, so to speak, than a Verity."

Ulfric shook his head. "I've thought of that, but I fear it would give the Dyrraks more doubts than it would subdue them. Vaka Aster simply doesn't bother with the affairs of her creations. History has born that out. If she—I were to suddenly take such intimate control of things, they could be tipped off that there is something different about this vessel than others."

"Doubt it," Stave said. "They're so blinded by fanaticism that they'd think it was just Vaka Aster showing them the attention they always thought they deserved, they will."

Ulfric thought it over. With a gesture at the tray of goblets, he offered the others a drink. Stave poured one, but Safran and Mallich declined with shakes of their heads.

"When this is all over," Ulfric said, "we'll need to do something about the rift the Dyrraks created with Ivoryss, find a way to salve the ire of Arch Keeper Beatte." He sighed and took a drink. "Or perhaps this won't be over for a hundred turns or more and Beatte will be long gone before Vaka Aster's vessel is ever seen in Ivoryss, or Yor, again."

Mallich chuckled dryly. "The squabbles of politics and politicians never seem to amount to much when viewed through the lens of a few hundred turns, do they?"

Ulfric joined him with an unamused laugh of his own. "It's settled, then. I'll let Eisa and the Ecclesium sort out this rulership contest on their own. Perhaps it will benefit us. If we're lucky, it'll mean we don't need to leave Dyrrakium. It's unprecedented that a Knight rule a kingdom, but then, what's happened over the last few weeks that isn't unprecedented? If things go awry between them, somehow, I'll still have this"—he waved at his eyes with his free hand—"to fall back upon and take control of Dyrrak myself. If it comes to that." With the sense of resolve that always followed a firm decision, Ulfric swallowed half the syke liquor in a long, satisfying gulp.

Something began to come over him. It started as a tickle in his throat, like a tiny hand was whisking a tiny feather against the walls of his esophagus. He forced a gentle cough, but that was a mistake. The tickle became a burn, and the burn quickly spiked into his stomach, then outward to his whole torso, growing hotter, searing him from inside out like fast-moving lava. It shot through him, growing in strength and filling him until he thought he'd burst into flame.

"Ulfric!"

Mallich's voice came from afar, or rather, it sounded distant while competing with the roar of agony Ulfric felt ripping through his insides. He clawed at his throat, his hand hooking his Mentalios chain. A spasm shot through him and the chain broke, sending his wystic lens across the room.

He blacked out for a moment, though he wasn't sure if it *was* only a moment. He wasn't sure of anything. What had just happened to him?

He felt...different. His body seemed weightless, unattached. Not naked, just not...there. He forced open his eyes, but his vision was cloudy, gray, as if a veil lay over his face—and no longer the shifting, chromatic Verity-enhanced vision he'd finally started to get used to. There were shapes on the other side of the grayness, but it was all out of whack. He couldn't recognize the shadowy forms.

One thing was brighter than the rest, a large square of hazy light. But it was below him, and off to the side. He reached up to rub his eyes to try and clear this odd distortion, but he couldn't feel his arms. He couldn't feel anything.

"Mallich? Safran, what's happening?" he asked, then realized he couldn't hear his own voice. "Mallich!"

Frantic and growing more so, he tried to push himself up. He had fallen, hadn't he? The only thing that happened was the cloudiness of his sight diminished just slightly, and new forms appeared, as if he had moved. The white square of light was now directly in front of him. He gazed into it, hoping it would somehow burn away the fog.

Far away, more images began to take shape. Tall and reddish, like buildings. Off in the south lay a flatter space, like…like…the field where he'd seen the Dyrrakium military's fighter crafts, perhaps. Was he standing in front of the window?

He spun around, and this time he knew he was moving. The shadows spun with him, and his sight cleared more. He *was* in front of the window. But he wasn't standing—he knew this because he couldn't feel any floor beneath him. In fact, he was…hovering, like a wraith.

In front of him lay his own body, Mallich crouched beside him, shaking him, saying his name. The Knight released one of Ulfric's shoulders and grasped his Mentalios in a death grip, clearly channeling through it. But Ulfric couldn't hear him through his own lens link. He couldn't do anything but gasp in silent, horrified shock at what he was seeing—

Himself, supine, gray-fleshed, collapsed on the floor. Yet, at the same time, he was here, several paces away.

How can this be? Vaka Aster, what's happening to me?

The silence answering him was without question the deepest, hollowest emptiness he'd experienced in his long life. He was cut off— from his own body, from the vessel that bore his creator, and from the creator herself.

In the time it would take to blink, panic, despair, rage, and desperation washed through him in a hurricane gale. He couldn't protect the vessel, or himself, if he was unable to move. But then, he was beyond being unable to move, he wasn't even *him*. He was ephemeral, not physical, not…alive? Was that it? Had he died? No, that wasn't possible. If he had died, Vinnr would have ceased to exist. Had Vaka Aster taken over? No, again, the same thing seemed to be true. She'd told him she couldn't take over his form without taking over his mind and breaking it. Breaking it would break the world, and he wouldn't be standing, *floating* here having this conversation with himself.

Try to speak with Mallich, explain what's going on, even though I don't understand it.

Stave, kneeling beside Ulfric's form, brayed, "What in Balavad's blacktrack happened to him?"

Mallich's eyes suddenly fastened on the doorway, and they all, including Ulfric—albeit incalculably slower—turned to look.

The door guard stood there, looking inside with his brow furrowed. He must have heard Ulfric yelling and opened the door. Nothing in his demeanor had shifted from the stoic, at-the-ready pose and expression he and all the Dyrraks constantly assumed. But that made his creased eyebrows, and the confusion that danced in the eyes below them, all the more extreme.

"Bar the door," Mallich said, almost mildly.

Safran moved to the guard, pushed him out, and quickly secured the door. When she turned back, the others watched her intently, as if she were speaking. If she was, Ulfric couldn't hear her either.

Knights! Stave, Safran! Mallich! Listen, hear me! he yelled uselessly. One cannot yell without lungs and a mouth to yell through.

"His pallor suggests an illness or poison," Mallich was saying. "But that doesn't make sense. No plague or poison could affect a Knight so suddenly."

At the mention of "poison," their eyes fell on the shattered goblet of syke liquor that lay next to Ulfric's body. The remaining liquid had dampened the floor in scattered puddles. Looking at it, Ulfric realized it was different from the syke liquor the Knights had been served previously. The color was a cobalt blue and nearly opaque. He'd thought it had been the same honey brown as before when he drank it. Was there some kind of enchantment on it?

Stave hurled his own untouched goblet at the wall, deep blue liquid splattering everywhere. He muttered, "That's..." All three of the Knights seemed to draw the same conclusion at once, but none said a word aloud.

What?! What is it? Ulfric shouted in vain.

"Balavad's consecration elixir. He's here," Mallich stated as he rose from Ulfric's side to his feet. "Somehow he's infiltrated Dyrrakium."

Stave stepped toward the ewer of remaining liquid and kicked it. The pottery flew directly toward Ulfric, or where he perceived himself to be, then through him, smashing into fragments against the wall as well.

The Knight turned back. "So, somehow Ulfric is now one of Balavad's slaves? But how would that work with him being the vessel, eh? How?"

"I don't know. I don't understand either," Mallich answered.

They looked to Safran, then Stave said, "She's right, she is. That guard won't keep his mouth shut for long, and any Dyrrak who already harbors any doubts about what Ulfric is—or dare I say, *was*—will start talking, too. Like that Ecclesium. We'll have a rebellion on our hands, I'll wager, or worse. These painted zealots know a thing or two more about fighting than any Ivoryssian I've ever met."

Mallich said to Safran, "She's…attending to a delicate matter before High Halls and the Conquestum."

"Well, we need Eisa to put aside her delicacies and get Ulfric out of Dyrrakium, we do," Stave said. "Besides Ulfric, she's the only one who knows where the interrealm well is. And we need to go, now. Where is she, then?"

Safran must have spoken again, and Stave said, "Good point." He reached for Vaka Aster's Scrylle and continued. "Maybe we should open a starpath to Himmingaze. Feed two birds with one scone and take the novice and his people back there with us. The whole lot of it may be sinking into the sea, but there may be no better reason for them to get back on their own soil, or what they have for soil, than having that bogtrotting black-breathing Verity on ours. It'll buy us time and—ah, slag it. Does anyone know where Bardgrim is?"

A voice, speaking loudly, came from outside the barred door. "No one is to see the—wait—Stop! Stop!"

There was no mistaking the sound of clashing weapons. Galvanized, Mallich ordered, "Stave, grab Ulfric. Safran, the artifacts—all of them. And draw your klinkí stones. We'll try to reach the Himmingazians at the base of the citadel and hope Eisa can get to us there."

Stave slung Ulfric's form like a sack over his shoulder. Prepared to do battle, they rushed to the door. Ulfric attempted to follow, but his will, or whatever he still controlled of who he was, was sluggish. He could only turn in a slow revolution as the Knights flung open the door and stepped out. In the agonizing moments it took him to turn, he caught the rapid lights of flying klinkí stones through the corner of his ethereal eye. But by the time he'd made the full turn, he heard the Knights' footsteps retreating through the antechamber and into the hallway beyond.

With a monumental effort, he pushed himself toward the doorway, eventually seeing the smattering of bodies they'd left in their wake. The guard, unfortunately, was among them, killed by the attackers, he assumed. There were a half-dozen others. They were clearly Dyrrak, all of them, with the telltale skin markings that denoted their rise through their social caste. But there was more. Their blood had turned from red to a sludge-like gray-black, and their skin had faded to the same gray wanness of the Raveners he'd seen aboard Balavad's ship.

It was true. The usurper had found him. And it seemed, through trickery and deception, he had at last won the prize he sought.

CHAPTER THIRTY-SEVEN

Eisa feinted left, then dodged right just before striking the Ecclesium. He stood before Lillias in a wide-footed, bent-kneed pose ready for her, but striking him wasn't what she meant to do. That would have been stupid, and he should have known better than to expect it of her. She was no First Phase novice or new Conservatum acolyte. Eisa's only goal was to put him off balance, force him to spin and face her—

—and then knock out as many of his teeth as she could with the dragør statue she swept up from the foot of Lillias's seat.

He grunted heavily and reeled backward into the Speaker, knocking into her hard, one hand covering his jaw. Lillias's body shifted, her hands falling free to dangle over the chair's sides. Blood gushed between Starkas's fingers, glistening like oil in the dim room. Eisa could have finished him off right then but chose to wait and see how he'd react. If Balavad was here, she had questions, and Starkas would answer them before she was through with him.

He recovered immediately, as she knew he would. Pushing himself off the chair, he bent his knees once more, ready for her next onslaught. Their eyes locked, neither speaking. She was about to tell him her terms, but then he did the last thing she'd have ever in a million turns expected.

The coward ran.

He was out the doorway before she could believe what she was seeing. Giving chase instantly, she crossed the room so fleetly it seemed her feet never hit the floor. She hurled herself through the doorway, for once not pausing to ensure she wasn't flinging herself into a trap.

It wasn't a trap. It was worse.

As her feet crossed the threshold, she *did* leave the floor. Her body was picked up by an unseen force and flung against the stone wall on the other side of the passageway. She spun halfway around before hitting hard enough to get the wind knocked out of her and landed on her knees. Gasping, she looked up.

A monstrous being unlike any she'd ever seen stood before her. A woman, the Battgjaldic creature stood easily a foot over her, her black hair a wild tangle that writhed around her head like the smoke of an inferno. Her obsidian eyes were unnaturally large and pulsed with some deep inner glow. Eisa knew this being with unquestioning certainty. This was Balavad in a new Battgjaldic vessel.

The new vessel the Verity had chosen was obscene, loathsome. No other reaction, not fear, not terror, not even anger coursed through Eisa at the sight of it. Nothing but a disgust so heavy she almost gagged on it. Her hundreds of turns of life had trained her to revere Verities to her core, but it wasn't in her to revere this one.

"Knight Eisa Nazaria," the being said with a voice like embers in her ears. "I know all about you. Your Domine Ecclesium has been very forthcoming."

Balavad's new form swept toward Eisa as she rose to her feet and stopped a couple of paces away. Eisa smelled char, a heavy odor that nearly overwhelmed her. It was the smell of worlds burning.

"And he has been wise. I'll offer you the same as I offered him, and offered your Stallari before you. Join me in making Vinnr the haven I can promise it will become, and you will be a leader of your world, worshipped and exalted almost as highly as I am to be."

She had to swallow before she could respond, and even then her jaw twitched and bunched with fury with every word she spat out. "Vaka Aster will destroy you again, fiend. Go back to your swamp in the Cosmos and corrupt it with your base vulgarity." It was foolish; she knew it. To challenge and insult a celestial being was a death sentence. But she'd rather be dead than at Balavad's mercy.

The Domine Ecclesium stood behind the Verity, his back to the wall, blood running freely down his chin and chest. He caught Eisa's glance and shook his head as if to say, *Don't damn yourself, Eisa. You have only this one chance.*

Balavad followed her gaze and turned around, and Eisa took it as her opening. She lunged. Again, she was flung backward into the wall, though the Verity had not turned. Heaving to pull air into her locked lungs, she could do nothing else for the moment. Balavad gestured to the Ecclesium, and he pulled Eisa's klinkí stones from a pouch and handed them over. Balavad faced her again.

Grotesquely, she smiled at Eisa. Her teeth were spikes. "Your Vaka Aster has already succumbed to my rule. She is shackled, as I intended, and the flesh she wears now belongs to me too. Your Stallari has been consecrated and he is mine. Everything, mine. Except you. But only for a little bit."

Balavad flung the stones at her, and she reflexively threw her arms over her face to block them, knowing she couldn't and this was likely the death she expected to come. Instead, the stones encircled her, holding her in a net that she could not escape. She tried anyway and reached forward, but it was like touching hot, smooth, solid granite.

With Balavad's hand outstretched to hold the net, the Verity said to the Ecclesium, "Go, send word to all Dyrrakium that your empire's time is at hand. Today instead of meeting their new ruler, they shall meet their new Verity."

"You slag worm, you won't get away with this!" Eisa screamed, her voice ringing like a bell inside the net.

The Ecclesium gave her a final look, then turned and began climbing the stairs.

Balavad, with the same amused smirk, said, "Nothing outside your new cage can hear you, little bird. Make as much music as you like."

The Verity lifted her hand, and a river of black vapor began to filter out of the air like poison being drawn from a wound. It condensed around the blue sphere of Eisa's prison, blocking her sight from the outside. Eisa stilled as dread wormed through her. Then all at once, the miasma pushed past the net and enveloped her. She could feel it on her skin, like oil the moment it combusts into flame, and she swore at Balavad again.

As the dark vapor slid down her throat, the net rose from the floor, closing beneath Eisa's feet and shrinking around her until she was wrapped as tightly as a swaddled infant. Struggling like a worm on a hook, Eisa continued screaming every curse and oath she knew as the usurper levitated her, new prison and all, up the stairwell after the Ecclesium.

CHAPTER THIRTY-EIGHT

Trying to tell himself he was overreacting, Jaemus listened to the footsteps and concluded he'd simply borrow a lamp from whoever was approaching when they got to him. Surely just a group of Dyrraks.

But that sound he'd heard, that had been no Dyrrak.

The footsteps were growing closer. No longer hedging, Jaemus did the one remaining thing he could think of. He looked for somewhere to hide. He was running from shadows while practically buried in shadows, though the irony of this did nothing to amuse him.

He turned to head back up the stairs. Just then, he saw a glow below. It wasn't the soft white glow of an illuminate orb like there were in other places in the citadel. Rather, the color splashed the walls in a shifty, sickly green, moving in a pattern like water, turning the red ore in the wall an oily purple. His steps faltered at the sight.

Whatever the light was, it was too close. If he started running up the stairs, there was no way he'd be unheard. He wasn't like Eisa or the Dyrraks, fleet footed and silent. Whoever was down there would give chase. He'd be caught. Then what? He found himself uninterested in following that train of thought to its conclusion.

The light was being cast far enough that he could make out the opening to a secondary passage just a few steps up. Without thinking, he tiptoed to it and diverted inside, moving as silently as possible, seeking any doorway or alcove he could press himself into until the light-bearer passed.

The passage gave way to a T-junction only a few steps in, and he instantly turned down the left tunnel, walked a few paces, and stopped, listening to the echoing footsteps. The light, though diffused as it slid down his escape passage, was bright enough now that he could see the bumps of frightened flesh on his arms.

His breath didn't need to be held. He was too scared to draw one.

"My newly consecrated Raveners tell me that they haven't yet acquired the vessel," a voice said from the main stairway. It was feminine but deep, with a liquid roiling quality that Jaemus recognized not with his mind but with some deep, primitive sense organ that all beings rely on for survival. It wasn't a Ravener he'd heard after all. This was Balavad's voice, even if feminine. There was no mistaking it.

"It will be done, Your Holiness. The rest of the citadel venerates will be brought into your fold easily. Even if the Knights reach the main level, they will not get the Stallari's body out of the fortress."

"When captured, bring my quin outside. You will denounce Aldinhuus to the empire, tell the Dyrrak people his claims to be the vessel are untrue."

"It...it is not in the Dyrrak people to lie, Your Holiness."

"It is not a lie to show them Aldinhuus's deceptions. Your people must be led to the truth gently. Tell them only that Vaka Aster has abandoned them. A simple, unaltered truth. When I am ready, I will give the Dyrrak people the Verity they are worthy of. Until Dyrrakium is fully consecrated, it is for their own good that they still believe in Vaka Aster's invincibility—you don't want them to believe there can be weakness to their own creator. They will lose hope, and you will lose control of them. Have I made myself clear, Ecclesium?"

The voices were diminishing, and with a slowness that felt intentional, as if it were waiting for him to reveal himself, the light began to fade up the stairway as well. Jaemus didn't move until he was in pitch-blackness again and the only sound was his own panicked heartbeat.

Unless I've gone full muddlemind, that was the Ecclesium working hand in hand with Balavad. I need to warn the Knights, he thought.

Which he couldn't do without his damned Mentalios.

After what felt an eternity, a wan kind of bravery compelled him to leave his sanctuary. Grudgingly, he slid his hands along the feeder passage until he was again in the main. He counted back to the last step he'd been on and dropped to a knee, sweeping his hands back and forth across the floor in search of his dropped wystic lens.

The stones were remarkably smooth, whether by time or by design, he couldn't tell. And their coolness was considerably unlike the citadel's upper floors and what seemed like the kingdom's general climate.

But it was no use. He'd have to sweep every stone from here to the Speaker's chamber if he was going to find his Mentalios. And, he realized, why take that time when he knew a faster way? If his recollection of the map was right, though he had to admit after his little moment of excitement that it wasn't likely to be, he was close to his original destination. Another two hundred yards and one final right fork. Then he'd have the final piece of Fenestros. Even without his Mentalios, he might be able to join the three broken shards and conjure some light from it the way Ulfric was able to.

What does it matter? You heard Balavad, Ulfric is being hunted.

But what choice did he have but to go down? If he went up, he could easily run into either the usurping Verity or her minions, and he really preferred to avoid being stabbed again. So, with slow, deliberate steps, he continued down, feeling the edge of each stair with his soft-soled Ivoryssian boots. Not long later, the smell of lamp oil and smoke grew stronger. Then there was light, lamplight rather than whatever Balavad had projected.

As soon as he realized he was almost there, he stopped again, listening for anything that might be as bad, or worse, than what he'd felt pass earlier. But it was quiet. As a grave.

Sucking in a breath, he took the last few steps. A door stood ajar at the end of the passageway, and the dim, smoky light came from within.

He paced inside and immediately saw the strange woman. Unlike her rigid, awkward posture from aboard the *Gildr*, her body was now draped over a formidably built wooden chair, her hands dangling.

Notably, a black, empty cavity adorned the center of her chest.

Jaemus could have wept. Eisa had already been here, apparently. The Fenestros shard was gone, and so was she. In addition, Balavad appeared to be loose in Dyrrakium, and Jaemus was for all intents and purposes now buried hundreds of feet underground with no way to warn the Knights. To say the day had taken a turn for the worse was a criminal understatement.

After a moment, he sighed. "Well, at least this is the worst that can happen. Things really can't go more wrong. The Knights and Ulfric will simply open another starpath and spirit themselves and the 'Nauts away while I end my days as a puppet for a demented star sprite," he told himself. "Lucky me."

He gazed around the chamber, feeling a helpless malaise settle into him. His eyes were drawn once more to the Speaker. In the flickering oil lamps, another difference about her stood out. Her face, which before had been pale and rigid as if she were in great pain, was relaxed now. Peaceful even. Something about the sight jolted him out of his doldrums.

Buck up, Jaemus. Stop acting as if you're dead like her. You're special, after all, sprinkled with star sprite dust and immortal. Even Mylla didn't die when Balavad attacked her. Not right away, at least.

That last thought gave him a shiver, yet he took a resolute breath and considered what to do next. Perhaps Eisa had left him a message? Spinning around in a slow turn, he scanned the chamber, but aside from the chair, some statuettes, and the Speaker, the only other objects in it were the lamps.

Except...

He stepped forward and picked up a figurine, about the length of his forearm, that lay on its side near one wall. Turning it over in his hands, he marveled at how similar to a slangarook it was. Except where a slangarook had long, trailing fins and a more fish-like hooked jaw, this had wings and a snout unlike any creature he could identify. And—a spot of dark liquid splattered along one side.

He dropped the figure. It was blood. He was certain.

He had to get out now, find his Mentalios. He swept a lamp from its emplacement and took one last look at the Speaker, considering going through her crimson robe to look for anything that might come in handy. Then his eye caught on something shiny lying beside the chair. He hadn't seen it in the shadows before. A stony object, rounded on one side.

Was it...?

He rushed to it and picked it up. Oh sparkling celestials, it was! The last piece of Fenestros shard. Maybe whoever had been fighting in here had knocked it loose, or maybe it was left behind by accident. What was certain was that the time had come to get out of here.

With too much to lose if he stayed down here, and too much to gain if he didn't, he tucked the shard into his satchel with the other pieces of Fenestros and Lífs's Scrylle map. No time to mess with magic he didn't yet understand, not when there were lamps available to light his way. With one in hand, Jaemus sped from the chamber and started up the steps to the citadel two at a time.

CHAPTER THIRTY-NINE

No sense of powerlessness, in seventeen centuries, had ever been so burdensome and crushing. Ulfric wanted to throw himself through the window, into a wall, against the floor, whatever he could, just to feel *something*, just to know he could move, to know he wasn't eternally trapped in this state of being nothing but consciousness without senses or the ability to affect his world in any way, any way at all.

He did all he could think of. Willing himself to move, he pushed toward the doorway through what felt, only in his mind, like frozen honey. The drudge of it would have been exhausting if he'd been able to experience it in any kind of physical way—but he couldn't.

After what seemed a hundred turns, he finally reached the opening. Looking through the antechamber at the hallway beyond, he lingered on the threshold for a moment as he considered what he would do now. By the time he made it even across the outer room, the Knights and the vessel could be anywhere in the citadel or beyond. If he couldn't move faster, everything that might be about to happen already will have. It was a hopeless position, and he despaired the way a caged wild animal must the moment before it gives up completely.

In vain, he pushed himself around, searching the throne chamber.

For what, he couldn't guess. He couldn't hold a weapon, couldn't search for answers in a Scrylle, couldn't even spit in someone's eye if he wished to. He was—

Wait.

There—his Mentalios. He remembered his hand catching on it and pulling it free from his neck as he'd choked on the poisoned syke liquor. With the distraction at the doorway by hostile and probably Balavad-controlled Dyrraks, Stave must not have seen it when lifting Ulfric.

A noise from the dais drew his attention. Urgo and Yggo perched there still, and, to his astonishment, were eyeing him closely. *Him.* They, descendants and evolutionary children of the dragørs of the Howling Weald, were ordained by Vaka Aster as well. As bruhawks, though, what unique gifts they were endowed with was unknowable. But they could see him, he was sure.

He had an idea.

In his agonizingly impeded way, he pushed himself to the wystic lens. On reaching it, he forced himself down to the floor, drifting as slowly as if he were snowflake. The two predators had plenty of time to observe him, their large yellow eyes blinking slowly on occasion as if amused at his pitiful ethereal wobbling. When he was close enough to the lens that it was his sole visual focus, he muttered the words he'd taught Safran four hundred turns ago that would link one's sight to the bruhawks, focusing sharply on only one bird, Urgo. *With thy eyes, these eyes too see.* He had no reason to believe it would work, but he had hope, and by the Verities, he had the *will* to make it work.

But it didn't. At least, not in the way he expected.

The first sensation he experienced since becoming disembodied was what he thought it would feel like to be shot from a bow. He *whooshed*—he could think of no other way to describe it. And then, he was not only seeing through Urgo's eyes, it seemed he *was* Urgo. He felt his body as a bird's body, with strange appendages sprouting from his back, flesh covered by a soft down and topped by heavier feathers, eyes that *pierced* the world rather than merely *saw* it, and, strangest of all, his mind was split, partly his own, partly a predatory, honed cognizance that buzzed with a singular focus.

Urgo did not appear to approve of his impromptu possession. The bird launched into the air so suddenly and violently that it looked to Ulfric as if he, or rather *they*, were going to smash into the ceiling.

NO! he cried, and Urgo echoed him with a shrill screech of his own. Fortunately, the bruhawk thought better of self-destruction and banked hard, soaring through the tall open window.

Panicked, Ulfric closed his eyes, and the world went dark as Urgo did as well. *Verities have mercy! Open your eyes, Urgo! Watch where you're taking us.*

The world came back into sight, though it was speeding below them so far and so fast that Ulfric almost wished it hadn't. Getting ahold of himself, he realized what had happened. Urgo had heard him and responded. He thought as calmly as he could, *Well done, well done. Vaka Aster willing, we'll get through this together...as partners. Listen, Urgo, please. You know my voice. It's Ulfric. We've been friends for many turns.*

The panic he and the bruhawk shared ebbed somewhat. *Better, better. I'm not going to hurt you, boy. I don't know how, but...let's just say we're in this together for now. Can you help me?*

The bird's thoughts were not accessible to him, but his senses seemed to be, and Urgo gradually grew somewhat calmer, more in control. *Good, okay, that's good. I think we're getting somewhere. Thank you, Urgo. Can you take me back to the citadel and retrieve Yggo? We have some hunting to do.*

As the bruhawk banked back toward the massive structure, Ulfric wondered: Would he be able to leave Urgo again, or was being joined with the creature his destiny now? He recognized the cruel twist of irony—sharing a body and mind had already become a familiar happenstance. Now, though it seemed he'd lost Vaka Aster, he'd gained a new form. The question was, what could he do with it?

CHAPTER FORTY

On the way up from the bowels of the citadel, through sheer luck Jaemus came across his Mentalios. He swept it up and found it remarkably undamaged. Not even a scratch notched the crystal face. The moment he dropped it over his head, a thrill shot through him. He could warn the Knights now!

Before the thrill wore off, though, Stave's agitated voice came to him: *On your left, your left!*

He jerked his eyes left, but saw only wall. Stave must have been talking, *yelling* rather, to one of the other Knights. By the sound, the battle he'd feared since hearing Balavad in the stairway had already begun. Doubling his pace, he used his lens to try to reach his new companions.

Knights? Stave? he sent.

Slag it, novice, where the—bleeding Verities, you bastirt! Stave's voice faded for a moment, then came back. *Bardgrim, get to the 'Gazians. Ulfric's in trouble. We're holding them back but—*

His voice kept breaking off as if he were speaking through a damaged wave-speaker, but his urgency came through with perfect clarity.

Jaemus had to get to Cote.

If feet were capable of flying, he swore his were doing it. By the time he reached the door to the main floor, his ragged breaths stung like needles in his raw throat and a stitch in his side might as well have been the same sword that had skewered him days before. He was about to burst through the doorway but halted just outside the fall of light from the passage beyond. If he ran willy-nilly out there, he might run directly into one of Balavad's Raveners, what Jaemus had heard the Verity call a "consecrated." Or worse—he could run into Balavad himself (or was it *herself* now?). He'd left Winter's Bite behind with Cote and was thus now armed with a single thing: his sole klinkí stone.

In a moment of rueful self-reflection, he thought, *Gramsirene Vreyja always told me I should become a librarian. No danger, endless interesting things to learn. Why didn't I listen?*

Cautiously, he peeked beyond the doorway, trying to mute his hard breathing. The hallway outside was empty. The most direct way to the Himmingazians' chamber was twisty, but it wasn't too far.

Mustering what speed he had left, he wove through two more hallways, encountering as much stillness as when he'd come through last time. The citadel along with the city were preparing for the event Eisa had mentioned. Or were they already under Balavad's thumb? He had one final chamber to pass through, and on the other side an antechamber led to his friends and his lifemate.

Outside the final chamber, his progress ended. The unnatural stillness of the citadel was broken by the sound of fighting, a lot of it, pouring through the archway leading to the room as wild hisses, grunts, clanging weapons. Peering carefully past the arched opening into the spacious room, he caught a brief glimpse of the Safran, Stave, and Roibeard surrounded by what resembled a Glister Cloud storm. Streaking blue lights, the Knights' klinkí stones, shot everywhere, many times passing through bodies of misshapen Dyrrak warriors, who just kept charging as if they felt nothing. For a moment he grew dizzy, thinking he'd somehow been transported back to the warship, back into the battle that had ended with him being impaled by a sword and then shot through time and space into another realm.

But this was no warship, and this time, the Knights were alone in their fight. No captive Vinnrics were here to face this new Ravener horde. In fact, the only ally they had was Jaemus and his single wystic stone.

And if he went in there, who would be left to protect Cote and the others?

There was another way to the Himmingazians' chamber, a longer route that took him around several other rooms and down lengthy halls. He knew the way from memorizing Eisa's map.

His choices, such as they were, were two: join the Knights' fracas or try reaching Cote and the Himmingazians.

Stave, he sent, *I'm sorry but I have to see to my friends.* He was beyond caring if the Knight thought him a coward. Yet the response he got surprised him.

That's what I said, get to the 'Gazians. Ulfric's with them. He has the Scrylle. You have to starpath them out of here.

As if chased by a fleech, Jaemus rushed toward the Himmingazian chamber's secondary entrance. Through smaller passages he assumed were used by servants and down a couple of additional detours, he wound away from the fight and arrived at the final short hallway leading to his destination.

Where he found his path blocked.

A man nearly Jaemus's height and easily three times his girth stood at the door, his back to Jaemus. He carried a heavy club with a metal cap on the end and was beating it against the narrow door, trying to break it down. His skin was marked with a galaxy of the Dyrrak brands, showing he was both accomplished and well trained in their Phases—so, of course, he could break Jaemus like a twig. And Jaemus assumed that was his imminent fate, as the man's skin had also taken on the ashen pallor of a Ravener.

Jaemus froze to the spot. He couldn't run. Where on Vinnr would he go? And he couldn't attack the man without a weapon. Of course, he had his klinkí stone, but it was too new to him, too small to do much with, too—ah, to the Verities with it. He had to do *something*! He couldn't simply let the Dyrrak Ravener slaughter the Himmingazians.

"Excuse me!" he yelled, his voice a reedy whistle. He tried again. "Heyo! Brute-force man! Back here!"

The Dyrrak Ravener turned, saw him, and held his club out as if to tap Jaemus on the shoulder.

Down the hallway, Jaemus stood with his arm extended, his lone wystic stone sitting in his palm. It occurred to him that to an observer it might look like he and the Dyrraks were offering to trade weapons.

Come on, Jae, think, concentrate, make this stone do what Ulfric threatened he'd do to you all those times.

Unfortunately, his powers of concentration were being sorely tested by the muscular and definitely violence-seeking Dyrrak who was now taking slow, deliberate steps toward him.

"Ssss..." the creature hissed, sizing him up.

"Erm, now that I have your attention—" With a heroic effort, Jaemus simultaneously focused as hard as he could on making the stone fly and flung it toward the cursed Dyrrak's chest with all his force.

Where it struck! Then clattered to the ground and lay still, not the least bit of light in its wystic heart.

Too distracted and frightened to call upon his will and channel his Verity spark, Jaemus might as well have tossed the wystic stone into the ocean for all the good it would do him now.

The Dyrrak didn't even acknowledge the stone's impact and lunged toward Jaemus.

Jaemus took a lumbering backward step, managed to turn, then felt the club hammer him between the shoulders, sending him reeling forward uncontrollably. His legs tangled and he splatted to the ground, breathless and nearly paralyzed with pain. Still, Stave's ruthless training must have kicked in, and he shoved himself onto his back and threw his hands up to block the finishing blow he knew would be coming.

The Dyrrak loomed over him, seeming to want to take his time to enjoy finishing Jaemus off. Though empty, his gray eyes still seemed to be assessing him, maybe as curious as all the Vinnrics about Jaemus's green-tinted skin.

Never going to live this difference down, I guess. Especially since I've only got a moment of living left.

The Dyrrak began to swing the club up over his head for a final blow. As it reached the apex of its arc, Jaemus got his knees up and feet on the floor and scooted himself backward, using his elbows to help propel him—

But his head was blocked. Not by a wall but by…boots?

He looked up. Directly into the crotch of another Dyrrak.

"Get up, Knight," the woman standing above him said.

"But there's a—" he began, wondering how it was she didn't notice the marauding Dyrrak Ravener about to turn him into mush.

The next instant, an angry hiss came from the enemy, and the woman stepped over Jaemus and began rushing down the hallway to meet it. Several more Dyrrak fighters followed, all vaulting Jaemus or passing beside him as if he were no more than an awkwardly placed vase.

He reached out to the wall and pulled himself to his feet as down the hall the Dyrrak warriors who, thank the Verities, hadn't become monsters set upon the one who had in a brutal melee. The sounds of clubs hitting flesh and the Ravener hissing made Jaemus's stomach turn. After a decidedly wet and heavy thud, it was over and the Ravener lay in a bleeding, broken, unmoving heap.

Jaemus got his breath back and felt only a twinge of the original pain between his shoulder blades. Despite this, he could think of no words to say when the woman whose boots he'd met pushed through the crowd of fighters and stepped up to him. It was Chancellor Aoggvír.

"Do you know what's happening, Knight?" she asked.

"You mean beyond…" His eyes fell on the bleeding mass. "That?"

"Hysteria is running through the citadel. Half, maybe more, of the citadel venerates have been turned into those things, and the Ecclesium is missing."

Jaemus realized he was about to have to be the bearer of what would likely be the worst news anyone in this empire had ever heard. But she needed to be warned. Clearing his throat, he said, "Balavad, the

Verity of Battgjald, has somehow returned and he's changing your people into…those. Raveners is the name I've heard the most. If you can, you have to warn the people of Dyrrakium. And—sorry about this, but I think the Ecclesium is helping him, er, her. Balavad, I mean."

Her hard eyes never left his face as he spoke, but she listened without interruption. When he stopped, she looked to the fighter beside her.

The woman said, "The Ravener in the vaults… it would explain what happened to Venerate Edizriis, Chancellor."

The chancellor nodded, then returned her gaze to Jaemus. "Why is Vaka Aster doing nothing to help us?"

"I, uh, I don't know?" This was partially true. Stave had said Ulfric was in trouble, but he had no idea what kind. He was sorry for the state of confusion he'd caused the woman, but he needed to get to Cote. "Chancellor, the other Knights are in a huge fight on the other side of the Himmingazians' chamber. I have to stay here to keep them safe, and I owe you—"

Where are you, novice?

Stave's voice in his Mentalios link distracted him, and it took him a moment to finish his statement. "I owe you my life, but now I've got to get in there." He pointed to the door at the end of the hall. "Take your troops and join the Knights. Roibeard—you know, the tall pale one— he'll be able to give you better instructions than I can."

Without hesitation, she moved her hands and weapon in an elaborate gesture he at first thought was an attack, then realized was a salute of sorts, and said, "See to your people. Faith eternal, Knight." Then she waved at her group and they sped away back down the hall, leaving him alone with the red pulped Dyrrak Ravener.

Sidestepping around the dead man and doing everything he could to look nowhere but straight ahead, he reached the door. Before entering, he leaned over to scoop up his klinkí stone. *For whatever good it will do me.* Just then the door was pulled open from the inside.

With a greeting on his lips, he stood up—and was immediately struck in the face by a ceramic pitcher.

"Stop!" he yelled, jumping back. "It's me, it's me!"

Heleina, a Glisternaut navigator, dropped the container—or what was left of it—immediately. "Oh, Glint Engineer! I'm so sorry."

He rubbed his temple and his hand came away slightly bloody. One thing about being smacked in the head, he no longer felt the stitch in his side or his bruised back. "It's okay. I'll be okay," he said. And he would, wouldn't he? As soon as his sprite spark kicked in. It wasn't as comforting a thought as he would have expected.

He stepped in and barred the door quickly behind him. "It's not safe out there. Where's Cote?"

Heleina waved toward the front of the room, where Cote was kneeling over one of the pallets, the only one left that wasn't shoved in front of the main entrance's set of double doors to bar anyone from breaking in.

"Jae!" he said as Jaemus ran up to him. The two fell into an embrace. After a moment, Cote pulled free and said, "The Knights are fighting the Dyrraks, who seem to have become more of those foul Battgjaldic beasts. They left Ulfric here when we were attacked. What do we do with him now?"

On the pallet next to Cote lay the Stallari. His normally dark brown skin was now as gray as wet ash. His eyes were open as if he were dead, and they too had a slight sheen covering the glow they'd lately acquired, dimming the Verity influence almost completely. Jaemus recognized the beginnings of the transformation that created the Raveners.

"Do with him?" he raved. "What happened to him?"

"They said he was tricked into drinking a poison sent by Balavad."

"Is he dead?" Deep in his mind he knew Ulfric couldn't be dead, because that would mean Vinnr would cease to exist. And Jaemus still existed enough to have been brained by a pitcher, so...

Cote was looking at him, just as eager for answers as Jaemus was. His lifemate looked remarkably well, if thinner, for a man who'd been close to death yesterday, but that wasn't what Jaemus focused on. He looked confused, out of his depth. *Makes two of us.*

Bardgrim! Bardgrim! It was Roibeard's voice this time. *You have to open the starpath. Get Ulfric and your people to safety. We're not going to be able to hold them off much longer!*

"Jaemus?" Cote asked. "The Knights told us to bar the door from anyone but them. Do you know what we should do?"

He did, but he was having trouble believing it. He held up a finger to Cote and sent: *I'm almost sure you just said I should open a starpath, but I'm also sure you've mistaken me for someone else, because there's no way I—*

Just—oh Verities, it's Balavad! Watch out!...Stave, Safran, group up—we...

And that was the last Roibeard had to say for the moment.

"Jaemus," Cote asked again.

Trembling, Jaemus whispered, "Did the Knights by chance give you a bag or container holding a bunch of celestial junk?"

Cote shook his head. Exasperated now, as well as frightened, Jaemus sent: *Roi, Master Knight? I seem to be without the necessary tools for the starpath.*

He waited but received no response. Trying to come up with a plan, *any* plan, he suddenly remembered what Stave had said—Ulfric had the Scrylle. Then he remembered the map case.

Bending down, he swept aside the unconscious man's robe. The case! He pulled the artifacts free. As he lifted the Fenestros, a boom came from the chamber's door followed by a clatter of smaller sounds. Startled, Jaemus dropped the celestial stone. Afraid he'd broken it, he barely reined in his panic.

"Oh lightning..." he breathed and picked it up. Unmarred. Huffing with relief, he tried again: *Knight Roibeard, if you could just...?*

Still nothing. Shaking, he began the process of converting the Scrylle into a setting for the Fenestros, thus turning the assemblage into a celestial scepter awaiting its crowning jewel. He'd watched Ulfric do it in Himmingaze and the Knights here in Vinnr once or twice. They'd warned him that it took a significant amount of practice and mental discipline to be able to "read" the Scrylle archaeology, that unprepared minds could break from the strain.

And now his mind was about to be tested. *Couldn't even manage a klinki stone...*it now yammered at him unhelpfully.

More hammering came from the doors. It seemed someone was trying to break in.

Cote's eyes rested on the Scrylle. "Can you get us home, Jae?" he asked, his voice calm.

Jaemus looked around and saw the same fear and anxiety in the face of each of his crew. It was this or nothing. There was no way the Himmingazians could fight the Dyrraks, even if they hadn't been wystically enhanced by whatever corrupt brew Balavad had served them.

It's just reading, he told himself. *Smart fellow like you shouldn't have any trouble.*

He grabbed Cote's hand. "Okay, I'm not-not really sure what's going to happen. But the plan is to get us back to Himmingaze the same way we left. You know what to expect. Um, everyone, just grab each other's hands like when we went through the interrealm well and get as close to me as you can. Cote, I'm going to need to hold the Scrylle, so you hold my shoulders or my waist."

"Will that work?" one of the 'Gazians asked.

Through a rapidly tightening throat, he squeaked, "Absolutely." The effect, according to their expressions, wasn't as reassuring as he'd hoped.

Here goes, he thought and dropped the Fenestros into its setting.

The globe began to glow immediately with a soft yellow-blue light, the same though more subdued version of Ulfric's eyes. He wasn't sure if that was encouraging. With a deep breath, he focused his mind the way Safran had spent hours showing him to and "looked" into the Fenestros.

It seemed as if he were whisked off his feet by a strong but unfelt wind. One moment his feet were planted on the ground beside Ulfric, the next he was skidding into a vast white field of nothingness. Aside from the weightless and uncontrollable careening, the overall experience wasn't too terrible.

Then the firebolt struck.

A cascade of blazing lightning-like information exploded in his head like all the lights of the Glister Cloud at once. His mind whipped like a shredded flag in a torrential wind, every thread being yanked separately by the gale, nearly ripping it to pieces. The cavalcade was too much, he feared he would combust into embers at any moment.

All sensation of his body left him. All he knew was the tumbling Cosmos, all of its history, experiences, creations thundering inside his head. He tried to retreat, look away, let go of the celestial cylinder, but he could do none of these. He was lost in a maelstrom and there was no way out.

Jaemus...Jaemus, can you hear me? a thready voice whispered through the chaos. *Bardgrim, where are you? Are you with Ulfric?*

Jaemus's mental jaws opened in a scream, trying to plead for help. His own wail was lost in the wystic thunder of the Scrylle.

He's got us, Jaemus, the speaker continued, and Jaemus realized it was Roibeard. *We're being taken somewhere, but we still have our lenses. If you can hear me, if you can still get to the Scrylle, pay attention. The three of us will help you seek the starpath invocation. Listen to me, Jaemus. Can you hear me?*

Listen, Jaemus, it's Safran. I'm here too.

As am I, novice. If you're hearing us, send us something. Let us know.

As the Knights spoke, their voices grew louder, stronger, and they began to buffer the cacophony that deluged him.

*Help...*he finally managed.

Oh Verities, you're there! Roibeard cried. *And the Scrylle?*

Brain, he mentally moaned, *on fire. Help.*

He's inside, said Safran. *He won't last much longer.*

Hold our voices in your mind, Jaemus. We'll channel the threads to follow to show you the way to open the starpath.

The Knights began to speak as one, their voices twining together—but it wasn't just their voices he was receiving. Images and ideas formed in his head, around him, coalescing into a shield that slowly blocked the onslaught of thousands of turns of Vinnr's lore. Jaemus latched on to their directions as if they were the only candle in a universe of darkness, a candle that, as they continued to mindlink to him, turned into a torch, then a blazing fire. He felt them echoing around him, and after a passage of time he couldn't guess at, the lore of the Scrylle began falling into place. The assault slowed and became endurable.

As he regained the ability to focus, he recognized things in the slowing deluge that made sense. Here, the way to build an airship that could be made nearly invisible through some sort of painted coating made of a rare stone; there, a history of a city that, he understood, had fallen to ruin a thousand turns before this day. It was like everything that had ever been a part of Vinnr was recorded in the Scrylle, every person, every emotion that person had experienced, every invention that had existed, every animal that walked the world's earth. It was, in a word, awesome.

Maybe there was a good reason to remain a Knight after all.

A form began to loom in front of him. Another sphere but huge, as big as Balavad's warship. Unlike that ship, though, it was not solid and it blazed like a blue-white sun.

I think this is it, he sent, distantly thrilled he could articulate thoughts again. *Do you see it?*

...Knights? Still there?

Inside his mental ocean, pressure began to build, the same pressure as at first. Archaneology began to batter into him again, whipping wildly like a striking fleech. He felt less and less of the other three's minds with him. They were growing reedy, thinning...leaving.

KNIGHTS! Don't go, I don't know how to get out. I don't know how to open the starpath!

A final thought from Roibeard reached him. *A starpath is a bridge, Jaemus. Just cross it...*

Cross it? Cross how? I have no feet at the moment! Like a silk sheet, the last of the Knights' thoughts slipped away. The Scrylle's contents blurred around him, threatening to sweep him off with it in an instant. The only thing left he could make sense of was the blazing blue-white starpath, its edges already losing definition as if the storm of everything past and present was tearing it apart.

Before he could be whipped away in the frenzy, Jaemus did the one thing he'd learned that might help, the same thing that had worked for him last time—if not in the exact way he'd hoped.

He leaped.

CHAPTER FORTY-ONE

Ulfric was able to goad Urgo back inside the throne room, though the bruhawk needed little compelling to sweep Ulfric's Mentalios lens up in one of his talons. He seemed to understand innately that the lens was their link, and with Yggo's help, the lens's chain was draped around his neck to leave his talons free.

However, he and Yggo refused to take the inside passages through the citadel to chase down the Knights and join their fight. Ulfric pushed the bird in every way he could think of—promises of reward, plays to Urgo's loyalties, threats—but bruhawks were not known for their tenacious and persevering nature for nothing. The bird would not be urged past the doorway of the throne room, and in the end, Ulfric had to settle for cajoling Urgo back outside to fly down toward the structure's base with Yggo soaring beside them.

As they dropped like a stone toward the earth, Ulfric cringed at what he saw. A group of Dyrrak warriors swarmed out from the main hall onto the jutting pavilion overlooking the citadel's amphitheater. They moved with the speed and decisiveness that spoke of a mission. The bruhawk's beyond-human eyesight showed Ulfric more than he could detect on his own, and he saw clearly that the Dyrraks had undergone the same change his own body had. They were now puppets of Balavad.

His first impulse was to direct Urgo and Yggo to assault them. The birds were the size of people, with claws and beaks that would shred someone into strips of bleeding flesh no sword-wielder could ever emulate. But he thought better of it. There were at least a dozen shapeshifted Dyrraks, and Ulfric didn't know what would become of him if Urgo were killed. The bruhawks were as much a part of the Order as any Knight, and he wouldn't sacrifice them if he didn't have to.

But he had to get to Roibeard, Stave, and Safran. Balavad was enslaving the Dyrraks, and the Knights would already be outnumbered. They had to flee, take his body and Vaka Aster somewhere the usurper wouldn't find them. Their one choice now was to use Vaka Aster's Scrylle to open a starpath and spirit away—and if they'd made it to the Himmingazians' chamber, they may already be preparing to do exactly that. If he wasn't with them when they did—his incorporeal self, that was—he may never get his body back. Then what would happen to Symvalline and Isemay? What would happen to Vaka Aster and Vinnr? And the Himmingazians? And last but in no way the least to *him*?

Yggo swept close to Urgo, near enough that the air streaming over their wings ruffled each other's feathers. They lofted higher, speaking to each other, he assumed, with squawks and churrs. Something was coming. He sensed it too—a crackling in the air that sent pinpricks tingling over his skin. The same feeling as when—

A brilliant column of cerulean flame rent the sky above the citadel, spearing it through the middle like a comet.

A starpath well.

With mighty flaps, the bruhawks sped away from the column of light toward the south. Frantic, Ulfric didn't know whether to try to force Urgo to go back or to let him keep fleeing. But in a moment, it wasn't a question anymore. The well closed as quickly as it opened, leaving the citadel itself whole and undamaged.

He had no idea who'd come. Or who'd gone. Was he now alone in Vinnr, formless and helpless?

The only way to know was to get closer and see for himself. At his urging the bruhawks swooped low toward the row of massive arches that spanned the citadel's long column-lined pavilion like ribs. Urgo complied readily, much to his relief. They were getting used to each other. Just as the hawk was about to dip between two arches, he faltered and flapped away. Ulfric sensed his fear, a palpable sensation like tacks being driven into his mind. The birds did a tight half circle and rose upward again.

Calmly now, stay close, Urgo. We have to learn what's happened, what's still happening. As he sent this thought to his copilot, a thick smoke rolled out through the archway over the citadel's entrance, across the wide landing in front, to the end of the column-lined pavilion and down the steps toward the courtyard arena. Its torpid thickness was like a slow-moving forest fire. He knew that miasma. The agony of being enveloped in it had almost made him wish for death aboard Balavad's warship.

The usurper was here.

The smoke thinned enough to reveal the Domine Ecclesium step out to the dais at the end of the citadel's lined pavilion. He was carrying a satchel. Safran's satchel, the one she'd collected the artifacts in.

Dread tightened around him like a noose. If the usurper had the bag, he must have the Knights as well. Safran would never have given it up. Or had she abandoned it for some reason and taken the starpath away from Vinnr? Vaka Aster's Scrylle was in the map case he'd been carrying before his body had been taken from him, but Balavad's Scrylle and two Fenestrii might still be in that satchel, as were the rest of Vaka Aster's celestial stones. If the usurper had them, many of the tools the Knights could use to protect Vaka Aster's vessel would be gone. Ulfric had to get that bag back.

Desperately, he pressed Urgo to swoop down and snatch the satchel from the Ecclesium. As the bird turned to line up his trajectory, the usurper himself emerged—but in a new form, a woman's. Somehow, a

Battgjaldic had survived the destruction of Balavad's realm. There was no mistaking this being came from there, and no mistaking the celestial light that shone from her eyes. Balavad had a new vessel.

Again, Urgo veered away from the dreadful Verity—nothing could compel the hawk to get close to her. The bruhawk instead flew to a spire a few dozen yards over the citadel's line of columns and landed, Yggo setting down nearby, making both themselves and Ulfric witnesses to what was coming.

Throughout the amphitheater that surrounded the lower courtyard arena, thousands of Dyrrak people sat in silence. Their faces showed a rapt sense of awe, confusion, and perhaps, though their stoic nature made it hard to know, a hint of fear. None had ever seen a starpath well. Knowing the Dyrraks' devotion to Verity lore, it was almost a certainty that they knew what it was. But knowing of something and witnessing that something in person, especially something as staggering as a path between the Cosmic realms, was very different.

Yet no Dyrrak fled. They waited for whatever was coming. And though it terrified and infuriated him, Ulfric could do nothing but wait with them.

Unnoticed, the bruhawks stood as still as sentinels as Balavad emerged. The Verity was hidden from the amphitheater in the shadows cast by the arches and columns, but Ulfric could see into the dim space from Urgo's perch perfectly as Balavad waved a hand to someone behind her.

Ulfric tried to call the Knights again, hoping that because he was in a sense once more embodied, his mental voice might have some power in the Mentalios. *Knights, Roibeard, can you hear me? Eisa? Jaemus? What's happened to everyone?*

As he waited for a response, a rumbling noise that sounded like great wooden wheels came from inside the hall. The answer to his fellow Knights' fates was given to Ulfric then. In the form of a contraption being pulled out to the end of the citadel's pavilion.

It resembled a gallows in every way that mattered. Being dragged with ropes by eight Dyrrak Raveners, the rectangular wheeled platform, the length of three grown horses, had stout vertical beams on each end with a crossbeam laid overtop. From the crossbeam dangled five cages, each only large enough for something the size of a human head. And that was what each contained.

The Knights themselves hung like meat in a butcher shop from their necks, which protruded through the cages' bottoms, leaving all their body weight suspended from their caged heads. Ulfric could see their neck muscles stretched as taut as ship sails in a frantic gale, his imagination gruesomely suggesting that it would only be a matter of a firm yank by someone heavy to tear their heads from their bodies. He could see no movement nor a sign of life among them, though they were all there. Safran, Stave, Mallich, Eisa. And when he saw the last body hanging from the crossbeam, he wanted to weep.

It was his own.

Then who summoned the starpath...? Jaemus? The thought was whipped away quickly by the frenzy of rage and horror at seeing his friends in such ghastly circumstances.

The Birdcage was an inhumane device, though its construction preceded Balavad. The Dyrraks had long been known for their methods, the Birdcage included, of keeping order among both their own and those who tried, or even considered trying, to imperil them. And now it was being used on the Knights of Vaka Aster by the Dyrraks. And willingly, it appeared to Ulfric, at least in the case of Ecclesium.

From his vantage, he could see the leader of the Dyrraks had not been turned into one of Balavad's puppets. His physique and countenance hadn't changed, yet he was working for the Verity as if he had become a Ravener himself. Dyrrakium had sunk to an unknown low. And with this development, Ulfric could see Balavad's plan clearly. The Verity was carefully, methodically pushing her septic consecration elixir among the Dyrrak people, at least to those who needed more coercion than whatever she'd offered the Ecclesium. She'd gotten to Ulfric, maybe before she even knew Ulfric was present in the citadel. The syke liquor that every Dyrrak favored was the perfect vector. And soon, if Ulfric had to guess, the entirety of Elezaran would be asked to drink, too.

The fact that Dyrrakium's own leader had needed no more persuasion than Balavad's poison words to follow her was the thing that most turned Ulfric's guts into ice. What had she told the Ecclesium? That the Dyrrak forces would at last be freed to fulfill their purpose and prove to the rest of Vinnr that they were the most favored among Verities? Was a promise of war and dominion all the Ecclesium needed, and did it not matter to him what Verity he followed, so long as the promise was kept?

Ulfric had every indication to think this was the truth.

His attention turned back to the Knights. Their bodies were limp and eyes closed. Unconscious—he *hoped*. As proof, he looked at his own body. As long as his flesh lived, Vinnr was spared. But there was no telling what Balavad would do to him now. One thing seemed without question: Vaka Aster must still be shackled to his former self. She had fought Balavad last time Ulfric had been out of his wits. But this time…nothing.

More Dyrrak Raveners began to filter from the citadel and moved down the side stairs toward the open gates that were built into Citadel Suprima's outer walls in regular intervals. In quiet, orderly rows, they lined the walls expectantly. Many of the unchanged Dyrraks sitting in the amphitheater stands glanced at them but all remained where they were. *Sheep about to be slaughtered,* Ulfric thought.

Balavad motioned to the Ecclesium and said something Ulfric didn't catch. The Dyrrak leader gave orders to the eight Dyrraks who'd brought out the Birdcage, and they lowered and unharnessed Ulfric's body from its height.

A stone slab large enough for the bodies of two adults lay at the top of the dais, visible to everyone in the courtyard stands. The Ecclesium had Ulfric's body placed atop it, the cage still encompassing his head. For the first time, the Dyrraks reacted. Shocked, muted murmurs started among those with the best view of the dais. Most of the population of Elezaran had come out to watch Ulfric's procession from the docks to the citadel over the course of three hours. Few would have forgotten the face of the one they believed to be the vessel of their creator.

Next to Ulfric's slack body, the Ecclesium spread the Verities' artifacts, and Ulfric and Urgo watched raptly. Among Vaka Aster's artifacts, there were only four Fenestrii. Ulfric's eyes shot to his body, which had been stripped of its cloak and map case. Secondly, the Ecclesium laid out Balavad's Scrylle and the two celestial stones belonging to him. Ulfric wanted to have Urgo swoop down and grab as many of them as he could, but he doubted even a creature as swift as the bruhawk could outfly Balavad's malevolence. He had to stay put, as difficult as it was. *Look for a chance to free the Knights.* But what he was seeing began to look more and more like the preparations for a sacrifice.

The Ecclesium stepped forward and raised his arms. The crowd's silence came as swiftly as a blade through a neck.

"Warriors and servants of Dyrrakium." His voice echoed inside the amphitheater bowl. "Our unending faith and devotion make us, all of us, the worthiest of all people in the Great Cosmos. We have never wavered in our devotion or service to our maker, and came to the aid of Vaka Aster herself when called. Because we are loyal! Because we are faithful! Because we do not shun our duty no matter how difficult or how much we must sacrifice. Is this not true, people of Dyrrakium?"

A cry of assent rose up, then stopped when the Ecclesium chopped his hand down. "For seven hundred and fifteen turns, we have listened to the wisdom of the greatest living Dyrrak, the Nazarian Most High, and we exiled ourselves from the lessers of Vinnr, not allowing their false faith to stain our six pure Lines or sully our own faith."

He paced back and forth in front of the stone platform. "And so, it will pain every one of you as much as it pains me when I tell you that we, all of us, have been deceived." He stopped and swept his cold stare over the crowd from the center of the dais, his black hair glistening under Halla. Voices began, a grumble of confusion that slowly, insidiously became one of anger.

"Vaka Aster has abandoned us!" he roared, drowning out the people. "You saw it yourselves just now. The maker fled from Vinnr, forsaking all of her people! This wilted flesh before you"—he waved a dismissive hand at Ulfric's body on the slab—"is nothing but a false idol. And why were we deceived? To further distance the great and ever-faithful Dyrrak people from our destiny! This vessel behind me is a lie!"

The Ecclesium spun around and yanked Ulfric from the platform with such force that his body hit the first step, then began to roll down the stairway, gaining momentum. The amphitheater would have been dead silent, but the clanking sound of the iron cage on his head smashing against stone shattered it. When his body finally hit the base of the stairs, it lay motionless with his limbs bent awkwardly. From his perch, Ulfric saw blood coming from wounds on his head and arms.

"That is no Vaka Aster," the Ecclesium proclaimed.

The Dyrrak people began to push forward toward the body, jostling each other down the stands' aisles and into the stairways, some with murder in their eyes, others with tears.

The lies the Ecclesium spewed were incredible. Even if the Dyrrak leader believed Ulfric was not the vessel, that didn't change the fact that he was—and if the Dyrraks carried out some misbegotten vengeance for deceiving them on his body, they would inadvertently destroy themselves, and everything else. Ulfric looked to Balavad, who remained shadowed in the background beneath the arches, where none would see him clearly. Surely, she would stop the Dyrraks from attacking Ulfric's body, wouldn't she? If she wanted Vinnr destroyed, she'd had ample opportunity to do so.

Ulfric couldn't chance it. He poised Urgo to dive and protect the vessel, but it was the Ecclesium who stopped the Dyrraks.

"Stay back!" the Dyrrak leader commanded. "There is justice to mete out, yes! Not just to this cozening Knight Corporealis who faked divinity, but also to these other Knights for abetting this most abominable lie."

He let the crowd settle as he turned and gestured for the Dyrrak Raveners on the platform to retrieve Eisa's dangling body. She was brought forward and laid on the slab next and her cage removed. The Dyrrak leader then produced a vial from his robes and dumped its contents into her mouth. Eisa sputtered and choked, rolling off the flat stones as she heaved to get a breath. She seemed to come to and groggily used the platform to pull herself to her feet, swaying and blinking at the Ecclesium as if she barely knew who he was. She looked gravely ill to Ulfric, though not transformed into one of Balavad's pets. Unable to stand by herself, she gripped the slab and breathed in gasps.

The Ecclesium eyed her warily for a moment, then turned back to the crowd. "But there is one witness to this abominable lie whose word is more sacrosanct than even my own. Our Nazarian Most High, heir to the Sixth Line, and kin to the last vessel of Vaka Aster before our maker abandoned Vinnr and abandoned *us*.

"You all came here today to see the Nazarian challenge me, the Venerable Domine Ecclesium who has longed served Dyrrakium as one of its most devoted leaders. Instead, it is we the *faithful* who challenge this betrayer. The Nazarian's grace may have been stripped by her own duplicity, and we shall judge her not only as her own people, but as the greatest people in the Cosmos."

He turned to face the ailing Knight. "What do you have to say for yourself, Nazarian? Why has our maker forsaken us? Was it the Knights Corporealis who created this rift between her creations and Vaka Aster? Did the Knights defy their oaths because you all lusted for the power to rule Vinnr yourselves?"

He grabbed Eisa by the back of the neck and dragged her to the edge of the steps. Her feet slid and caught, and she barely stayed upright. He held her before him like an offering and spoke in a tone that echoed throughout the amphitheater.

"Speak, Nazarian, and be judged by your betters for your crimes."

CHAPTER FORTY-TWO

As a willful and determined nine-year-old, Eisa had once scaled halfway up the Citadel Suprima's outside wall to prove to her trainer she was stronger and more agile than he thought she was. He'd warned her it was impossible and forbid her from trying it. So she did.

Going up had been easy. But coming down, she'd lost her footing sixty feet aboveground and crashed to the hard-packed arena courtyard. The only thing that had saved her life was the fact that the citadel's outer walls angled slightly toward the pyramid peak overhead, slowing her descent just enough. She'd broken twelve bones and bruised her lungs, liver, and kidneys. But she'd never lost consciousness and had lived with the pain for several thirty-nights as she'd finally grown strong enough to walk again.

That sharp, driving pain from head to foot during that first few hours after she'd hit the ground was the closest she'd ever felt to this.

She wobbled unsteadily, grasping Penitence Rock—where those found guilty of high crimes or dishonors were flogged—for balance. The suffering induced by Balavad's vile miasma still raced through her, wrapping her bones and tissues in febrile tendrils beneath her skin, but it was diminishing. The cool healing juice of the ong fruit, presumably administered to her by the Domine Ecclesium, had reduced the pain in her throat. Now it was the only part of her that didn't ache, but she didn't have the luxury of attending to her complaints. Not with the Ecclesium's accusations ringing in her ears.

"Was it the Knights Corporealis who created this rift between us and Vaka Aster? Did you defy your oaths because you lusted for the power to rule Vinnr yourselves? Speak, Nazarian, and be judged by your betters for your crimes."

Thanks to the ong, the curdled laugh that rumbled out of her was tolerable. The bitter irony of being accused of the very thing she'd slain the Himmingazian Mystae for was too rich to hold it back. But then she glimpsed Balavad in the entryway, and her laughter dried up.

"Whatever that slaghammer told you is a lie, Starkas," she grated out. "You'll kill us all if you put an end to Aldinhuus."

The Ecclesium released her and she staggered but stayed on her feet. Facing her, he spoke low so the crowd wouldn't hear. "I know your Stallari is the vessel, Nazarian. And I know how easily and readily he turned on Vaka Aster, on his own maker. But he lied, you lied, all of you. The Knights are faithless and don't deserve to be treated as anything but. Balavad of Battgjald, however, has not lied to me. Why should he? We Dyrraks have waited long enough for our maker to acknowledge us. Balavad did not make us wait, and he'll give Dyrrakium everything we've ever desired."

"You blaspheme. The usurper will only give you shackles and death. He's a broken, corrupted piece of a greater whole. They all are."

"Who's blaspheming now?" He spun back to the crowd and said, "The fallen Nazarian has words." Then back to her: "Tell them of the Knights Corporealis and their lies. Tell them who our redeeming Verity is, Eisa, and that they should trust and follow Balavad now. Not the Knights, not you. This is the only way to bring Dyrrakium back the world, and to better it."

"Better which? The world or Dyrrakium? Or you?"

The cold grin on his face showed her that the answer hardly mattered.

She ground her teeth together and looked over her shoulder at her companions hanging like animals, then back down to the foot of the stairs at Ulfric's battered form. If only he had trusted her more, and she him. If he'd shared the rite to build the Verity cage, perhaps she could use the celestial artifacts now lying on the platform and imprison Balavad. If only Griggory had found Lífs's Scrylle and the banishment spell. If only she hadn't killed Himmingaze's Mystae and caused them to be lost in the first place. So many regrets.

Not the least of which was her regret for failing not herself but her companions. Stave, he was the stoutest man she'd ever met, and though she'd questioned his temperance, she'd never questioned his loyalty to his companions. And Safran, a child really, but the wisest woman Eisa knew, and always seeing straight to the heart of any matter. She'd been proud to be a Knight with the Ivoryssian woman, even if she'd never said it. And Roibeard...Roibeard. His stalwart devotion, his nobility, none could match them. He was a man she could have loved if their paths had been different. She could not denounce her companions, each as strong and as honorable as a Dyrrak, and each as devout. They should not be forced to pay for her mistakes, or for Ulfric's.

Now, she was the last Knight standing. The last one who could make any difference. And her home, her birthplace and the empire she'd left out of duty, was the only thing remaining that still mattered to her. She didn't know Bardgrim's fate or his people's, but it wasn't hard to guess at it. Doomed like the rest of their kind. She had failed everything and everyone.

And it all led to this moment, with this one last chance to do something right.

"Let the other Knights go," she demanded. "And I will proclaim your lies."

"No. There is a price for what Aldinhuus did, and the Knights Corporealis must pay it."

"Why am I addressing you, blackguard?" she spat. With more strength of will than of flesh, she leaped onto the slab and raised her voice, looking to Balavad behind her. "I will speak to you now, usurper.

If you release the Knights and give them their freedom, I will not only renounce Vaka Aster, but I will serve you. Hear me? I will serve."

She sensed the Ecclesium behind her prepared to grab her if told to but refraining. Waiting for orders like a good little pup. For the first time since Eisa had come to, Balavad showed herself. With a gait that seemed to be more float than footsteps, the Verity approached. Eisa held herself steady with the last of her fortitude. She would not cower. She would *never* cower.

The Verity did not need to step onto the stone to look her in the eye. Her body simply rose into the air and hovered before Eisa, an arm's-length distant. Eisa found she could not help but stare into her illuminated eyes, no longer black but a cerulean so deep and liquid she thought she could drown in them. That burning smell struck her nostrils again potently, and she blinked, breaking the spell. As Balavad's expression turned from thoughtful to decisive, Eisa's heart beat crazily.

"Yes," the usurper said, "creation of my quin, you will serve."

Her arm extended, and from the corner of her eye, Eisa saw the Battgjald Scrylle lift from the slab and fly into her hand. Lightning fast, the Verity shot toward her and punched the celestial cylinder forward at Eisa's chest, directly at her breastbone. Then *into* her chest.

Eisa screamed.

And screamed more.

The Verity drew back and pulled her hand away, leaving the cylinder in place, embedded between Eisa's ribs. She collapsed on the slab, every rib splintered, her breastbone all but disintegrated. She could feel her heart beating like a caught hare's against the celestial metal. Each pulsing brush of her heart's meat against it burned like coals. Her throat locked and her vision blurred and broke into black dots. She welcomed the moment of death, the only thing that could make this pain bearable.

But she didn't die. Something worse was happening. Filaments that felt like embers began to grow from the embedded Scrylle outward, crawling along her ribs, her heart, her lungs, and then onward. She felt the bone splinters knitting themselves together in an abnormal way, around the Scrylle itself, as if joining the metal and absorbing it as part of her body. And the tendrils of heat continued, to her fingertips and toes, her head, her hair. Whether she was breathing or not, she couldn't tell, but she no longer felt the need to. She was simply living, her body becoming something new that had no need for air.

The agony had been replaced by the crawling sensation—which was so much worse—and she pushed herself to her hands and knees. Raising her head, she met the Ecclesium's eyes, and the horror she saw in his face spread to her. What was happening to her? She looked toward Balavad, who now stood back with her feet on the ground, watching Eisa. The Verity clutched one of the onyx Fenestrii. Eisa could read the silvery runes that glowed on its surface.

"What did you do to me?" she whispered.

"I need a warrior to protect these," Balavad said simply, waving a hand at the other celestial artifacts. "And you did offer to serve me." She lobbed the Fenestros lightly upward, and the next instant, it shot into Eisa's chest between her collarbones just above the Scrylle. The two artifacts connected. She was hurled off the dais and into one of the beams of the Birdcage, coming to rest on her back with her horrorstruck eyes wide open. Moments later, Balavad's face peered down at her, and she heard her speaking—but not aloud. Her voice crept into Eisa's thoughts as if they were her own.

What you did to that Vinnric woman was remarkable. A creature with your strength will be useful to me, but your creativity is the true fortune.

Somehow, she found some fight still in her. *Get out of my head, fiend.*

It is not yours anymore, Nazarian. In another moment, you'll be completely mine.

She only had a second left, and she would use it. With a Scrylle at her disposal—in fact, actually part of her being—she chanted the words to open a starpath well. The sky was split open by a beam of light. As it reached for Penitence Rock, Eisa let her eyes find the rest of the Knights, and the beam seized them.

Find Griggory and Bardgrim and save us, friends, she thought. *For Vinnr's sake, keep your faith in this fight.*

The last thing she saw before her mind gave in were the bruhawks,

Urgo and Yggo, flying toward the starpath. Remarkably, draped around Urgo's neck was...was it Ulfric's Mentalios lens?

The world crackled around her as the starpath pulled the Knights inside—and then she knew herself as Eisa, Stallari Regent of the Knights Corporealis of Vinnr, no more.

CHAPTER FORTY-THREE

Jaemus hadn't had the chance to ask the all-important questions about returning to Himmingaze, such as where would they arrive and what should they expect?

However, as the wash of Cosmos-traveling energy dissipated and he opened his eyes, he realized how silly those questions were—because he was about to arrive the same way Ulfric had just a few short cycles ago. Face-first on the stone floor of the Creatress's temple after a sudden and short fall from the ceiling.

THUNK.

Every iota of air left his body as though shot from a cannon. He rolled to one side and pulled his knees into his chest and wheezed and wheezed. Speckles of something struck him, and he looked up in time to see bits of broken masonry clattering down. Unlike Ulfric's arrival, however, he seemed to have come *through* the roof rather than appearing suddenly beneath it.

The last loosened chunk landed nearby without harming him. As he looked up into the Glister Cloud, strange bright flashes lit up and faded, followed by a boom of thunder so loud it shook the ancient building. Then the sky began to literally rain people.

Before he could do anything to get out of the way, the Glisternauts poured through the hole in the ceiling and, unfortunately, through parts that had still been intact, coming to rest all around him with similar bumps and thumps. As much as he could while covering his head with his arms, he counted them. When the sound of landing bodies had ceased for more than a few moments, he finally tallied those he'd seen and those he'd heard and quickly deduced all were accounted for.

Amid the Himmingazians' groans of pain and gasps of astonishment, finally, his chest unlocked and he pulled in much-needed air. "Cote? Glisternauts? Is anyone hurt? Is anyone missing?"

One by one, the returned Himmingazian people stirred and began to call out their condition. None seemed badly hurt. Jaemus stood, finding himself also none the worse for wear.

He could make out little in the gloom inside. The Glister Cloud was in the dim part of its cycle, and only the flashes of lightning and the illuminated gasses that comprised much of the Cloud gave them any light at all.

"Cote?"

"Here!" His lifemate paced toward him, and Jaemus could have wept with joy.

A particularly fierce flash lit up the interior, and biting wind hurled itself through the hole in the roof, so cold and piercing it felt malevolent. They'd arrived in the midst of a Glister Cloud storm apparently, as strong as, or more so, any he'd ever witnessed. *Weeks or even just days left, Eisa said,* he thought, and for the first time he believed it not just in his mind but in his bones.

Cote hugged him hard. "You did it, Jae. We're home." His eyes rose to take in the stormy sky. "What's left of it, anyway."

"Now then," Jaemus said, stepping back. "Time to find—wait, where's Ulfric?"

Suddenly frantic, he scanned the floor near him, but the strobe-like effect of lightning and distracting drums of thunder made seeing much of anything impossible. He reached for the Mentalios lens hanging from his chest—still there, thank the sky sprites, and in one piece—and mouthed the words to illuminate it and shed a more regular light around the ancient decrepit structure.

And light came, but not the kind he was expecting. The next thing he knew, he was lifted off the ground inside a glowing cerulean sphere that sent waves of oddly pleasant vibrations over his skin. The effect was not unlike traveling through a starpath well, but muted and far less discombobulating. *I guess you can get used to anything when you're on a better-than-passing acquaintanceship with the creators of the Cosmos,* he realized.

Jaemus knew the sphere for what it was and was relieved, for once, to be engulfed within it—a net of klinkí stones, Ulfric's most likely. But why Ulfric had him thus encumbered wasn't immediately clear.

It wasn't until he noticed the Glisternauts, all but Cote, had scattered that he realized he might be making a mistaken assumption about his predicament and who was causing it.

"Your gramsirene would have been proud of you, Jaemus Bardgrim," a voice from the gloom said. "She always told me you were destined for more than the Glisternauts. It seems you've become a...a Cosmosnaut!"

"Release him, old man," Cote demanded, holding steady next to Jaemus's bubble, but not quite touching it.

Jaemus couldn't see clearly through the wavering blue envelope, but that voice, and the snicker that came after... "Griggory?" he asked. "That's you, isn't it?"

Despite being saved the effort of finding the old Vinnric, Jaemus wasn't confident such a convenience was going to do him any good. The Knight had never seemed the most...balanced of men.

A moment passed, then he was lowered gently back to the floor. The klinkí stone net widened and rose overhead to become a shield to keep out the wind and rain pouring through the roof.

Cote grabbed his elbow. "Are you all right?"

Jaemus nodded and stared toward the doorway. In the wystic stones' blue shimmer, he could make out the form of Griggory standing before it.

"Master Knight," Jaemus began, nearly melting with relief, "I can't believe my luck, but you are exactly who I'm looking for. I don't think I have time to explain everything, but I came because—"

"You never give up hope," Griggory cut in. "Like a Knight Corporealis, you keep your faith in the fight."

He'd always been an odd one, the old man. A friend to Jaemus's gramsirene Vreyja since Jaemus's childhood, but reclusive, always shying away from the company of others, sometimes absent for annicycles. Jaemus had always thought he was just an unwell hermit his gramsirene pitied, but he'd been there for most of Jaemus's life, if distantly.

Yet, after the revelations of the last few days, Jaemus had new questions. Had his gramsirene known who—and what—Griggory was? Had she learned everything she'd taught Jaemus, all that forbidden lore and history of the ancient beliefs that could have seen both her and Jaemus charged with crimes against Himmingaze, from Griggory himself? Jaemus had the dawning realization of just how much his life had directed him to this moment, here, now, with this Knight Corporealis from another realm, and prepared him to serve this all-important purpose.

He brushed the fractured bits of roof stones from his trousers and turned around to give the frightened Glisternauts what he hoped was a reassuring smile. "It's okay," he said to them. "He's a Knight. Like Ulfric and the others. Perfectly friendly." *I hope.*

Turning back, he said to Griggory, "I won't argue with that old saw, faith and fights and so on, I guess," he said. "But listen, Eisa told me everything, and I hope you can help me find the Creatress's Scrylle because I think we might actually be able to save Himmingaze." *And where is Ulfric?* he wondered.

Stepping up to Jaemus, Griggory smiled, his gaunt face and large teeth bathed in a blue glow that gave the illusion he was some vicious sea creature. Jaemus had never seen the man look so wild, almost dangerous. "You are cleverer by far than I'd guessed, Jaemus, though your gramsirene said you were. And with just as much grit as Glint. But I wonder, I do, why have you brought me these?" He reached into his Himmingazian uniform, which was tattered and dripping wet, and pulled free Vaka Aster's Scrylle, still bearing the Fenestros.

"Erm, well I didn't exactly. But have them. They're more yours than mine, anyway." Jaemus could see he was going to have to get right to the point. If anyone was going to be prone to wandering and losing focus, it wasn't going to be him, for once. "Master Knight, please listen. There are some...Verity issues in Vinnr we will need to attend to soon, but first, we're going to find the Creatress's Fenestrii and bring Himmingaze out of the Cloud for good."

He began to reach into his pocket for the Scrylle map when the old Knight's hand darted forward, fast as a fleech. He didn't even have time to flinch before Griggory's fingers plucked the Mentalios from his chest and held it up, eyeing Jaemus through it as if it were a monocle. "Young Ulfric made this," he said. "And you"—his eyes widened—"are ordained!"

Nodding, feeling oddly self-conscious, Jaemus said, "I am, yes. It was kind of an accident. Part of that explanation I don't think we have time for."

Griggory dropped the Mentalios again, scowling at Jaemus. "One is not ordained by a Verity by accident, 'Gazian."

"No, I know, I just meant, it wasn't something I meant to happen. You see..." Despite his wish for urgency, he clearly wasn't going to press Griggory to action without some explanation, so he launched into the briefest version of events he could manage. When through, he held his tongue as Griggory rubbed his chin star and paced a short circle, scowling harder, occasionally flicking an unreadable glance at the rest of the Glisternauts.

Finally, the old Knight regathered his klinkí stones and tucked them away, muttering cryptically, "So with Balavad's realm destroyed, he will be more focused on preventing the Syzyckí Elementum than ever."

Jaemus started to ask what he meant and where Ulfric was, and whether Griggory had some ideas on how to rescue the Knights—and the rest of Vinnr—from Balavad's takeover but stopped when a familiar sensation began to whisper along the hairs of first his arms, then his head and eyebrows and eyelashes. That tingling, energetic feeling...

"Get back!" he cried and hooked Cote's arm. With a leap, he pulled Cote toward the wall of the temple as the beam of a new starpath struck the floor where they'd been standing.

Moments later, three figures fell from above and the starpath disappeared.

As the charged air dissipated, Jaemus looked over the new arrivals. Safran, Stave, and Mallich Roibeard, each with a bizarre metal contraption on their head.

With a wild holler, Stave leaped up. "Slag rotter, get offa me!" He began yanking the metal cage with brute force, and Jaemus worried he'd dislocate his jaw.

"Stave, wait!" he said and stepped to where the Knight could see him. "Let me see if I can help."

"Novice?" Stave said, marginally calming down. "You survived? Where are we?"

Roibeard and Safran began to rouse, and Stave rushed to Safran before Jaemus could answer. As he helped her to her feet, Jaemus reached a hand out to Mallich.

"Steady," he said, pulling the laconic Knight up.

Mallich gave him a nod of thanks, then pressed his hands to the cage enclosing his head, feeling for a release or lock. As he did, he gazed around the confines of the temple. "Himmingaze," he muttered in a low voice. "Eisa, I don't know how, but you got us here." He turned to Jaemus. "Where's Ulfric?"

It was becoming increasingly clear to Jaemus that the leader of the Knights hadn't made it. Somehow, Jaemus had included the Himmingazians in the starpath but left Ulfric behind. With a sick feeling, he thought hard about whether he'd been in contact with Ulfric's unconscious form when he'd looked into the Scrylle, but it was all a haze. Either he'd failed the Stallari, or for some reason Vaka Aster had not let Ulfric leave Vinnr.

"I don't think he's here," he said simply.

Roibeard stared at him through the bars of the head cage for so long Jaemus began to wonder if he was going to need to defend himself. He patted his pocket containing his lone klinkí stone and nearly laughed at himself for his foolishness. But before it came to that, Griggory spoke.

"Mallich Roibeard, my old friend and Yorish fisherman of the highest caliber. Never met a chelbiefin shark you couldn't outswim."

Roibeard spun toward the old man with wide eyes. "Griggory?" He took a short step toward the old Knight, then stopped. "Is it truly you?"

Griggory stepped forward and lowered his lit wystic stones. When he smiled, it was the first time Jaemus had seen such a genuine expression cross the man's face. "Hold still now, Roi, let me get that ugly thing off."

Through the use of the klinkí stone lock-melting technique, like Jaemus had witnessed Ulfric once use, the cages were soon removed from all three Knights. Safran and Stave introduced themselves to the ancient Vinnric. Then the four Knights, five if he counted himself, Jaemus supposed, stood in a circle beneath the battering rain. *Is this what warriors do when they're the last to survive a battle?* Jaemus wondered, both loathing the feeling and curiously contented by it at the same time.

"That's it then," Roibeard said. "We've lost Ulfric and Vinnr. And we've lost Eisa."

Safran sent: *And Mylla, Symvalline, and Isemay.*

Stave and Roibeard nodded, and Roibeard concluded, his voice an anvil, "We've simply…lost."

Jaemus looked to Stave, who seemed good at offering options, even when they were bad ones, but the gruffest of the Knights remained unusually quiet.

"Wait," he said, desperate for something to stir up some hope. "We still have Vaka Aster's Scrylle. That's a good thing, right? And there are still five of us, plus…" He trailed off, unable to come up with any further items to salve their collective wounds. And he definitely wasn't going to mention the chance that Himmingaze might be brought back from the brink of doom as the bright side. It wasn't, not for them.

"The Vinnr Scrylle can't help us now, Bardgrim," said Roibeard. "It was Balavad's that contained the key to unlocking Ulfric and Vaka Aster's cage, and that Scrylle is empty. Only Mylla and Ulfric ever looked inside it, and if Ulfric didn't know the way, Mylla couldn't have either. Not that it matters, given her fate." He lapsed into silence then, leaving them even grimmer than before.

"Jaemus," Cote said from beside him, tipping his head to the rest to get their pardon for his interruption. "I can't entirely understand what's being said, but we have another concern. The Glisternauts, and you and I, need to get home. We have no ship here, but perhaps he does." His eyes shifted to Griggory and back to Jaemus. "Can you ask him if he can get word to the Council of Nine at Vann that we've... returned?"

Jaemus nodded, glad to have something to do that seemed achievable. But as he turned to speak to Griggory, the Knight began pacing hurriedly toward the temple's entrance. The doors were askew, the hinges having been bent sometime recently, and a sky-splitting flash of green-white light burst outside, practically on the structure's steps. Jaemus's eyelids slammed shut. When he opened them again, the massive head of a sea monster was poking through the opening.

He let out a caw like a wounded raven and backpedaled, too quickly, falling hard on his rear. "Run, everyone!" he wheezed, too frightened to get enough force behind the words to be heard.

But Griggory, instead of running, stood in front of the beast and calmly reached out to pat its snout. "Let's retrieve her now, shall we, Hither?"

I-I must have hit my head when I fell from the starpath, Jaemus told himself. And—was Griggory speaking to the monster? To his clearly starpath-scrambled mind, it appeared Griggory had actually *named* the thing, not to mention *tamed* it. What kind of name was Hither, anyway?

The monster's head withdrew, then Griggory stepped out into the storm after it. Jaemus looked at the Knights incredulously. Each of them shared his expression.

"What in Vaka Aster's eyes?" Stave asked.

"A slangarook, that's all. Just a monster that could swallow each of us and have room for another. What, you don't have these in Vinnr?" Jaemus said lightly, dizzy from having been so close to the terrifying sea monster.

Roibeard lowered a hand this time, and Jaemus took it. Just as he rose, the creature's head once more filled the doorway. Still holding Roibeard's grip, he stayed upright this time. Small victories.

Griggory squeezed in the doorway beside its head. "Lay her there, Hither. Thank you."

And that's when Jaemus realized the beast carried something, or rather, *someone*, in its jaws, which it released with an unceremonious thud.

Heedless of the monster, Safran was first to find her feet and ran to the person's side. *Mylla?!* she cried, all who wore a Mentalios hearing her.

As Jaemus stared in shock, Safran reached Knight Evernal, who, though drenched and unconscious looked very much, if not alive, at least not dead.

Safran knelt down and scooped Mylla's head in her arms. A moment later, she looked up at them. *She's breathing!* And a smile of equal parts happiness and relief spread across her lips.

Watching another profound impossibility prove that it wasn't, Jaemus figured surely everything would make sense soon. He'd just ride this latest surprise out and give in to what had been passing for his fate since the day he'd stolen his first celestial artifact. Oh, he thought wistfully, that day had changed many things, *everything* in fact. And if he was about to be eaten by a giant sea dragør—or not?—and this was the way to save Himmingaze, and maybe Vinnr as well, it could have been worse he guessed. It could have been a fleech.

———

AFTERWORD

To my treasured reader, I'm deeply grateful for your readership your presence in my wordy world. If my book has touched your heart with magic or transported you to another realm, would you consider sharing your thoughts through a review on your favorite retailer? Your voice carries immense value and can guide fellow readers to a tale that resonates with them too. Together, we can build a community of kindred spirits, connected through the power of storytelling. Thank you for your kindness and support.

Don't forget to join my newsletter at www.tammysalyer.com/news letter to stay up to date on new releases and receive a free collection of stories. Cheers!

ABOUT THE AUTHOR

Tammy is an inveterate verbarian, who spends her days surrounded by the written word, both hers and others'. As an ex-paratrooper with the 82nd Airborne Division, her stories are often as gritty as a grunt's pile of three-week-old field gear. Her military science fiction Spectras Arise series debuted to acclaim in 2012, and her epic fantasy adventure series The Shackled Verities was launched in 2020. She's currently five books deep in a Weird West series called Otherworld Outlaws, featuring half-fae sawbones, a necromancer gnome, and a hoodoo cowgirl galavanting into mischief in the Old West.

When not hunched like a Morlock over her writing desk, Tammy runs and bikes silly miles with her super-cool weirdo partner in the Pacific Northwest playground and spends an inappropriate amount of time watching Henry Rollins videos on YouTube. Contrary to whatever ideas her last name might conjure, she's never really been much of a Slayer fan.

Fantasy, space opera, satire, and snark fans will feel right at home with Tammy. Learn more about her and her books by visiting www.tammysalyer.com. She hopes you enjoy reading her works and welcomes your reviews.